For years, the fictional town of Blackstone and its inhabitants lived in John Saul's imagination, as he wondered how to best capture the spirit of this ever-evolving tale of terror. Then he found his answer: the serial novel.

Thus, *The Blackstone Chronicles* emerged from the mind of the bestselling master of terror to haunt his readers' nightmares. The first chilling installment, *Part I: An Eye for an Eye: The Doll,* was launched in January 1997. The book became an instant *New York Times* bestseller, leaving us waiting at the edge of our seats for the next five installments, which were published one by one in each consecutive month—until the serial's explosive finale, *Part VI: Asylum,* in June 1997.

Now, for the first time, this *New York Times* bestselling serial thriller is complete in one volume. And the six parts make one terrifying whole. . . .

By John Saul:

SUFFER THE CHILDREN
PUNISH THE SINNERS
CRY FOR THE STRANGERS
COMES THE BLIND FURY
WHEN THE WIND BLOWS
THE GOD PROJECT
NATHANIEL
BRAINCHILD
HELLFIRE
THE UNWANTED
THE UNLOVED
CREATURE
SECOND CHILD
SLEEPWALK
DARKNESS
SHADOWS
GUARDIAN*
THE HOMING*
BLACK LIGHTNING*
THE BLACKSTONE CHRONICLES:
   Part 1—AN EYE FOR AN EYE: THE DOLL*
   Part 2—TWIST OF FATE: THE LOCKET*
   Part 3—ASHES TO ASHES:
     THE DRAGON'S FLAME*
   Part 4—IN THE SHADOW OF EVIL:
     THE HANDKERCHIEF*
   Part 5—DAY OF RECKONING:
     THE STEREOSCOPE*
   Part 6—ASYLUM*
THE PRESENCE*

*Published by Fawcett Books

THE BLACKSTONE CHRONICLES

John Saul

Fawcett Columbine
The Ballantine Publishing Group • New York

A Fawcett Columbine Book
Published by The Ballantine Publishing Group

Copyright © 1997 by John Saul

Map by Christine Levis

Originally published in 1997 by The Ballantine Publishing Group as a six-part serial under the titles: *An Eye for an Eye: The Doll*, *Twist of Fate: The Locket*, *Ashes to Ashes: The Dragon's Flame*, *In the Shadow of Evil: The Handkerchief*, *Day of Reckoning: The Stereoscope*, and *Asylum*.

http://www.randomhouse.com

Library of Congress Catalog Card Number: 97-97060

ISBN 0-449-00192-X

Cover design by Dreu Pennington-McNeil
Cover illustration by Danilo Ducak

Manufactured in the United States of America

First Trade Edition: February 1998
10 9 8 7 6 5 4 3 2

For Linda,
with love and gratitude,
with hugs and kisses,
with peaches and cream,
with hearts and flowers,
with emeralds and diamonds,
now and in the future

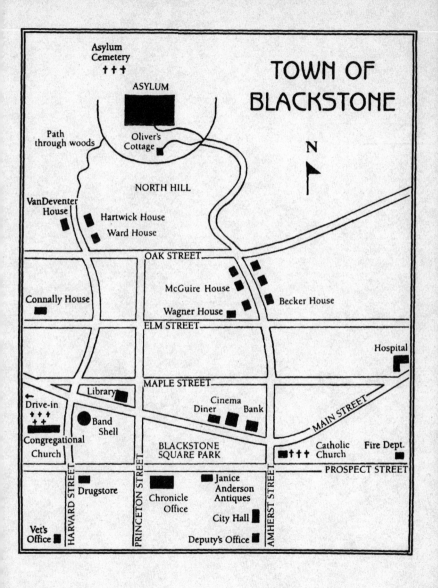

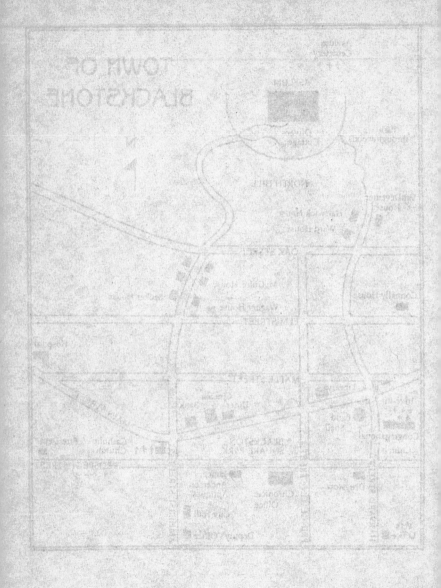

The Connally Family

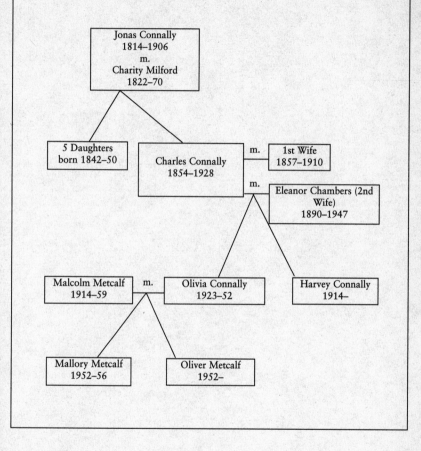

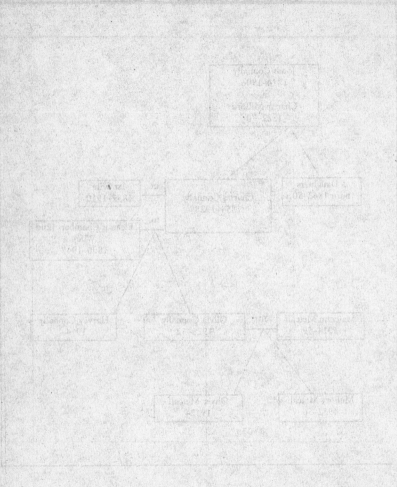

Dear Reader,

Over the past twenty years, it has been my pleasure to entertain you with books relating tales of terror and mayhem. But, as I'm sure you've suspected, there are at least as many stories I haven't yet told, for the very simple reason that they have never fit comfortably into the publishing form we call "the novel."

Now, thanks to Stephen King and his groundbreaking serial novel, *The Green Mile*, a newly revitalized form of publication has become available to us all. The form of the serial is far from new—its history stretches from Dickens's serialized novels in the 1850s and '60s through the Saturday afternoon adventures that my generation enjoyed in movie theaters. But serial novels haven't appeared since my grandfather's day—until *The Green Mile*.

So it was with mounting excitement that I watched as subsequent installments of King's tale proved that the form is as fresh today as it was when Dickens employed it. For ever since I wrote my first novel, *Suffer the Children*, I have been living with the fictional town of Blackstone in my head. I clearly see the village in New Hampshire, right down the road from Port Arbello; its shady tree-lined streets, its even more shadowy history.

Its characters are vivid to me. (In fact, over the years, some characters from my other novels have moved to Blackstone, as you shall see.) Their secrets, their sins, and the sins of their fathers seem so real they are more like memories than inventions.

There are several leading families in my imaginary Blackstone—the Connallys, the Beckers, the McGuires, the Hartwicks. All have a part to play as the drama unfolds. Over the generations their lives have intertwined: births, marriages, deaths, business dealings, rivalries, hardships, and occasional triumphs (all the stuff of our lives, in other words) have created among them the connections—and separations—shared by these prominent citizens of my little town. Above all, one person, one series of shocking and secret circumstances, has bound them together. But how could I explain those relationships, those events—and the catalyst that set in motion the evil that now shadows their lives? What was the best way to tell these separate stories, each of them linked to long-hidden moments in the past, each of them linked to each other, each of them linked to a powerful force that is about to make its insidious presence known?

It seemed to me that this "new" form, the novel conceived in parts, or installments, provided the answer, and *The Blackstone Chronicles* finally began to take place for me on the printed page, as did the objects—artifacts of evil, if you will—that symbolized for me each of the stories I wanted to tell. *The Doll* is the first of these, and it arrives on the doorstep of the McGuire family in Part One. Who sent this gift to Elizabeth and Bill McGuire—and why—I leave you to discover. But I warn you that you won't know the full story until the very end, some months from now! In the meantime, several more presents from the past will have made their way to various carefully selected denizens of Blackstone. And I hope that as you finish the last page of each part another piece of the puzzle will have been revealed—and that you will experience the delicious thrill of anticipating the next installment. And as you finish each volume of *The Blackstone Chronicles*, perhaps you will let your imagination conjure up the terrors that might await in future installments.

So, without further ado, I offer you *An Eye for an Eye: The Doll*, the first of the half dozen gifts I've prepared for you this year.

I hope you enjoy them as much as I've enjoyed wrapping them.

—JOHN SAUL
October 10, 1996

PART 1

AN EYE FOR AN EYE:
THE DOLL

The Beginning

*T*he old Seth Thomas Regulator began to chime the hour. Oliver Metcalf kept typing only long enough to finish the sentence before abandoning the editorial he was composing to gaze thoughtfully at the wood-cased clock that had hung on the wall of the *Blackstone Chronicle*'s one-room office for far more years than Oliver himself could remember. It was the clock that first fascinated him when his uncle brought him here more than forty years ago and taught him how to tell time, and the clock still fascinated him, with its rhythmic ticking, and because it kept time so perfectly that it had to be adjusted by no more than a single minute every year.

Now, after marking the thousands of hours of his life with its soft chime, it was reminding Oliver that the hour had come for him to perform his part in an event that would take place only once.

Today, the town of Blackstone was going to take the first, significant step in the destruction of part of its history.

Oliver Metcalf, as editor and publisher of the town's weekly newspaper, had been asked to make a speech. He'd made preparatory notes for several days but still had no idea precisely what he would say when the moment finally arrived for him to stand at the podium, the great stone structure rising behind him, and face his fellow townsmen. As he picked up the sheaf of notes and tucked it into the inside pocket of his tweed jacket, he

3

wondered if inspiration would strike him when at last he had to speak, or whether he would stare speechlessly out at the gathered crowd as they gazed, waiting, at him.

Questions would be in their minds.

Questions that no one had spoken aloud for years.

Questions to which he had no answers.

He locked the office door behind him and stepped out onto the sidewalk. Crossing the street to cut through the town square, he considered turning back, skipping the ceremony entirely and instead finishing the editorial upon which he'd been working all morning. It was, after all, exactly the kind of day that was meant for staying indoors. The sky was slate gray, and the previous night's wind had stripped the last of the leaves from the great trees that had spread a protective canopy above the town from spring through fall. In early spring, when the enormous oaks and maples first began to bud, the canopy was the palest of greens. But as summer progressed, the foliage matured and thickened, darkening to a deep green that shaded Blackstone from August's hot glare and sheltered it from the rain squalls that swept through on their way toward the Atlantic seacoast several miles to the east. Over the last few weeks, abundant green had given way to the splendor of fall, and for a while the village had gloried in autumn's shimmering golden, red, and russet tones. Now the ground was littered with leaves, already a dead-looking brown, already beginning the slow process of decay that would return them to the soil from which they'd originally sprung.

Oliver Metcalf started toward the top of the hill where most of the townspeople would soon be gathered. Snow had not yet fallen, but a sodden, chill rain had accompanied last night's wind. It seemed to Oliver that a damp, freezing winter was about to descend. The gray light of the day seemed perfectly to reflect his own bleak mood. The trees, with their huge, naked limbs, raised their skeletal branches grotesquely toward the sky, as if seeking to ward off the lowering clouds with fleshless, twisted fingers. Ducking his head against the ominous morning, Oliver walked quickly through the streets, nodding distractedly to the people who spoke to him, meanwhile trying to focus his mind on what he would say to the crowd that would soon be gathered around the best-known building in town.

The Blackstone Asylum.

Throughout Oliver's life—throughout the lives of everyone in Blackstone—the massive building, constructed of stones dug from the fields surrounding the village, had loomed at the top of the town's highest hill. Its long-shuttered windows gazed out over the town not as if it were abandoned, but rather as though it were sleeping.

Sleeping, and waiting someday to awaken.

A chill passed through Oliver as the thought crossed his mind, but he quickly shook it off. No, it would never happen.

Today, the destruction of the Blackstone Asylum would commence.

A wrecking ball would swing, hurling its weight against those heavy gray stones, and after dominating the town for a full century, the building would finally be torn apart, its stone walls demolished, its turrets fallen, its green copper roof sold off for scrap.

As Oliver stepped through the ornate wrought-iron gates that pierced the fence surrounding the Asylum's entire ten acres, and started up the wide, curving driveway leading to its front door, an arm fell across his shoulders and he heard his uncle's familiar voice.

"Quite a day, wouldn't you say, Oliver?" Harvey Connally said, his booming, hearty voice belying his eighty-three years.

Oliver's gaze followed his uncle's, fixing on the brooding building, and he wondered what was going through the old man's mind. No point in asking; for despite their closeness, he'd always found his uncle far more comfortable discussing ideas than emotions.

"If you talk about emotions, you have to talk about people," Harvey had told him back when he was only ten or eleven years old, and home from boarding school for Christmas. "And talking about people is gossip. I don't gossip, and you shouldn't either." The words had clearly signaled Oliver that there were many things his uncle did not want to discuss.

Still, as the old man gazed up at the building that had risen on North Hill only a few years before his birth, Oliver couldn't help trying one last time.

"Your father built it, Uncle Harvey," he said softly. "Aren't you just a little sorry to see it go?"

His uncle's grip tightened on his shoulder. "No, I'm not," Harvey Connally replied, his voice grating as he spoke the words. "And neither should you be. Good riddance to it, is what I say, and we should all forget everything that ever happened there."

His hand fell from Oliver's shoulder.

"Everything," he said again.

Half an hour later Oliver stood at the podium that had been erected in front of the Asylum's imposing portico, his eyes surveying the crowd. Nearly everyone had come. The president of the bank was there, as was the contractor whose company would demolish most of the old Asylum, keeping only the facade. The plan was to replace the interior with a complex of shops and restaurants that promised to bring a prosperity to Blackstone that no one had known since the years when the institution itself had provided the economic basis for the town's livelihood. Everyone who was involved in the project was there, but there were others as well, people whose parents and grandparents, even great-grandparents, had once worked within the stone walls behind him. Now they hoped that the new structure might provide their children and grandchildren with jobs.

Beyond the assemblage, just inside the gate, Oliver could see the small stone house that had been deeded to the last superintendent of the Asylum, upon the occasion of his marriage to the daughter of the chairman of the Asylum's board of directors.

When the Blackstone Asylum had finally been abandoned and its last superintendent had died, that house, too, stood empty for several years. Then the young man who had inherited it, having graduated from college, returned to Blackstone and moved back into that house, the house in which he'd been born.

Oliver Metcalf had come home.

He hadn't expected to sleep at all on that first night, but to his surprise, the two-story stone cottage seemed to welcome him back, and he'd immediately felt as if he was home. The ghosts he'd expected had not appeared, and within a few years he almost forgot he'd ever lived anywhere else. But in all the years since then, living in the shadow of the Asylum his father had once run, Oliver had not once set foot inside the building.

He'd told himself he had no need to.

Deep in his heart, he'd known he couldn't.

Something inside its walls—something unknowable—terrified him.

Now, as the crowd fell into an expectant silence, Oliver adjusted the microphone and began to speak.

"Today marks a new beginning in the history of Blackstone. For nearly a century, a single structure has affected every family—every individual—in our town. Today, we begin the process of tearing that structure down. This signifies not only the end of one era, but the beginning of another. The process of replacing the old Blackstone Asylum with the new Blackstone Center will not be simple. Indeed, when the new building is finally completed, its facade will look much as the Asylum looks today; constructed of the same stones that have stood on this site for nearly a hundred years, it will look familiar to all of us, but at the same time, all of it will be different. . . ."

For half an hour Oliver continued speaking, his thoughts organizing themselves as he spoke in the same simple, orderly prose that flowed from him when he sat at his computer, composing a feature or an editorial for the newspaper. Then, as the bell in the Congregational church downtown began to strike the hour of noon, he turned to Bill McGuire, the contractor who would oversee the demolition of the old building and construction of the new complex of shops and restaurants as well.

Nodding, Oliver stepped away from the podium, walked down the steps to join the crowd, and turned to face the building as the great lead wrecking ball swung for the first time toward the century-old edifice.

As the last chime of the church bell faded away, the ball punched through the west wall of the building. A sigh that sounded like a moaning wind passed through the crowd as it watched half a hundred fieldstones tumble to the ground, leaving a gaping hole in a wall that had stood solid through ten decades.

Oliver, though, heard nothing of the sigh, for as the ball smashed through the wall, a blinding flash of pain shot through his head.

Through the pain, a fleeting vision appeared . . .

A man walks up the steps toward the huge double doors of the Asylum. In his hand he holds the hand of a child.

The child is crying.

The man ignores the child's cries.

As man and boy approach the great oaken doors, they swing open.

Man and boy pass through.

The enormous doors swing closed again.

Prologue

*T*he previous day's clouds had long since swept out to sea, and a full moon stood high in the sky. Atop North Hill the Asylum was silhouetted against a sky sparkling with the glitter of millions of stars while the night itself seemed infused with a silvery glow.

No one, though, was awake to see it, save a single dark figure that moved through the ruptured stone wall into the silent building that had stood empty for nearly forty years. Oblivious to the beauty of the night, that lone figure moved silently, intent on finding a single chamber hidden within the warren of rooms enclosed by the cold stone walls.

The figure progressed steadily through the darkness, finding its way as surely through those rooms that were utterly devoid of light as it did through those whose dirt-encrusted windows admitted just enough moonlight to illuminate their walls and doors.

The path the figure took weaved back and forth, as if it were threading its way through groupings of furniture, although each room was bare, until it came at last to a small, hidden cubicle. Others would have passed it by, for its entrance was concealed behind a panel, the sole illumination provided by the few rays of moonlight that crept through a single small window, which itself was all but invisible from beyond the Asylum's walls.

The lack of light in the chamber had no more effect on the dark-clad figure than had the blackness of the rooms through which it had already passed, for it was as familiar with the size and shape of this room as it was with the others.

Small and square, the hidden cubicle was lined with shelves, each of which contained numerous items. A museum, if you will, of the Asylum's past, containing an eclectic collection of souvenirs, the long-forgotten possessions of those who had passed through its chambers.

The figure moved from shelf to shelf, touching one artifact after another, remembering the past and the people to whom these things had once been dear.

A pair of eyes glinted in the darkness, catching the figure's attention. The memory attached to these eyes was bright and clear.

As clear as if it had happened only yesterday . . .

The child sat on her mother's lap, watching in the mirror as her mother brushed her hair, listening as her mother sang to her.

But a third face appeared in the mirror as well, for the little girl held a doll, and anyone who saw the three of them together would have noticed the resemblance.

All three—the doll, the child, and the mother—had long blond hair framing delicate, oval faces.

All three had the same lovely blue eyes.

All their cheeks glowed with rouge, and their lips shone brightly with scarlet gloss.

As the brush moved through the child's hair in long and even strokes, so also did the brush in the child's hand mimic the motions of the mother, moving through the hair of the doll with the same single-minded affection that flowed from the mother.

As her mother sang softly, the child hummed, contentedly crooning to her doll as her mother crooned to her.

Through the open window the gentle sounds of the summer afternoon lulled them. In the street, half a dozen of the neighbor boys were playing a pickup game of baseball, and in the next block the melody of the ice-cream truck chimed its tune.

The mother and child were barely aware of it, so content were they in their own little world.

Then, from downstairs, the sound of the front door slamming interrupted their idyll, and as heavy footsteps thudded on the stairs, the mother began wiping the lipstick from the child's face.

The child twisted away, dropping the brush with which she'd been stroking her doll's hair, but clutching the doll itself close to her chest. "No! I like it!" the child protested, but still the mother tried to wipe away the gloss.

Then the child's father was towering in the bedroom doorway, his face flushed with anger. When he spoke, it was with a voice so loud and harsh that both mother and child shrank away from him.

"This was not to happen again!"

The mother's eyes darted around the room as if she was seeking some avenue of escape. Finding none, she finally spoke, her voice breaking. "I'm sorry," she whispered. "I couldn't help it. I—"

"No more," her husband told her.

Again the mother's eyes darted wildly around the room. "Of course. I promise. This time—"

"This time is the last time," her husband said. Striding into the room, he swept the child from her lap, his arms closing around fragile shoulders. Though his wife reached up as if to take the child back, he moved out of her reach. "No more," he repeated. "Didn't I tell you what would happen if this continued?"

Now the woman's eyes filled with panic, and she rose to her feet. "No!" she pleaded. "Oh, God, don't! Please don't!"

"It's too late," the man told her. "You leave me no choice."

Pulling the doll from the child's arms, he tossed it onto

*the bed. Then, ignoring the child's shrieks, he carried
her out of the bedroom and started downstairs. Moving
down the long central hall on the lower floor, he passed
through the butler's pantry and the large kitchen, where
the cook, frozen in silence, watched as he strode toward
the back door. But before he could open it, his wife
appeared, holding the doll.*

*"Please," she begged. "Let her take it. She loves it so.
As much as I love her."*

*The man hesitated, and for a moment it seemed as if he
would refuse. But as his child cried out in anguish and
reached for the doll, he relented.*

*The woman watched helplessly as her husband carried
her child out of the house. Instinctively, she knew she
would never see her child again. And she would never be
allowed to have another.*

*The man carried the child through the great oak doors of
the Asylum, and finally set the small, trembling figure on
her feet. A matron waited, and she now knelt in front of
the child.*

*"Such a pretty little thing," she said. As the child,
holding her doll, sobbed, the matron looked up at the
man. "Is this all she brought with her?"*

*"It's more than will be necessary," the man replied.
"If anything else is ever needed, please let my office
know." He looked down at his child for a moment that
stretched out so long a spark of hope glowed briefly in
the child's eyes. Finally, he shook his head.*

*"I'm sorry," he said. "Sorry for what she did, and
sorry you let her do it. Now there is no other way."
Without touching his child again, the man turned and
strode through the enormous doors.*

*Without being told, the child knew she would never see
her father again.*

*When they were alone, the matron took her by the
hand and led her through a long hallway and then up*

some stairs. There was another long hallway, and finally she was led into a room.

Not nearly as nice as her room at home.

This room was small, and though there was a window, it was covered with heavy metal mesh.

There was a bed, but nothing like the pretty four-poster she had at home.

There was a chair, but nothing like the rocking chair her mother had painted in her favorite shade of blue.

There was a dresser, but it was painted an ugly brown she knew her mother would have hated.

"This will be your room," the matron told her.

The child said nothing.

The matron went to the dresser and took out a plain cotton dress that looked nothing like the pretty things her mother had given her. There was also a pair of panties, and some socks that had turned an ugly gray color. "And these will be your clothes. Put them on, please."

The child hesitated, then did as the matron had instructed. Taking off the frilly pinafore in which her mother had dressed her that morning, she lay it carefully on the bed so as not to wrinkle it. Then she pulled off her underthings, and was about to put on the panties when she heard the matron utter a strange sound. Looking up, she saw the woman staring down at her naked body, her eyes wide.

"Did I do something wrong?" the child asked, speaking for the first time.

The matron hesitated, then shook her head. "No, child, of course you didn't. But we got you the wrong clothes, didn't we? Little boys don't wear dresses, do they?" The matron picked up the doll. "And they certainly don't play with dolls. We'll get rid of this right now."

The child screamed in protest, then fell sobbing to the bed, but it did no good. The matron took the doll away. The child would never see it again.

Nor would anyone beyond the Asylum's walls ever see the child again.

The dark figure cradled the doll, gazing into its porcelain face in the moonlight, stroking its long blond hair, remembering how it had come to be here. And knowing to whom it must now be given. . . .

Chapter 1

*E*lizabeth McGuire was worried. It had now been nearly twenty-four hours since her husband had gotten the call from Jules Hartwick. Though the banker told Bill that the "small problem" that had come up about the Blackstone Center wasn't particularly serious, Bill had been brooding ever since. All through yesterday afternoon his agitation had grown worse. By dinnertime even Megan, who in the six short years of her life had rarely failed to bring a smile to her father's face, was unable to extract anything more than a grunt from him.

Bill spent most of the night pacing the house, finally coming to bed only when Elizabeth had come downstairs, rubbing her distended belly, and informed him that not only was she lonely, but their soon-to-be-born baby was too. That had at least brought Bill to bed, but she was aware that he hadn't really slept. By dawn he was already dressed and downstairs, getting in Mrs. Goodrich's way.

Worse, when Megan came down ten minutes ago, the first thing she wanted to know was if her daddy was sick. Elizabeth assured the little girl that her father was all right, but Megan wasn't convinced, and volunteered to take care of her daddy if he was sick. Only when Bill himself had given her a hug and declared that he was fine had she gone off to the kitchen to help Mrs. Goodrich with the breakfast dishes.

Now, as she poured Bill a second cup of coffee, Elizabeth tried to reassure him one more time. "If Jules Hartwick said it's nothing serious, I don't see why you don't believe him."

Bill sighed heavily. "I wish it were that simple. But everything was all set. I mean, everything, right down to the wrecking ball day before yesterday—"

"Which was mostly ceremonial," Elizabeth reminded him. "It's not like you're tearing the whole building down. You told me yourself the ball was mostly for show."

"It was still the beginning," Bill groused. "I'm telling you, Elizabeth, I just have a bad feeling about this."

"Well, you'll know in another twenty minutes," Elizabeth told him, glancing at the clock. "It'll be all right, I know it." She heaved herself up from the table, suppressing a groan. "This has to be the heaviest baby in history. It feels like it weighs forty pounds."

Bill slipped an arm around her, and together they walked to the front door. "See you in an hour or so," he said. He kissed her distractedly and was just reaching for the doorknob when the bell rang. He opened the door to the mailman, standing on the porch, holding a large package. "Another present, Charlie?" he asked. "Is this one for Christmas, or the new baby?"

The mailman smiled. "Hard to say. Christmas is only a couple of weeks away, and the package just says McGuire. Take your pick, I guess. Don't weigh too much, for whatever that's worth."

"It means I can take it," Elizabeth said, reaching for the package as Bill started down the steps. "Thank you, Charlie."

"Just doing my job."

The mailman touched his cap almost as if saluting, and Elizabeth had to resist the urge to return the salute. Contenting herself with a wave, she called a good-bye to her husband and went back into the house, quickly closing the door against the early December chill.

Taking the package back to the dining room with her,

she stared at it, puzzled. Just as Charlie had said, it bore no other name but McGuire, and their address, written in neat, block letters.

There was no return address.

" 'Curiouser and curiouser,' " she quoted softly as she tore away the brown paper that enclosed the parcel. She was just opening the box itself when Megan came in.

"What's that, Mommy? Is it for me?"

Elizabeth peered into the box, then lifted out a doll.

A beautiful, antique doll with blue glass eyes and long blond hair.

Save for the doll, the box was empty.

Her eyes went once more to the empty spot where the sender's name should have been. "How strange," Elizabeth said.

Chapter 2

*B*ill McGuire started down the hill toward the center of Blackstone. Elizabeth is right, he told himself. Whatever prompted Jules Hartwick's call yesterday morning was no more serious than Jules claimed.

"We need to have a meeting," Hartwick had explained. "And I think you should hold off on the project for a day or two, at least, until we can talk."

Though Bill had asked any number of questions, trying to find out precisely what was on the banker's mind, Hartwick refused to answer, saying only that he wasn't ready to go into it yet; that Bill shouldn't worry.

Meaningless platitudes that had triggered even louder alarms in Bill's mind. How on earth could he *not* worry? Blackstone Center was the biggest project he'd ever taken on. He'd turned down two other jobs—one in Port Arbello, the other in Eastbury—in order to concentrate on the conversion of the old Asylum into the sort of commercial center that could revive what had been a slowly dying town. The Center, in fact, had been in large part his own idea. He had thought about it for more than a year before even suggesting it to the directors of the Blackstone Trust. The one person he'd talked to almost from the start was Oliver Metcalf, because he'd known that without Oliver's support, the plan would never have gotten off the ground. A couple of tepid editorials in the *Chronicle*, and that would have been that. But Oliver was enthusiastic about the Blackstone Center from the very beginning, with a single major reservation.

"What about me?" he'd wanted to know. "Am I suddenly going to be living on the busiest street in town?"

Bill had already thought of that. Grabbing a pencil from Oliver's cluttered desk, he'd quickly sketched a rough map to show that the most logical approach to the site was not through the front gates, but from the back, where the old service entrance had once been. Appeased, Oliver immediately backed the project, pushing for it not only in the paper, but with his uncle as well. Once Harvey Connally had been won over—albeit reluctantly— the rest was easy. By the day before yesterday, when the wrecker's ball had made its ceremonial swing, puncturing the Asylum's west wall in preparation for the expansion of the building, most of the opposition to the project had evaporated.

Bill McGuire, and his entire crew, had been all set to go to work the next day.

Yesterday.

But only hours after the ceremony, Jules Hartwick made his ominous call. "Hold off for a day or two," indeed! "Not to worry"—fat chance of that. Bill McGuire was worried, all right. Worried nearly out of his mind.

Now, as he walked the three blocks down Amherst Street to the corner of Main, where the redbrick, Federal-style building that housed the First National Bank of Blackstone stood, he felt an anticipatory rush of fear. His nerves gave an additional jump when he spotted Oliver Metcalf at the bank's door.

"You know what this is all about?" Oliver asked.

"He called you too?" Bill replied, trying to betray nothing of his ballooning sense that something very serious had gone wrong.

"Yesterday. But he wouldn't say what it was about, which tells me that whatever it is, it's not good news."

"Did he tell you not to worry?"

The editor nodded. His eyes searched McGuire's face. "You don't have any idea at all what this is about?"

McGuire glanced in both directions, but they seemed to be alone on the sidewalk. "All he told me was to hold off on the Center project. You can guess how that made me feel."

"Yes," Oliver said with an ironic smile, "I certainly can."

Together the two men entered the bank, nodded to the tellers who stood behind old-fashioned frosted-glass windows, and made their way to Jules Hartwick's office at the back.

"Mr. Hartwick and Mr. Becker are waiting for you," Ellen Golding told them. "You can go on in."

Bill and Oliver exchanged another glance. What was Hartwick planning to tell them that required the presence of his lawyer?

Jules Hartwick was on his feet as they entered the walnut-paneled office, and he came around from behind his desk to greet both men with no less warmth than ever. The gesture did nothing to ease Bill McGuire's sense of foreboding. He'd learned long ago that a warm handshake and a friendly smile meant absolutely nothing in the world of banking. Sure enough, as Hartwick retreated around his desk and lowered himself into his deeply tufted red-leather swivel chair, his smile faded. "I don't suppose there's any easy way to tell you this," he began, looking from Bill McGuire to Oliver Metcalf, then back again.

"I assume it has to do with the financing for the Blackstone Center project, right?" the contractor asked, his worst fears congealing into a hard knot in his belly.

The banker took a deep breath, then slowly let it out. "I wish it were that simple," he said. "If it were only the Center project, I suspect I could arrange a bridge loan for a few—"

"Bridge loan?" McGuire interrupted. "For Christ's sake, Jules, why would I need a bridge loan?" He rose from his chair, his hands unconsciously clenching into fists. "The financing's supposed to be all set!" But even as he spoke the words, McGuire knew that no matter how true they might have been only a few days ago, they no longer were. Nor would getting angry help the situation. "Sorry," he said, slumping back into his chair. "So what is it? What's happened?"

"We don't really think it's very serious," Ed Becker said, but there was something in his tone that told both McGuire and Oliver Metcalf that whatever was coming was going to be very bad indeed. "The Federal Reserve has put a temporary hold on loans by the bank, and—"

"Excuse me?" Oliver Metcalf cut in. "Did you say the Federal Reserve?" His eyes shifted from the lawyer to the banker. "What exactly is going on, Jules?"

Jules Hartwick shifted uncomfortably in his chair. For twenty years, ever since he'd taken over the bank after his father suddenly died, the worst part of the job had been having to tell a customer—usually someone he'd known most of his life—that he couldn't give him a loan. But this was worse.

Far worse.

The construction account had already been set up; the first funds had been transferred into it. And Bill McGuire had already begun hiring a crew; two of the men who would be working on the project, Tom Cleary and Jim Nicholson, had come into the bank only yesterday to make small payments on debts the bank had been carrying for months. Just as he—and his father before him—always had, Jules told both men to wait until after Christmas. What, after all, could be the harm? The bank had already been carrying Tommy for a year and a half, and Jim for nine months.

What would another month matter?

Let the men and their families enjoy the holiday.

Except that now there would be no more paychecks for those men, for the simple reason that the routine audit the

Federal Reserve was working on had turned up what it considered a "disproportionately large percentage" of inactive loans.

So many, in fact, that the Fed had put a hold on all new lending by the Blackstone bank until the bank could demonstrate how it was going to handle the loans.

But to Jules Hartwick, they weren't simply "inactive loans." They were loans to people he'd known all his life, people who had worked hard and always done their best to meet their responsibilities. Not one of them had purposely quit a job, or been lax in looking for a new one. They had simply been caught in an economy that was "downsizing"—a word Jules Hartwick had come to hate—and would make good on their debts the moment things got better for them.

Now, thanks to his own decision to carry all those loans, the bank wasn't going to be able to fund the Center project. Ironically, the Fed had seen to it that at least some of the men whose loans were a source of concern to the auditors would no longer have the jobs that would allow them to make their loans current.

"It seems the auditors are worried about the way we do business," he said, forcing himself to meet Bill McGuire's gaze straight on. "For the moment, we're going to be unable to continue funding the construction account." He turned to Oliver Metcalf. "The reason I wanted you here is so that Ed can explain exactly what's happening. The bank isn't insolvent, and I'm sure we'll be able to straighten all this out in a couple of weeks. But if word gets out that the Fed is nervous about us—well, I'm sure you can imagine what would happen."

"A run," Oliver said. "Could you stand one?"

Jules Hartwick shrugged. "Probably. If it got bad, we might lose our independence. In the end, none of our depositors would lose a cent, but we'd be folded into one of the big regional banks and become just one more small branch with no flexibility to do things our way."

"Your way seems to have gotten us all into a fine mess, if you ask me," Bill McGuire said. "What am I supposed to tell my people, Jules? That the jobs they've been counting on have simply evaporated? Not to mention my own job." Though this time he managed to stay in his chair, his voice began to rise. "Do you have any idea how much work I turned down to make this project happen? Any idea at all? I'm already stretched tight, Jules. The new baby's due in a month, and I—" Abruptly, he cut short the tirade he'd been working up to, recognizing the genuine pain the banker was feeling. What, after all, was the point of yelling at Jules? Once again he forced himself to calm down. "Do you have any idea how long it might be?" he asked in a more reasonable voice. "Is this just a temporary funding freeze, or is the project done for?"

Hartwick was silent for a long time, but finally spread his hands helplessly. "I don't know," he said. "I'm hoping it's only for a week or so, but I can't promise you anything." He hesitated, then forced himself to finish. "There's a possibility it could be months."

The banker kept talking in an effort to explain, but Bill McGuire was no longer listening. Instead his mind was already working, trying to figure out what to do next.

This afternoon he'd drive up to Port Arbello and see if there was any chance of bidding on the condominium project he'd turned down three weeks ago. Although that project wasn't supposed to start until spring, if he could secure the job, its financing would tide them over for a while. And while he was up there, maybe he'd talk to the developers behind the condo project about finding new financing for the Blackstone project.

"Well, what do you think?" he asked Oliver Metcalf twenty minutes later as they left the bank. "Is it all over even before it starts?"

Metcalf shook his head. "Not if I have anything to do with it. All I'm going to run is a small article to the effect that the project is being held up, maybe imply that there are some permits not in place yet. Then we'll see what happens."

Nodding, McGuire turned away and started up Amherst Street. He hadn't taken more than a couple of steps when Metcalf called out to him.

"Bill? Give my love to Elizabeth and Megan. And try not to worry. Things will work out."

McGuire forced a smile, wishing he could share Oliver Metcalf's optimism.

Chapter 3

*O*liver Metcalf was already starting to compose his editorial as he left the bank building, but instead of going directly back to his office, he turned in the opposite direction, walking a block farther down Main Street to the corner of Princeton, where the old Carnegie Library still stood in the center of the half acre of land that Harvey Connally's father had donated nearly a century ago. Though most of the old Carnegie libraries that had sprung up in small towns all over the country had been replaced decades ago by far more modern "media centers," the one in Blackstone remained as unchanged as the rest of the town. Part of the reason for its preservation was Blackstone's sense of historic pride; part was lack of funds for modernization. Though there were a few new buildings—"new" being defined as less than fifty years old—most of the town still looked as it had a hundred years ago, some peeling paint and other signs of wear and tear notwithstanding; and some of it had gone unchanged for more than two centuries.

In Oliver Metcalf's own memory, nothing about the library had changed at all. Perhaps the trees were a little bigger than they'd been when he was a boy, but even then the maples on the front lawn had been fairly mature, spreading their limbs wide, providing plenty of shade for the Story Lady, who had read to the children of the town every Thursday afternoon of the summer months. Now, forty years later, there was still a Story Lady, and she still entranced the children of Blackstone on warm summer Thursdays. Oliver suspected there would always be a Story Lady. Anyway, he hoped so.

Today, though, there was no storyteller or cluster of children in evidence as Oliver mounted the steep flight of concrete steps, deeply worn by generations of feet moving up and down, and pushed through the outer set of double doors that provided a buffer between the chill of the December day outside and the comforting heat from the old-fashioned radiators whose occasional clanging was the loudest sound ever heard within the walls of the building. The radiators provided too much heat, really, but nobody objected because Germaine Wagner, who had been the head librarian for nearly twenty years now, always insisted, "A warm room leads to the appreciation of good books." Oliver had never been able to figure out what the connection between temperature and literature might be, but Germaine was willing to work for a salary that was no more modern than the building itself; if she wanted the heat turned up, so be it.

Now, as Oliver pushed through the second set of doors, Germaine looked up from the stack of books she was checking back into the library—still with old-fashioned cards bearing the due date and the signatures of the people who had borrowed them tucked into envelopes glued to the inside covers. Peering at Oliver over the tops of her half-glasses, Germaine stuck her pencil into the thick bun of hair that was neatly pinned to the top of her head and beckoned him over to the desk.

"I'm hearing rumors that there might be a problem with Blackstone Center," she said in the professional whisper with which she could silence rowdy high school students from seventy feet away.

Oliver's mind went over the possibilities. He supposed that Germaine had seen him go into the bank with Bill McGuire and immediately assumed the worst. The assumption would have been typical of her. Or someone else had seen them and told Germaine.

More likely, Germaine was on a fishing expedition, looking for a juicy tidbit to take home to her mother. Old Clara Wagner, wheelchair bound, hadn't been out of the house in at least a decade, but she loved a good piece of gossip even more than Germaine.

To say nothing at all to Germaine was tantamount to guaranteeing that whatever rumor she passed on would henceforth have his name attached to it ("I asked Oliver Metcalf point-blank, and he did *not* deny it!"), so he decided the best thing to do would be to send her off in the wrong direction. "Well, I know Bill's been pretty busy with some other projects," Oliver said. "I suspect that once he gets them wound up, he'll be pitching into the Asylum full-tilt."

Germaine pursed her lips suspiciously. "It seems to me that leaving equipment idle up there is something Bill McGuire wouldn't do," she replied, her sharp eyes boring into him. "He's never been one to waste a dime, Oliver."

"Well, I'm sure he knows what he's doing," Oliver said. Then, before the librarian's cross-examination could continue, he rushed on. "Actually, the Center project is the reason I came by. I'm thinking of running a series on the history of the building."

The librarian fixed on him darkly. "I would have thought you'd have all the material you need right in your own house," she observed, "given who your father was."

Suddenly, Oliver felt like a little boy who'd come to school without his homework. "I'm afraid my father didn't keep much in the way of memorabilia," he said.

The librarian's eyes narrowed slightly, and her already narrow nostrils took on a pinched look. "No, I don't suppose he would have, would he?" There was a coldness in her tone that made Oliver flinch, but he tried to pretend that neither the look nor the words affected him.

Just as he'd tried all his life to pretend that looks and words such as Germaine Wagner's had no effect on him.

"It's only gossip, Oliver," his uncle had told him over and over again. "They have no more idea of what really happened than anyone else. The best thing to do is simply ignore them. Sooner or later they'll find other things to talk about." His uncle had been right. As the years had gone by, fewer and fewer people gave him that curious look, or tried to ask him thinly veiled questions about what had *really* happened to his sister all those years ago. But of course Oliver had never known any more about it than anyone else. By the time he'd come home from college and gone to work for the paper, it had all but been forgotten.

Except that every now and then, with people like Germaine Wagner, he still found that a look could slice open old wounds, a tone of voice could sting. But there was nothing he could do about it; like Oliver himself, the Germaines of this world were going to have to go to their graves still not knowing the truth.

"I really don't remember that much about my father," he said carefully now. "Which, I suppose, is part of why I'm here. I thought that maybe now that the Asylum's finally going to be put to a good use, it might be time for me to write up a history of how it came to be here in the first place."

"Caring for the mentally ill was a perfectly good use for the building," Germaine replied. "My mother was very proud of her work there."

"As she should have been," Oliver quickly assured her. "But it's been so long since it was closed that I really don't know much about it myself. And I suspect that whatever historical material still exists is upstairs in the attic here. I thought I'd see what I could find."

He waited as the librarian pondered his request. Germaine Wagner, over the years, had come to think of the contents of the library as her personal property, and tended to consider so much as a one-day-overdue book as a personal affront. As to letting someone paw through the boxes and boxes of old documents, diaries, and memoirs that had migrated into the library over the course of the eight decades since it had been built, Oliver suspected that she would take his request as an invasion of her privacy.

"Well, I don't suppose there's any real reason why you shouldn't be able to see what's there," Germaine finally said in a sorrowful tone as if she was already regretting having to make the admission. "I suppose I could have Rebecca bring down whatever we have."

As if the librarian's mere mention of her name was enough to summon her, a girl appeared from the back room.

Except that she wasn't a girl; not really. Rebecca Morrison was in her late twenties, with a heart-shaped face that radiated a sweet innocence, framed by soft chestnut hair that fell in waves from a part in the center. Her eyes, slightly tilted, were a deep brown, and utterly guileless.

Oliver had known her since she was a child, and when he'd had to write the obituary after the automobile accident that left sixteen-year-old Rebecca an orphan, tears had streamed down his face. For weeks after the fatal car crash, Rebecca hovered between life and death. Though there were many people in Blackstone who had fallen into the habit of referring to her as "Poor Rebecca," Oliver was not among them. It had taken months for the girl to recover from her injuries, and while it was true that when she emerged from the hospital her smile was sad and her mind was slower, to Oliver the sweetness that imbued Rebecca's personality more than made up for the slight intellectual damage she had suffered in the accident.

Now, as she smiled at him, he felt the familiar sense of comfort her presence always gave him.

"Oliver wants to see if there is any information about the Blackstone Asylum in the attic," Germaine Wagner briskly explained. "I told him I wasn't certain, but that perhaps you could look."

"Oh, there's a whole box of things," Rebecca said, and Oliver was sure he saw a flash of disapproval in the librarian's eyes. "I'll bring it down right away."

"I'll help you," Oliver immediately volunteered.

"You don't have to," Rebecca protested. "I can do it."

"But I want to," Oliver insisted.

As he followed Rebecca to the stairs leading up to the mezzanine and the attic beyond, he felt the librarian's eyes following him, and had to resist the urge to turn around and glare at her. After all, he thought, most of her problem undoubtedly stemmed from the simple fact that in her whole life, no man had probably ever followed her up the stairs.

Ten minutes later a large dusty box filled with file folders, photo albums, letters, and diaries was sitting on one of the immense oak tables that were lined up in two precise rows in the front of the library, close by the windows. Oliver settled onto one of the hard oak chairs, reached into the box, and pulled out a photo album. Setting it on the table in front of him, he opened it at random.

And found himself staring at a picture of his father.

The photograph had been taken years ago, long before Oliver had been born. In it, Malcolm Metcalf stood in front of the doors of the Asylum, his arms folded across his chest, scowling straight into the camera almost as if he were challenging it.

Challenging it to what? Oliver wondered.

And yet, as he stared at the black-and-white photograph, he felt a shudder take form inside him. As though it were Oliver himself who had brought forth Malcolm Metcalf's piercing look of disapproval.

But, of course, it was the unseen photographer upon whom his father had fixed that look; he had not wanted the camera any closer to the Asylum than it already was.

In the photograph, Malcolm Metcalf was guarding the doors of his Asylum against the prying eye of the camera.

Oliver flipped the pages quickly, as if to escape his father's stern stare, when suddenly an image seemed to leap forth from the pages of the book.

A boy is tied down to a bed.
His hands are tied, his ankles are strapped.
Across his torso, a shadow falls.
The boy is screaming. . . .

Blinking, and shaking his head, Oliver quickly flipped back through the pages, searching for the picture.

Only there was no such picture in the book.

Chapter 4

As he had often done before, Bill McGuire paused on the sidewalk in front of his house for no better reason than to gaze in satisfaction upon the structure in which he'd spent almost all his life. The house was a Victorian—the only one on this particular block of Amherst Street—and though Bill was perfectly well aware of the current fashion of turning houses such as his into pink, purple, or lavender Painted Ladies, neither he nor Elizabeth had ever been tempted to coat the old house with half a dozen colors of paint. Instead, they had faithfully maintained the earthy tones—mustards, tans, greens, and maroons—of the period, and the elaborate white trim, meant by the original builders to resemble lace that gave the house a feeling of lightness, despite its mass.

The house was one of only six on the block, and all of them had been as well taken care of as the McGuires'. Amherst Street, which sloped gently up the hill, eventually turning to the left, then back to the right, and finally ending at the gates of the old Asylum, could easily have been set aside as a sort of living museum of architecture. There was a large half-timbered Tudor on one side of the McGuires', and a good example of Federal on the other. On the opposite side of the street were two houses that had been built early in the Craftsman era, separated by a large saltbox that, to Bill at least, appeared slightly embarrassed by the Victorian effusiveness of its across-the-street neighbor. Still, all six houses sat on spacious enough grounds and were surrounded by so many trees and shrubs that the block was unified by its parklike look, if not its architecture.

Today, though, as he gazed up at his house, with its profusion of steeply pitched roofs and dormer windows, Bill had a strange sense that something was not right. He searched the structure for some clue to his uneasiness, but could see nothing wrong. The paint wasn't peeling, nor were any shingles missing. He quickly scanned the ornate trim work that he'd always taken special pride in keeping in perfect repair, but every bit of it looked exactly as it should. Not a spindle missing, nor a lath either split or broken. Telling himself his discomfort was nothing more than his own bad mood after the meeting at the bank, Bill strode up the brick pathway, mounted the steps that led to the high front porch, and went inside.

The sense that something was wrong grew stronger.

"Elizabeth?" he called out. "Megan? Anybody home?" For a moment he heard nothing at all, then the door leading to the butler's pantry at the far end of the dining room opened and he saw Mrs. Goodrich's stooped form shuffling toward him.

"They're both upstairs," the old woman said. "You might want to go up and talk to the missus. I think she might be a little upset. And I'm fixing some lunch for the whole family." The old woman, who had been with Elizabeth since she was a child in Port Arbello, gazed at him worriedly. "You'll be here, won't you?"

"I'll be here, Mrs. Goodrich," he assured her. As the housekeeper made her slow way back to the kitchen, Bill started up the stairs. Before he was even halfway to the second-floor landing, Megan appeared, gazing down at him with dark, uncertain eyes.

"Why can't I have my dolly?" she demanded. "Why won't Mommy give her to me?"

"Dolly?" Bill repeated. "What dolly are you talking about?"

"The one someone sent me," Megan said. Her eyes narrowed slightly. "Mommy won't let me have her."

At that moment Elizabeth, still dressed in the night-gown and robe she'd been wearing when Bill left the house three hours earlier, appeared behind their daughter, smiling wanly. "Honey, it's not that I won't let you have the doll. It's just that we don't know who it's for."

"Would one of you mind enlightening me about what's going on?" Bill asked as he came to the top of the stairs. He knelt down to give Megan a kiss, then stood and slid his arm around his wife. The smile his kiss had put on Megan's face disappeared.

"It's for me!" she declared. "When you see it, you'll know."

"Come on," Elizabeth said. "It's in our room. I'll show it to you."

With Megan reaching up to put her hand in his, Bill followed his wife into the big master bedroom. On the old chaise longue, once his mother's favorite place to sit and read, was the box the mailman had delivered this morning. Reaching into it, Elizabeth lifted out the doll, automatically cradling it in her arms as if it were a baby. "It's really very beautiful," she said as Bill moved closer to her. "I think its face must be hand-painted, and the clothes look like they were handmade too."

Bill looked down into the doll's face, which had been painted so perfectly that for the briefest of moments he almost had the feeling the doll was looking back up at him. "Who on earth sent it?"

Elizabeth shrugged. "That's the problem. Not only wasn't there any return address, but there wasn't any card with it either."

"It's mine!" Megan piped, reaching up for the doll. "Why would anybody send a doll to a grown-up?"

Elizabeth, seeming to hold the doll a little closer to her breast, turned away from the little girl. "But we don't know that it was sent to you, darling. It might be a present for the new baby."

Megan scowled deeply and her chin began to tremble. "But the baby's going to be a boy," she said. "You said so. And boys don't play with dollies!"

"We *hope* the baby is going to be a boy," Elizabeth explained. "But we don't know. And if you have a little sister, don't you think she'll love the doll as much as you do?"

Megan's features took on a look of intransigence that almost made Bill laugh. "No," she declared. "Babies don't even play with dolls. All they do is eat and cry and wet their diapers." She turned to her father, and her eyes opened wide. "Please, Daddy, can't I have her?"

"I'll tell you what," Bill said. "Why don't we put the doll away for a while and see if we can find out who sent it? Then, if it turns out it was meant for you, it'll be yours. And if it turns out it was meant for the baby, we'll wait until the baby is born, and if it's a little boy, then the doll can be your first present from your little brother. How does that sound?"

Megan looked uncertain. "Where are we going to put her?"

Bill thought for a moment. "What about the hall closet, downstairs?"

Megan brightened. "All right," she agreed. "But I get to carry her downstairs."

"Sounds fair enough," Bill agreed. He winked at Elizabeth. "After all, you've gotten to have it all morning. Don't you think it's only fair that Megan should get to carry it?"

For a moment he almost thought he saw hesitation in his wife's eyes, as if she wasn't quite ready to give up the doll, but then she smiled. "Of course," she agreed. She knelt down and handed the doll to Megan. "But you have to cradle it, just like I did. Even though it's not a real baby, you could hurt it if you dropped it, and it's very valuable."

"I won't drop her," Megan declared, holding the antique doll close to her chest just the way her mother had a moment earlier. "I love her."

Together, the family went downstairs and opened the hall closet. "She'll get cold in here," Megan said. "We have to wrap her in a blanket." She darted back up the stairs, returning a minute later with the small pink blanket that had first been in her crib, and since then at the foot of her bed. "She can use this," she said, carefully wrapping the doll in the blanket. Then she surrendered it to her father, who put it up on the shelf, nested among the woolen ski caps, gloves, and scarves.

"There," he said. "Now she'll sleep until we find out who she belongs to." But as they moved toward the dining room, where Mrs. Goodrich was putting their lunch on the table, he saw Megan turn back to look longingly at the closet.

He had a suspicion that before the afternoon was over, the doll would somehow have found its way from the closet to his daughter's room.

That, however, would be something Elizabeth would have to deal with, since he himself would be in Port Arbello.

"Do you really have to go?" Elizabeth asked when he told her what had happened at the bank that morning and what he had to do now.

"If we want to eat, I do. I'm pretty sure I can still get the job. But I'm probably going to have to hole up in a motel for the night, putting together numbers so I can nail it down in the morning." He glanced at his wife's swollen belly, which seemed—impossibly—to have grown even larger just in the few hours he'd been gone. "Will you be all right?"

"I have a whole month yet before he's due," Elizabeth said, instantly reading his thoughts. "Believe me, I'm not going to deliver early just because you're out of town. So go, do what you have to do, and don't worry about Megan and me. Mrs. Goodrich has been taking care of me all my life. She can do it one more night."

"Mrs. Goodrich is almost ninety," Bill reminded her. "She shouldn't even be working."

"Try telling her that," Elizabeth replied, laughing. "She'll eat you for supper!"

An hour later, when he was ready to take his overnight bag and portable computer out to the car, Bill's earlier uneasiness returned. "Maybe I better not go," he said. "Maybe I can do it all over the phone."

"You know you can't," Elizabeth said firmly. "Go on! Nothing's going to happen to us."

But even as he drove away from the house, Bill found himself looking back at it.

Looking back, and still feeling that something was wrong.

Chapter 5

*E*lizabeth was holding her baby—a perfect, tiny boy—cradling him gently against her breast. She was sitting on the porch, in a rocking chair, but it wasn't the porch of the house in Blackstone, nor, oddly, was the day nearly as cold as it should have been, with Christmas only three weeks away.

The summer mists seemed to part, and she realized where she was—back home in Port Arbello, on the porch of the old house on Conger's Point, and it was a perfect July day. A cool wind was blowing in off the sea, and the sound of surf breaking against the base of the bluff was lulling her baby into a contented sleep. She began humming softly, just loud enough so her baby could hear her, but quietly enough not to disturb him.

"Rockabye baby,
In the tree tops,
When the wind blows,
The cradle will rock . . ."

The words died away to nothing more than a murmuring hum, and Elizabeth began to feel drowsy, her eyelids heavy. But then, just as the song faded completely from her lips, a movement caught her eye.

A child was emerging from the woods across the field. Megan.

Elizabeth was about to call out to her daughter, but as

the child grew closer, she realized this little girl wasn't blond, sunny Megan at all.

It was her sister.

It was Sarah!

But that wasn't possible, for Sarah looked no older now than she had on that day so many years ago when she'd been taken away to the hospital.

Yet as the little girl drew closer, walking steadily across the field, directly toward her, Elizabeth felt a terrible chill.

Sarah was carrying something cradled in her arms. She was holding it out now, offering it to her, and Elizabeth recognized it instantly.

An arm.

Jimmy Tyler's arm . . .

Reflexively, Elizabeth looked down at her baby.

Her son was no longer sleeping. Instead, his eyes were wide open, and he was screaming, though no sound came out of his mouth. But worse than the silent scream, worse than the terror in the infant's eyes, was the blood spurting from her child's left shoulder, where the arm had been hacked away.

Elizabeth felt a scream rise from her lungs, but at the same time a terrible constriction closed her throat, and her howl of anguish stayed trapped within her, filling her up, making her feel as if she might explode into a million fragmented pieces. There was blood everywhere now, and Sarah, still holding the bloody arm that had been torn from the baby's body, was drawing closer and closer.

Elizabeth tried to turn away; could not. Finally, with an effort that seemed to sap every ounce of her energy, she hurled herself out of the chair and—

Elizabeth jerked awake. For an instant the terrible vision still hung before her. Her heart was pounding and she was gasping for breath. But as the dream quickly retreated, and as the hammering of her heart eased and her breathing returned to normal, she realized she wasn't back in Port Arbello at all.

She was in her room in Blackstone, on a December afternoon, and her baby was still safe in her womb. Yet, as if from a great distance, she once again heard the lullaby she had been crooning in the dream.

"When the bough breaks,
The cradle will fall,
And down will go baby,
Cradle and all . . ."

Elizabeth rose from the chaise on which she'd been sleeping and stepped out into the hall. The lullaby was louder now, and coming from Megan's room. Moving silently down the wide corridor that ran two-thirds of the length of the second floor, Elizabeth paused outside her daughter's door and listened.

She could still hear Megan, humming softly.

As she herself had been humming.

She opened the door a crack and peered inside.

Megan was sitting on her bed.

She was cradling the antique doll in her arms.

Elizabeth pushed the door wide. The lullaby died on Megan's lips as her eyes widened in surprise. Her arms tightened reflexively, pressing the doll close to her chest.

Elizabeth crossed the room until she was standing over her daughter. "We decided the doll would stay in the closet, didn't we?"

Megan shook her head. "You decided," she said. "I didn't."

"We all decided," Elizabeth told her. "Daddy, and Mommy, and you. So I'm going to put the doll away again. Do you understand?"

"But I want her," Megan protested. "I love her."

Reaching down, Elizabeth took the doll from her daughter. "She's not yours to love, Megan. Not yet. Perhaps someday, perhaps even someday soon. But not now. I'm putting it back in the closet," she said. "And you're not to touch it again. Do you understand?"

Megan looked up, saying nothing as Elizabeth left the room and closed the door. For a moment Megan felt hot tears flood her eyes. Then she realized: It didn't matter where her mother hid the doll. She would find it, and it would be hers.

Elizabeth carried the doll back downstairs and was about to put it back in the closet when she changed her mind. The closet would be the first place Megan would look. Leaving the hall, she went through the arched entry into the living room, then beyond it, in the library, saw the perfect place to put the doll: the top shelf of one of the pair of mahogany cases Bill had built to stand on either side of the fireplace.

The top shelf—one she could barely reach herself—was empty. Even if Megan spotted the doll up there, she wouldn't be able to get to it without a ladder. Positioning the doll as far back on the shelf as she could, Elizabeth was about to leave the library and return upstairs when her eyes fell on a portrait.

Along with the treasured books Elizabeth had brought with her from Port Arbello, there were framed pictures of her family and Bill's, and even an old Ouija board she and Sarah had played with when they were children. The portrait to which her eyes had been drawn was of one of Bill's aunts—the one named Laurette, Elizabeth dimly remembered, who had killed herself long before Bill had been born. Though Elizabeth had seen the portrait dozens of times before, this time something about it caught her eye. She stared at it, trying to understand what had captured her attention. Then her eyes returned to the doll that now sat on the top shelf of the mahogany case.

There was an odd resemblance between the doll and the woman in the portrait, Elizabeth realized.

The same blue eyes.

The same long blond hair.

The same pink cheeks and red lips.

It was as if the doll were a miniature version of the woman in the painting.

A thought flitted through Elizabeth's mind. Could it be possible that the doll had actually been modeled on this woman? Perhaps even been owned by her? As quickly as the thought came, Elizabeth dismissed it.

Going back upstairs, she stretched out on the chaise once more, and this time, when she slept, she didn't dream.

Megan McGuire's eyes opened in the darkness. For a moment she was startled, unsure what had awakened her, but then, on the far wall of her bedroom, she saw a shape.

The shape of a witch, inky black, with pointed hat and flowing gown, astride a long broomstick. In her hand—held high aloft—she grasped a sword.

The witch was moving now, flying higher, moving up toward the ceiling, hurtling through the air, then down toward Megan.

The little girl shrank into her pillow, pulling the covers tight around her neck as a shiver of fear passed through her.

Closer and closer the witch came, sword brandished.

Megan pressed deeper into the pillow.

Then, just as Megan could feel the first tingling of the sorceress's touch, the apparition vanished as suddenly as it had come, snatched away by an enormous flash of light.

As she always did, Megan lay still for a moment, savoring the delicious thrill that the shadow always gave her, even though she knew perfectly well that the soaring witch was no more than a momentary vision produced by a car driving up Amherst Street, then vanquished by its headlights the instant the car passed by the house.

The room returned to its familiar shape as the sound of

the car faded away, but as Megan released her grip on the blanket that covered her, she heard something else.

A sound so soft she almost couldn't hear it at all.

The sound grew louder as she listened, and then she knew exactly what it was.

Someone was crying.

A little girl with long blond hair, pink cheeks, and blue eyes.

A little girl wearing a ruffled white pinafore and a garland of flowers in her hair.

A little girl who wanted to be her friend, but whom her mommy had sent away.

Getting up from her bed, Megan pulled her robe over her flannel nightgown and slipped her feet into the woolly slippers Mrs. Goodrich had given her for Christmas last year. Pulling the door to her room open a crack, she peered out into the hallway. Farther down the hall, halfway to the stairs, she could see the door to her parents' room.

It was closed, and no light shone from the crack beneath it.

Silently, Megan crept along the hall, then down the stairs.

The little girl's crying was louder now. When Megan reached the bottom of the stairs, she peered through the dining room and butler's pantry, into the kitchen.

No light came from any of the rooms, nor could she hear the television droning in Mrs. Goodrich's room.

Save for the sound of the little girl's sobbing, the house was as silent as it was dark.

A last, sorrowful sob faded away, and a moment later Megan heard something else.

A voice calling her name.

"Megan . . . Megan . . . Megan . . ."

It was as if the voice had become a beacon. Megan followed it away from the kitchen and the housekeeper's quarters to the other side of the house. Through the darkness of the entry hall, she moved, through the deep shadows of the large living room, gliding as easily as if it were daylight, then pausing at the door to the library.

The voice grew louder: *"Megan . . . Megan . . ."*

The library was almost pitch-black. Megan stood in the darkness, listening. Then, through the French doors leading to the flagstoned side patio, the first rays of the rising moon crept into the room. In that first instant of faint illumination, Megan saw them.

The eyes of the doll, gleaming in the moonlight, gazing down at her from the top shelf of the tall case that stood against the wall to the right of the fireplace.

So high that her mother thought she wouldn't be able to reach it.

But Megan knew better. As silent and surefooted as she'd been when she crept through the upstairs hall and down the stairs, she crossed the library and began climbing up the shelves of the cabinet as easily as if they were the steps of a ladder.

Elizabeth jerked awake, not from the terror of another nightmare, but from a loud crash, immediately followed by a terrified shriek. Then, a long, wailing cry.

Megan!

Heaving herself out of bed and ignoring the robe lying on the chaise longue, Elizabeth stumbled through the darkness toward the bedroom door. She fumbled with the two old-fashioned light switches set in the wall next to the door. A second later the overhead fixture in the center of the ceiling came on, filling the room with harsh white light. Blinking in the glare, Elizabeth jerked the bedroom door open and stepped into the hall, now lit brightly with its own three chandeliers.

Megan's door was closed, but as Elizabeth started toward her daughter's room, another scream rent the night.

Downstairs!

Megan had gone downstairs and—

The doll! She'd found the doll and tried to get it, and—

Heart beating wildly, Elizabeth lurched to the top of the long flight and started down. When she was still three steps from the bottom, the lights in the entry hall came on, illuminating Mrs. Goodrich, wrapped in a tattered chenille bathrobe, shuffling toward the living room.

As still another cry echoed through the house, Elizabeth came to the bottom of the stairs and rushed through the living room. At the door to the library, she reached for the bank of switches, pressing every one her fingers touched. As the lights flashed on and every shadow was washed from the room, the vision Elizabeth had seen only in her mind a few moments before was now revealed in its terrible reality.

The mahogany case had fallen forward. Beneath it, Elizabeth could see Megan struggling to free herself from the massive weight pressing down on her. The pictures and curios that had filled the case's shelves were scattered everywhere, shards of glass from broken picture frames littered the carpet, and figurines lay broken all around her.

Megan's shrieks had deepened to a sobbing cry.

Choking back a scream, Elizabeth rushed across the room and bent down, her fingers curling around the front edge of the cabinet's top.

From the doorway, realizing what Elizabeth was about to do, Mrs. Goodrich cried out. "Don't! You mustn't!"

Ignoring the old housekeeper's plea, Elizabeth summoned every ounce of strength she could muster and heaved the case upward, lifting it off her daughter. "Move, Megan," Elizabeth cried. "Get out from—" Her words cut off by a terrible flash of pain that felt as if a knife had been thrust into her belly, Elizabeth struggled to hold on to the cabinet while Megan, finally responding to her mother's voice, squirmed free. A second later the weight of the cabinet overwhelmed her and it crashed back to the floor. Elizabeth sank down onto the carpet as

another wrenching pain ripped through her and she felt
something inside her give way.

"Call . . . ambulance," she gasped, her hands clutching
protectively at her belly. "Oh, God, Mrs. Goodrich.
Hurry!"

Wave after wave of pain was crushing her. Elizabeth
felt a terrible weakness come over her, and the light
began to fade.

The last thing she saw before darkness closed around
her was Megan, on her feet now and looking down at her.

In Megan's arms, utterly undamaged by the accident
that had smashed everything else the cabinet had held,
was the doll.

Chapter 6

*B*ill McGuire turned into the nearly deserted parking lot of Blackstone Memorial Hospital and pulled the car into the space closest to the emergency entrance. He'd driven for nearly three hours, leaving the motel in Port Arbello minutes after he'd gotten the call from Mrs. Goodrich, pausing only long enough to drop the room key through the mail slot in the office's locked front door. Throughout the frantic drive to Blackstone, he'd had to force himself time and again to slow down, reminding himself that the objective was to get home as quickly as possible, but in one piece. Still, the drive seemed endless. He managed to reach the hospital three times on his cellular phone, but all three connections ended in a frustrating crackle of static.

All he'd been able to find out was that Elizabeth had gone into labor, and that things were "going as well as can be expected."

Oh dear God, let her live, he prayed. Dear merciful God, let the baby be all right.

Oh God, why, *why* did I have to leave them tonight, of all nights?

Tensed over the wheel, he felt sharp, stabbing needles of guilt as he raced through the darkness, returning from a trip that now seemed utterly unnecessary. He'd won the condo project, but even while putting together the final figures in the motel room, he'd known he could have

47

done the whole thing on the phone from his desk in the library at home.

Slamming the car door behind him, barely able to wait for the automatic glass doors to open for him, Bill raced into the waiting room and immediately spotted Mrs. Goodrich, still wearing her old chenille bathrobe, sitting on a sagging green-plastic upholstered sofa, her arm wrapped protectively around Megan, whose forehead was partially covered by a bandage. Mrs. Goodrich, in her fear for the welfare of the person she loved best in the world, looked almost as small as Megan, but as Bill approached he saw a determined glimmer in the old woman's eyes, and she made a gesture as if to shoo him away.

"We're all right," she told him. "Just a little cut on Megan's forehead, but it doesn't even hurt anymore, does it, darlin'?"

Megan bobbed her head. "I just fell off the shelves, that's all," she said in a small voice.

"You go see to Elizabeth," Mrs. Goodrich went on. "We'll be right here. You tell Elizabeth we're praying for her."

A few seconds later Bill was following a doctor down the hall, listening to a brief explanation of what had happened. Then he was in the room where Elizabeth lay in bed, her face ashen, her blond hair, darkened only slightly over the years, spread around her head like a halo.

As if sensing that at last he was there, Elizabeth stirred in the bed, and when Bill took her hand, he immediately felt her respond with a weak squeeze. But it was enough.

She was going to be all right.

For Elizabeth, waking up was like trying to rise through a pool of molasses. Every muscle in her body felt exhausted, and even breathing seemed an almost impossible chore. Slowly, she began to come back to consciousness, and then, feeling Bill's hand in her own, she forced herself to open her eyes.

She was not in her bed.

Not in her home.

Then the nightmare began to come back to her.

"Megan," she whispered, straining to sit up, but barely managing to raise her head from the pillow.

"Megan's fine," Bill told her. "She and Mrs. Goodrich are out in the waiting room, and all Megan has is a little cut on her forehead."

"Thank God," Elizabeth sighed. She dropped her head back onto the pillow, and her left hand moved to touch her belly in the nearly unconscious gesture she'd developed during both of her pregnancies.

At the movement, fear lurched inside her.

Then it came back to her: the terrible flash of pain, the breaking of her water, and the first violent contractions of labor. Contractions so unbearably painful that they'd caused her to pass out.

"The baby," she whispered. Her gaze fastened on her husband's, and though Bill said nothing for a second or two, Elizabeth could read the truth in his eyes. "No." The word emerged as a despairing moan. "Oh, please, no. The baby can't be . . ." Her voice faded away as she found herself incapable of uttering the final, terrible word.

"Shhh," Bill whispered, holding a finger to her lips, then brushing a lock of hair away from her suddenly clammy forehead. "The important thing is that you're all right."

The important thing. The important thing . . .

The words ricocheted through Elizabeth's mind, leaving bruises everywhere they went.

. . . you're all right . . .

But she wasn't all right. How could she be all right if their baby—their son—was . . . was . . .

"I want to see him," she said, her hand tightening in Bill's. "Oh, God, please let me see him." Her voice started to break. "If I can see him, I can make him all right." She was sobbing now, and Bill moved from the chair to the bed, gathering her into his arms to hold her close and comfort her.

"It's all right, darling," he whispered. "It's not your fault. It's just something that happened. We knew it might happen. It was hard enough when you had Megan, and maybe we just shouldn't have tried again. But it's not your fault. Don't ever think it's your fault."

Elizabeth barely heard the words. "The case," she whispered. "I put the doll in the case, and it fell on her. My fault. My fault."

"It was an accident," Bill said. "It wasn't anybody's fault."

But Elizabeth still heard nothing of her husband's words. "I lifted it off her. I lifted it up so she could get out. And it killed our son. It killed our son. . . ." Her words dissolved into broken sobbing. For a long time Bill held her, stroking her hair, soothing and comforting her. Finally, after nearly half an hour, her sobbing began to ease, and the terrible convulsive shaking that had seized her slowly lost its grip. A little while later Bill heard her breathing drift into the long rhythmic pattern of sleep, and felt her body at last relax in his arms. Kissing her gently, he eased himself up from the bed, then tucked the sheet and blanket close around her. He kissed her once more, then quietly slipped out of the room.

The strange numbness had already begun to set in as he walked back down the corridor toward the waiting room.

His son—for indeed the baby had been a boy, just as he and Elizabeth had hoped—was dead.

Dead, without having ever taken a breath.

Should he ask to see the baby?

The thought alone made him wince, and instantly he knew he would not. Better to keep an image in his mind of what might have been: a happy, grinning, gurgling son for whom no dreams would be too great.

Better to cling to the memories of a future that might

have been than to gaze directly at the tragedy that had just befallen him.

To see the child who might have been would bring far more pain than Bill McGuire could bear, and in the days to come Elizabeth—and Megan too—were going to need everything he had to give.

He pushed through the doors to the waiting room, and it seemed to him that neither Megan nor Mrs. Goodrich had moved at all. The old housekeeper still held his daughter close, and though Megan's head rested against Mrs. Goodrich's ample bosom, her eyes were open and watchful.

Cradled in her arms, she held the doll.

For an instant, and only an instant, Bill was tempted to snatch the doll from Megan's arms, to tear it apart and hurl it out into the night, to destroy utterly the thing that had come into their house only this morning and already done such damage to their lives. But that thought, too, he discarded from his mind. The doll, after all, was not at fault, and Megan, at least, seemed to be taking a certain comfort from it.

Pulling a chair close to the sofa, he sat down and took his daughter's hands.

"Is he here?" the little girl asked. "Has my brother been born?"

Bill felt a sob rise in his throat, but determinedly put it down. "He's been born," he said quietly. "But he had to go away."

Megan seemed puzzled. "Go away?" she repeated. "Where?"

"To Heaven," Bill said. A gasp of sorrow escaped from Mrs. Goodrich's throat. Her arm tightened around Megan, but she said nothing. "You see, Megan," Bill went on, "God loves little children very much, and sometimes He calls one of them to come and be with Him. Remember how He said, 'Suffer the little children to come unto me'? And that is where your brother's gone. To be with God."

"What about my Elizabeth?" Mrs. Goodrich whispered, her eyes wide with fear.

"She's going to be all right," Bill assured her. "She's asleep right now, but she's going to be just fine." He stood up. "Why don't I take you and Megan home?" he said. "Then I'll come back and stay with Elizabeth."

Mrs. Goodrich nodded and got stiffly to her feet. Her hand clutching Bill for support, she let him guide her out to the car. Megan followed behind them, the doll held tightly in her arms.

"It's all right," Megan whispered to the doll as they passed through the glass doors into the night. "You're better than any brother could be."

Chapter 7

*E*lizabeth McGuire stayed in the hospital for three days, and on the afternoon that Bill finally brought her home, the weather was every bit as bleak as her mood. A steel-gray sky hung low overhead, and the first true chill of winter was in the air. Elizabeth, though, hardly noticed the cold as she walked from the garage to the back door of the big house, for her body was almost as numb as her emotions.

The moment she entered the house, she sensed that something had changed, and though Bill suggested she go right up to their room and rest for a while, she refused, instead moving from room to room, unsure what she was looking for, but certain that she would know it when she found it. Each room she entered seemed exactly as it had been before. Every piece of furniture was in place. The pictures still hung in their accustomed spots. Even the mahogany case in the library was back where it belonged—screwed to the wall with much heavier hardware this time, so the accident could never be repeated—and even most of the objects it contained had been repaired and put neatly back in their places. Only the doll was gone. Elizabeth shuddered as she gazed up at the empty shelf where she'd placed it. Apart from the doll, all was as it should have been.

The photographs were back in their silver frames; the shattered glass all replaced.

Fleetingly, Elizabeth wondered if her spirit could be

repaired as easily as the damage to the pictures, but even as the question came to mind, so also did the answer.

The pictures might have been made right again; she would never be.

Finally she went upstairs, retreating wordlessly to her room.

Later that night, when Bill had come to bed, she remained silent. Though she could feel the warmth of his body lying next to hers, and his strong arms holding her, she still felt more alone than she ever had before. When finally he drifted into sleep, she lay awake gazing up at the shadows that stretched across the ceiling, and began to imagine them as black fingers reaching out to squeeze her sanity from her mind as her own body had squeezed her son from her womb. Elizabeth realized then that it wasn't the house that had changed. It was she who was different now. Long minutes ticked away the night while she wondered if she could ever be whole again.

Finally she left the bed, slipping out from beneath the comforter so quietly that Bill didn't stir at all. Clad only in her thin silk nightgown, but oblivious to the damp chill that had seeped into the room through the open window, she walked on bare feet through the bathroom that connected the master bedroom to the nursery next door. In the dim illumination from the street lamps outside, the bright patterned wallpaper had lost its color, and the animals that appeared to gambol playfully across the walls when she had hung the paper a few short months ago now seemed to Elizabeth to be stalking her in the night. In the crib, lying in wait on a satin comforter, lay a forlorn and lonely-looking teddy bear.

Alone in the darkness, Elizabeth silently began to weep.

"Maybe I should just stay home today," Bill suggested the next morning as the family was finishing breakfast.

Elizabeth, sitting across from him at one end of the huge dining table that could seat twenty people if the need should ever arise, shook her head. "I'll be fine," she insisted, though the pallor in her face and her trembling hands belied the words. "You have a lot to do. If I need anything, Mrs. Goodrich and Megan can take care of me. Can't you, darling?" she added, reaching out to put her arm around Megan, who was perched on the chair next to her.

The little girl bobbed her head. "I can take care of Mommy. Just like I can take care of Sam."

"Sam?" Bill asked.

"That's what I named my doll," Megan explained.

Bill frowned. "But Sam's a boy's name, honey."

Megan gave her father a look that declared she thought he was being deliberately dense. "It's short for Samantha," she informed him. "Everybody knows that."

"Except me," Bill said.

"That's because you're a boy, Daddy. Boys don't know anything at all!"

"Boys aren't so bad," Bill said quickly, his eyes flicking toward Elizabeth.

"I hate them," Megan declared. "I wish they were all d—"

"You wish they were all girls like you, right?" Bill interjected quickly, cutting off his daughter before she could quite finish the last word.

"That's not what I was going to say," Megan protested, but by now her father was on his feet and had come around the end of the table to lift her out of her chair.

He held her high up over his head.

"I don't care what you were going to say," he said, swinging her low, toward the floor, then lifting her up once again. "All I care about is that you take as good care of your mommy as you do of your dolly. Can you do that?" Megan, overcome by giggling, nodded, and Bill set her down on the floor. "Good. Now run along and let me talk to your mother for a minute." When she was gone, Bill dropped down next to Elizabeth. "You're sure you'll be all right?" he asked.

"I'll be fine," Elizabeth assured him. "You do what you have to do. Megan and Mrs. Goodrich will take care of me."

Rising from her chair, she walked with him to the door, kissed him good-bye, then stood watching until his car had disappeared around the corner. But when he was finally gone and she'd shut the door, she slumped against the wall for a moment, afraid she might collapse to the floor without its support. A moment later she heard Mrs. Goodrich behind her, clucking worriedly.

"Now you get yourself back upstairs and into bed, young lady," the housekeeper said, reverting to the same no-nonsense tone she'd used years ago, when she felt Elizabeth wasn't behaving in a manner she considered quite proper. "The best thing for you is a good long rest, and there's nothing in this house I can't take care of."

Too tired to do anything but agree with Mrs. Goodrich's command, Elizabeth mounted the stairs. But when she reached the door of the master bedroom, instead of going inside, she paused, gazing down the hall toward Megan's room, whose door stood slightly ajar. Though she heard no sound coming from her daughter's room, something seemed to be drawing her to it. A moment later she was standing in the doorway gazing at the doll, which sat on Megan's bed, propped up against the pillows.

It seemed to be gazing back at her. Something in its eyes—eyes that now seemed so lifelike she could hardly believe they were only glass set in a porcelain head—reached out to her, touched a nerve deep inside her, took hold of her. Elizabeth picked the doll up, cradled it in her arms, and walked slowly back to her own room, closing and locking the door behind her.

Sitting down in front of the mirror above her vanity table, she put the doll in her lap and began brushing its hair, humming softly. As the brush moved gently through the doll's hair in a soothing rhythm, the numbness within Elizabeth began to lift and the pain began to ease. When the brushing was finally done, Elizabeth moved to the chaise, stretching out on it, the doll resting on her breast, almost as if it were nursing. Warmed by the morning sun streaming though the window, and comforted by the doll resting against her chest, Elizabeth drifted into the first peaceful sleep she'd had since losing the baby.

Bill McGuire was starting to wonder if anything was ever going to go right again. Since the day Jules Hartwick had told him the Blackstone Center loan was on hold, it seemed as if everything that could go wrong, had. Worst of all, of course, had been Elizabeth's miscarriage. After Megan's birth they'd been told it was unlikely that Elizabeth would be able to conceive again, and they had all but given up hope of a second child when Elizabeth discovered back in April that she was pregnant. "But it's going to be tricky," Dr. Margolis told them. "And this will definitely be the last." So now it was over, and though Bill still felt a terrible sense of emptiness and loss, the agony of that first night when he'd come back to Blackstone to find that his son had been born dead had already begun to dull.

He knew he was going to survive it, and that somehow he would carry Elizabeth through the loss as well.

As if the loss of his son were not enough, it seemed the gods were somehow conspiring against him. He had raced home from Port Arbello thinking he'd won the condo project. But yesterday he'd received a call from the developer to tell him that the contract—the contract he'd counted on to carry him through until the Blackstone Center project came back to life—had gone to an outfit from Boston, which came in with a late bid that Bill knew he couldn't possibly undercut. In fact, he was certain the Boston firm had no intention of staying within the bid they'd submitted, and planned to make up their losses on change orders. He'd argued with the developer, but the man would not be convinced. So now he was back at the bank on the slim hope that Jules Hartwick might have some good news for him. As he pulled his car into a parking slot, however, he saw Ed Becker going into the bank. A preoccupied scowl on the lawyer's face was enough to tell him that whatever news might be coming out of Jules Hartwick's office would not be good.

Instead of entering the bank, Bill veered off the other way and walked down the street to the offices of the *Blackstone Chronicle*. An old-fashioned bell tinkled as he pushed the door open, and all three people in the office looked up.

Angela Corelli, the young woman who served as receptionist and secretary, and Lois Martin, who had been Oliver Metcalf's assistant editor and layout artist for fifteen years, greeted him with embarrassed smiles and quickly downcast eyes. Only Oliver immediately got up, came around from behind his desk, and took his hand. "I'm so sorry about what happened," he said. "I know how much you and Elizabeth were looking forward to the new baby."

"Thanks, Oliver," Bill said. "I'm just starting to think maybe I'm going to make it, but Elizabeth's taking it pretty hard."

The older of the two women in the office finally seemed to recover her wits. "I was thinking I should call her," Lois Martin offered. "But it's just so hard to know what to say."

"I'm sure she'd appreciate hearing from you," Bill told her. "But you might want to wait a couple of days."

"If there's anything any of us can do, just let us know," Oliver said. He gestured to the wooden chair in front of his desk. "Got time for a chat?"

"Actually, I was hoping I might be able to pick up some news," Bill said. "About the bank."

Oliver shrugged. "Your guess is as good as mine. I

keep calling Jules Hartwick, but I always get steered to Melissa Holloway instead."

Bill sighed. "Well, at least I no longer feel like I'm the only one. How can someone who looks that sweet be that efficient? And how'd she get to be second in command at her age?"

"Takes after her father," Oliver replied. "One of the smartest men I ever met, except when it came to picking a wife. Charles Holloway's a terrific lawyer, but his second wife was a terror. Hated Melissa. Melissa got through it, though."

But Bill McGuire had stopped listening, his mind already focusing on what to do next, calculating how much money he had in the bank—assuming the bank wasn't about to collapse—and how long it would last him. The numbers gave him no comfort. The fact of the matter was that the odds of finding a construction job that could carry him through till spring were pretty much zip. If he was going to avoid going broke, he was going to have to get to work on a new line of credit. He rose to his feet. "If you hear anything—anything at all—let me know, okay?"

"You'll hear it before I even start to write the story," Oliver promised.

As they walked toward the front door, it opened and Rebecca Morrison stepped inside. Taking in the number of people in the little newspaper office, though, she blushed crimson and turned to leave again.

"Rebecca?" Oliver said. "What is it? Can I help you with something?"

She hesitated, then turned back, her cheeks still flushed red. Her eyes nervously flicked from one face to another, but finally came to rest on Oliver. Taking a tentative step toward him, she held out her hand. "Th-this is for you," she said. "Just because you're always so nice to me." Her flush deepening once again, she turned away and quickly ducked out the door.

Oliver peered into the bag. Inside, wrapped in shiny silver foil, were a dozen chocolate Kisses. When he looked up again, everyone in the office was staring at him.

Staring, and smiling.

Oliver broke into a smile too, wishing Rebecca hadn't scurried out of the office quite so fast.

"Well, at least some people's lives are going right," Bill McGuire said, slapping Oliver on the back as he left the office.

Seeing how happy the little bag of silver-wrapped chocolates had made Oliver, his own troubles no longer seemed quite so grim. Maybe, Bill thought, he'd just stop at the candy store and pick up a bag for Elizabeth. No, make that three bags; no sense in leaving Megan and Mrs. Goodrich out.

Suddenly, Bill McGuire felt better than he had in days.

An hour later Elizabeth came awake again, stretching languorously, savoring the feeling of well-being that had replaced the terrible torpor she'd felt earlier this morning. But as the last vestiges of sleep were sloughed away and she came back to consciousness, she slowly became aware of someone moving around in the next room.

The nursery.

Megan?

But what would Megan be doing in the nursery?

Rising from the chaise and carrying the doll with her, Elizabeth went through the bathroom and into the nursery.

Mrs. Goodrich, her back to Elizabeth, was in the process of emptying the contents of the little dresser, which stood against the opposite wall, into a large cardboard box.

"Who told you to do that?" Elizabeth demanded.

Startled by Elizabeth's words, Mrs. Goodrich whirled around. "Oh, dear," she said. "You frightened me, popping out of the bathroom that way. You go on back to bed, dear. I can take care of all this."

"All what?" Elizabeth asked, moving out of the bathroom doorway into the middle of the room. "What are you doing?"

Mrs. Goodrich placed the tiny sweater she held in her hands into the box and took another from the dresser drawer. "I just thought I'd get all this packed away for you, and put away in the attic."

"No," Elizabeth said.

Mrs. Goodrich blinked. "Beg pardon?"

Elizabeth's voice hardened. "I said no, Mrs. Goodrich." Her voice began to rise. "How dare you come in here and start packing all my baby's clothes."

"But I thought you'd want—" Ms. Goodrich began. Elizabeth didn't let her finish.

"I don't care what you thought. Go back downstairs and leave me alone. And from now on, stay out of this room!" Mrs. Goodrich hesitated, but before she could argue, Elizabeth spoke again. "Just go! I'll take care of this."

Mrs. Goodrich stared at Elizabeth in shock, barely able to believe her ears. Should she try to argue with her? she wondered.

No, she decided. Better not to say anything right now. After all, given what she'd been through, Elizabeth couldn't be expected to be herself quite yet. It was her own fault, really. She should have given Elizabeth more time before she began packing away the things in the nursery.

Laying the sweater in her hand on the top of the dresser, Mrs. Goodrich quietly left the room.

When she was gone, Elizabeth went to the dresser and began removing the clothes—the little play suits and pajamas, the tiny overalls, bibs, and shirts—from the box, carefully smoothing each one out and refolding it before putting each item back in the drawer from which it had come.

"How could she do that?" she asked the doll, which she'd sat on the dresser so it was leaning up against the wall, exactly as if it were watching what she was doing. "Doesn't she realize you're going to need all these things?" Taking a small sweater out of the box, she shook it out, then held it up against the doll. "Still a little big, but in a few months it will fit perfectly, won't it? What could she have been thinking of?" Still talking to the doll, Elizabeth folded the sweater and put it in the drawer next to the bottom, with all the other sweaters. When the box was empty and all the baby clothes were back where they belonged, she picked up the doll and carried it to the crib, where she carefully tucked it under the comforter and kissed it softly on the cheek.

"Time for a nap," she whispered. "But don't you worry. Mommy will be right here." Settling into the blue rocking chair next to the crib, Elizabeth softly began crooning a lullaby.

From the open doorway to the hall, unnoticed by her mother, Megan watched.

Chapter 8

"Something's wrong with Mommy," Megan announced as her father came through the front door. She was sitting on the bottom step of the hall stairway, her face stormy. "She took Sam."

"Your doll?" Bill asked. "Why would she do that?"

"I don't know," Megan replied. "And she got mad at Mrs. Goodrich too. Real mad." Then she saw the paper bags tied with red ribbon, and got up. "Is that for me?"

"One bag's for you," Bill told her, "and one's for your mother, and one's for Mrs. Goodrich." He gave her one of the little bags of chocolate Kisses. "You can have one now. Then we'll put the rest away for later."

"Mommy shouldn't get any," Megan said. "If I were bad, you wouldn't let me have any."

Bill knelt down so his eyes were level with his daughter's. "Honey, Mommy isn't being bad. She's just very, very sad right now. And if she took your doll, I'm sure there's a good reason."

Megan shook her head. "She just wanted it. But Sam wants to be with me."

"I'll tell you what," Bill said. "I'll go up and talk to Mommy, and see if I can find out why she took Sam. Okay?" Megan nodded, her hand disappearing into the bag, emerging with a fistful of Kisses. "Only one now," Bill said. "You can have another after lunch. And we'll save the rest for later."

Megan hesitated, calculating the odds of getting her

way if she begged for more of the candy right now. Reluctantly, she dropped all but one of the chocolates back in the bag. As her father started up the stairs, though, she quickly sneaked another one, and then a third.

Bill headed for the master bedroom, expecting to find Elizabeth either in bed or lying on the chaise. But the room was empty. Then, through the open door to the bathroom, he heard the soft creaking of the antique rocker in the nursery. Why would Elizabeth have gone in there? Since the miscarriage, even he hadn't been able to bring himself to go into the room they'd been preparing for the new baby. And for Elizabeth, going into the nursery had to be agonizing. Yet something had drawn her into it.

He crossed the bedroom and stepped into the connecting bathroom. Though the door opposite him stood ajar, he could see little of the room beyond. And now in addition to the creaking rocking chair, he could hear Elizabeth, quietly humming a lullaby.

He pushed the door to the nursery farther open.

Elizabeth was seated in the chair. Her back was to him, but he could see that she was holding something in her arms.

Something to which she was humming the quiet song.

"Elizabeth?" he asked, starting toward the chair.

The rocking stopped, as did Elizabeth's humming. "Bill?"

He bent over to kiss her on the cheek, but pulled back abruptly.

In her arms, wrapped in the soft pink and blue woolen blanket they had bought only a week earlier, was the doll. Its blue eyes were staring up at him, and for the tiniest fraction of a second Bill had the feeling that they were watching him. But then the moment passed and he brushed his lips against Elizabeth's cheek.

Her flesh felt oddly cold.

"Honey? Are you all right?"

Elizabeth nodded, but said nothing.

"I brought you something."

A flicker of interest came into her eyes, and she stood up. "Let me just put the baby back in his crib."

The baby . . . The words echoed in Bill's mind as Elizabeth gently laid the doll in the crib and tucked the little blanket around it. "How come you brought Megan's doll in here?" he asked as she turned back to face him. A flash of confusion appeared in Elizabeth's eyes, and then they cleared.

"Well, we don't really know the doll was meant for her, do we?" she asked, but there was a brittleness to her voice that sent a warning chill through her husband. "It could have been for the new baby, couldn't it?"

"I suppose it could," Bill conceded uneasily. "But don't you think—"

"Can't we just leave it here for now, at least?" Elizabeth pleaded. "When I came in here this morning, the room just seemed so empty, and lonely, but when I brought Sam in, it just seemed to fill right up." Her eyes flicked toward the crib. "Sam," she repeated. "What a nice name. I always thought if we had a boy, it would be nice to name him Sam."

Another warning current tingled through Bill. Though he and Elizabeth had discussed a lot of names, he couldn't remember either one of them ever mentioning Sam. "I think Megan really—" Bill began, only to be quickly interrupted by his wife.

"Megan can get along without the doll for now," she said. "And it will only be for a day or two." She smiled at him, then moved close, putting her arms around him. "I can't explain it, really," she whispered, her lips close to his ear. "It just makes it easier for me. Can't you understand that?"

Bill's arms closed around her and he wished there

were something—anything—he could do to ease her pain. "Of course I can understand," he replied. "If it makes you feel better, there's no reason you can't keep the doll in here for a little while. I'm sure Megan will understand."

In the hall outside the nursery, Megan scowled angrily. Her father hadn't taken the doll away from her mother after all.

In fact, he'd told her she could keep it.

And Megan didn't understand.

She didn't understand at all.

✳

Chapter 9

*T*he moment Bill awakened, he knew Elizabeth was no longer beside him, but as the big clock downstairs began to strike midnight, he still reached out to his wife's empty place in the hope his instincts might have betrayed him.

They had not. The bed was empty, the sheets almost as cold as the room itself.

He lay in bed for a moment, trying to decide what to do. The evening had not been easy for any of them. First he'd had to try to explain to Megan that right now her mother needed the doll more than she did. "Mommy's sick," he'd told her. "And she needs the doll to take care of her."

"But she's always sick," Megan had protested. "And I need Sam to take care of me!"

"In a few days," he'd promised, but he could see the doubt in Megan's eyes, and when Elizabeth finally came down for supper, the three of them sat tensely at the table. Megan, usually full of chatter about what she'd been doing all day, barely spoke at all, and Elizabeth was utterly silent.

After dinner he'd tried to interest his wife and daughter in watching a videotape, but Megan quickly retreated to her room, and although Elizabeth sat beside him on the sofa in the library, he knew she wasn't paying attention to the movie. Finally, a little after nine, they both came up to bed.

While he stopped in to kiss Megan good night, Elizabeth went directly to their room. He told himself she'd sensed

Megan's anger and was simply giving her daughter some
time to get over it, but deep inside he suspected that Elizabeth had simply not been able to consider Megan's feelings, any more than she'd been able to concentrate on the
movie.

"Mommy doesn't love me anymore, does she?" Megan
had asked when he'd gone in to say good night. Her voice
was quavering, and though he couldn't see her face in the
shadowy room, he'd tasted the saltiness of tears when he
kissed her cheek.

"Of course she loves you," he'd assured her. "She's
just not feeling well, that's all."

But Megan had not been consoled. "No, she doesn't,"
she insisted. "She just loves Sam."

He'd tried to assure her that things would be better
tomorrow, when the two of them would go and find a
Christmas tree, but even that hadn't cheered Megan up.
When he left her room, she'd already rolled over, turning
her back to him.

Things had been no better with Elizabeth. She was
already in bed, and though he knew she wasn't asleep,
she hadn't responded when he tried to cuddle her close to
him. At last he'd given up, contenting himself with lying
next to her and holding her hand, determined to stay
awake until he heard her breath drift into the steady
rhythms of sleep.

But he hadn't been able to stay awake, and now he'd
awakened to find himself alone.

The last gong of the hour struck, leaving the house in
silence. Then he heard the squeak of the rocking chair.
Slipping out of bed and putting on the thick woolen robe
Elizabeth had given him two Christmases ago, he went
through the bathroom into the nursery.

Elizabeth was sitting in the rocking chair she had res-
cued from the attic and painted pale blue.

Once more, she was humming a soft lullaby to the
doll, as she had when he'd come home in the afternoon.

But tonight she was doing something else as well.

The pale skin of her bare breast gleamed in the moonlight, and he could see the doll's head pressed firmly against her nipple.

He went to her and knelt beside the rocking chair. "Come back to bed, darling," he whispered. "You're so tired, and it's so late."

For a moment he wasn't sure she heard him, but then she turned her head and smiled at him. "In a minute," she said. "I have to finish feeding the baby, and then put him down for the night."

Though she'd spoken the words softly, in a voice so sweet it broke his heart, they still sliced through him like tiny knives.

"No, darling," he said. "It's not a baby. It's just a doll." He rose to his feet and reached down as if to take the doll from her, but she shrank away from him, and he saw her arms tighten. "Elizabeth, please," he said. "Don't do this. You know it's not a—"

"Don't say it!" she commanded, her voice rising. "Just go back to bed!"

"For God's sake, Elizabeth—" he began again, but once again his wife cut his words off.

"Leave me alone!" she shouted. "I didn't ask you to come in here! And I know what I'm doing! I can take care of my baby!" She was on her feet now, and there was a look in her eye that frightened Bill.

"It's all right," he said, forcing his voice back to a gently soothing tone. "Of course you know what you're doing, and of course you can take care of the baby. It's just late, that's all. I thought maybe I could help you."

"I can do it," Elizabeth said, her voice taking on an edge of desperation. "I can take care of my baby. I know I can. Just leave us alone and we'll be fine." Her eyes met his now, beseeching him. "Please? Can't you just leave us alone for a little while?"

Suddenly Bill felt utterly disoriented. Was his wife losing her mind? What should he do?

Take the doll away from her? No! That would only make things worse.

The doctor. He should call Dr. Margolis. Dr. Margolis would know what to do. "All right," he said, taking care to keep his voice perfectly level. "I'll go back to bed, and you take care of—" He faltered for a moment, but then managed to finish the sentence. "—the baby. And when he's gone to sleep, you'll come back to bed. All right?"

Elizabeth nodded, sinking back into the rocking chair. His throat constricting as a sob formed in his chest, Bill turned and hurried back through the bathroom, carefully closing the door behind him. But instead of going back to bed as he'd told Elizabeth he would, he went downstairs to the desk in the library, and the telephone.

After the twelfth ring he finally heard the sleepy, and faintly annoyed, voice of Dr. Margolis.

An hour later Elizabeth was back in bed, the pills the doctor had given her already taking effect. "I'll be all right," she said as she began to drift into sleep. "Really I will. All I need to do is take care of my baby and I'll be all right." Then, as Bill kissed her gently, her eyes closed.

Leaving Mrs. Goodrich to watch over Elizabeth, Bill led the doctor down to the library, where he poured each of them a shot of his best single-malt scotch. "I don't know about you, but I really need this," he said, handing Margolis one of the glasses, then draining half the other.

"I'm not sure it's as bad as you think it is," the doctor observed, taking a sip of the whiskey, rolling it around in his mouth, then swallowing it.

"For God's sake, Phil! She thought the doll was a baby. *Our* baby!"

The doctor's brows arched slightly. "She's had a terrible shock, Bill. I don't think any man can truly understand how hard it is for a woman to lose a baby.

Especially when she knows there's no chance of having another one, and she thought she was long past any danger."

"But to fantasize that a doll is—"

"But isn't that what little girls do all the time? Don't they pretend their dolls are real babies?"

"It's hardly the same thing."

"Isn't it?" Margolis countered. "Why not? The way I see it, Elizabeth is in so much pain right now that she simply can't deal with it. So tonight she projected all her maternal feelings—the ones she's been storing up, ready to shower on your son—onto the doll. I suspect it was far more an emotional release than a true delusion."

"And you don't think I should be worried?" Bill asked, hope mingling with his doubt.

"Of course you should be worried," the doctor replied. "Hell, if you weren't worried, I'd be more concerned about you than about Elizabeth. All I'm saying is that I think right now you need to cut Elizabeth a lot of slack. I suspect that by morning she'll be feeling a lot better. But even if she wants to pretend the doll is her baby for a day or two, where's the real harm? Right now she's got hormones raging through her, causing all kinds of confusion, and she's in just as much turmoil emotionally as she is chemically. Let's just give her another day to calm down, and then take another look at how she's doing. Deal?"

Bill hesitated, but as he turned Margolis's words over in his mind, he began to see their wisdom. Finally he took the doctor's outstretched hand. "Deal."

In her room, Megan lay in her bed, watching the shadows on the ceiling. She'd been awake a long time, listening through the nursery door, hearing every word her mother and father had said.

And now, as she lay gazing at the dark shapes above her, she heard another voice.

The voice of the doll.

But tonight it wasn't calling out to her.

Tonight it was whispering.

As it spoke, Megan listened, and began to understand what she must do.

Chapter 10

*T*he next morning dawned bright and clear, with no trace of the slate gray overcast that had gathered like a shroud over Blackstone nearly every day of the past week. Leaving Elizabeth to sleep as long as she could, Bill was dressed and at the desk in the library by six. By eight, when Megan came in to report that Mrs. Goodrich was going to throw his breakfast away if he didn't come to the table *right now*, he'd reached the conclusion that if he and Elizabeth were reasonably careful about what they spent, they might just make it through until Jules Hartwick's problem at the bank was cleared up. At the worst, only a small loan would be needed, and there was far more than enough value in the house to secure whatever loan might become necessary. Then, as he and Megan were finishing breakfast half an hour later, the phone rang and the need for a loan suddenly evaporated.

"I'm wondering if you might have any free time," Harvey Connally said. It was clear in the old man's voice that he was aware of the problems with Blackstone Center.

"Depending on the project, I might be able to work you in," Bill replied.

"I thought you might," Connally observed dryly. "Here's the deal. My nephew Oliver has been wanting to do some remodeling down at the *Chronicle*. Seems he's decided he needs a private office, and I thought it might make a nice Christmas present for him."

"It would make a nice Christmas present for me too," Bill said.

"Always like to spread the cheer around." Connally chuckled. "Hate to see anyone get their holidays ruined. Why don't you meet me down at Oliver's little place in about an hour?"

As Bill hung up the phone and went back to the dining room, the load of worries he'd been carrying for the last few days seemed just a little lighter.

Megan watched from the front porch until her father had disappeared down Amherst Street, then she went back into the house, closing the door silently behind her. In her mind she could still hear the doll whispering to her, just as it had last night.

"Go to the kitchen," the doll's voice instructed. *"See what Mrs. Goodrich is doing."*

Obeying the voice, Megan moved through the dining room and the little butler's pantry, and pushed open the kitchen door. Mrs. Goodrich was sitting at the table, mixing a large bowl of batter.

"No tasting," the old woman warned as Megan reached a finger into the bowl, scooping out a large dollop of dark brown dough studded with chocolate bits. "Well, maybe just one," the housekeeper amended as the lump of dough disappeared into the little girl's mouth. "But that's enough," she added, rapping Megan's knuckles lightly with a wooden spoon as she reached for a second helping. "Now, you just stay out of my way for half an hour, and then we'll start getting the Christmas things out. And this year you can set the crèche up on the mantel all by yourself."

Snatching one last morsel of the batter, Megan left the kitchen.

"Half an hour," the voice in her head said. *"That's a long time."*

As the voice whispered to her, Megan went upstairs

and paused outside her parents' bedroom. The door was closed, but when she pressed her eye to the keyhole, she could see that her mother was still in bed.

Megan waited, watching. After a full minute had passed, she decided that her mother was still asleep. Moving farther along the hall, she passed the door to the big linen closet, then went through the next one.

The nursery was filled with morning sunlight, and as Megan gazed around at the new wallpaper and all the new furniture her parents had bought for the baby, she wondered if maybe she shouldn't listen to the doll after all, if she should ignore the voice. But even as the thought came into her mind, she heard the voice whispering to her once again.

"This room is much nicer than your room," it said. *"They didn't buy you new furniture."*

Megan carefully closed the door, then crossed to the crib.

The doll lay beneath the pink and blue blanket. Its head was turned so that it seemed to be looking directly at her.

"Pick me up," the doll commanded.

Megan obeyed.

"Take me to the window."

Cradling the doll, Megan walked over to the window.

"Open the window."

Setting the doll down, Megan raised the window as high as she could. Then, still following the instructions being whispered in her head, she picked up the doll and crept out onto the roof that pitched steeply away from the gabled window. Holding on to the sill with one hand, she laid the doll as far from the window as she could.

The doll slid on the wet shingles of the roof. Megan's heart raced as it tumbled closer to the edge. Then its skirt caught on the rough edge of one of the shingles and it came to a stop six inches from the rain gutter and the straight drop to the flagstone terrace below.

Pulling herself back into the nursery, but leaving the window open, Megan ran through the bathroom and into her parents' room.

"Mommy!" she cried. "Mommy, wake up!" Rushing to the side of the bed, Megan began shaking her mother. "Mommy! Mommy!"

Elizabeth jerked awake, the voice of her baby still echoing in her ears. Even after she opened her eyes, the voice persisted. Finally, through the haze of sedatives, Elizabeth recognized it.

Megan.

"Honey?" she said, struggling to sit up as her daughter tugged at her. "What is it? What's wrong?"

"The baby," Megan told her. "Mommy, something's wrong with the baby. Come on!"

The baby! Then it hadn't just been a dream—her baby really had been calling to her. Throwing the covers back, Elizabeth climbed out of bed and stumbled through the bathroom to the nursery.

The crib was empty!

"Where is he?" Elizabeth cried, her voice rising as panic welled up in her. "What's happened to him?"

"He's outside, Mommy," Megan said, pointing to the open window. "I tried to stop him, but—"

Elizabeth was no longer listening. Rushing to the window, she peered out into the bright morning sunlight.

There, lying on the shingles only a few inches from the edge of the roof, was her baby. How had it happened? How had he gotten out there?

Her fault.

It was all her fault! She never should have left him alone. Never!

If he tried to turn over—tried to move at all—surely he'd fall.

Elizabeth leaned out the window, reaching as far as she could, but her baby was just beyond her reach. Gathering her nightgown around her hips, she crept out onto the steep roof, hanging on to the casement of the window.

"Help me," she told Megan. "Just hold on to my hand." As Megan came close to the window and gripped her mother's wrist in both her hands, Elizabeth released her grip on the casement.

"Now," the voice whispered in Megan's head.

Obeying the voice without question, Megan let go of her mother's wrist. Elizabeth began to slide, her bare feet finding no purchase on the wet shingles. A second later her right foot caught in the rain gutter. For an instant she thought she was going to be all right. Reaching out, she snatched up the doll, but it was already too late. Her balance gone, and with nothing to catch herself on, Elizabeth pitched forward, plunging headfirst onto the flagstone terrace, the doll clutched protectively against her breast.

Leaving the window wide open, Megan left the nursery, made her way down the stairs, then ran through the living room to the library. Unlocking one of the French doors, she stepped out onto the terrace.

Her mother lay sprawled on her back, her head twisted at a strange angle, blood oozing through her blond hair.

In her arms was the doll, still pressed protectively against her breast. Squatting down, Megan carefully pried her mother's hands loose from the doll, then cradled it against her own chest.

"It's all right, Sam," she whispered to the doll as she took it back into the house, quietly closing and relocking the French door. "It's all right," she repeated as, without so much as a glance back through the glass of the French doors, she left the library and carried her doll back up to her room. "You're mine now. Nobody's ever going to take you away from me again."

Bill McGuire sensed nothing amiss when he came back to the house an hour later. The sweet smell of chocolate chip cookies was wafting from the back of the house; Mrs. Goodrich was taking the last batch out of the oven as he entered the kitchen.

"Well, isn't this good timing," the old woman said as Bill helped himself to one of the cookies that were piled high on a platter on the table. "I was just going to take some up to Miss Elizabeth, but I'm not really sure my old bones could get me up there."

"Don't even think about it," Bill told her. Putting half a dozen cookies on a smaller plate, he left the kitchen and went upstairs. As he was about to go into the room he and Elizabeth shared, though, he heard Megan singing softly.

Singing a lullaby.

Turning away from the master bedroom, he continued down the hall to his daughter's room. The door stood wide open, and Megan was lying on her bed, propped up against a pile of ruffled pillows.

In her arms she held the doll.

When she saw her father standing in the doorway, the lullaby she'd been singing faded into silence.

"I thought we decided Sam could stay in the nursery for a while," Bill said.

Megan smiled at him. "Mommy changed her mind," she said. "She gave Sam back to me."

"Are you sure?" Bill asked. "You didn't just take her out of the crib?"

Megan shook her head. "Mommy said she knows Sam isn't a real baby, and that she doesn't want her anymore. She told me to take good care of her and always love her."

As Bill listened to the words, a sense of uneasiness began to come over him. "Where is she?" he asked.

Megan shrugged. "I don't know. After she gave Sam back to me, she went back in the nursery and closed the door."

Bill's uneasiness turned to fear. Telling Megan to stay in her room until he came back, he went to the nursery.

Opening the door, he was greeted by a blast of cold air surging in through the open window.

The doors to both the bathroom and the master bedroom beyond stood wide open. "Elizabeth?" he called. "Elizabeth!"

Going to the window, he started to close it. Before he could pull it shut, however, his eyes fixed on the roof outside.

Some of the shingles appeared to be hanging loose.

As if something had disrupted them, and then—

"Elizabeth!" he shouted, then turned and ran from the room.

A few seconds later he was in the library, at the French doors. Through the windows, he saw his wife, and a moment later, as he cradled her lifeless body in his arms, a terrible howl of grief erupted from his throat.

Upstairs in her room, Megan smiled at her doll. And the doll, she was almost certain, smiled back at her.

Chapter 11

*B*ill McGuire was utterly unconscious of the icy chill in the air on the day he buried his wife, for he was far too numb to be aware of anything as insignificant as the weather. Bareheaded, he stood at the head of Elizabeth's grave. Megan was on one side of him, holding on to her father with her left hand as she clutched the doll in her right, pressing it against her breast almost as if to prevent it from seeing the coffin that stood only a few feet in front of them. On Bill's other side was Mrs. Goodrich, one of her hands tucked into the crook of his arm, her face covered by a thick veil. The old woman seemed to have shrunk since Elizabeth died three days earlier, and though she had continued to go through the motions of taking care of Bill and Megan, the spirit had gone out of her. Bill could not help thinking that the Christmas rapidly approaching would be her last.

Even the house seemed to have gone into mourning; a silence had descended over it, broken only by Megan, for whom, Bill suspected, the truth of what had happened had not yet sunk in. Each night, as he tucked her into bed, she looked up into his eyes and repeated the same words.

"Mommy's all right, isn't she?"

"Of course she is," Bill assured her. "She's with God, and God is taking care of her."

Last night, though, Megan had said something else: "Sam's sorry," she'd whispered.

"Sorry?" Bill had asked. "About what?"

"She's sorry Mommy had to go away."

Bill had assumed that, like so many children who lost a parent when they were very young, Megan was afraid that somehow she might have been the cause of her mother's death. But the thoughts were far too painful to face directly, so she was projecting them onto the doll. "You tell Sam not to worry," he told her. "What happened to Mommy wasn't Sam's fault, or your fault, or anyone else's. It was just something that happens sometimes, and all of us must try to help each other get through it."

But how was Megan going to help him get through it? How was he ever going to be able to forgive himself for leaving Elizabeth alone that morning? How must she have felt when she awakened?

Alone.

Grieving.

Bereft.

And remembering what had happened the night before, when she'd thought the doll was her baby. What must have gone through her mind? Had she thought she was going insane? Was she afraid she was going to end up like her sister, confined for the rest of her life in a sanitarium? And he hadn't even been there to comfort her.

Surely he could have put Harvey Connally off for a few hours.

But he hadn't, and for that he would never forgive himself.

Bill heard Lucas Iverson begin the final prayer, and as Elizabeth's coffin began to descend slowly into the grave, Bill closed his eyes, unable to watch these final moments. When Rev. Iverson fell silent once again, Bill stooped down and picked up a clod of soil. Holding it over the coffin, he squeezed his fingers and the lump broke apart, dropping into the open grave.

The same way his life was breaking apart and falling away.

His eyes glazing with tears, he stepped back from the grave's edge and stood silently as one by one his friends and neighbors filed past to pay their last respects to Elizabeth, and offer their condolences to him.

Jules and Madeline Hartwick had come, along with their daughter and her fiancé. The banker paused, laying a gentle hand on Bill's shoulder. "It's hard, Bill. I know how you feel."

But how could Jules know how he felt? he wondered. It wasn't his wife who had died.

Ed Becker was there too, with Bonnie and their daughter, Amy, who was only a year younger than Megan. While Bonnie Becker murmured sympathetic words to him, he heard Amy speaking to Megan.

"What's your dolly's name?"

"Sam," he heard Megan reply. "And she's not a little boy. She's a little girl, just like me."

"Can I hold her?" Amy asked.

Megan shook her head. "She's mine."

Bill knelt down. "It's all right, honey," he said. "You can let Amy hold Sam."

Again Megan shook her head, clutching the doll even tighter. Bill looked helplessly up at Bonnie Becker.

"You can hold her another time," the lawyer's wife said quickly, taking Amy by the hand. "Just tell Megan how sorry you are about her mother, and then we'll go home. All right?"

Amy's large dark eyes fixed on Megan's. "I'm sorry about your mother," she said.

This time Megan made no reply at all.

Rebecca Morrison, accompanied by her aunt, Martha Ward, was next. As Martha stood glaring at her niece, Rebecca struggled to speak, her eyes downcast in shy embarrassment.

"Thank you for coming, Rebecca," Bill said, taking her hands in both his own.

"Tell him what you wanted to say, Rebecca," Martha Ward urged her niece, causing Rebecca's face to flush.

"I—I'm just so sorry—" Rebecca began, but her voice quickly trailed off as the words she and her aunt had rehearsed vanished from her memory.

"We're so terribly sorry about poor Elizabeth," Martha said, her eyes flicking toward her niece in disapproval. "It's always such a tragedy when something like this happens. Elizabeth was never a very strong woman, was she? I always think—"

"Elizabeth bore more in her life than most of us have ever been asked to," Bill cut in, his eyes fixed on Martha Ward. "We'll all miss her a great deal." He put just enough emphasis on the word "all" to throw Martha off her stride. Then, seeing how mortified Rebecca was by what her aunt had said, he managed to give her a friendly hug before turning to the next people in line.

The faces began to run together after a while. By the time Germaine Wagner approached, pushing her mother in a wheelchair, he barely recognized them. When Clara Wagner informed him in a stern voice that he "must come for dinner one night," he had no idea how to respond. He knew Germaine from the library, of course, but had never been inside the Wagners' house, and certainly had no desire to go there now.

"Thank you," he managed to say, then turned quickly to Oliver Metcalf and Harvey Connally.

"Watch out for that one," Connally warned dryly, watching Germaine push her mother away. "As far as she's concerned, you've become fair game."

"Jesus, Uncle Harvey!" Oliver Metcalf protested. "I'm sure Mrs. Wagner didn't mean anything like—"

"Of course she did," the old man cut in. "And don't tell me I'm saying something inappropriate, Oliver. I'm eighty-three years old, and I shall say what I please." But as he turned back to Bill McGuire, his tone softened. "It's a terrible thing you're going through, Bill, and there's nothing any of us can say that's going to make it easier. But if there's anything I can do, you tell me, understand?"

Bill nodded. "Thanks, Mr. Connally," he said. "I just keep wondering if maybe—" The words died on his lips as he felt Megan slip her hand into his.

"Don't think that way," Harvey Connally advised. "Things happen, and there's no explaining them, and no changing them. All any of us can do is play the hand we're dealt, the best way we can."

Ten minutes later, when the little cemetery was empty save for the three of them, Harvey Connally's words still echoed in Bill McGuire's mind.

Play the hand we're dealt, the best way we can.

Gazing one last time at his wife's coffin, Bill McGuire finally turned away from the grave and started out of the cemetery.

Mrs. Goodrich, leaning slightly forward, dropped a single rose onto the coffin, then reached down to take Megan's hand.

But Megan lingered for a moment, and though she still faced the coffin, her eyes were fixed on the doll.

The doll gazed back at her.

Now they truly belonged to each other, and no one would ever take the doll away from her again.

Late that night, as Blackstone slept, the dark figure moved once more through the silent corridors of the abandoned Asylum, at last coming again to the room in which the secret trove of treasures was stored.

Glittering eyes flicked from one souvenir to another, and finally came to rest on a single sparkling object.

A hand, smoothly gloved, reached out and picked up a locket, holding it high so it glimmered silver in the moonlight.

It would make a perfect gift.

And the dark figure already knew who its recipient would be.

To be continued . . .

PART 2
TWIST OF FATE: THE LOCKET

PART 2

TWIST OF FATE:
THE LOCKET

Prelude

*T*he full moon stood high in the night sky above Blackstone, bathing the stones of the old Asylum atop North
Hill in a silvery glow, even penetrating the thick layers of
grime that covered its windows so that its dusty rooms
were suffused with a dim light. Though the dark figure
who moved silently through these rooms needed no light
to guide him, the luminescence allowed him to pause
now and then to savor the memories this place held for
him: vivid memories. Images as sharp and clear as if the
events they depicted had occurred only yesterday. He
was their keeper, even if those same memories had faded
from the minds of the very few in Blackstone who might
have shared them.

And this room, with its shelves filled with mementos,
was his sanctuary, his museum, to which he had added
something new.

It was an ancient ledger, which he'd come upon in one
of the basement storerooms. Covered in faded red leather,
it was like the ones used in years gone by, in which were
recorded all the minutiae of the Asylum's busy life.
Taking the book to the shelf-lined, square room, he
stroked its cover with all the sensual gentleness with
which a man might stroke the skin of a beautiful woman.
Hoping it might jog delicious memories even his brilliant
mind might have mislaid, he finally opened its cover,
only to feel a pang of bitter disappointment: despite its age,
its yellowed leaves proved blank. Then disappointment

gave way to a tingling excitement. There would be a new use for the book, an important use.

An album!

An album containing accounts of the madness unleashed upon the town that had spurned him.

Now, hunched over the album in the dim moonlight, he opened its cover and read once more the familiar words of the two articles he had painstakingly clipped and carefully pasted to the brittle pages within.

The first described the suicide of Elizabeth Conger McGuire, despondent over the premature birth—and death—of her son.

Nowhere had the newspaper account mentioned the beautiful doll that arrived at the McGuires' a few short days before Elizabeth's death, returning at last to the house from which it had been carried so many years ago in the arms of a child who had entered this very building, never to leave it again.

The second article, lovingly pasted into the album, had appeared three days later, noting the burial of Elizabeth McGuire and listing all the people who had gone to the cemetery to mourn her.

People who, soon enough, would be mourned themselves.

Closing the album, the dark figure caressed its cover once again, shivering with anticipation as he imagined the stories it would soon contain.

Then, as the moon began to drop in the sky and dark shadows edged up the walls, he touched again the object he had decided to deliver next.

The beautiful heart-shaped locket, in which was contained a lock of hair . . .

Prologue

"*Lorena.*"

It wasn't her real name, but it was a name she decided she liked. For today at least, it would be hers.

Perhaps she would use it again tomorrow, but perhaps not.

And no last name. Never a last name.

Not even a made-up one.

Too easy to make a mistake if you used a last name. You could accidentally use your real initials, and give yourself away. Not that Lorena would ever make such a mistake, since she hadn't even risked using a first name that started with her real initial since she'd come here.

They'd told her it was a hospital, but the moment she saw the stone walls, she knew they were lying. It was a prison—and dressing the guards as doctors and nurses hadn't fooled Lorena for a minute. It hadn't fooled the people who were watching her either. They were already there, waiting for her. She'd felt their eyes on her from the moment she came through the huge oak door and heard it slam shut behind her—imprisoning her.

Over the months she'd been here, though, Lorena developed a few tricks of her own. She'd never spoken her real name out loud; trained herself even to keep from thinking it, since some of her enemies had learned to read her mind. She'd learned to make herself inconspicuous, doing nothing that would draw attention to herself, barely moving, never speaking.

She spent most of her time simply sitting in the chair. It was an ugly chair, a horrible chair, covered with a hideous green material that felt sticky when she touched it, which she tried not to do: that sticky stuff might be some kind of poison with which her enemies were trying to kill her. She thought about finding another chair to sit in, but that would only let them know she'd caught on to what they were trying to do, and inspire them to try something else.

Lorena sat perfectly still. The slightest movement, even the blink of an eye, could give her away almost as quickly as using her real name. Some of them had been watching her for so long that she was certain they could recognize her by the slightest gesture.

The way she brushed her hair back from her face.

Even the way she tilted her head.

Her enemies were everywhere. And still they came.

Ever watchful, never letting down her guard, today she'd spotted a new one.

This time it was a well-dressed woman—exactly the kind of woman who used to pretend to be her friend back in the days before she'd caught on to the plot. This woman was younger than her, forty, with long dark hair that she had swept into an elaborate French twist at the back of her head. She wore a silk dress in the darkest shade of midnight blue. Lorena immediately recognized its distinctive cut and flair, which could only have come from Monsieur Worth in Paris. Lorena herself had been fitted in his salon when she'd traveled on the Lusitania *to Europe the year before they sank it.*

The woman was talking to the warden, who still pretended he was a doctor even though Lorena had made it perfectly clear to him that she knew exactly who he really was. Every few minutes the woman's eyes flicked in her direction. Each time, Lorena wondered if the woman was truly foolish enough to think she didn't notice.

Another surreptitious glance.

Lorena felt the familiar fear quicken inside her. They were watching her, talking about her. Despite the charade they were playing out—that they had eyes only for each other—they weren't fooling her at all.

They weren't just watching her.

They were plotting against her.

A plot Lorena wouldn't—couldn't—let succeed.

The woman's eyes flicked nervously to the patient who had been sitting in the dayroom, unmoving, from the moment she and the doctor slipped in to steal a few minutes alone together. When the doctor had first suggested to the woman that she volunteer to spend a few hours each week at the Asylum, the idea hadn't appealed to her at all. In fact, though she'd never admitted it to anyone, she'd always been a little afraid of the forbidding building on the top of North Hill. But the more she thought about it, the more convinced she became that her lover was right—as a volunteer, no one would question her reasons for coming up here. Her husband would be none the wiser, and her friends would be completely thrown off the scent.

Today, as she had nearly every day since the affair had begun a month ago, she'd driven up the hill to offer her services. She had talked to some of the patients, read a story to an odd little boy, played cards with a sad-eyed old man. All the time waiting for her lover to appear. Then, there he was, taking her gently by the arm, escorting her through the corridors until finally, a little while ago, they'd come into this room, which was empty save for the woman in the chair.

"She doesn't even know we're here," he assured her, slipping his arms around her and pulling her toward him, his lips nuzzling at her throat. Despite the thrill of *excitement that ran through her body, the woman pulled away from him, her eyes flicking toward the patient in the chair.*

"What's wrong with her?" she asked. "Why doesn't she move?"

"She's delusional." He glanced at the patient. "She thinks if she holds still, her 'enemies' can't see her." Reaching into the pocket of his white coat, he pulled out a small box. "I have something for you." He put the box into her hands. "Something to celebrate our being together."

The woman gazed at the pale blue box, recognizing its origin immediately. Her heart beating a little faster, she undid the white silk ribbon and lifted off the lid. Inside there was a soft velvet pouch; inside the pouch was a tiny locket.

In the shape of a heart, it was covered with silver filigree, and when she pressed on the tiny catch to open it, the woman found a lock of hair pressed under the glass where a picture could have gone.

Taking the locket from the woman's hands, the doctor unhooked its chain and, as she turned around, placed the chain around her neck and fastened it. As she turned back to face him, he leaned down and pressed his lips against her neck.

A flush of heat coursed through her body; the woman closed her eyes.

Lorena watched it all—watched them whisper to each other, watched them glance at her, then watched them whisper again. She watched the woman open the box and take out the locket; watched her open it. As the "doctor" put it around the woman's neck, Lorena suddenly knew what was contained inside the silver heart.

Lies.

The locket was filled with lies about her, lies that the woman would carry out and spread among her enemies.

As the "doctor" bent down once more to whisper into the woman's ear, Lorena leaped from the chair and scuttled across the room, her fingers already extended so that before the woman could turn away, Lorena had already snatched the locket from her neck, the thin silver chain breaking.

She backed away, the locket clutched in her hand, her wary eyes watching to see what they would do.

The "doctor" moved toward her. "Give it to me," he said quietly, holding out his hand.

Lorena backed farther away, her fingers clenched on the tiny locket.

"What's she going to do with it?" she heard the woman ask.

As the "doctor" moved toward her once again, Lorena edged backward until the wall stopped her, then scrabbled crabwise along the wall until she could go no farther. Cornered, she watched the "doctor" move closer to her. Her eyes flicked over the room, searching for some means of escape, but there was none. The "doctor" reached toward her once again, but Lorena, far more clever than he, had already figured out what to do.

Before his hand could close on her wrist, then pry her fingers loose from the tiny piece of jewelry, her own hand went to her mouth.

In an instant, she swallowed the locket.

"You shouldn't have done that," she heard the "doctor" say, but it didn't matter, because now the locket was safely out of his reach.

Lorena, knowing she'd won, began to laugh. Her laughter built, filling the room with a raucous sound that didn't die away until three "orderlies" came in and circled around her. Then Lorena's laughter suddenly became a scream of terror.

* * *

They were in a room in the basement of the Asylum. It was equipped with a metal table. Above the table a bright light was suspended.

The orderlies, having strapped the patient to the table, had disappeared. Now, as the woman gazed at the patient's terrified eyes, she wished she'd never come here today.

Indeed, she wished she'd never met the doctor at all.

"Perhaps you should wait outside," he said.

Making no reply, the woman started out of the room, but before she passed through the doorway, she turned around and glanced back.

A scalpel glimmered in her lover's hand.

Stepping quickly out of the room, the woman pulled the door closed behind her as if the act alone could shut what she'd just seen out of her mind. But the scream she heard a moment later seared the scene into her memory forever.

The first scream was followed by another, and then another, and for just an instant the woman was certain that someone would appear, would burst from the stairs at the end of the corridor to stop whatever was happening behind the closed door.

But no one came. Slowly, the screams died away, to be replaced by a deathly silence.

At last, when she thought she could take it no more, the door opened and the doctor stepped out. Before he pulled the door closed behind him, the woman caught a glimpse of the room beyond.

The patient, her face gray, still lay strapped to the operating table.

Her eyes, open and lifeless, seemed to be staring at the woman.

Blood oozed from her eviscerated belly, and crimson

threads were strung from the edge of the table to the scarlet pool on the floor.

The door closed.

The doctor pressed the locket into the woman's hand, still warm with the heat of the patient's body.

The woman gazed at it for a second, then dropped it to the floor. Turning, she staggered toward the stairs, not looking back.

When she was gone, the doctor picked the locket up, wiped it clean, and dropped it in his pocket.

Chapter 1

*T*here was nothing about the First National Bank of Blackstone that Jules Hartwick didn't love. It was a passion that had begun when he was a very small boy and his father brought him down to the Bank for the first time. The memory of that first visit remained vividly sharp through the half century that had since passed. Even now Jules could recall the awe with which, as a child of three, he had first beheld the gleaming polished walnut of the desks and the great slabs of green-veined marble that topped all the counters.

But the brightest memory of that day—brighter than any other memory he had—was of the fascination that came over him when he'd seen the great door to the vault standing open, the intricate works of its locking mechanism clearly visible through a glass plate on the inside of the door. Every shiny piece of brass had captivated him, and over and over he'd begged Miss Schmidt, who had been his father's secretary right up until the day she died, to work the combination yet again so he could watch the tumblers fall, the levers work, and the huge pins that held the enormous door fast in its frame move in and out.

Half a century later, nothing had changed. The Bank (somehow, Jules always capitalized the word in his own mind) was no different now than it had been back then. Some of the marble showed a few chips, and there were some nicks in the walnut, but the tellers' cages were still fronted by the same flimsy brass grills that offered little in the way of security but a great deal in the way of atmosphere, and the huge vault door still stood open all day, allowing the Bank's customers to enjoy the beauty of its inner workings as much as Jules had on that long-ago day. Had he been forced to make a choice, Jules would have been hard put to say which he could live better without: his wife, or the Bank. Not that he'd thought of it much, until the last few weeks, when the auditors from the Federal Reserve had begun to raise disconcerting questions about the Bank's lending practices.

Now, as he sat in his office with Ed Becker, trying to concentrate on what his attorney was saying, his eyes fell on the desk calendar and the small notation in the box marking off this entire evening: "Dinner Party for Celeste and Andrew."

It was a party he'd been looking forward to for weeks, ever since Andrew Sterling had formally requested permission to marry his daughter. To ask for Celeste's hand in marriage was exactly the kind of endearingly anachronistic gesture Jules had come to expect of Andrew, who had been working at the Bank for almost five years, rising from teller to Chief Loan Officer not only on the merit of his work—which was considerable—but because Andrew, like Jules himself, preferred the old-fashioned way of banking.

"I know it's an idea the business schools don't approve of," he'd told Jules when they were discussing his promotion to the job he now held, "but I think there are far better ways to judge a man's worth than by his credit application."

It was precisely the philosophy upon which the Hartwicks had founded the Blackstone bank, and it confirmed Jules's judgment that Andrew, though only five years out of college, was perfectly qualified for the loan officer's job.

Now, the engagement of Andrew and Celeste was to be formally announced that night, though Jules suspected there were few people in Blackstone who weren't already aware of it. The bethrothal of his only daughter to this upstanding young man was the frosting on Jules's cake: a few more years and he might be able to consider the possibility of retirement, knowing the Bank would be in Andrew's capable hands, and that Andrew would be part of the family.

The continuity of First National of Blackstone would be ensured.

"Jules?"

Ed Becker's voice jerked the banker out of his reverie. When Jules shifted his eyes back from the calendar to his attorney, he saw the lawyer looking at him with a worried frown.

"Are you all right, Jules?"

"I'd be a lot righter if this audit were behind us," Hartwick replied, leaning forward. "Going to be some party tonight, isn't it? It should be one of the happiest nights of my life, and now I have this ruining it." He gestured to the stack of papers in front of them. The auditors were questioning nearly one hundred loans—and they were still at work. Jules could see no end in sight.

"But it's nothing more than a nuisance, when you get right down to it," Ed Becker said. "I've been over every one of these loans, and I haven't found anything illegal in any of them."

"And you won't," Jules Hartwick replied. He leaned forward in his chair, folding his hands on his desk. "Maybe," he said with a smile, "you were down there in Boston a little too long."

Becker grinned. "About five years too long, at least," he agreed. "But who knew I was going to get sick of— what did you used to call them?"

" 'Slimeballs,' " Jules Hartwick instantly replied. "And that's what they were, Ed. Murderers and rapists and gangsters. I'll never understand how—"

Ed Becker held up a hand in protest. "I know, I know.

But everyone deserves a defense, no matter what we might think of him. And I *did* get fed up with the whole thing, remember? I quit. I came back home to set up a nice quiet little practice, with nothing messier than the occasional divorce to deal with. But Jules, you probably know more than I do about business law. Sue me, or educate me. Why are you so worried about this? If there really isn't anything illegal about any of these loans, why are you making yourself sick over this?"

A brief and hollow chuckle emerged from Jules Hartwick. "If this weren't an independent bank, it wouldn't matter a damn," he said. "And maybe I've been wrong all these years. Maybe I should have sold out to one of the big interstate banks. God knows, it would have made Madeline and me far richer than we are today."

"I've seen your accounts, Jules, remember?" the lawyer put in archly. "You're not exactly suffering."

"And I haven't cashed out for a few hundred million like a lot of other bankers I won't name," Hartwick replied, the last trace of good humor vanishing from his voice. "I've always felt that this is more than just a bank, Ed. To me, and to my father, and to my grandfather, this bank has been a trust. We never thought it existed just for us. It's not just a business, like any other. This bank has always been part of the community. A vital, life-giving part. And to keep Blackstone alive over the years, I've made a lot of loans that a lot of other bankers might not have made. But I know the people I loan money to, Ed." He picked up one of the stacks of papers from his desk. "These are not bad loans."

The lawyer's eyes met those of the banker. "Then you have nothing to worry about, do you? It sounds like you should give the auditors what they're asking for before they start issuing subpoenas."

Hartwick's face paled slightly. "They're talking about subpoenas?"

"Of course they are."

Hartwick stood up. "I'll think about it," he said, but the reluctance was evident in his voice. The material the auditors wanted would show no criminal behavior on his part, but certainly it could be used by anyone who wished to make a case that his banking methods did not always conform to the standards that were currently considered prudent. That, he knew, could easily shift the balance on his Board of Directors, a majority of whom might finally be convinced that it was time that First National of Blackstone—like practically every other little bank in the country—sold out to one of the interstates.

If that happened, rich though he may be, he would no longer be in possession of the one thing he loved most.

Under no circumstances would Jules Hartwick allow that to happen.

He would find a way to keep his bank—and his life—intact.

Oliver Metcalf checked himself in the mirror one last time. It had been years since the last time he'd put on a necktie for dinner—only the very fanciest restaurants down in Boston and New York still required them—but Madeline Hartwick had been very specific. Tonight's dinner was going to be a throwback to days gone by—all the women were dressing, and all the men were expected to wear jackets and ties. Since he knew as well as everyone else that this was the night Celeste Hartwick and Andrew Sterling were announcing their engagement, he'd been more than happy to comply. His tie—the only one he owned—was more than a little out of date, and even his jacket—a tweed affair that had struck him as very "editorial" when he'd bought it—was starting to look just a bit shabby, now that it was entering its twentieth year. Still, it should all pass muster, and if Madeline began needling him about how a wife might be able to do wonders with his wardrobe, he'd simply smile and threaten to woo Celeste away from Andrew.

Leaving the house, he considered whether it was too cold to walk across the Asylum grounds and follow the path that wound through the woods down to the top of Harvard Street, where the Hartwicks lived. Then, remembering that he'd left the gift he'd found for Celeste and Andrew in his office, he abandoned any idea of walking and got into his car—a Volvo almost as ancient as his tweed jacket.

Five minutes later he slid the car into an empty slot in front of the *Blackstone Chronicle* and left the engine idling while he dashed inside to pick up the antique silver tray he'd come across last weekend, and which Lois Martin had insisted on rewrapping for him this afternoon. Peering into the large shopping bag where Lois left the tray, Oliver had to admit she'd done a far better job than he: the leftover red and green Christmas paper he'd used had been replaced with a silver and blue design printed with wedding bells, and no ragged edges showed anywhere, despite the cumbersome oval shape of the tray. Scribbling a quick thank-you note that Lois would find first thing in the morning, he relocked the office door, got back in his car, and headed toward Harvard Street. As he slowed to make at least a pretense of obeying the stop sign at the next corner, he saw Rebecca Morrison coming out of the library, and pulled over to the curb.

"Give you a lift?" he asked.

Rebecca seemed almost startled by the offer, but came over to the car. "Oh, Oliver, it's so far out of your way. I can walk."

"It's not out of my way at all," Oliver told her, reaching over and pushing the passenger door open. "I'm going up to the Hartwicks'."

Rebecca got into the car. "Are you going to the dinner?"

Oliver nodded. "You too?"

"Oh, no," Rebecca said quickly. "Aunt Martha says I mustn't go to things like that. She says I might say the wrong thing."

Oliver glanced over at Rebecca, whose face, softly illuminated by the streetlights, seemed utterly serene, despite the less than kind words she was repeating about herself.

"What does Martha want you to do?" Oliver asked. "Spend the rest of your life at home with her?"

"Aunt Martha's been very good to me since Mother and Father died," Rebecca replied. Though she had neatly sidestepped his question, he still failed to hear even the slightest note of discontent in her voice.

"You still have a life to live," Oliver said.

Rebecca's gentle smile returned. "I have a wonderful life, Oliver. I have my job at the library, and I have Aunt Martha for company. I count my blessings every day."

"Which is what Aunt Martha told you to do, right?" Oliver asked. Martha Ward, whose younger sister had been Rebecca's mother, had retreated deep into her religion on the day her husband moved out twenty-five years earlier. Her only child, Andrea, had left home on her eighteenth birthday. It had been just a few months after Andrea's departure that Rebecca's parents died in the automobile accident that nearly killed Rebecca as well. Aunt Martha had promptly taken her young niece in. And there, twelve years later, Rebecca remained.

There were even a few skeptical souls in Blackstone who thought that the accident had occurred in answer to Martha Ward's own prayers. "After all," Oliver once heard someone say, "first Fred Ward got out, and Andrea left as soon as she could. And since the accident, Rebecca hasn't been quite right in the head, so Martha has someone to pray over, and Rebecca has a place to live."

Except that Rebecca was perfectly all right "in the head," as far as Oliver could see. She was just a little quiet, and totally without guile. She said whatever came into her mind, which could sometimes be unnerving—at least for some people. Edna Burnham, for instance, had yet to recover from the day that Rebecca stopped her on the street and announced in front of three of Edna's best friends that she loved Edna's new wig. "It's so much better than that other one you used to wear," Rebecca assured her. "It always looked like a wig, and this one really does look real!"

Edna Burnham had never spoken to Rebecca again.

Oliver, who'd had the good fortune to be only ten feet away when the incident occurred, still hadn't stopped laughing about it.

And Rebecca, as utterly innocent as the sixteen-year-old she'd been on the day of the accident that killed her parents, had no idea why Edna Burnham was upset, or what amused Oliver so.

"But it *is* a wig, and it *does* look nice," she'd insisted.

Now, in reply to his question about her aunt, Rebecca told him exactly what she thought. "Aunt Martha means well," she said. "She can't help it if she's just a little bit odd."

"A little bit?" Oliver echoed.

Rebecca reddened slightly. "I'm the one everyone says is odd, Oliver."

"No you're not. You're just honest." He pulled the Volvo over to the curb in front of Martha Ward's house, next door to the Hartwicks'. "How about if you come to the dinner with me?" he suggested. "Madeline told me I could bring a date."

Rebecca's flush deepened and she shook her head. "I'm sure she didn't mean me, Oliver."

"I'm sure she didn't mean *not* you," Oliver replied. As

he got out and went around to open the door for her, he tried once more. "I didn't tell her I was coming alone. Why don't you just put on your prettiest dress and come with me?"

Rebecca shook her head again. "Oh, Oliver, I couldn't! Not in a million years. Besides, Aunt Martha says I make people uncomfortable, and she's right."

"You don't make me uncomfortable," Oliver retorted.

"You're sweet, Oliver," Rebecca said. Then, giving him a quick peck on the cheek, she added, "Have a good time, and tell Celeste and Andrew that I'm very happy for them."

Just then Martha Ward opened the front door of her house and stepped out onto the porch. "It's time for you to come in, Rebecca," she called. "I'm about to begin evening prayers."

"Yes, Aunt Martha." Rebecca turned away from Oliver and started up the walk toward her aunt's house.

Taking his gift out of the backseat of the Volvo, Oliver strode past the Ward house and turned up the Hartwicks' driveway. But as he neared the porte cochere he suddenly had the sense that he was being watched. Looking over his shoulder toward the Ward house, he saw that Rebecca still stood on the porch.

She was gazing at him, and even at this distance he could see the wistfulness in her face. But then he heard Martha Ward's voice call her once again. A moment later Rebecca disappeared into the house.

Suddenly wishing very much that he were not going to the party alone, Oliver mounted the Hartwicks' front steps and pressed the bell. Madeline Hartwick opened the door to greet him with a hug.

"Oliver," she said. "How wonderful." As she stepped back to let him in, her eyes flicked toward the house next door. "For a moment I thought you might be bringing poor Rebecca with you."

Oliver hesitated, then decided to be as truthful as

Rebecca would have been. "I asked her," he said. "But she turned me down." Though he tried to tell himself he was mistaken, Oliver was certain he saw a look of relief pass over Madeline Hartwick's perfectly made-up face.

Chapter 2

*J*ules Hartwick leaned back in his chair and gave Madeline an almost imperceptible nod, the signal that it was time for Madeline to let her toe touch the button on the floor beneath her end of the dining room table. It would summon the maid who had been hired for the evening to clear the dessert plates while the butler—also hired only for the evening—served the port. The dining room had always been one of Jules's favorite rooms in the house he'd grown up in, and into which he and Madeline had moved a decade ago, after his father, widowed for fifteen years, retired to a condo complex in Scottsdale. "It's perfect for me," the elder Hartwick had declared. "Full of Republicans and divorcées with enough money that they don't need mine."

Like all the rooms in the house, the dining room was immense, but so perfectly proportioned that it didn't seem overly large even when the party, like tonight's, was small. A pair of chandeliers glittered from its high-beamed ceiling, and the plaster walls above the mahogany wainscoting were hung with tapestries so luxuriously heavy that even the largest parties never seemed overly noisy. One wall was dominated by an immense fireplace, in which three large logs blazed merrily, and there was a sideboard built into the opposite wall, which served perfectly for the informal buffets that were this generation's preferred way to serve. "So much less ostentatious than the staff Jules's grandfather used to have," Madeline was fond of explaining, never mentioning that economics might have something to do with the scaled-back festivities that were now the rule in the house. Still, every now and then—on occasions such as tonight's—Jules liked to hire a full staff and do his best to roll the calendar back a generation or two. Tonight, he decided, had been a total success.

All the men save Oliver Metcalf had worn black tie, and, since no one had expected Oliver to appear in anything except his old tweed jacket, he didn't seem the least bit out of place. The women were resplendent in their evening dresses, and while Madeline looked even more elegant than usual in a long black sheath set off by a single strand of perfect pearls, Celeste had stolen the limelight in a flow of emerald green velvet that was a perfect complement to her auburn hair. She wore a single stunning piece of jewelry: a small spray of emeralds set in gold that had belonged to Jules's mother glittered near the heart-shaped neckline of her dress. Seated opposite her at the center of the long table, Andrew Sterling, Jules observed, had been unable to keep his eyes off his fiancée for more than a few seconds at a time. Which, Jules reflected, was exactly as it should be.

The rest of the party—all except one—seemed to be nearly as happy as Celeste and Andrew. Aside from Oliver Metcalf and Ed and Bonnie Becker, Madeline had invited Harvey Connally—"to represent the older generation, which I think gives a nice continuity to things"— and included Edna Burnham as the old man's dinner partner. She'd also managed to persuade Bill McGuire to come out for the first time since Elizabeth's death, and included Lois Martin as part of her ongoing plan to match Oliver with his assistant outside the office as well as in. When Jules suggested that perhaps Oliver and Lois spent enough time together at the *Chronicle*, Madeline had given him the kind of wifely look that informed him very clearly that while his banking skills might be excellent, he knew nothing about matchmaking.

"Lois and Oliver are perfect for each other," she'd said. "They just don't know it."

Though Jules suspected Oliver's interest in Lois ended at the office door, he'd kept his own counsel, just as he had when his wife decided to invite Janice Anderson to fill the seat across from Bill McGuire. Not that Jules didn't like Janice. With a perfect combination of business acumen and a winning personality that made her immediately seem like everyone's best friend, Janice had built her antique shop into a business strong enough to bring people to Blackstone from hundreds of miles around. It had been Bill McGuire who convinced her to move her shop into Blackstone Center as soon as the new complex was completed.

Tonight, though, even Janice's sunny disposition didn't seem to be working on Bill. The poor man appeared to Jules to have taken on an unhealthy gauntness since Elizabeth's death two months ago. Still, he seemed glad he'd come, and on balance, Jules decided that Madeline had been right: if anyone would be able to take Bill's mind off his troubles for a little while, it would be Janice.

"Shall we take the port into the library?" Madeline asked as the butler finished filling the glasses. "We found something in the attic last week that we've been dying to show off."

"So that accounts for the library door being closed when we came in," Oliver Metcalf said. He'd risen to his feet to help Lois Martin move her heavy chair back from the huge marble-topped table. The guests all followed their hostess out of the dining room and through the reception room where they'd gathered for drinks—then across the great entry hall that was dominated by a sweeping staircase that led to the second floor mezzanine.

While the dining room had always been Jules's favorite, the library was Madeline's. Its ceiling vaulted up two full floors, and the walls, save for the areas where family portraits hung, were lined with floor-to-ceiling bookcases, their upper shelves so high that to reach them required the use of a wheeled ladder hung from a polished brass guide rail at the top. For Madeline, though, the bookcases were not the room's most distinguishing feature.

Directly above the double doors through which she had just led her guests was a minstrel's gallery large enough to hold a string quartet, and paneled in mahogany linenfold. Tonight, in honor of her daughter's engagement, she had hired a quartet, which was already playing softly when the company entered the room.

"Fabulous," Janice Anderson told Madeline. "It's like going back in time. I truly feel as if I've stepped into another century."

"Just wait till you see what we found in the attic—something amazing from yesteryear," Madeline promised her. "When the Center is done, of course we're going to donate it, but for now we just couldn't resist hanging it in here."

She led them to the far end of the room, where a picture, covered by a black cloth, had been hung. When everyone had gathered around, she signaled to Jules to lower the lights until the only illumination in the room was provided by a spotlight on the picture. As an expectant hush fell, Madeline pulled a cord and the picture's covering fell away.

From an ornately gilded frame, an aristocratic woman of perhaps forty gazed down on the room. She was wearing a dark blue dress of shimmering silk. Despite her elegant bearing and expensive clothing, her eyes gazed out from the canvas accusingly, as if she had resented having her portrait painted. Her hair was pulled severely back from her high forehead, apparently done in an elaborate twist at the back, and she stood beside a chair. The fingers of one hand clutched tightly to the back of the chair, while the other hand, though hanging at her side, appeared to be clenched in a fist.

"It's your mother, isn't it, Jules?" Janice Anderson asked. "But what a strange costume to have a portrait painted in. What is that she's wearing?" Indeed, though the woman in the portrait wore an elegant blue dress, over it was a pale gray apronlike affair that looked to be made of a heavy cotton material.

"We think it's her uniform from the Asylum," Jules replied. His eyes were fixed on the portrait, and he was frowning deeply, as if trying to figure out why his mother appeared so angry. "Apparently she volunteered her services as a Gray Lady at some point. Oddly enough, though, I don't ever remember seeing her wear that uniform. Until last week, I had no idea the portrait even existed." He turned to Oliver. "Do you remember ever seeing my mother like that?"

But Oliver Metcalf wasn't listening. The instant he'd seen the picture, a sharp pain flashed through his head, and a vision appeared in his mind.

The boy, naked and terrified, is shivering in the huge room.

His thin arms are wrapped around his body in a vain effort to keep himself warm.

The man appears, and the boy shrinks away from him, but there is no escape. The man holds a sheet in his hands—a wet sheet—and though the boy tries to slip past the man and dash from the room, the man catches him in the sheet as easily as a butterfly is caught in a net. In an instant the icy cold sheet engulfs the boy, who opens his mouth to scream—

* * *

"Oliver?" Jules Hartwick said again. "Oliver, is something wrong?"

Abruptly, the strange vision vanished. His headache eased and Oliver managed a small smile. "I'm fine," he assured Jules. He looked up at the portrait once more, half expecting the pounding pain behind his eyes to return, but this time there was nothing. Just the painting of Jules's mother in the uniform the volunteers at the Asylum had worn decades ago. Vaguely, he remembered reading somewhere how it had once been the fashion for people of means to have portraits done that reflected their professions or avocations. The costume, he ventured a guess to Jules, was Mrs. Hartwick's way of proclaiming her service to the town.

"I suppose so," Jules agreed. "But the weird thing is, I don't even remember Mother volunteering. But she must have, mustn't she?" He glanced up at the portrait again, then shook his head. "Easy to see why she put it up in the attic the minute it was done. But I think it could be kind of fun up at the Center, don't you? Maybe we can find pictures of some of the other women, and make it the centerpiece of an exhibit. Call it 'The Do-Gooders of Blackstone' or something."

"Jules!" Madeline exclaimed. "Those women took their work very seriously, and did a lot of good."

"I'm sure they did," Jules said. "But you still have to admit that Mother looks pretty unhappy about the whole thing."

"I'm sure her expression had nothing to do with her work at the Asylum," Madeline insisted. But then she relented, and a smile played around her lips. "Actually, she looks almost as disapproving as she did the day you married me."

"Well, she got over that," Jules said, slipping an arm

around his wife as the quartet in the minstrel's gallery began playing a waltz. "Marrying you was still the best thing I ever did." Pulling Madeline close, he swept her across the library floor in a few graceful steps. A moment later the rest of the party had joined in the dancing.

The portrait on the wall, and Jules's mother, were quickly forgotten as the party swirled on.

Rebecca felt as though she were going to suffocate.

The air in the room was thick with smoke from the rows of votive candles that lined the altar, and heavy with the choking perfume of incense.

The droning of Gregorian chants didn't quite drown out the sound of her aunt's voice as Martha Ward, on her knees next to Rebecca, mumbled her supplications and fingered the rosary beads she held in trembling hands.

An agonized Christ gazed down from the cross on the wall above the altar. Rebecca cringed as her eyes fixed on the trickle of painted blood oozing from the spear wound in his side. Feeling his pain as vividly as he must have felt it himself, she quickly moved her gaze away from the suffering figure.

It had been nearly two hours since they finished supper, and her aunt had led her here to beg forgiveness for the thoughts she had harbored during the meal. But how could Aunt Martha have known what crossed her mind when she caught a glimpse of the party going on next door? She'd barely had time to think at all before Aunt Martha, seeing her gazing out the kitchen window at the Hartwicks' brightly lit house, had pulled the blinds down, taken her by the arm, and marched her into this downstairs room that served as her aunt's private chapel.

It wasn't really a chapel at all, of course. Originally it had been her uncle's den, but shortly after Fred Ward left, her aunt had converted it into a place of worship, sealing the windows that once looked out on a lovely garden with curtains so heavy that no light penetrated them. Where there had once been a fireplace—which on a night like this might have blazed with crackling logs— there was now an ornate fifteenth-century Italian altar that Janice Anderson had discovered somewhere in Italy. Venice, maybe? Probably. Rebecca had found a book in the town library with a picture that showed a piece very much like Aunt Martha's. For all Rebecca knew, it might be the very same one.

The pungent aroma of incense and smoking candles filled Rebecca's nostrils and stung her eyes. Finally, when she was certain that her aunt was so far lost in her prayers that she wouldn't notice her absence, Rebecca eased herself onto the hard wooden bench, the only furniture in the room except for the altar and the prie-dieu upon which her aunt often knelt for hours at a time. As soon as her knees stopped hurting enough that she trusted them to hold her, she slipped out of the chapel and up to her room.

After changing into her nightgown, Rebecca was about to turn back the coverlet on her bed when she heard the sound of an automobile engine starting, and went to the window. It had begun to snow, and the night had turned brilliant in the glow of the streetlights. Next door, the party was breaking up, and Rebecca easily recognized all the guests as they said their good-nights to the Hartwicks. Maybe, after all, she should have accepted Oliver's invitation, she reflected. But it wouldn't have been right—Madeline Hartwick meticulously planned every detail of her dinners, and the last thing she'd have been able to cope with would be the last-minute appearance of an uninvited guest.

Still, it would have been nice to have gone, and spent an evening with smiling people, and pretend that they were her friends.

That's unkind, Rebecca told herself. Besides, Oliver *is* your friend!

As if he'd heard her thought, Oliver, who was seeing Lois Martin into her car, suddenly looked up. Smiling, he waved to Rebecca, and she waved back. But then, as first Janice Anderson and then Bill McGuire followed Oliver's glance to see who he was waving at, she felt a hot surge of embarrassment and quickly stepped back from the window. If Aunt Martha caught her, she would spend the next whole week repenting in the chapel!

Going to bed, Rebecca turned off the light and lay in the darkness, enjoying the glow from beyond her window and the shadow play on her ceiling and walls. Soon she drifted into a sleep so light that when she came awake an hour later she was barely aware that she'd been sleeping at all. She listened to the utter silence in the house. No chants drifted up from downstairs, which meant that her aunt, too, had gone to bed. It must be very late, Rebecca thought.

What had awakened her?

She listened even more intently, but if it had been a noise that had startled her awake, it wasn't repeated.

Nor had any strange shadows appeared on her ceiling.

Yet something had disturbed her sleep. After several minutes, Rebecca slipped out of her bed and went to the window, this time leaving the light off.

The night was filled with snow. It swirled around the streetlights, burying the cars in the street and covering the naked trees with a glistening coat of white. Next door, the Hartwicks' house had all but vanished, appearing as nothing more than an indistinct shape, though a few of its windows still glowed with a golden light that made Rebecca think of long-ago winter evenings when her parents had still been alive and her family snuggled in front of the fireplace and—

A sudden movement cut into her reverie, and then, out of the shadows of the Hartwicks' porte cochere, a dark figure appeared. As Rebecca watched, it went quickly down the driveway to the sidewalk, crossed the street, then vanished into the snowstorm.

Save for the footprints in the snow, Rebecca wouldn't have been sure she'd seen it at all. Indeed, by the time she went back to bed a few moments later, even the footprints had all but disappeared.

As the grandfather clock in the Hartwicks' entry hall struck the first note of the Westminster chime, the four people in the smallest of the downstairs rooms fell silent. The big, encased timepiece in the entry hall was only the first of a dozen clocks in the house that would strike one after the other, filling the house with the sounds of gongs and chimes of every imaginable pitch. Now, as the clocks Jules had collected from every corner of the world began marking the midnight hour, Madeline slipped her hand into her husband's, and Celeste, on the sofa opposite her parents, snuggled closer against Andrew. None of them spoke again until the last chime had finally died away.

"I always thought the clocks would drive me crazy," Madeline mused. "But now I don't know what I'd do without them."

"Well, you'll never have to," Jules assured her. "Actually, I've got a line on an old German cuckoo that I think might go nicely on the landing."

"A *cuckoo*?" Celeste echoed. "Dad, they're so corny!"

"I think a cuckoo would be fun," Jules said. Then, sensing that not only was Madeline going to take Celeste's side, but Andrew was too, he relented. "All right, suppose I put it in my den?" he offered in compromise. "They're not *that* bad, you know!"

"They are too, and you know it," Madeline replied. Rising from the sofa with a brisk movement that conveyed to Andrew that the evening was at an end, she picked up Jules's port glass, despite the fact that half an inch of the ruby fluid remained in it.

"I guess I'm done with that," Jules observed.

"I guess you are," Madeline agreed. She leaned down to give him an affectionate kiss on his forehead.

"I hope Celeste takes as good care of me as Mrs. Hartwick does of you, sir," Andrew Sterling said a few minutes later as he and Jules stepped out into the snowy night.

"I'm sure she will," Jules replied, throwing an arm around his prospective son-in-law's shoulders. "Or at least she'll come close. Nobody could take as good care of a man as Madeline takes of me." His voice took on what seemed to Andrew an oddly wistful note. "I've been a very lucky man. I suppose I should count my blessings."

They were at Andrew's car now, and as Andrew brushed the snow off its windshield, he glanced quizzically at the older man. "Is something wrong, sir?"

For a moment Jules was tempted to mention the audit, then decided against it. He'd managed to get through the entire evening without talking at all about his worries at the Bank, and he certainly had no intention of burdening Andrew with them now. None of it, after all, was this young man's fault. If there was blame to be borne, Jules thought, he would certainly bear it himself. "Nothing at all," he assured Andrew. "It's just been a wonderful evening, and I am, indeed, a very lucky man. I have Madeline, and Celeste, and I couldn't ask for a better son-in-law. Get a good night's sleep, and I'll see you in the morning."

As Andrew drove away, Jules swung the big wrought-iron gate across the driveway, then started back toward the house. But coming abreast of Madeline's car, still free of snow under the porte cochere, he noticed that the driver's door was slightly ajar. As he pulled it open in preparation for closing it all the way, the interior light flashed on, revealing a small package, neatly wrapped, sitting on the front seat. Frowning, he picked it up, closed the car door tight, and continued back into the house. Pausing in the entry hall, he turned the package over, looking for some clue as to where it had come from.

There was nothing.

It was simply a small box, wrapped in pink paper and tied with a silver ribbon.

Had Madeline bought it as a gift for him?

The pink paper was enough to put that idea out of his mind. Nor was his wife the kind of woman to leave a gift sitting in her car, not even concealed in a bag.

As he stood at the foot of the stairs, Jules realized that Madeline had not bought the gift at all.

No, she was the intended recipient of the gift, not the giver.

But who was it from? And why had it been left in Madeline's car?

Without thinking, Jules found himself pulling the ribbon from the package, and then the paper. A moment later he'd opened the box itself and found himself looking at a small silver locket.

A locket in the shape of a heart.

His fingers shaking, he picked the locket up and opened it.

Where a picture might have been—should have been—there was nothing.

Nothing, save a lock of hair.

Closing the locket, Jules clutched it in his hand and gazed up the stairs toward the floor above. Suddenly an image came into his mind.

An image of Madeline.

Madeline, whom he'd loved for more than a quarter of a century.

Whom he'd thought loved him too.

But now, in his mind's eye, he could see her clearly.

And she was in the arms of another man.

As he put the locket in his coat pocket, Jules Hartwick felt the foundations of his world starting to crumble.

Chapter 3

"**M**other, for Heaven's sake, look outside!" Celeste Hartwick said as she came into the breakfast room the next morning and poured herself a cup of coffee from the big silver carafe on the table. "It's fabulous!"

But even with her daughter's urging, Madeline barely glanced at the sparkling snowscape that lay beyond the French doors. Every twig of every tree and bush was laden with a thick layer of white, and the blanket of snow that covered the lawns and paths was unbroken save for a single set of bird tracks, apparently made by the cardinal that was now perched on a branch of the big chestnut tree just outside the window, providing the only splash of color in the monochromatic scene.

"Okay, Mother," Celeste said, seating herself in the chair opposite Madeline. "Obviously something's wrong. What is it?"

Madeline pursed her lips, wondering exactly what to say to Celeste, for the truth was that though something was, indeed, wrong, even she herself had no idea what it was. It had begun last night, when Jules had come up after seeing Andrew out and closing the gate. When he entered their bedroom, he'd barely looked at her, and when she'd spoken to him, asking if something was wrong, he positively glared at her and informed her that if something were wrong, she would know it better than he. Then, before she could say another word, he'd disappeared into his dressing room and not come out for nearly thirty minutes. When he finally appeared in his pajamas, he slid into bed beside her, then turned out the light without so much as a good-night, let alone a kiss. Having picked up very clearly that he was in no mood to communicate with her, she'd decided that rather than make this unexpected situation worse by trying to drag the problem out of him in the middle of the night, she would let it go until morning. She'd managed to sleep—at least sporadically—but every time she awakened, she could feel him lying stiffly next to her. Though she'd known by the rhythm of his breathing that he was as wide awake as she, he'd made no response when she'd spoken to him.

Now she asked her daughter, "Were you still up when your father came in last night?"

Celeste nodded. "But I didn't see him. I heard him come up, but I was in my room. Did something happen?"

"I don't know—" Madeline began. "I mean, I think something must have happened, but I haven't the slightest idea what. It was the most peculiar thing, Celeste. When your father came to bed last night, he was barely speaking to me. He—"

"Do you tell *everyone* what happens in our bed, Madeline?"

Recoiling from his words as if she'd been slapped, Madeline's whole body jerked reflexively. Coffee splashed from her cup onto the table. As Celeste quickly blotted the spill with a paper napkin, Madeline shakily set the cup back onto its saucer. "For heaven's sake, Jules, will you please tell me what's going on? Did Andrew say something last night that upset you?"

Andrew, Jules thought. His hand, shoved deep in his pocket, closed on the locket, its metal so hot it seemed to burn into his palm. Could it be Andrew? But Andrew was in love with Celeste, not with Madeline. Or was he? It wouldn't be the first time a young man had fallen in love with a woman old enough to be his mother. "Why do you ask?" he said aloud.

The shock of his words giving way to impatience, Madeline picked her napkin off her lap and began folding it slowly and neatly, pressing each crease flat with the palm of her right hand. It was an unconscious gesture that both Celeste and Jules had long ago learned to recognize as a sign that Madeline was annoyed. Though Celeste threw her father a warning glance, it seemed to have no effect whatsoever.

"I ask," Madeline said in a perfectly controlled voice that made Celeste brace herself for a breaking storm, "because I do not know what is going on. When I asked you last night if something was wrong, you said I would know better than you. Now you are implying that I am in the habit of discussing our bedroom activities with other people, which is something you are well aware that I would never do. If something is wrong, Jules, please tell me what it is."

Jules's eyes flicked suspiciously from his wife to his daughter. How much did Celeste know? Probably everything—didn't mothers always confide in their daughters? "What's his name, Madeline?" he finally asked. "Or should I ask Celeste?" He turned to his daughter. "Who is it, Celeste? Is it someone I know?"

Celeste glanced uncertainly from one of her parents to the other. What on earth was going on? Last night, when she'd gone up to bed, everything had been perfect. What could have happened? "I'm sorry, Daddy," she began. "I don't—"

"Oh, please, Celeste," Jules said, his voice carrying a knife edge she'd never heard before. "I'm not a fool, you know. I know all about your mother's affair."

Now it was Celeste whose coffee splashed across the table as her cup fell from her hand. "Her *what*?" she asked. But before Jules could say anything more, she'd turned to her mother. "He thinks you're having an affair?"

Madeline was on her feet, her eyes glittering with anger. "Tell me what this is all about, Jules," she demanded. "Where on earth did you get such an idea? Did Andrew say something last night to put such a ridiculous idea into your head?"

"Don't be stupid, Madeline," Jules cut in. "Andrew didn't say anything." His hand, still in his pocket, squeezed the locket so tightly he felt its filigree digging into his flesh. "He'd be the last person to say anything, wouldn't he?"

Now Celeste was on her feet too. "Stop it, Daddy. How can you even think such a thing? Andrew and Mother? That's the most disgusting thing I've ever heard!"

Jules's eyes, narrowed to little more than slits, darted back and forth between his wife and his daughter. "You didn't think I'd find out, did you?" he asked. "But I did find out, didn't I? And I'm damn well going to find out all the rest of it too." Leaving Madeline and Celeste staring speechlessly after him, Jules Hartwick turned and strode out of the breakfast room.

"It's the Devil's work!"

Martha Ward's words were uttered with such sharpness that they made Rebecca flinch and instinctively wonder what sin she might have committed this time. But then the wave of guilt receded as she realized the words hadn't been directed toward her at all. Martha was on the telephone, and this time, at least, it was her cousin Andrea who was the recipient of her aunt's lecture.

"I warned you," Martha continued, holding the phone in her left hand as she used her right to gesture to Rebecca to pour her another cup of coffee. "When I first met that man, I recognized him for what he was. Didn't I say, 'Andrea, that man has the face of Satan'? Of course I did, whether you want to remember it or not." She fell silent for a moment, then clucked her tongue in a manner not so much sympathetic as disapproving. "You must go to church, Andrea," she admonished. "You must go and pray for your immortal soul, and beg for forgiveness. And the next time, perhaps you'll recognize the Devil when you see him!"

Hanging up the phone, Martha Ward scooped three teaspoonsful of sugar into her coffee, added some cream, then sighed as she sipped at the steaming mixture. "I think this time I truly put the fear of the Devil into that child," she declared. "But it's true, Rebecca. The first time I saw Gary Fletcher, I warned Andrea about him. I told her never to bring him to this house again. I am a woman of the Church, and I will not countenance evil in my presence."

"But how can you recognize Satan, Aunt Martha?" Rebecca asked, an image still fresh in her mind of the dark figure she'd seen in the snowstorm last night.

"You know him when you see him," Martha stated. "It doesn't matter what guise he takes on, a person of virtue can always recognize the Devil."

"But what does he look like?" Rebecca pressed. "How would I *know* if I've seen him?"

Martha Ward set her coffee cup down and regarded her niece suspiciously. There was a lot of her father in Rebecca, and Martha Ward had never approved of the man her sister, Margaret, had married, any more than she did of the man her daughter, Andrea, was living with. Mick Morrison, as far as Martha had been concerned, was evil incarnate. It had always been her firm belief that the accident that killed both him and her sister was nothing short of God's retribution for Mick Morrison's sinning ways, and Meg's countenancing those sins. Rebecca, she assumed, had been spared her life because she was so young, but there was still more of Mick Morrison in her niece than Martha would have preferred. The vigilance required to prevent Rebecca from giving in to the wickedness inherited from her father was just one more of the crosses she'd been called upon to bear. Martha sighed heavily. "Just what are you trying to get at, Rebecca?"

"I saw something last night," her niece replied. "It was after the Hartwicks' party." She described the figure she'd seen emerging from the porte cochere next door. "And he just vanished into the snow," she finished. "It was almost like he hadn't been there at all."

Martha Ward's face pinched in disapproval of her niece's recitation. "Perhaps he wasn't there, Rebecca," she suggested. "Perhaps you merely invented this mysterious person to justify having been spying on our neighbors. The Hartwicks are good, decent people, and they don't need you peeping at them in the middle of the night. I suggest you go to the chapel and say three Hail Marys in repentance. And as for the Devil," she added pointedly as Rebecca hurried to obey her order, "I think you should look very carefully at Oliver Metcalf."

There, she told herself as Rebecca left the room. I've done my duty, and if anything bad happens to her, it's nobody's fault but her own.

Jules Hartwick could feel them watching him.

It started the moment he left the house. Even as he walked down the driveway to the sidewalk, he'd known that Martha Ward and Rebecca Morrison were watching. Twice he turned to glare accusingly at them, but both times they were too quick for him, stepping back from their windows before he caught even a glimpse of them.

But they weren't fooling him—he knew they were there!

Just as he knew the rest of his neighbors on Harvard Street were watching him as he made his way down the hill toward Main. How long had they been watching him? Years, probably. And he knew why.

They were all his enemies.

He understood it all this morning with a clarity he'd never had before.

They knew about the problems at the Bank.

They knew about the affair Madeline was having.

And they were laughing at him, laughing at his humiliation, laughing at the indignity, the dishonor that was about to befall him. But he wouldn't give them the satisfaction of seeing him suffer, wouldn't even let them know he'd finally caught on to them. He held his head high as he turned onto Main Street and walked right past the Red Hen Diner, where half the leading businessmen in Blackstone gathered every morning for coffee.

Their real purpose, of course, was to plot against him, to plan the downfall of not only his bank, but himself as well. And they'd been clever, going so far as to ask him to join their group in order to keep him from guessing its true purpose. But this morning, finally, he understood why some of them were always already there when he arrived, and others always lingered after he left. They were talking about him, whispering to each other behind his back, plotting every detail of his downfall.

But he wouldn't let it happen.

Now that he knew what they were doing, he could out-maneuver them. He'd always been smarter than the rest of them, and that was another reason they hated him.

Well, they might hate him, but they wouldn't beat him!

Now, as he stepped through the door of the Bank, he could feel the whole staff watching him, even though they were pretending not to be.

The tellers were behind their windows, ostensibly

counting their cash drawers, but he knew they were secretly observing him, following every step he took as he started toward his office at the back of the Bank in the corner next to the vault.

But it wasn't just the tellers who were watching him. The guards were all following his progress too. The hairs on the back of his neck were standing on end, and he felt a shiver pass through him that didn't release him from its cold grip until he was inside his office and had closed the door behind him. He leaned against it for a moment, waiting for the tension that had been building inside him from the moment he left the house to ease.

Now, for the first time, he felt his heart pounding.

Had Madeline put something in his coffee this morning?

No, he'd fooled her and hadn't had any coffee.

Finally moving away from the door, he went to his desk and dropped into the big chair that had been his father's and grandfather's before him. He was about to press the button on the intercom and ask Ellen Golding to bring him a cup of coffee, but quickly thought better of it. Whatever was going on at the Bank—and it was clear now that the Federal Reserve audit was only part of a much larger conspiracy—surely they would have recruited Ellen at the very beginning.

Better to get his own coffee before that sneaking bitch could doctor it!

Stepping out of the office, he went to the coffeepot Ellen always kept on the credenza that contained all his files and started to pour himself a cup.

"Why didn't you call me, Mr. Hartwick?" Ellen asked. "I could have done that for you."

He'd been right! She would have put something in it. Should he fire her right now? Better not to let them know he was on to them yet. "I'm not totally helpless, Ellen," he said. "Besides, isn't asking your secretary to bring you coffee considered grounds for a lawsuit these days?"

Ellen Golding stared at her boss. What on earth was he talking about? She'd been his secretary for nearly ten years, and brought him a cup of coffee every single morning. It was part of her job, for God's sake! "Are you all right, Mr. Hartwick?"

"Don't I look all right?" Jules shot back. "Do I look like something's wrong with me? Well, I can assure you, Miss Golding, that nothing is wrong with me, and nothing is *going* to be wrong with me, no matter how clever you might think you are." Taking the cup of coffee with him, he retreated to his office, closing the door behind him once more. Back at his desk, he took a sip of the coffee.

It had a bitter flavor to it that instantly put him on his guard. Had Ellen put something in the pot?

He pushed the cup aside.

Suddenly, the feeling of being watched swept over him again. But how? He was alone in his office.

Wasn't he?

What if someone was hiding in his private bathroom? Rising abruptly, he moved to the bathroom door, listened for a moment, then pulled the door open.

Empty.

Or was it?

What about the shower?

His heart pounding harder, he crossed the tile floor.

The shower curtain was closed, but he could almost feel the presence behind it.

Who?

In a movement so quick it surprised even himself, he reached out and snatched the curtain aside with so much force that three of its rings tore loose from the plastic fabric.

The stall was empty. Venting his frustration by jerking the rest of the curtain loose, he left it crumpled on the bathroom floor and went back to his office. And the moment he was back inside the paneled room, he knew where the watchers were hiding.

The security cameras!

There were two of them, set up six years ago not because Jules thought them necessary but because the insurance company had offered a reduction in premiums if they were installed. Now, however, he understood the real reason the insurance company had wanted the cameras put in. It wasn't to protect security at all.

It was so they could spy on him!

He picked up the phone and punched in the extension for his executive vice-president. "I want the security cameras in my office turned off," he said without so much as a good morning.

"I beg your pardon?" Melissa Holloway asked.

"You heard me!" Jules snapped. "I want the cameras in my office off right now, and taken out completely by lunchtime!" Slamming the phone back onto its cradle, he glowered up at the mechanical eye that stared at him from the corner. Then, unable to bear being watched a moment longer, Jules Hartwick left his desk once more.

Ten seconds later, having failed for the first time in his life to respond to every employee who spoke to him, he was on his way home.

Once again his right hand was buried deep in his pocket, clutching the locket.

Chapter 4

*E*d Becker knew something had gone wrong the moment he walked into the bank that morning. Though there was only one customer at the tellers' windows, there were whispered conversations going on everywhere, nearly all of which quickly died away as people became aware of his presence. At first he assumed that something had happened with regard to the audit, but when he glanced into the glass-fronted conference room in which the audit was taking place, the man and two women from the Fed were hard at work, each of them poring over a thick stack of computer printouts, just as they'd been doing for weeks. He was about to head for Jules Hartwick's office when Melissa Holloway beckoned him to her desk.

"Was Mr. Hartwick all right last night?" she asked.

Ed Becker felt eyes watching him from every direction. "He was fine," he assured the executive vice-president. "But I assume from the question that he isn't this morning. Is he in his office?"

Melissa Holloway shook her head. "He was here for about ten minutes," she told him. "First, he almost bit Ellen Golding's head off and then he called me and ordered—"

"Ordered?" Ed Becker echoed. In all the years he'd known Jules, he'd never heard the banker utter any instruction in terms that could be construed as an "order." Countless times he had heard Jules request that things he needed be done, but Ed had never witnessed even a hint of the kind of authoritarian behavior implied by the word Melissa Holloway had used.

Melissa shrugged helplessly. "I know. It's not like Mr. Hartwick at all. But he ordered me to turn off the security cameras in his office—immediately—and have them completely removed by noon."

Had it not been for the pallor of Melissa's complexion and the worry in her expression, Ed Becker would have suspected she was pulling his leg. Obviously, though, she wasn't. "And then he left?"

Melissa nodded. "Without speaking to anyone. And he didn't speak to anyone when he came in either. Ed, he *always* speaks to everyone. It might not be more than a word or two, but he always has at least a 'good morning.' But not today. It was like—" She hesitated, floundering, then shook her head. "I don't know what it was like. It was crazy!"

"What about the auditors?" Ed asked, lowering his voice so it would carry no farther than Melissa's ears. "Could they have found something that might have upset him?"

"It's the first thing I thought of, but none of them even said hello to him. I was hoping maybe you might know what's going on."

Before Ed could say anything else, Andrew Sterling came over, his face red, a vein throbbing in his forehead. "Do you have any idea what the hell is going on with Jules?" he demanded, his voice harsh.

Ed Becker braced himself. "What did he say to you?"

"Nothing. But I just got a call from Celeste. For some reason her father seems to think that—" He fell silent for a moment, and it was apparent to both Ed Becker and Melissa Holloway that he had to force himself to continue. "He seems to have gotten the idea in his head that Celeste's mother is having an affair."

"Madeline?" Ed Becker gasped. "Come on, Andrew. You've got to be kidding!"

"I wish I were. But it gets worse. It seems he thinks *I'm* the person she's—" Again he went silent. This time, it was apparent Andrew wasn't going to be able to finish the sentence at all.

"Jules actually *said* that?" Ed asked. When Andrew made no answer, Ed took a deep breath, then slowly let it out. "I guess I'd better go up there and see what's going on."

The gate at the foot of the Hartwicks' driveway stood open. Madeline's car was gone, so Ed pulled his Buick under the porte cochere and strode up the steps. Ringing the bell, he shivered in the cold as he waited for Jules Hartwick to open the door. When the banker hadn't appeared after a full minute went by, he rang the bell again. When there was still no response, Ed went back to the Buick, pulled his winter coat out of the backseat and put it on, then went around to the back of the house.

Peering through one of the windows in the garage, he saw that Jules's black Lincoln Town Car was inside. Of course, that didn't necessarily mean that Jules himself was at home; like almost everyone in Blackstone, Jules walked to work unless the weather was truly horrible, and it had been Melissa Holloway's impression that Jules had, indeed, walked down to the bank that morning. Mounting the steps to the large glassed-in back porch, Ed let himself though the storm door, then tried the back door.

Locked.

He looked for a bell, found none, and knocked loudly.

There was no more response from within than there'd been at the front door a few minutes earlier.

Leaving the back porch, Ed circled the house to the other side, past the breakfast room, then moved onto the broad terrace. There, sets of French doors, one at each end, led into the library and the large formal living room. He cupped his hands around his eyes in an attempt to peer into the shadowy rooms beyond the doors, but the shirred material covering the panes defeated his efforts.

He moved on around the house, his shoes now squishing with icy water and the bottoms of his pants heavy with snow. Rounding the far corner, he came to the protrusion next to the library that housed Jules Hartwick's den.

Heavy drapes had been drawn over both the windows flanking the small fireplace that was the room's dominant feature, and the windows were far too high for Ed to have seen through them even had curtains not covered them. He made his way around to the front door again and jabbed the bell three more times, but got no more response than before. Finally giving up, he returned to his car, got in, and started the engine. It wasn't until he'd reached the street that he saw it: smoke curling from the chimney that vented the fireplace in Jules Hartwick's den.

Ed Becker pulled back into the driveway, then sat staring at the drifting smoke. The den, he knew, was the one room in the house that neither Madeline nor Celeste ever went into. "I don't have even the slightest desire to go in there," he remembered Madeline saying a few months ago. "He has it exactly the way he wants it, and if he doesn't mind the stink of those awful cigars he thinks I don't know he smokes, so be it. He keeps the door shut, and I stay out. Which is fine, since I think we all need a place to go when we want to hide. I have my dressing room, and Jules has his den, and we share the rest of the house. It works perfectly."

And it also meant that if there was a fire on the den's hearth, then Jules was there.

Ed turned on his cellular phone and dialed Jules's private number. On the fourth ring the answering machine came on. He listened patiently as Jules's recorded greeting played through. When the machine beeped, Ed began talking. "You might as well pick up the phone, Jules. I'm outside, sitting in my car, and I can see the smoke from the fireplace. I don't know what's troubling you, but whatever it is, we can work it out. But I can't do anything for you if you won't talk to me." He paused, giving the banker a chance to pick up the phone, but nothing happened. He began talking again. "I'm your lawyer, Jules. That means that whatever's happening, I'm on—"

"You're fired, Becker. Get out of my driveway."

The harsh words erupted from the cell phone's speaker, startling Ed Becker into silence for a moment. He quickly recovered. "What's going on, Jules? What's happened?"

"A lot's happened," Jules Hartwick replied. "But you know all about it, don't you, Ed? Well, guess what? I know all about it too now. I know what's going on at the Bank, and I know what Madeline's been up to. And I know all about you. So just get off my property before I call the police."

The cellular phone went dead, leaving Ed Becker staring at the Hartwicks' mansion in stunned disbelief.

Twenty minutes later, with Jules Hartwick still refusing to answer either the door or the telephone, he finally gave up and started back down to the village. Somewhere, he was sure, there had to be someone who knew what had upset Jules so badly.

Unless, as Melissa Holloway had suggested, he'd just plain gone crazy.

* * *

"Oliver?" Lois Martin asked. Ed Becker had left the offices of the *Blackstone Chronicle*, having found out nothing more about what might be bothering Jules Hartwick than he'd known when he'd arrived half an hour earlier. Oliver had been sitting silently, head in hands, ever since. "Oliver?" Lois repeated. "Are you all right?"

The *Chronicle*'s editor and publisher pressed his fingers against his temples in a vain effort to stem the rising tide of pain. The headache had begun ten minutes ago, and was now threatening to overwhelm him not only with throbbing pain but with nausea as well. He leaned back in his chair and closed his eyes. The fluorescent light in the office, though no brighter than usual, was suddenly blinding him. "Have you ever had a migraine headache?" he asked.

"A long time ago," Lois replied, grimacing at the memory. "I had a few when I was in college. Worst thing I've ever been through." She lowered herself onto the chair that Ed Becker had vacated just minutes before, and regarded her boss worriedly. "You sure it's a migraine?"

"My head throbs, the lights are killing my eyes, and I'm starting to feel queasy. It's like someone's driving a spike right into the center of my head."

"Sounds like a migraine," Lois agreed. "When did it start?"

"This one? Maybe ten minutes ago. But this is maybe the third or fourth one I've had in the last month."

"Maybe you'd better go see Dr. Margolis."

"Or maybe Jules Hartwick ought to," Oliver countered. "Did you hear much of what Ed was saying?"

"I heard, but I can't believe it," Lois replied. "It just doesn't sound like Jules. I mean, the whole idea of Madeline Hartwick having an affair is ludicrous! And even if there's a major problem at the bank, Jules just isn't the type to go off the deep end."

"He's not the type to fire his lawyer over the phone either." Oliver sighed. "But he did it. What the hell is going on around here, Lois? Last month Elizabeth McGuire commits suicide, and now it sounds like Jules Hartwick is turning paranoid."

Lois Martin frowned. "You're not suggesting there's any connection between the two, are you?"

Before Oliver could reply, another stab of pain slashed through his head. He felt his skin turn cold and clammy, and his stomach began to churn. "Is there anything going on you can't handle?" he asked weakly when the wave of agony had receded to the point where he trusted himself to speak.

"There hasn't been anything going on that I couldn't handle for the last five years," Lois told him. "Go see the doctor, Oliver. Or at least go home, close the curtains, and lie down for a while." Oliver managed a nod and got shakily to his feet. "Can you drive?" Lois asked anxiously as Oliver used the desk to brace himself against the dizzy spell that struck him as he stood fully upright. "Maybe I better lock the office up for a few minutes and—"

"I'll be all right," Oliver assured her as the dizziness passed. He took a couple of experimental steps toward the front door, then managed a weak smile. "See? Perfectly steady."

"Just be careful," Lois cautioned as she helped him pull on his coat. "And call me when you get home. Otherwise, I'll come up to your house and fuss over you like an old hen. You'll hate it."

"I'll call," Oliver promised.

Getting into his Volvo, he winced as the engine caught and surged into noisy life, but a moment later, as the motor settled down to its normal rough idle, the throbbing pain in his head eased slightly. Pulling out of the parking space in front of the *Chronicle* office, he drove down Prospect to Amherst and started up the long slope of North Hill. Though the road was slick with packed snow, the Volvo threatened to go into a skid only once, and less than five minutes later Oliver pulled through the gates of the old Asylum and turned left, onto the side road that led to his cottage.

He pressed the remote control as he approached, and the door to his garage drew fully open just as he pulled into it. Getting out of the car, he opened the door that led directly into the laundry room of his house, but as he reached for the wall button that would close the garage door, he caught sight of the Asylum itself, looming on the crest of the hill half a hundred yards away at the top of the wide, curving drive.

Something about it seemed somehow different.

Abandoning the garage, Oliver stepped out into the bright, late morning sunlight and gazed up at the old building.

Its steeply pitched copper roof was covered with a thick blanket of glistening white snow. For a fleeting second he was almost able to imagine the building as it must have been a century ago, when it had first been built as a private home. He tried to envision it at Christmastime, when brightly colored sleighs drawn by horses laden with silver bells would have come up the hill bearing women in furs and hugely bustled dresses, and men in top hats and morning coats, to call on Charles Connally, who had originally built the huge mansion as a gift for his first wife and a slap in the parsimonious face of his father, Jonas, who had never willingly parted with so much as a nickel of the fortune he had accumulated.

The glory days of the mansion hadn't lasted long. The patriarch of the Connally clan had died only a dozen years after the mansion was completed, and when Charles's wife died as well, the house was soon converted to the only other use it had ever known.

A shelter for the insane.

Or had it actually been little more than a prison?

Oliver had never been sure, though over the years he'd certainly heard plenty of stories from people who may or may not have known what they were talking about.

All he truly knew was that the imposing stone structure had always terrified him. Terrified him to the point where he'd been utterly unable to bring himself even to enter it. Yet this morning, with his head throbbing and his stomach churning, he found himself being drawn toward the long-abandoned building.

The cold of the morning forgotten, Oliver made his way through deep drifts and up the curving driveway toward the great oaken doors. A silence seemed to have fallen over North Hill, broken only by the sound of snow crunching beneath his feet.

Coming to the steps, he hesitated for a moment, then climbed up to the broad porch. He gazed for a moment at the huge wooden panels before reaching out to the great bronze lever that would release the latch.

As Oliver's fingers touched the ice cold metal, another wave of nausea seized him, and his hand jerked reflexively away as if the hardware had been red hot. His gorge rising, Oliver turned away once more and lurched back down the steps.

Falling to his knees, he retched into the snow, then, gasping for breath, got back to his feet and stumbled down the hill to his house. Unwilling to stay outside even long enough to unlock his front door, he went through the garage and into the laundry room, slamming the door behind him.

His heart pounding, Oliver leaned against the washing machine and tried to catch his breath. Slowly, the nausea in his belly eased and his breathing returned to normal, and even the stabbing pain in his head began to recede. When the telephone rang, he was able to make his way into the kitchen and pick up the extension with trembling fingers.

"Oliver?" Lois Martin said. "Is that you?"

"I-it's me," Oliver managed.

"Thank God," Lois breathed. "This is the third time I've called. If you hadn't answered, I was going to come up there. Are you all right?"

"I'm fine," Oliver said, though even as he uttered the words, he knew they were a lie.

Chapter 5

*M*adeline Hartwick turned off the interstate and slowed her Cadillac to precisely seven miles an hour above the posted speed limit. Another twenty minutes and they would be safely back in Blackstone, despite Celeste's insistence this morning that driving down to Boston today was insane. Madeline had been determined; they were both far too upset to sit at home all day, worrying over Jules's unprovoked outburst, and waiting tensely for him to return home from the bank.

"We'll go down to Boston, do some shopping, and have a nice lunch," she'd informed Celeste no more than ten minutes after Jules had left the house. Celeste had objected, but Madeline prevailed, and by the time they began browsing the shops on Newbury Street, Madeline had already convinced herself that Jules's crazy accusations had undoubtedly been brought on by the pressure he was under from the audit at the bank; when he got home, it would all have been forgotten. Nor had she killed anyone with the Cadillac as Celeste had so uncharitably insisted she was bound to do, given last night's snowstorm.

Shifting in the seat to ease the tension that always built up in her when she drove on the interstate, Madeline breathed a sigh of contentment. "I don't know about you," she said, glancing at her daughter, "but I feel a lot better."

Celeste—not nearly as sanguine about her father as her mother obviously was—rolled her eyes. "I'm not sure why bankrupting Daddy makes you feel better," she said. "And I certainly don't see how it makes up for the awful things he said this morning."

"It's really very simple, dear," her mother explained. "I vented my anger with my credit cards. Your father has atoned for what he said by buying me a perfectly lovely Valentino coat."

"But he doesn't know he bought it!" Celeste protested.

"He will when he gets the bill," Madeline reminded her. "And by then he'll feel so guilty about what he said that he won't even blink at how much it cost."

"But to have implied that you were having an affair—"

"Oh, pooh!" Madeline removed a hand from the steering wheel just long enough to brush her daughter's words dismissively away. "When you think about it, it's rather a compliment that he still thinks I'm attractive enough that someone would want to have an affair with me. Especially someone as young and handsome as Andrew!"

"Mother!"

"Oh, for Heaven's sake, Celeste—don't be such a prude. By the time you and Andrew have been married as long as your father and I, you'll understand that things are not always easy. If you don't, you'll already be divorced several times by the time you're my age. There are lots of rough patches in any marriage, dear. You have to learn to deal with them without cutting and running."

"But what Daddy said was unforgivable—" Celeste began.

But Madeline, having heard it all three times already today, didn't let her finish. "Everything is forgivable, if you wish to forgive," she cut in. "And I don't wish to discuss it any further. Let's just go home and see how your father is when he comes home from the bank today. All right?"

The sigh Celeste uttered was far more out of resignation than from contentment, but she decided to let the argument go, at least for now. If her mother was determined not to see that something had gone seriously wrong with her father, there would be no talking her out of it. At least not right now. Lapsing into silence, she contented herself with gazing at the wintery scene outside the car. Maybe this weekend she and Andrew would drive over to Stowe and do some skiing. Assuming, of course, that she and Andrew were still together by the end of the week. If her father started spreading his horrible story around the bank, there was no telling what Andrew might do. But maybe her mother was right, and by now the whole terrible incident was over with.

A few minutes later, though, as they pulled into the driveway, Celeste saw the smoke curling up from the den's chimney and glanced at the clock on the Cadillac's dashboard. Just a little after four. What was her father doing at home? He never came home before six.

As the Cadillac pulled up under the porte cochere, Celeste saw the tracks in the snow that still marked the path Ed Becker had taken that morning. "Something's wrong, Mother," she said. She got out of the car, but instead of going to the trunk to help Madeline carry the packages in, she walked farther up the driveway until she could clearly see the path someone had beaten into the snow. "Mother, it looks like someone was trying to get into the house," she called out.

"Well, I'm sure there's a reasonable explanation for it," Madeline said a moment later as she stood next to her daughter, her arms laden with packages. "Perhaps your father—"

"Why would Daddy be trying to break into his own house?" Celeste asked. "Maybe we shouldn't even go in! Maybe we should call the police—"

"Nonsense!" Madeline declared. "For heaven's sake, child, we'd look like perfect fools. Besides, you yourself just pointed out the smoke coming from the fireplace in your father's den. Unless the world has changed a great deal more than I think it has, burglars do not build fires to keep them warm while they rifle your house! Bring the rest of the packages in from the car while I go see what's been going on here."

Ignoring Celeste's protests, Madeline mounted the steps to the porch, then fumbled with her keys until she found the right one. "Jules?" she called out as she set her packages down on the table in the entry hall. "Jules, are you here?" When there was no answer, she crossed the foyer to the library and rapped sharply on the closed door to her husband's den. "Jules? May I come in?" There was no answer. "Jules!"

A muffled voice came from the other side of the door. "Go away."

Madeline's hand closed on the doorknob and she tried to turn it.

Locked.

"Jules, I want to talk to you!"

When there was no response from inside the den, Madeline mounted the stairs, heading for her dressing room. She kept a spare set of keys to every door in the huge old house in the top drawer of her vanity. But when she came to her dressing room she stopped abruptly. The door was ajar. Beyond it, every drawer and every closet door stood open, and her lingerie had been scattered across the carpeted floor. The anger she'd so deliberately dissipated in the shops along Newbury Street came flooding back. Jules never came into her dressing room, just as she never went into his den. Today, though, he'd not only entered her sanctuary, but searched through her things! Surely he hadn't actually expected to find proof of the affair he imagined she was having! It was ludicrous! Intolerable!

Ignoring the tangle of clothes on the floor, Madeline went to her vanity. Though it was clear that every drawer had been gone through, everything still seemed to be there, and she quickly found the ring of keys.

Celeste was just coming into the foyer when she got back to the foot of the stairs. Together the two women returned to the locked door to the den. Madeline once again knocked loudly on the mahogany panels, and when there was no reply, she began trying the keys on the ring until one fit. She heard the bolt click back and turned the knob once more. The door swung open.

Jules glowered at her from behind his desk. A nearly empty bottle of scotch sat at his elbow.

She crossed to the desk. "I don't know what's wrong, Jules," she said softly. "But I do know that finishing that bottle won't help."

"You know what's wrong, you tramp!"

As if acting under its own volition, Madeline's hand flashed out and slapped her husband across the face, but even before the sting on her palm had died away, she regretted her action. "Oh, God, Jules, I'm sorry. I didn't mean—"

"You've been wanting to do that for years, haven't you?" Jules growled, his words slurring. "Do you think I haven't known? Well, I know, Madeline. I know everything."

Madeline bit her lower lip to keep her temper in check, then took a deep breath. "All right," she said. "I can see there's no point in talking to you right now. Dinner will be ready at seven. Come to the table or not, as you see fit." Picking up the bottle of scotch and taking it with her, Madeline left the study, pulling the door closed behind her.

"What is it?" Celeste asked. "Mother, what's wrong with him?"

"I don't know," Madeline replied. "But I think it's time to call Dr. Margolis."

The two women went back through the library to the foyer, where a telephone sat on a table near the base of the wide staircase. Picking up the receiver, Madeline dialed Philip Margolis's office. His nurse answered on the second ring.

"Nancy?" Madeline said. "It's Madeline Hartwick. I would like to speak to Philip, please."

"I'm afraid he's in Concord, Mrs. Hartwick," Nancy Conway told her. "Is there something I can do for you?"

Madeline hesitated. Though she'd known Nancy Conway for twenty years, and liked her, she was well aware that Nancy had never kept a secret in her life, and never passed on a story without embellishing it. If she even hinted at the things Jules was doing and saying, by tomorrow morning everyone in Blackstone would have heard that he'd lost his mind. Better to deal with Jules herself tonight, she decided, and talk directly to Philip Margolis in the morning. "I don't think so, Nancy," she said. "It's nothing that can't wait."

Chapter 6

*A*s the symphony of chimes signifying the dinner hour echoed through the Hartwicks' vast house, Madeline carried the last plate into the breakfast room, where she, Jules, and Celeste invariably ate when they were alone. Tonight, in a special effort to please her troubled husband, Madeline had covered the table with one of her best lace cloths, set out the sterling candelabra that had belonged to Jules's mother—the same candelabra that could be seen in the portrait of her that they'd found in the attic, and which now hung in the library— and gotten out the Limoges china with the hunting pattern that had always been his favorite. Celeste had even found a dozen roses at the florist that perfectly matched the red of the burgundy Madeline had opened half an hour ago.

Madeline turned the outside lights on, transforming the dark landscape beyond the windows into a brilliantly sparkling winterscape. As she waited for her husband and daughter to join her, she decided that no matter how bad Jules's mood had been today, the dinner she'd prepared, and the setting she created in which to serve it, couldn't possibly fail to cheer him up. But when Celeste came into the room as the last of the clocks' chimes died away, her father was not with her.

"Do you think he'll come at all?" Celeste asked as she took her seat while her mother poured the wine.

"I don't know," Madeline replied, sounding far more calm than she felt.

"But—"

"But nothing," Madeline cut in, perfectly matching the level of wine in the third Waterford goblet to that in the other two. "If he won't tell us what's wrong . . ." Her voice died away as she heard Jules's footsteps coming through the dining room.

When he appeared in the doorway, she forced a smile that managed to mask the many emotions that had been churning through her all day. "I've fixed all your favorites," she said, moving toward Jules to take his arm and draw him into the room. When he pulled away from her, she chose to ignore it, and pulled his chair out for him. "Filet mignon, just on the medium side of medium rare, a baked potato with all the things that are bad for you, green beans with almonds, and a Caesar salad. And I broke out a Pauillac, one of the 'eighty-fives."

Jules eyed the table carefully, as if searching for something that might be ready to strike out at him, and for a moment Madeline was afraid he was going to bolt from the room. But then he moved away from his chair and seated himself in her own. He looked up at her, his eyes glinting in the candlelight. "Suppose I sit in your chair tonight?" he asked, a strange smile twisting his lips—one that seemed to Madeline to be oddly triumphant, as if he'd just won some kind of victory over her. "Would that be all right with you?"

"Of course," she replied, immediately settling herself into what was ordinarily Jules's place at the table. It felt distinctly odd, but if this was what it would take to soothe her husband, so be it. She picked up her knife and fork, cut off a small portion of the steak, and put it in her mouth.

Jules abruptly stood up. "I've changed my mind. I'll sit there after all."

Her jaw tightening, but saying nothing, Madeline stood and picked up the plate in front of her.

"Leave it there," Jules commanded.

Celeste, who until now had said nothing at all, finally broke her silence. "For heaven's sake, Daddy, what are you doing? Did you think Mother poisoned your food or something? It's as if . . ." Celeste's words died away as her father's eyes bored into her, glowing with a feverish light she'd never seen in them before. She quickly shifted her own gaze to her mother, who shook her head just enough for Celeste to understand that she would do well to change the subject. "Maybe we could talk about the wedding," she began, realizing the moment the words were out of her mouth that she'd made a mistake.

"And what wedding would that be?" her father demanded, his voice ice cold.

"M-mine and Andrew's," Celeste stammered, her words barely audible.

Jules's gaze pierced her. "Really, Celeste, how stupid do you think I am?" Once again Celeste glanced at her mother, but this time her father saw the movement of her eyes. "Don't look at her, Celeste. She can't help you this time. I'm on to her, and I'm on to Andrew. I'm even on to you."

Celeste set down her fork. She had begun to tremble. "Why are you doing this, Daddy? Why are you talking like everyone's out to get you? Why are—"

"Aren't they?" Jules suddenly bellowed, slamming his fist down on the table so hard his wineglass fell over. A dark stain spread like blood from a wound. "There won't be a wedding, Celeste! Not to that bastard Andrew Sterling, anyway. And as of tomorrow morning, he'll be out of the Bank. Do you understand? How dare he think he can take over my own Bank! And how dare you even think of marrying him! Don't you understand? He wants everything I have. My Bank, my wife, my daughter—

everything! Well, he won't get it! None of it! None of it, goddamn it!"

Bursting into tears, Celeste fled from the table. Madeline rose as if to follow her daughter, but as she heard Celeste's feet pounding up the stairs, she turned back to face her husband, her own eyes now almost as angry as his. "Have you gone out of your mind, Jules?" she demanded. "I called Dr. Margolis earlier, and I'm going to call him again in the morning. In the meantime, I suggest—"

"You'll suggest nothing!" Jules stood, plunging his right hand deep into the pocket of his pants. "What are you planning to do, put me in the Asylum? Well, you won't get away with it, Madeline! When I tell people what you've been up to—you and Andrew, and Celeste too—you'll all be in jail! Or have you got everyone else in the plot too?" His eyes narrowed to tiny, suspicious slits. "You'd better tell me what you're planning, Madeline. I'll find out, you know. One way or another, I'll find out everything."

He edged toward her, but Madeline turned and strode from the breakfast room. By the time he'd moved through the dining room and the small parlor, she had reached the foot of the broad staircase.

"I'm going upstairs, Jules," she told him, her eyes fixed steadily on him, her voice calm. "I'm not having an affair with anyone, and I'm not out to ruin your life, and neither are Celeste and Andrew. We all love you, and we all want to help you." She paused, then spoke again, using the soothing tones that had always calmed Celeste when she was a child. "It's going to be all right, Jules. Whatever is wrong, I'm going to fix. Right now, I'm going to go up and take care of our daughter. Then, in a few minutes, I'll be back downstairs, and you and I can figure it all out." When he made no reply, she turned and hurried up the stairs.

Jules, clutching the locket tightly in his right hand,

watched her disappear onto the second floor. Take care
of Celeste, indeed! He could almost hear them, whispering together in Celeste's room, scheming against him.

Scheming what?

Would Madeline really call Margolis and have him
locked away in the Asylum?

Of course she would! She'd do anything to get rid of
him, so she and Andrew could take over the Bank.

And Celeste was part of it too, of course!

How stupid he'd been not to have seen it coming
months ago! But of course that had been the genius of
their plot—Celeste would pretend to be in love with
Andrew so he'd never suspect what Andrew and Madeline were up to! But he'd figured it out in time.

And he'd stop it too.

He was at the foot of the stairs; suddenly, one of the
lights on the telephone went on.

They were trying to call someone! One of their co-
conspirators, no doubt!

He started up the stairs, intent on stopping them, then
realized they'd have locked Celeste's door against him.

The phones!

He could tear out the phones!

Instead of going up, he dashed back through the dining
room and into the kitchen, then down the back stairs to
the basement. Groping in the dark, he found the light
switch. The bright glare of a naked bulb pierced the darkness around him.

The laundry room.

That's where the main electrical box was, and he was
almost sure that's where they'd put the box for the new
phone system he'd had installed last year.

He darted into the laundry room, felt for the light
switch, and a moment later found the telephone's control
box right where he remembered it.

Dozens of wires sprouted from the connector boards
that were mounted on the wall next to the controller, and

Jules, after staring at them for a split second, began indiscriminately jerking them loose.

Through nothing more than pure chance, the very first wires he tore free from the boards were the lines coming in from the outside. Though he kept tearing at the wires, the phones throughout the house had already gone dead.

※

Chapter 7

*T*he last wire jerked free from the panel next to the control unit. Jules Hartwick stepped back, breathing hard, staring at his handiwork, listening to the silence that had descended on the house.

What had they thought he'd do? How big a fool did they take him for? Even as he sat in his den all day, he'd been able to hear them. Hear them as clearly in his own mind as if they'd been in the room with him.

Talking about him.

Laughing at him.

Plotting against him.

But he'd outsmarted them. Now he was in control, and they had no one to talk to but each other.

Who had they been calling?

The traitor, Andrew Sterling?

The quack, Philip Margolis?

Or someone else?

There were so many of them out there.

Enemies.

They weren't just in his home and in his Bank.

They were all over town. Watching him. Whispering about him.

And plotting. Always plotting.

How long had it been going on? How long had they all been able to fool him, making him think they were his friends? Well, it was all over now. Everything was crystal clear, and finally he was in control of his own life again. And it would stay that way.

Jules left the laundry room, careful not to turn off the lights, not to offer his enemies any darkness in which to hide. He moved through the basement, turning on every light until the warren of dusty rooms beneath the house was free from any shadows in which his enemies might lurk. Then, satisfied that no lights remained unlit, he went back up to the kitchen. There, too, he turned on every light, filling the room with a brilliant glow.

From the huge rack above the carving counter, he chose a knife with a ten-inch blade, honed to razor sharpness by years of perfect care. Its smooth haft, carved from ebony nearly a century earlier, fit perfectly in his hand, and as his fingers tightened on it he felt the strength of the hardwood seep from the weapon into his body. Fingering it now as he'd fingered the locket a few minutes earlier, he left the kitchen and moved through the butler's pantry and into the dining room, still turning on every light he found, washing the house free of any dark corners in which his enemies might conceal themselves.

Moving as silently as a wraith, Jules Hartwick prowled the main floor of his house, banishing the darkness from its rooms as the locket he carried with him had banished reason from his mind.

Madeline and Celeste listened to the silence of the house.

When the phone had suddenly gone dead in Madeline's hand while she was waiting for Philip Margolis's answering service to come back on the line, she'd assumed that the connection had merely been lost by the service itself. But when she pressed the redial button and nothing happened, her impatience with the incompetence of the answering service gave way to fear. Surely she was wrong!

Jules was upset, but he wouldn't cut the phone lines—would he?

She stabbed at the buttons that should have connected to one of the other lines that came into the house. None of the lights came on. There was a deadness to the silence in the receiver that told her the phones were no longer working at all. She slammed the handset back onto its cradle. Her thoughts darted first one way then another, like mice in a maze.

Raise the window and call for help?

She cringed at the mere thought of the kind of talk that would cause. If the problems at the bank were bad now, they'd be ten times worse by tomorrow, when everyone in town would know that Jules had gone—

She cut herself off, refusing to use the word "insane" even in the privacy of her own mind. Jules was under a strain—a severe strain—but he was *not* insane! Therefore, whatever had upset him could be dealt with. *She* could deal with it. Taking a deep breath to steady her nerves, she turned to Celeste. "Stay here," she instructed her daughter. "I'm going downstairs to talk to your father."

"Are you crazy?" Celeste asked. "Mother, he's cut off the phones! You don't know what he'll do next."

Madeline steeled herself against the fear that was creeping through her, knowing that if she gave in to it even for a moment she would lose her courage entirely. "Your father won't hurt me," she said. "We've been married for twenty-five years, and there's never been a hint of violence in him. I don't think he's going to start now." She started toward the door.

"I'm coming with you," Celeste told her.

Madeline was tempted to argue, but as she remembered the look she'd seen in Jules's eyes as he glared at her from the foot of the stairs, she changed her mind. Opening the door to Celeste's bedroom, she stepped out into the hall.

The house was as silent as a tomb.

Unconsciously taking her daughter's hand in her own, Madeline moved to the head of the stairs. She was just about to peer over the banister to the entry hall below when the silence was shattered by the gong of the grandfather clock striking the half hour. As both Madeline and Celeste jumped at the noise, all the other clocks in the house began sounding as well, the rooms resonating with a cacophony of chimes and bells.

Then, as quickly as it had begun, it was over, and once more a shroud of silence dropped over them.

"Where is he?" Celeste whispered. "What's he doing?"

Before Madeline could answer, Jules appeared at the bottom of the stairs. His hands behind his back, he glowered up at them.

"Stay here," Madeline instructed Celeste firmly. "I'm going to try to talk to him. If anything happens, lock yourself in your room. You'll be safe in there."

"Mother, don't," Celeste pleaded, but Madeline was already starting slowly down the long flight of stairs, her eyes fixed on her husband.

Do not be afraid of him, she told herself. He won't hurt you.

From her room in the house next door, Rebecca Morrison watched curiously as every window on the main floor of the Hartwicks' house blossomed into light.

Were the Hartwicks going to have another party?

Surely not—no catering truck had arrived, nor had she seen any of the waiters Madeline always hired when she was having a big party. And it was already seven-thirty, long after the time the parties next door invariably began.

Yet she was certain that something unusual was happening, for except when the Hartwicks were having a party, the lights in the rooms they weren't using were never left burning, any more than they were in her own house.

"Rebecca? What are you doing, child?"

Rebecca jumped at her aunt's words and instantly dropped the curtain she'd been peeping through. As she turned to face her aunt, Martha Ward's eyes narrowed and her lips pursed in disapproval.

"Are you spying on the neighbors again, Rebecca?" Martha demanded.

"I was just looking," Rebecca said. "And the oddest thing is happening, Aunt Martha. All the—"

"I do not wish to hear," Martha interjected, her own words neatly cutting her niece's short. "Nor do you need to watch. We shall go to the chapel and pray for your forgiveness."

"But Aunt Martha," Rebecca began again, "I think maybe—"

"Silence!" Martha Ward commanded. "I shall not be tainted with your sins, Rebecca. Come with me."

Rebecca, with one last glance toward the curtained windows that looked out at the house next door, silently, obediently, followed her aunt to the chapel. As the Gregorian chants began to play, she knelt before the altar and the glowing candles whose heat and smoke seemed to draw the very air from the room. Her aunt began mumbling the prayers, and Rebecca tried to close her mind to whatever might be happening next door.

It's none of my business, she told herself. I must remember that it is none of my business.

Madeline Hartwick came to the bottom of the stairs. Her husband's eyes were still fixed on her, and in the brilliant light of the chandelier suspended from the ceiling of the great entry hall, she could see clearly the hatred emanating from them.

"Go back to your room, Celeste," she said, once again steeling herself to betray none of the fear that was suddenly coursing through her. Whatever had happened to Jules—whatever madness had seized him—had worsened in just the few minutes she'd been away from him, and though she refused to betray her terror to him or to their daughter, she had to protect Celeste. "Lock your door. You'll be safe there."

For the smallest instant she was afraid Celeste was going to ignore her words, and when she saw Jules's gaze flicker toward the stairs, she uttered a silent prayer.

Leave her alone! If your madness demands a victim, take me!

As if he'd heard her unspoken words, Jules's eyes fixed once more on her. In the silence that followed, she heard Celeste's door thud shut and, a second later, the hard click of the lock snapping into place. "What is it, Jules?" she asked softly. "What is it you want of me?"

Without warning, Jules's left arm snaked out, spun her around, and clamped her against his chest. At the same instant, she saw the blade of the knife glimmering in the light of the chandelier, then felt cold steel caress her neck with a touch as light as a feather.

A deadly feather.

She froze, her nostrils flaring, every muscle in her body going rigid.

Then she felt Jules's hot breath on her neck and smelled the whiskey he'd been drinking all through the day.

"I could kill you," he whispered. "All I have to do is pull the knife across your throat. It would be easy, Madeline. And you deserve it, don't you?"

When she made no reply, his grip on her tightened, and she felt the blade of the knife etch her skin. Her mind raced and she began speaking, the words boiling up out of some well of defense she hadn't known she possessed. "Yes," she heard herself saying. "I didn't think you'd find out. I didn't think you were smart enough. But I was wrong, Jules. I should have known I couldn't fool you. I should have known you'd find out. And I'm sorry, Jules. I'm so very, very sorry."

She began crying then, and let herself go limp in his violent embrace. Once again his grip on her tightened. He steered her across the entry hall, then through the parlor, the dining room, and the kitchen. Then they were at the top of the stairs leading to the basement. Madeline gazed down the steep flight at the concrete floor below.

"Lies!" she heard Jules whisper harshly in her ear. "All of it has been nothing but lies, without so much as a tea-spoon of truth!" He released her, the knife dropping away from her throat as he hurled her away from him. Madeline reached out frantically, groping for the wall, the banister, anything that might stop her as she pitched forward.

There was nothing.

As she plunged headfirst down the stairs, the fear that had been rising within her broke through the dam of self-control she had struggled to hold intact. A scream of terror erupted from her throat, shattering the silence in the house, only to be cut off a second later as her head struck the concrete floor.

As Madeline's body lay broken at the foot of the stairs, Jules—his right hand still clutching the knife—slowly descended to the basement.

In the Hartwick mansion at the top of Harvard Street, all that could be heard was an eerie quiet.

A silence as deep as the grave.

Chapter 8

*A*ndrew Sterling punched Celeste Hartwick's number into the keypad of his portable phone for the third time, and listened with growing worry to the continuous ringing at the other end of the line. The line had been busy when he'd first dialed her number fifteen minutes ago, but when he'd tried again, he'd gotten no answer. It made no sense: he was sure Celeste had been planning to have dinner with her parents tonight. Why was no one answering the phone? The memory of Jules's strange behavior at the bank that morning only increased Andrew's mounting uneasiness. Following the tenth unanswered ring on Celeste's line, he hung up and dialed the operator. After waiting thirty seconds he heard a laconic voice inform him that "that line is currently out of order, sir. Would you like me to connect you with repair service?" Unwilling to get involved in what he suspected would turn into an impenetrable bureaucratic maze, Andrew hung up.

He pulled a parka on over the flannel shirt into which he'd changed after leaving the office an hour ago, and, gulping down the last bite of the microwaved pizza that had served as dinner, he went out to his five-year-old Ford Escort—all his bank salary could support in the way of a car—and prayed there was enough tread left on the tires to let him get up Harvard Street to the Hartwicks' house.

A few flakes of snow drifted down as the Escort's

engine coughed into reluctant life. By the time Andrew pulled away from the curb, a sharp wind had come up. The light dusting of a minute or two earlier was rapidly developing into a heavy snowfall. He'd gone only a block when the night filled with a swirling white cloud that cut visibility down to a few yards. As the wiper struggled to keep the windshield clear, Andrew crept toward North Hill, praying that the Escort would find the power to make it up the snow-slicked grade of Harvard Street.

It seemed to Celeste as if hours had passed since she'd heard her mother's muffled scream, cut off almost the instant it had begun.

Oh God! Had her father hurt her mother?

Maybe even killed her?

But that couldn't be possible—could it? Her parents adored one another! But as she stood rooted to the floor behind the locked door to her room, images of her father flashed through her mind.

This morning at the breakfast table, his eyes burning with jealousy as he hurled insane accusations at her mother . . .

This afternoon when they'd come home and found him drinking in his den . . .

A few minutes ago at the dinner table, accusing not only her mother, but herself as well . . .

Insane! It was all insane!

He was insane!

Rattling the doorknob to be certain the lock was secure, she went to the window and peered out into the night. Snow was falling rapidly now, and though she could still make out Martha Ward's house next door, and even the VanDeventers' across the street, no lights showed. But maybe if she yelled, someone would hear her. She struggled with the window, finally managed to lift it, then began wrestling with the storm window outside. But what was the use? Every house on the street had storm windows, and even if she succeeded in opening hers, her voice would be all but lost in the snowstorm.

Out!

She had to get out! If she could just get to the garage and her car—

Her heart sank as she remembered that her mother's car was still sitting in the porte cochere. Even if the snow hadn't made the driveway impassable, her mother's car did. But she could still get to a neighbor's—*someone* had to be home; if not the VanDeventers, then in the house next door. Martha Ward never went anywhere except to church, and Rebecca went only to the library.

She went back to the door and pressed her ear against it, listening.

Silence.

Her fingers trembling, she twisted the key in the lock. When the bolt clicked back, it seemed unnaturally loud.

Again she listened, but still the house was silent.

Finally she risked opening the door a crack and peered out into the wide corridor.

Empty.

She stepped out of her room and started toward the top of the stairs, then heard a door close downstairs. Celeste stopped dead in her tracks, close enough to the head of the stairs that she could gaze down into the entry hall below.

Her father appeared from the dining room. Even from where she stood, Celeste could hear him muttering to himself. His clothes were smeared with blood. When he abruptly stopped and looked up as if sensing her presence, his eyes seemed to have glazed over.

"Whore!" he said, his voice rasping as he spat the word at her. "Did you think I'd never figure it out?"

He was at the foot of the stairs now. Celeste gasped as

she saw him lunge forward, taking the steps two at a time. Panic galvanizing her into action, Celeste fled back into her room, slamming the door and throwing the lock, then collapsing against the thick mahogany panel, her heart pounding.

Only as she heard her father grasp the knob and rattle the door did she realize her mistake. Instead of retreating back to her room, she should have fled past it to the back stairs. By now she'd be out of the house and into the street.

She'd be safe.

Instead she was trapped in her room like a rat in a cage.

How could she have been so stupid?

Her father stopped rattling the doorknob, and once again silence fell over the house. Celeste remained where she was, her heart pounding. Was he still out there? She didn't know. The seconds dragged on, turning into minutes. Should she risk unlocking the door and peeking out? But then, even as she reached for the knob, she froze. She could feel him on the other side of the door, feel his insane rage as palpably as if it were seeping through the wood to engulf her.

"Daddy?" she whimpered. "Daddy, please. Tell me what's wrong. Tell me what's happened to you. I love you, Daddy. I love—"

Her words were cut off by something—something hard and heavy—striking the door. The force of the blow, transmitted directly through the wood, was sharp enough to startle her into jumping back from the door, and as she stood staring at it, trying to fathom what was happening on the other side, she heard the sound again.

Pounding!

He was pounding with a hammer!

Trying to break the door down?

The pounding stopped for a moment, then began again,

and suddenly Celeste realized that he wasn't trying to break the door down at all!

He was nailing it shut.

A wave of hopelessness overwhelmed her. The phones were gone, the snow was too heavy and the neighbors too far away for anyone to hear her calling for help.

Stupid! How could she have been so stupid?

Andrew Sterling automatically steered into the skid as the Escort slewed to the left, threatened to spin around and slam into a parked car, then found its traction again. Making no further attempt to keep the car on the right side of Harvard Street, he nosed it slowly up the hill. The snow, packing under the pressure of the tires into a slick glaze of ice, kept threatening his control of the vehicle. By the time he could finally make out the gate to the Hartwicks' mansion, his body was knotted with tension and his hands ached from gripping the steering wheel too hard. But at last he was able to turn the car into the driveway. Leaving it close to the gate, he got out and started toward the house, which was blazing with light. Even as he watched, more lights came on on the second floor, but when he mounted the steps to the front porch and rang the bell, there was no response.

But someone was home.

Madeline's Cadillac was under the porte cochere, and someone had been turning the lights on upstairs.

He rang the bell again, waited a few more seconds, then tried the knob. The door was locked.

Pulling the hood of his parka up, Andrew tramped up the driveway, slogging through the drifting snow, which by morning would block it completely. Banging as hard as he could on the kitchen door, he called out, but his words sounded muffled even to himself, and he was sure they would be utterly inaudible to anyone inside the house. He started to turn away in order to go back to the front door, then changed his mind.

Someone was inside, but no one was answering the door.

The phones weren't working.

And something had been wrong with Jules Hartwick this morning.

Making up his mind, Andrew Sterling stepped back, lowered his left shoulder, and hurled himself against the kitchen door. Though the door held, he heard the distinct sound of wood cracking. On the second try the frame gave way and the door flew open as the striker plate clattered to the floor.

Andrew Sterling stepped into the kitchen.

For a moment everything appeared normal. Then he saw them.

Spots on the floor.

Bright red spots.

Blood red.

His pulse quickening, Andrew followed the trail of blood through the butler's pantry, the dining room, the parlor, and into the entry hall.

The trail stopped at the bottom of the stairs.

Andrew paused. Though the house was silent, he felt danger all around him.

Danger, and fear.

"Celeste?" he called. "Celeste!"

"Andrew?" Her voice was muffled, coming from somewhere on the second floor. Racing up the stairs, Andrew called out to her again as he reached the second-floor landing. His words died on his lips when he saw the door to her room.

Nails—three of them—had been clumsily pounded into the wood at a steep enough angle to pin the door to its frame. Andrew rattled the knob, then spoke again. "Celeste? Are you all right?"

"It's D-Daddy!" Celeste replied, her voice catching.

"He's—oh, God, Andrew, he's gone crazy! He's done something to Mother—"

"Unlock the door," Andrew told her.

As soon as he heard the click of the lock, he hurled his weight against the door, but the thick mahogany frame was stronger than the frame of the kitchen door had been. By the time the wood finally split away and allowed the door to open, his shoulder was aching and he was panting.

"Where's your mother?" he said, ignoring the stab of pain that shot through his shoulder as she pressed herself against him, sobbing.

"I don't know—downstairs, I think. They were at the foot of the stairs, and he—he had a knife, and—"

Andrew suppressed a groan. He'd followed the trail of blood the wrong way. Jules must have taken Madeline down to the basement. "Where is he now?" Andrew asked, his voice urgent.

"I—I don't know," Celeste stammered. "He nailed my door shut, then he—oh, God, Andrew, I just don't know!"

Suddenly Andrew remembered. The lights. It had to have been Jules turning on the lights. If he was still up here—

Both of them froze as they heard footsteps.

Footsteps from above. "He's on the third floor," Celeste whispered. "What are we going to do? Did he take Mother up there?"

"The basement," Andrew told her. "Come on. We've got to find her and get out of here!"

Half pulling and half supporting Celeste, Andrew led her downstairs, then into the kitchen. When they were at the door to the basement, he held her by the shoulders and looked directly into her eyes. "I'm going to go down and see if I can find your mother. If you hear your father coming down, go outside." Fishing in his pocket, he found his car keys. "My car's in the driveway. I'll try to catch up with you, but if I can't, take the car and get away."

Celeste shook her head. "No. I won't leave you and Mother with him."

Andrew started to argue with her, then changed his mind, knowing it would be useless. "I'll get back as soon as I can." Leaving her standing in the kitchen, he raced down the stairs.

He found Madeline in the laundry room. Her dress was soaked with blood, and she lay on the floor, her wrists and ankles bound with duct tape. Another piece sealed her mouth.

Her eyes were closed and she lay still, and for a moment Andrew was afraid she might be dead. But when he knelt down and pressed a finger against her bloody neck, he felt a pulse. Ripping the duct tape from her mouth, he lifted her in his arms and started up the stairs. A moment later he emerged into the kitchen. Celeste, her face ashen, lurched toward him.

"Mama?" she gasped, unconsciously using a word that hadn't crossed her lips since she was a child. Her eyes flicked to Andrew's. "Is she—" Her voice failed her and she left the question unspoken.

"She's alive," Andrew said. "We've got to get her to the hospital."

With Madeline in his arms, he followed Celeste through the dining room and parlor, and into the entry hall. Celeste was just opening the front door when there was a roar of rage from the stairs.

"Bastard!" Jules bellowed. "How dare you come here?" He was standing halfway up the stairs, the knife clutched in one hand, and what looked like some kind of necklace dangling from the other. His face was twitching, and his eyes, burning like coals, seemed to have sunk deep into his head.

For one brief instant Andrew was frozen in place, but then he met Jules Hartwick's insane gaze. "I'm taking them away from here, Mr. Hartwick," he said very quietly. "Don't try to stop me."

"Traitor," Jules Hartwick snarled. "Fornicator. Adulterer. I should kill all of you. And I could, Andrew. I could kill you as easily as I cut the whore's throat." He started down the stairs, moving slowly, his eyes never leaving Andrew.

Celeste, still at the door, stared in horror at her father. There was nothing left of the man she'd known only yesterday. The person who was advancing toward her now, spittle drooling from one corner of his mouth, his hair matted to his scalp, his eyes glittering insanely, bore no resemblance to her father at all. "Hurry, Andrew," she said. "Please."

Pulling the front door open, she stumbled out into the snow and ran for Andrew's car. Andrew, still carrying Madeline's unconscious body, strode out onto the porch, then turned back to look at Jules once again. He was at the foot of the stairs now, and starting toward the door.

Wordlessly, Andrew turned and hurried out into the night. By the time Andrew got to the car, Jules had emerged onto the porch. "Liars!" he shouted. "Prevaricators! I'll kill you all! I swear, I'll kill you all!"

As Andrew laid Madeline on the backseat, then slid into the front seat next to Celeste, Jules stumbled down the driveway toward them, bellowing curses, the butcher knife held high. Celeste put the car in gear and began backing out of the driveway. Jules lunged toward the car, but it was too late. He sprawled out onto the driveway, facedown, then pulled himself to his knees.

"Celeste, wait," Andrew said as Jules stared mindlessly into the glare of the headlights. "Maybe we'd better help him. Maybe—"

But Celeste kept her foot on the accelerator, backing the car out of the driveway, then slewing it around so it was pointed downhill. "No," she said as she started down the steep slope. "That's not Daddy. That's not anyone I know."

As he watched the car disappear into the snow, Jules Hartwick let out one more bellow of rage. The fingers of his left hand closed on the locket, and then, with a howl of frustration, he hurled it after the departing car.

And as the locket left his fingers, his mind cleared.

The paranoia that had robbed him of his sanity drained away as suddenly as it had come over him.

But the memories of what he'd done did not.

Every word he had uttered, every accusation he had made, echoed in his mind. But what horrified him most was an image.

An image of Madeline, crumpled at the bottom of the basement stairs, her neck bleeding, her body broken.

Sobbing, Jules Hartwick staggered to his feet. He lurched down the driveway, the hand that had held the locket only a moment ago now reaching out as if to call back the car that was carrying away everything he'd ever loved. He stood in the street, watching until it completely disappeared, then turned and began walking the other way.

A moment later he too disappeared into the snowy night.

Chapter 9

"*Liars! Prevaricators! I'll kill you all! I swear, I'll kill you all!*"

Although muffled by the closed and curtained windows of Martha Ward's chapel, the furious words still cut through the soft drone of Gregorian chants, startling Rebecca Morrison out of the reverie she'd fallen into as her aunt's prayers droned on. Her knees protesting painfully as she rose from the kneeling position her aunt always insisted upon, Rebecca moved to the window and pulled the curtain aside just far enough to get a glimpse of the house next door.

Every light had been turned on; even the tiny dormers in the roof glowed brightly through the falling snow. A car—Rebecca was almost certain it was Andrew Sterling's—was backing out of the driveway. For a moment Rebecca wasn't quite sure from where the shouted words had come, but then Jules Hartwick suddenly appeared in the glare of the car's headlights.

He was lurching down the driveway. Through the swirl of falling snow Rebecca could make out the contortions of his face.

And see the knife he held in his hand.

She watched, transfixed, as he stumbled toward the retreating car, then collapsed into the snow.

As he rose back up to his knees, howling like a wounded animal, then staggered away, Rebecca's mind raced.

167

What had happened next door?

Had Mr. Hartwick killed someone?

Who had been in the car?

Call someone.

She had to call someone.

Her fingers releasing the edge of the curtain, she backed away from the window, only to find herself facing her aunt.

Martha, eyes shining with the rapture of her prayers, was glaring furiously at her. "How dare you!" the older woman said in a furious whisper. "How could you commit the very sin for which you were praying for forgiveness! And in the chapel!"

"But something's wrong, Aunt Martha! Mr. Hartwick has a knife and—"

"Silence!" Martha commanded, holding her finger to her niece's lips. "I will not have the chapel vilified by your gossip! I will not have—"

But Rebecca heard no more. Brushing her aunt's hand away, she hurried out of the chapel and made her way to the front parlor on the other side of the foyer. Picking up the telephone, she was about to dial the emergency number when she hesitated.

What if she was wrong? Her mind echoed with everything she'd been told over the years, first by her aunt, then by librarian Germaine Wagner, then by almost everyone she knew:

"You don't understand, Rebecca."

"No one expects more of you than you can do, Rebecca."

"It's all right, Rebecca. Let someone else worry about it."

"Now, Rebecca, you know you don't always understand what's happening. . . ."

"Just do as you're told, Rebecca."

"You don't understand, Rebecca!"

But she knew what she'd seen! Mr. Hartwick had been holding a knife and—

"You don't understand, Rebecca! You don't understand. . . ."

Her hand hovered over the telephone. What if she was wrong? It wouldn't just be Aunt Martha who would be angry with her, then. It would be the whole town! If she called the police and got Mr. Hartwick in trouble—

Oliver!

She could call Oliver! He never told her she didn't understand, or shouldn't worry about something, or treated her like a child. Picking up the telephone, she dialed his number. On the fourth ring she heard his voice. "Oliver? It's Rebecca."

Oliver Metcalf listened carefully as Rebecca told him what she'd seen. As she talked, he recalled Ed Becker's visit to his office that morning, when the lawyer had hinted that Jules Hartwick was behaving strangely. Though Becker hadn't quite come out and said so, it had sounded to Oliver as if Jules was having a breakdown. "Here's what I want you to do," he told Rebecca now. "I want you to call Ed Becker. He's Jules Hartwick's lawyer. Tell him exactly what you've told me, and don't worry about what he might think. Whatever's happened at the Hartwicks', he'll help. All right?"

"But what if I'm wrong, Oliver?" Rebecca fretted. "Aunt Martha always says—"

"Don't worry about what Martha says," Oliver assured her. "If you're wrong, no one but Ed and me will know, and all you're trying to do is help. Just call Ed, and I'll be there as soon as I can." Finding Ed Becker's telephone number on the Rolodex he kept on the kitchen counter, he repeated it twice for Rebecca. He was about to hang up when he heard something in the background. "Rebecca? Do I hear a siren?"

"There's one coming up the street," Rebecca told him. "Just a second." He heard her put the phone down, then, increasingly clear, the wail of a siren. Then he heard Rebecca's voice on the line again.

"It's the police," she said. "A police car just pulled up in front of the Hartwicks'."

"All right," Oliver said. "Call Ed Becker. I'm leaving right now. I'll see you in a little while."

Hanging up the phone, Oliver grabbed his parka from the hook by the door to the garage. He was pulling it on when the phone rang again. This time it was Lois Martin.

"Oliver," she said, "Andrew Sterling and Celeste Hartwick just brought Madeline to the hospital. Apparently, Jules tried to kill her. Tried to slash her throat."

"Oh, Jesus," Oliver groaned. "Is she all right?"

"I hope so." Lois sighed. "She's lost a lot of blood and they don't know yet about internal injuries, but they think she has a chance. The nurse called me. I'm going over now to see what else I can find out."

"Good," Oliver told her. "The police just arrived at the Hartwick house. I'm on my way there now. Talk to you later."

Before the phone could ring yet again, he was in his car, turning the ignition key with one hand even as he pressed the remote control for the garage door with the other. He gunned the engine as the door slowly rolled open, sending a cloud of smoke and condensation billowing out of the exhaust pipe. Putting the car into reverse, he backed out, swinging around in the wide arc that would allow him to head straight down the driveway. But in midturn, as the headlights swept across the front of the Asylum, something caught his eye. He slammed on the brakes. The tires instantly lost their traction and the car swerved, leaving the building in darkness. Swearing under his breath, Oliver maneuvered the Volvo back around so that the headlights were once more shining on the building that loomed fifty yards farther up the hill.

Something—*someone*—was on the porch.

For an instant, just an instant, Oliver was confused. But then something in the figure's right hand glinted in the glare of the headlights. Suddenly, he understood.

Jerking the parking brake on but leaving the engine running, Oliver scrambled out of the car and ran up the slope toward the Asylum. He lost his footing in the snow, stumbled, fell to his knees. As he struggled to get up, the figure on the porch raised the knife. "No!" Oliver yelled. "Jules, don't!"

But it was too late. As Oliver watched helplessly, the knife arced downward, its blade plunging deep into Jules Hartwick's belly.

Finally regaining his footing, Oliver charged through the snow. With every step, his feet seemed mired in mud; he hurled himself on, feeling trapped in some terrible nightmare. At last, he came to the porch.

Jules Hartwick, his clothes already soaked with his own blood, was slumped against the Asylum's front door. As Oliver came close to him, his fingers tightened on the haft of the knife, and with a terrible effort he jerked it upward, laying his own belly open. As blood gushed from the gaping wound, he stared up at Oliver. His lips worked spasmodically, and then a sound gurgled from his throat.

"Evil . . ." he whispered. "All around us." His eyes closed and he moaned softly, but then he fixed Oliver with a beseeching stare. "Stop it, Oliver. You have to stop it before it—" He took a gasping, rattling breath. "—before it kills us all. . . ." His body went rigid and his eyes rolled back into his head.

As Jules Hartwick's body relaxed in death, his hands finally lost their grip on the knife. It fell to the porch, clattering eerily in the suddenly silent night.

For a long time Oliver crouched next to his friend. Finally, he stood up and started slowly back to his house. With every step, he heard Jules Hartwick's last words once again.

"You have to stop it . . . before it kills us all."

How, he wondered, was he going to honor Jules's last request when he had no idea what the words meant?

* * *

Midnight. The dark figure moved as silently as a wraith through the blackness of the Asylum, coming at last to the hidden room in which the treasures lay. It was once more the time of the full moon, and the room was suffused with a pale light just strong enough to allow him to admire his collection.

His fingers, sheathed in latex, touched first one object and then another, at last coming to rest on a golden oblong that glittered brightly even in the faint light.

It was an ornate cigarette lighter, cast in the shape of a dragon's head. Ruby red jewels were set in either side as eyes, and the mouth was slightly opened. As the gloved fingers tightened around a trigger in the dragon's neck, a spark flicked deep in its throat. Instantly, a tongue of fire shot from its gaping jaws.

The orange flame danced in the darkness as the shadowed figure pondered.

He already knew for whom the gift was meant; the question now was how to deliver it.

He eased his grip on the dragon's throat.

The flame flickered, then went out.

Soon—very soon—it would flare again.

And when it did, the dragon would strike.

To be continued . . .

PART 3
ASHES TO ASHES: THE DRAGON'S FLAME

Prelude

It was the kind of wintry March night that kept all but the most restless of Blackstone's citizens nestled within the warmth of their homes. Though the temperature hovered just above freezing, the wind that crept up on the town just after nightfall brought with it a chill of its own. Its gusts gathered force throughout the night, unleashing a howling monster that tore branches from the bare trees, clawed shingles from the roofs, and rattled the windows of every house, as if searching for ways to enact its fury upon the people within. Clouds, torn to shreds by the raging wind, scudded across the sky in grayish tatters, swirling across the moon so that dark shadows moved through the streets like thieves slithering from house to house.

In the Asylum atop North Hill the dark figure was oblivious to the menace of the night. Inured to the moaning of the wind and not feeling the cold, he crouched in his chamber, lovingly fingering the golden dragon. Its ruby red eyes seemed to blink with every darkening of the moon beyond the room's single tiny window. Cradling the dragon in his gloved hands, he cast his mind back to the time when he had first laid eyes on it. . . .

Prologue

It wasn't right.

It wasn't the way it was supposed to have been.

When she'd discovered she was pregnant, Tommy was supposed to insist that they get married immediately.

But instead of putting his arms around her and assuring her that everything would be all right, he'd looked at her with such pure fury blazing in his eyes that she thought he was going to hit her, that he would throw her out of the roadster right then, and she'd have to walk all the way home. "How could you be so stupid?" he demanded. They were parked on the lovers' lane on the slope of North Hill that faced away from Blackstone, and he'd yelled so loud that the people in the backseat of the only other car up there that night had rubbed a clear spot in the steamy window and peered curiously over at them.

She'd shrunk down in the seat, so embarrassed she wanted to die. Then Tommy started the engine and took off, slamming the car through the curves so fast she was terrified they were both going to get killed before they got back to town.

Maybe that would have been better than what happened next. He pulled up in front of her house, reached across and shoved the door open, then glowered at her one last time. "Don't think I'm going to marry you," he growled. "In fact, don't even think you're going to see me again!"

Sobbing, she stumbled out of the car, and he roared

176

away, tires squealing, and disappeared around the corner. A week later, when she heard that Tommy had joined the army and was going to Korea, she knew she had no choice. She had to tell her parents.

She expected her dad to go into a rage, threatening to kill whoever did this to his little girl. When she told him Tommy was in the army, his face blackened with fury and he swore that if the North Koreans didn't kill the stinking son-of-a-bitch coward, he would, no matter how long it took. Her mother demanded to know how a daughter of hers could ever let a man use her the way Tommy had, and sobbed that she would never again be able to look any of her friends in the face.

All of that, she had expected.

What she hadn't expected was what happened the next day: Her parents took her up to the top of North Hill and committed her to the Asylum.

She sobbed and begged. She raged at her father with every bit as much fury as he'd raged at her the day before.

But her parents were implacable. She would stay in the Asylum until the baby was born.

Only then would they decide what would be best for her to do next.

For the first two months, she lived in terror, afraid even to leave her room for fear of what might happen to her. All her life she and her friends had lived in quiet fear of the building at the top of North Hill. All through her childhood there were whispered stories of terrible things that went on up there, and she'd spent more than one sleepless night cowering under her quilt at rumors that one of the "lunatics" had escaped.

The first few nights in the Asylum were the worst. She was unable to sleep, for here there was no quiet at night; instead the hours of darkness were alive with the screams and moans of the tormented souls hidden away within the forbidding stone walls. But slowly her mind became inured to the howls of anguish that echoed through the small hours of the night. Finally she began to venture forth into the dayroom, where she joined the rest of the lower security patients, who whiled away their lives playing endless games of solitaire or thumbing through magazines whose pages they never actually read.

And they smoked.

During her second month in the dayroom, she began smoking too. It passed the time, and somehow numbed the pain of loneliness and hopeless desperation.

As the weeks turned into months, and her belly swelled with the child she was carrying, she began slowly, tentatively to make friends with some of the patients. She even tried to befriend the woman who always sat perfectly still, only her constantly darting eyes betraying her consciousness. But the woman never spoke to her.

One day, the silent woman simply vanished, and though there were stories that the woman had died somewhere in the secret chambers rumored to be hidden deep in the Asylum's basement, she didn't quite believe the talk.

Nor did she quite disbelieve it.

Her family had not come to see her. That was no surprise: Her father was far too angry, her mother too ashamed.

And her two little sisters, both much younger than she, would be far too frightened to brave a visit to the Asylum on their own.

So the months passed.

Today, on a cold March morning after a night in which the howling of the wind had been loud enough to drown out the cries and wails of the Asylum's occupants, she felt the first painful contraction.

She winced as it gripped her body, but didn't let herself cry out, for over the months of her pregnancy she had come to understand that the pain of childbirth would be nothing more than punishment for the sin she and Tommy had committed.

A punishment she had vowed to bear in silence.

Within an hour, though, the contractions were coming every few minutes, and she could no longer bear the pain without crying out. The women in the dayroom called out to one of the orderlies, and the orderly summoned a nurse.

With the pains coming every two minutes, and her body feeling as if it was about to be torn apart, she was strapped onto a gurney and wheeled into a white-tiled room. From the ceiling, three brilliant lights blazed down, nearly blinding her.

The room was cold—close to freezing. The orderlies began to strip her gown from her body. She begged them not to.

They ignored her.

The nurse came in, and the doctor.

As yet another contraction racked her body, she begged them to give her something for the pain, but they only went about their work, ignoring her pleas. "It's not an operation," the doctor curtly told her. "You don't need anything."

Her labor intensified, and then she was screaming, and thrashing against the restraints that held her strapped to the gurney. It seemed to go on forever, wave after wave of pain so intense she was certain she would pass out, until, with one last agonizing spasm, she felt the baby slip from her body.

She lay gasping, trying to catch her breath, her exhausted body still at last. Then she heard it: a tiny, helpless cry. Her baby, the baby for whom she had endured unimaginable pain, was crying out to her.

"Let me see it," she whispered. "Let me hold my baby."

The doctor, his back to her, handed something to the nurse. "It's better you don't," he said. "Better for both of you."

The nurse left the room, and she heard her baby's wails fade away into the distance.

"No!" she cried out, but her voice was pitifully weak. "I have to see my baby! I have to hold it!"

The doctor finally looked at her. "I'm afraid I can't let you do that. It would only make it much harder for you."

She blinked. Harder? What was he talking about? "I—I don't understand—"

"If you don't see it, you won't miss it nearly as much."

"Miss it?" she echoed. "What are you talking about? Please! My baby—"

"But it's not your baby," the doctor said as if talking to a small child. "It's being given up for adoption, so it's better that you not see it at all."

"Adoption?" she echoed. "But I don't want to give—"

"What you want doesn't matter," the doctor informed her. "The decision has been made."

Now a new kind of pain flooded over her—not the sharp pangs of the contractions, which, as violently as they'd seized her body, had quickly dissipated. This was a dull ache that she felt taking root deep within her, which she knew was never going to fade—a spreading coldness that would grow inside her cancerously, filling her with despair, slowly consuming her, leaving her no avenue of escape. She could already feel it uncoiling inside her, and someday, she knew, there would be nothing left of her at all.

There would be nothing left but the pain of knowing that somewhere there was a baby who belonged to her, whom she would never nurse, never hold, never see.

Left alone in the operating room under the cold, merciless lights, she began to cry.

No one came to comfort her.

When she awakened the next morning, she was back in her room, and though her blanket was wrapped close around her, it did nothing to protect her from the icy chill that had spread through her body.

Though she felt utterly exhausted, something drew her from her bed to the window. The landscape beyond the bars was no less bleak than the Asylum's interior: naked gray branches clawed at a leaden sky. Only a wisp of smoke that curled from the chimney of the incinerator behind the Asylum's main building disturbed the cold, silent morning. She was about to turn away when a movement caught her eye—a nurse and an orderly emerging from the Asylum and walking toward the incinerator. It was the same nurse who had been in the operating room yesterday, and the orderly was one of the two who had strapped her to the gurney.

The nurse was carrying an object wrapped in what looked like a small blanket, and even though she could see nothing of what was hidden within the blanket's folds, she knew what it was.

Her baby.

They weren't putting it up for adoption at all.

She wanted to turn away from the window, but something held her there, some need to see exactly what was going to happen, even though the scene had already played itself out in her mind. In the next few moments, as she stood shivering with cold and desperate fear, the scene she had just imagined unfolded before her eyes:

The orderly opened the access port of the incinerator, and the flames within the combustion chamber suddenly flared, tongues of fire licking hungrily at the iron lips of the door. As she watched, the nurse unfolded the blanket.

She beheld the pale, still form of the child she'd brought into the world only the day before.

A scream of anguish built in her throat, erupting in an agonized wail as the orderly closed the incinerator door, mercifully blocking her view of what had been done to her baby. As they turned away from the incinerator, both the nurse and the orderly glanced up at her window, but if they recognized her, neither of them gave any sign. A moment later they too vanished from view.

For a long time she remained at the window, gazing out at the lonely, lifeless landscape that now seemed a perfect reflection of the coldness and emptiness inside her.

Her own fault.

All her own fault.

She should never have told her parents about the baby, never have let them bring her here, never have let them make the decisions that should have been hers.

And now, because of what she'd done, her baby was dead.

At last she turned away from the window, and now her body, as well as her spirit, felt numb. As if in a dream, she left her room and went to the dayroom. Seating herself in one of the hard, plastic-covered chairs, she stared straight ahead, looking at no one, speaking to no one. Hours passed. Sometime late in the afternoon a nurse came into the dayroom and placed a small package in her lap.

"Someone left this for you. A little girl."

It wasn't until long after the nurse had gone that she finally opened the package. She peeled the paper away. Inside was a small box. She opened the box and gazed at the object inside.

It was a cigarette lighter.

Made of a gold-colored metal, it was worked into the shape of a dragon's head, and when she pressed a trigger hidden in its neck, a tongue of flame shot out of the dragon's mouth.

Click. There were the flames that had shot hungrily from the mouth of the incinerator. Click. The fire leaped and consumed her baby.

She held the flame to her arm, and though her nostrils quickly filled with the sickly smell of burning flesh, she felt nothing.

No heat.

No pain.

Nothing at all.

Slowly, methodically, she began moving the dragon's flame over her skin, letting the fiery tongue lick at every exposed piece of her flesh, as if its heat could burn away the guilt that was consuming her.

As the rest of the patients in the dayroom silently watched, she burned herself—arms, legs, neck, face— until at last there was no more flesh to torture.

The dragon, its flame finally extinguished, was still clutched in her hand when the orderlies finally came and took her away.

Within the hour, her own body had joined her baby's.

The dark figure's gloved hand closed on the dragon, and he smiled.

It was time.

Time for the dragon, after nearly half a century hidden in this dark lair, to emerge once more into the world beyond these cold stone walls.

Chapter 1

Oliver Metcalf turned up his collar, huddled deeper into his old car coat, and glanced up at the sky, which was rapidly filling with rain clouds. It was Sunday, and he'd intended to spend the afternoon in the *Chronicle* office, catching up on the unending details that always managed to pile up until they threatened to overwhelm the newspaper's small staff, no matter how hard they worked. He was wading through a sea of paperwork when, an hour ago, Rebecca Morrison had turned up with a shy smile and the suggestion that he give up his boring old work in favor of accompanying her out to the flea market that had taken over the old drive-in theater on the western edge of town. Her eagerness was infectious, and Oliver quickly decided that none of the bills and correspondence that had waited for his attention this long couldn't wait a day or two longer. Now, however, as he shivered in the chill of the late March day, he wondered if he hadn't made a mistake. They were still two blocks from the drive-in, and it seemed the sky might open up with a downpour at any moment. "How come they're open so early? Aren't they afraid they'll get rained out?"

Rebecca smiled serenely. "They won't," she said. "It's the very first day, and it never rains on the first day of the flea market."

"That's the Rose Parade," Oliver corrected her. "And that's on New Year's Day, in California, where it never rains. Unless it's flooding, of course."

"Well, it's not going to rain today," Rebecca assured him. "And I like the flea market on the first day. It's when all the things people find in the attic or the basement over the winter are for sale."

Oliver shrugged. As far as he was concerned, one man's junk wasn't another man's treasure at all: it just became someone else's junk for a while. There was one item he'd been eyeing for years now—a truly ugly porcelain table lamp, embellished with strange vines that snaked up from its gilt-painted base and were studded with pieces of purple, red, and green colored glass meant to look like grapes. The lamp was topped by a hideous stained-glass shade—three pieces cracked, at last count—intended to suggest the spreading leaves of the vine. When lit, the light filtering through the leaf-form glass cast a shade of sickly green that made anyone within its glow look deathly ill. So far, Oliver had seen it on three different tables at the flea market, watched as it was sold no fewer than four times at the Blackstone Historical Society Auction, and even found it displayed for a couple of days in the window of an antique shop—not, blessedly, Janice Anderson's. "Just promise me you won't buy the grape lamp," he asked.

"Oh, I already did." Rebecca giggled. "I bought it two years ago. I was going to give it to someone as a joke, but the more I looked at it, the less funny it seemed. So I gave it to the Historical Society."

"Did anyone buy it at the auction?" Oliver asked.

"You bet!" Rebecca said. "Madeline Hartwick snapped it right up! Of course, she only bought it because she knew I'd donated it and was afraid I'd be hurt if nobody bid on it." Her eyes clouded. "Do you think she's going to be all right?" Rebecca asked, her voice anxious.

"It's going to take a while," Oliver replied. Madeline was finally out of the hospital now, but still hadn't recovered from the terrifying night when her husband, Jules, almost killed her, and succeeded in killing himself. She and her daughter, Celeste, were staying in Boston with Madeline's sister. Oliver wondered if Madeline would ever come back to the big house at the top of Harvard Street.

The strangest thing was that no one yet knew exactly why Jules Hartwick had killed himself, nor had Oliver been able to fathom exactly what the banker had meant when he'd uttered his last words:

"You have to stop it . . . before it kills us all."

Stop what? Jules had said nothing else before he'd died on the steps of the Asylum. Though Oliver had asked Madeline and Celeste what Jules could possibly have meant, neither woman had any idea. Oliver inquired of others as well—Andrew Sterling, who had been at the house that terrible night; Melissa Holloway at the bank; Jules's attorney, Ed Becker. But no one had come up with an answer.

Only Oliver's uncle, Harvey Connally, had even ventured a guess. "Do you suppose he thought there was some connection between what happened to him and poor Elizabeth McGuire's suicide?" his uncle mused. "But that doesn't make much sense, does it? After all, even though Jules and Bill McGuire are some kind of shirttail cousins, Jules wasn't related to Elizabeth at all. From what I remember of *her* family, pretty much all of them were crazy, one way or another. But that didn't have anything to do with Jules. His parents were steady as a rock, both of them." The old man had sighed. "Well, I don't suppose we'll ever know, will we?"

So far, Harvey Connally had been proved right; no one yet had the slightest idea what had provoked Jules Hartwick's sudden mental breakdown and suicide. Even the problems at the bank were getting straightened out, and though they weren't all settled yet, nobody was saying that Jules had done anything illegal. Imprudent, perhaps, but the bank was in no danger of failing, and he'd been in no danger of being disciplined, either by the bank's board or by the Federal Reserve auditors.

"I keep feeling like I should have done something," Rebecca said, unconsciously slipping her hand into Oliver's as they neared the outskirts of Blackstone and the sagging stockade fence that had once protected the patrons of the drive-in movie from the glaring headlights of cars passing in and out of town on Main Street. "Maybe instead of praying with Aunt Martha, I should have—" She faltered for a moment, then looked helplessly up at Oliver. "Doesn't it seem like I should have done *some*thing?"

"I don't think there was anything anyone could do," Oliver told her, giving her hand a reassuring squeeze. "And I don't think we'll ever know exactly what happened that night." He put on a bright smile and changed the subject. "So, are we looking for something special, or are we just browsing to see what people are throwing out this year?"

"I want to find a present for my cousin," Rebecca told him.

"Andrea?" Oliver asked. "Do you even know where she is?"

"She's coming home."

"Home?" Oliver echoed. "You mean to your aunt's house?"

Rebecca nodded. "She called Aunt Martha the day before yesterday, and said she didn't have anywhere else to go."

Oliver remembered the last time he'd seen Andrea Ward. It was twelve years ago, the day before her eighteenth birthday, and Andrea had been talking about nothing except getting away from her mother.

Her mother, and Blackstone too.

Oliver had been sitting at the soda fountain in the drugstore near the square when Andrea and a couple of her friends had come in. Barely even noticing he was there, they'd huddled together on the three stools at the soda fountain's corner, and he was treated to at least one teenager's view of Blackstone.

"I can't believe I've survived this long," Andrea had said, impatiently brushing her long mane of blond hair away from her face, only to groan in exasperation a moment later as it fell right back over her forehead. "And the first thing I'm going to do is get this cut off. Can you believe my mother actually thinks it's a sin to cut your hair?" Then, with a brittle laugh, she proceeded to recite the long list of things Martha Ward had proclaimed sinful. "There's dancing and drinking and going to movies, just for starters. And smoking, of course," she added, lighting a cigarette with a defiant flourish. "And let's not forget dating either. How am I supposed to find a husband if I can't have a date?"

"Maybe she wants you to go to college," one of her friends suggested, but Andrea only laughed again.

"All she wants me to do is pray, just like she does," the girl declared. As she brushed her hair off her face again, Oliver had glimpsed how pretty she was, despite the heavy makeup she wore.

Or she would have been pretty, if she wasn't so angry. But Andrea had been angry for a long time, and over the years her anger had manifested itself in clothes that showed off her figure a little too perfectly, and makeup that hardened her face rather than accentuated its beauty.

And though she was forbidden to date, she'd always been popular with Blackstone's teenage boys.

Far too popular, according to Martha Ward.

Having heard Andrea's diatribe, when she disappeared from Blackstone the next day, leaving nothing behind except a note saying she'd gone to Boston and was never coming back, Oliver hadn't been surprised.

Martha Ward had been.

She'd been both surprised and furious. On the single occasion nearly three years ago, when Andrea had finally returned to visit Blackstone with her live-in boyfriend in tow, Martha refused to see her.

"I do not countenance sin," she proclaimed. "Don't come back until you've either married him or left him."

Andrea had not been seen in Blackstone since.

"What happened?" Oliver asked now, as he and Rebecca turned onto the grounds of the old drive-in movie and surveyed the two dozen tables that had been set up—only a third of what there would be later in the spring and in the summer, when the weather had warmed and the tourists began coming through.

"Her boyfriend left her, and she lost her job," Rebecca said. "I guess she really doesn't have anyplace else to go. So I thought I'd try to find something to cheer her up."

They meandered among the tables for a while, stopping now and then to wonder at some of the items that some people seemed to think other people might want. One of the tables was covered with tiny people constructed out of pebbles that had been glued together and painted with happy faces. PEBBLE PEOPLE, a small, badly lettered card on the table proclaimed. TO KNOW THEM IS TO LOVE THEM. To know them is to loathe them, Oliver thought, but kept silent, guessing that the elderly woman sitting hopefully behind the table had made the weird little humanoids herself.

Another table contained a collection of light-switch plates to which dozens of rhinestones had been glued, and yet another displayed religious icons constructed out of tiny shells.

None of it, they decided, was right for Andrea.

And then, sitting on a table that Janice Anderson was tending, they found it. Rebecca spotted it first, half hidden behind an antique picture frame that had a chip on it, thus disqualifying it from being displayed in Janice's shop on Main Street. "Look!" Rebecca cried. "Isn't it wonderful?"

Oliver looked curiously at the object in Rebecca's

hand. At first he wasn't quite sure what it was. It seemed to be a dragon's head, which Rebecca was holding by the neck. Two red eyes glared out from deep sockets. When Rebecca squeezed the dragon's neck, Oliver saw a spark deep in its throat, immediately followed by a flame that shot out of its mouth.

"It's a cigarette lighter," Rebecca exclaimed. "Isn't it perfect?"

"How do you know Andrea still smokes?" Oliver asked.

"Because I heard Aunt Martha telling her she couldn't smoke anywhere in the house." Rebecca's expression clouded. "That's why I want to give her this. She already feels terrible about the way her life is going, and now Aunt Martha wants her to feel bad about smoking too. At least I can let her know that *I* don't disapprove of everything she does." The flame died away as Rebecca eased her grip on the lighter. She held the lighter out to Oliver, and he reached out to take it from her, but the instant his fingers touched the metal of its snout, he reflexively jerked them away as if they'd been burned.

"Be careful!" Rebecca cautioned. With one fingertip she touched the dragon's snout herself. It was barely warm. "He must have bitten you, Oliver," she said. "It's not hot at all." Smiling, she dropped the cigarette lighter into Oliver's hand.

Just as Rebecca had told him, the lighter now felt perfectly cool. But that was impossible: it had been burning hot just a second before. As he turned the strange object over, searching for its price, he wondered whether the odd sensation of heat he'd just felt was a sign—like the troubling headaches he'd been having—of something wrong. Very wrong. Lost in his disturbing thoughts, he barely noticed that Janice Anderson had finished with the customer she'd been waiting on and turned to them. At a nudge from Rebecca, Oliver recovered himself and held out the lighter. "How much for the dragon?" he asked.

Janice gazed blankly at the object Oliver was holding. "Are you sure this was on my table?" she said.

Oliver nodded. "Right there, next to that frame."

Frowning, Janice took the cigarette lighter and examined it from every angle. There was a trade name stamped on the bottom, but it was far too worn to be legible. Though at first glance it appeared to be gold, she could see that the cheap plating was starting to peel away; and the "ruby" eyes were obviously glass, maybe even plastic. The question was, Where had it come from? She had no memory of having bought it, nor even of picking it up from the back-room clutter now spread out on the table in front of her. But then, surveying some of the other junk on the table, she realized she didn't know where most of these bits and pieces had come from. Many were the odds and ends purchased in lots from estate sales. Others, she could have bought from any one of the dozens of people who had come into her shop over the last year, offering for sale treasure they'd found hidden in their attics. Usually, Janice simply turned them away, but now and then, when she sensed that someone was selling something out of desperate need, she would knowingly buy a worthless object, simply as a way of allowing its bearer to keep his dignity and pocket a dollar or two.

That, undoubtedly, was how the lighter had come into her possession, she now decided, even though she had no memory of it. But how much might she have paid for it? Five dollars? Perhaps ten? "Twenty?" she suggested, knowing there was no chance Oliver would agree to her first price. To her dismay, it was Rebecca Morrison who replied without a second's hesitation.

"I'll take it! It's just the kind of thing Andrea will love!"

"For twenty dollars?" Janice Anderson heard herself say. "You will *not* take it for twenty dollars, Rebecca. It certainly isn't worth more than ten, and if you ask me, seven-fifty would be closer to fair."

"Great!" Oliver said. "How about five? Or would you like to counter at two-fifty?"

Janice tried to glare at him, but found herself laughing instead. "How about we stick to the seven-fifty my honest side thinks it's worth?"

Before she could change her mind, Oliver paid for the dragon's head lighter, and Janice wrapped it up for Rebecca in a piece of tissue paper.

"You really think your cousin will like it?" Oliver asked as they left the flea market a few minutes later.

"Of course she will," Rebecca assured him. Her face was alight with pleasure at her find. "It really is just perfect for her."

Oliver hoped that if Andrea shared his and Janice's judgment about the aesthetics of the lighter, the young woman would be kind enough to keep her thoughts to herself.

Chapter 2

*A*ndrea Ward moved nervously through the house she had grown up in and wondered how so many years could have passed with so little evidence of change.

The same drab furniture stood in the living room with antimacassars to protect the arms and backs of the horsehair upholstery still in place, though Andrea estimated that there hadn't been a guest in the house in at least twenty years.

Heavy curtains, the same ones that had hung at the windows when she was a child, still cut out all but the faintest rays of daylight, plunging the room into a deep gloom that obscured the fact that the wallpaper was faded and buckling, and the paint on the ceiling was peeling badly. It was dingier even than she remembered, in an even shabbier state of neglect, but otherwise exactly as depressing—and that was no surprise. Her mother never changed and nothing in her mother's house ever changed. All was exactly as it had been on the day she left. Even the chapel, with its dense, incense-laden air and garish statuary. Once, Andrea recalled, it had been her father's den, a cozy room with a thick shag rug, redolent with the inviting aroma of her father's cherry-flavored pipe tobacco.

But no more. Though she had been only five, Andrea could still remember as clearly as if it had been yesterday the morning Mr. Corelli, who ran the junk store, had arrived with his truck. At first she'd thought he must be looking for his daughter, Angela, who was her best friend back then. But she was wrong. Instead, Mr. Corelli carried all the furniture out of her father's den and loaded it into his truck. Andrea had pleaded with her mother, begged her to make Mr. Corelli put the furniture back: her daddy would be angry when he came home and found his den empty. That was when her mother told her that her father wasn't ever coming back.

"Even if he wants to, I won't have him," Martha had finished. "Your father is a tool of Satan, and I won't have him in my house again!"

Within a week, Fred Ward's snug sanctuary had been transformed into a retreat of another sort—her mother's chapel, where the little girl prayed just as hard as Martha did, begging God and the saints for her father to come home. For a long time she daydreamed while pretending to be rapt in prayer—pastel fantasies of her father taking her away from her mother's house, this cold, dark place that seemed to get darker and colder with every passing year. He would take her to live with him, in Paris, maybe, or in an orange grove in California, or on a sunny Caribbean beach.

But Fred Ward never did come back.

After Andrea ran away from Blackstone, she made an attempt to find him, searching the telephone directories in Boston and Manchester and even as far away as New York. But her resources were limited, and he seemed to have completely disappeared. Over the years, she had drifted from place to place, from one unsatisfying job to another, and into a succession of dead-end romances. Somehow, something always went wrong. Until, three years ago, she had met Gary Fletcher, who gave her a job as a waitress in the restaurant he managed. He was ten years older than she was. Handsome. Sexy. And in love with her.

Or so he said.

Until a month ago, when she'd told him she was pregnant. She'd been sure that they'd finally get married, and move out of their apartment and into a house, and for the first time she'd have a real family.

That was when he told her he couldn't marry her because of the simple fact that he'd never divorced his wife.

Andrea hadn't even known he'd been married.

The next day, instead of filing for a divorce from his wife, he kicked her out of their apartment.

The day after that, he fired her from the only job she'd ever managed to hang on to.

And the day after that, he withdrew all her savings from their joint checking account.

Panicked, Andrea tried to get another job, but was turned down at every interview she pursued. She tried to find a place to live, but she had no money. There were no friends to turn to: Gary had been her whole life.

With nowhere to turn, there was nothing to do but to swallow what little pride she had left and go home to Blackstone to try to start her life all over again.

First she would find a job—any job.

Then she would go back to school—and this time not quit until she'd finished.

And the next man she got involved with was going to have to be a lot more honest than Gary Fletcher had been.

Not rich.

Not even handsome.

Just honest, and decent, and willing to be a father to their kids. With these, the first hopeful thoughts she'd had in weeks, lightening her despair, Andrea had pulled her battered Toyota into the familiar driveway on Harvard Street, and breathed a sigh of relief when she realized that no one was home. She would not have to face her mother—yet.

The old key she had never quite had the courage to toss out still fit the lock. Inside, it was oppressive and dark—even darker and more oppressive than she remembered it. Now, wandering through the downstairs rooms, noting their unchanged appearance, she clung to her newly found resolve: Somehow, she would make it work out.

Retrieving one of the three worn suitcases that contained everything she owned, Andrea carried it upstairs, and discovered that one thing *had* changed. Her room— the room that had been her only retreat after her father left and her mother sank deeper and deeper into her own strange version of religion; the room that she simply assumed would be waiting for her, welcoming her even if her mother did not—was no longer hers. Her cousin Rebecca was living in it—Rebecca's clothes in the closet; Rebecca's slippers by the side of the bed; her raggedy teddy bear perched on the pillow. The knowledge stung her sharply. Her mother had cut her out of the house as thoroughly as she'd cut her father out twenty-five years before. The wound was almost as painful as Gary's betrayal had been, and for a moment a blinding jealousy seized her. Then reason returned. None of her problems, after all, were Rebecca's fault. She certainly couldn't ask Rebecca to disrupt her life just because she had messed up her own.

With renewed determination, Andrea went back downstairs and into the room next to the dining room. Small, little more than an alcove, really, it could be closed off with a pair of pocket doors, and still contained the daybed Andrea remembered her mother had always used for naps whenever she felt too tired to climb the stairs to her own room. At least she wouldn't be in anyone's way, she thought, and she didn't need much room anyway. Opening one of her suitcases, Andrea began hanging her clothes in the room's single, tiny closet.

"What do you think you're doing?"

Her mother's voice, even harsher than she remembered it, cut through her reverie. Andrea froze, the blouse she'd been about to hang up clutched to her chest.

She wanted to say, *Aren't you glad to see me? Don't you want to know why I've come home? Don't you want to give me a hug and ask me why I look so sad?* But all she could manage was, "I—I was just putting my clothes away, Mother."

"Down here?" Martha asked, her face hardening and her lips compressing into a tight line of disapproval.

Andrea glanced nervously around the room as if the walls might offer some clue to the reason for her mother's objection.

"If you think I'm going to allow you to live down here where you can come and go at any hour of the day or night with anyone you choose, you are very wrong. Do you think I'm going to tolerate your sins right here in my house?"

"Mother, I'm not going to—"

"You will sleep in your old room, next to mine," Martha decreed. She glanced around the little room. "There's no reason why Rebecca can't use this one."

"But Mother, that's not fair! Rebecca's been using my old room for years. She shouldn't have to move now!"

Martha glared at her daughter. "Keep a respectful tongue in your head, child. 'Honor thy mother,' " she quoted. "I know the Commandments mean nothing to you, but as long as you are under my roof, you will live by them. Do you understand?"

Andrea hesitated, then nodded. But as she began removing clothing from the closet, she wondered how she was going to tell her mother about her pregnancy. Well, there wasn't really any reason to tell her right now. After all, it wasn't as if she was showing yet. Maybe she'd just wait and—

No!

That was how she'd lived her life for way too many years already, letting herself drift along, thinking that everything would work itself out. But that was over. From now on she was going to face things squarely, and deal with them. Otherwise, she'd never have a life at all.

"There's something I have to tell you, Mother," she said. Martha's eyes narrowed to suspicious slits, and though Andrea wanted to run from the accusing glare, she made herself keep her gaze firmly on her mother's face. "Gary . . . the man I've been living with, the one I thought would marry me . . . He left me. And—he fired me from my job." She hesitated, willing herself not to burst into tears. Taking a deep breath and deciding that if her mother was going to throw her out, she might as well get it over with now, she said in a rush, "I'm pregnant too."

For what seemed an eternity, Martha Ward said nothing. As the seconds ticked interminably by, Andrea wondered if her mother was, indeed, going to banish her from the house.

Finally, Martha spoke. "You will pray for forgiveness. When the child is born, we'll find a family that will take care of it. Then I shall decide what you will do next."

Andrea took another deep breath. "I already told you what I'm going to do next, Mother. I'm going to get a job, and I'm going to go back to school."

"While you're pregnant?" Martha demanded. "I don't see how—"

Andrea decided to finish what she'd begun before she lost her nerve. "I'm not sure if I'm going to stay pregnant, Mother," she said. "But whatever I decide, it's going to be my decision, not yours."

Martha Ward could barely contain her fury. How dare Andrea speak to her this way? How dare she live in sin with a man who was married to another woman, then bring the fruits of her transgressions into Martha's own home?

Martha knew what she should do: she should cast Andrea out now, cast her out of her home lest her own immortal soul be put at risk.

But then she hesitated, remembering something she'd read recently.

It was the sin she was commanded to hate, not the sinner.

In a flash of insight, she understood.

She was being tested!

Andrea had been sent back to her as a test of her faith.

Her cross to bear.

She must not cast Andrea out. Instead, no matter how deeply her wayward child offended her, she must turn the other cheek and lead her prodigal daughter back onto the path of righteousness.

Reading her mother's silence as assent for her to stay in the house, Andrea Ward picked up her suitcases and started up the stairs to the room in which she'd grown up.

Martha Ward entered her chapel and fell to her knees. Her lips moving silently, she prayed for guidance on how best to cleanse her daughter's soul.

✳

Chapter 3

A cold drizzle was falling by the time Oliver and Rebecca got back to the *Chronicle* office. Oliver insisted on driving Rebecca home.

"You don't have to do that," she protested. "It's way out of your way. I can walk."

"Of course you *can*," Oliver told her. "But you won't. And it won't take more than a couple of minutes anyway." He fixed her with a mock glare. "Don't argue with me."

"I'm sorry," Rebecca said so quickly that Oliver immediately knew she hadn't realized he was joking. "I didn't mean—"

"No, *I'm* sorry," Oliver immediately cut in, opening the door to the Volvo for her. "You can argue with me all you want, Rebecca. About anything. But I'm still going to drive you home." This time he made certain his words were accompanied by a smile, and found himself inordinately pleased when Rebecca smiled back at him.

"I don't always get the joke, do I?" she asked as he slid behind the wheel.

"Maybe I don't make it clear enough when I'm kidding," he replied.

Rebecca shook her head. "No, it's me. I know everyone in town thinks I'm strange, but ever since the accident, I just don't seem to get things right away the way other people do."

"I don't think you're strange at all, Rebecca," Oliver

told her. Then he grinned. "But what do I know? Everybody thinks things about me too."

"No they don't."

"Sure they do. They just don't say anything to my face, that's all." Oliver pulled the Volvo up behind an old Toyota that was parked in the driveway of Martha Ward's house. "Looks like Andrea must have arrived. Do you think I should come in and say hello?"

Rebecca glanced worriedly toward the house. "Aunt Martha wouldn't like that. She—" Feeling suddenly flustered, Rebecca left the sentence uncompleted, but Oliver finished it for her.

"Is it just me she disapproves of, or is it any man at all?"

Flushing scarlet, Rebecca stared at her hands, which were kneading the brown paper bag in which Janice Anderson had put the cigarette lighter. "It's anyone," she said. "Aunt Martha doesn't trust men."

Oliver reached out and gently turned Rebecca's head so she couldn't help but look at him. "Don't believe everything Aunt Martha says," he told her. "I won't hurt you, Rebecca. I couldn't."

For a moment he thought Rebecca was going to say something, or maybe even burst into tears, but then she quickly got out of the car and hurried up the walk to the porch. At the door, she turned, hesitated, then waved to him. As he drove away, Oliver felt an overwhelming sense of relief that she hadn't gone into the house without looking back at all.

And that, he realized, told him something.

It told him that, despite his better judgment, despite telling himself that his affection for her was nothing more than friendly concern, he was falling in love with Rebecca Morrison.

How, he wondered, was he going to deal with that?

More important, how was she?

* * *

Rebecca closed the front door behind her, trading the gloom of the late afternoon for the gloom inside the house. She was about to call out to her cousin, but before Andrea's name could even form on her lips, she heard the insistent tones of the Gregorian chants that invariably accompanied her aunt's prayer sessions in the chapel. Moving quietly enough not to be heard over the music, Rebecca searched the lower floor of the house, but found no sign of Andrea. Then she realized where her cousin must be: in the chapel, praying with her mother.

But a minute later, as she was about to open the door to her room on the second floor, Rebecca stopped. She could hear something—a muffled sound like someone crying—and it was coming from inside her room. She hesitated, wondering what she should do.

It had to be Andrea, of course. But what was Andrea doing in her room? And then she remembered. The room used to be her cousin's, and Andrea had certainly expected to find it waiting for her.

Gently, Rebecca tapped at the door, but heard no response. She tapped again, a little louder this time. "Andrea? Can I come in?"

Now there was a distant sniffle, then Andrea's voice. "It's okay, Rebecca. It's not locked."

Turning the knob, Rebecca pushed the door open. Andrea was sitting on the bed, three suitcases spilling their contents on the floor around her feet. Her cheeks were streaked with tears, and she clutched a crumpled tissue in her hand.

Andrea looked thinner than Rebecca remembered her being, and tired. "Andrea?" she whispered. "You look—"

Terrible. She'd been about to say "You look terrible." But for once, instead of blurting out whatever came into her mind, Rebecca caught herself. But it was as if Andrea had read her mind.

"I look awful, don't I, Rebecca?"

Rebecca nodded automatically, and the tiniest trace of a smile played around Andrea's lips.

"I figured," her cousin said. "Apparently, I look too awful for Mom even to give me a hug. Or maybe she's just not very glad to see me."

"Oh, no!" Rebecca exclaimed. She hurried to the bed, dropped her purse and the paper bag onto it, and wrapped her arms around her cousin, then stood back and said, "You look fine! Aunt Martha doesn't hug anyone. And I'm sure she's glad to see you. She's just—"

Miraculously, Rebecca once again managed to censor herself, but once again Andrea had no trouble finishing the thought for her.

"Still crazy, right?" Her smile faded and she seemed to deflate. "I shouldn't have come back here, should I? Now it's not only going to be my life I mess up, but yours too."

Rebecca slipped her arm around her cousin in a quick hug. "You're not messing up my life. Why would you say that? I'm *glad* you came home."

"Then you haven't talked to my mother yet. She says if I stay here, I have to be in this room. She says you have to move into the room behind the dining room. Look, I feel really terrible about it. If you want me to, I'll go find somewhere else—"

"No!" Rebecca interrupted, holding a finger to Andrea's lips to silence her. "This is your home, and this was your room, and you should have it. And I really am glad you're here." She picked up the brown bag, now crumpled and sodden from the rain, and thrust it into Andrea's hands. "Look—I even bought you a present."

Andrea hesitated, and Rebecca had the strangest feeling that for some reason her cousin didn't feel she deserved whatever gift might be inside the bag.

"Please take it," Rebecca said softly. "It isn't much, but I thought you might like it. And if you don't, you don't have to keep it."

Now Andrea's eyes were shining with tears. "It isn't that at all, Rebecca. It's just—" She struggled for a moment, but couldn't hold the tears back. "Nobody's given me a present for so long that I forgot what it feels like. And I don't have anything for you. I—"

"Just open it," Rebecca begged. "Please?"

Blowing her nose into the crumpled Kleenex once more, Andrea finally opened the bag and took out the tissue-wrapped object inside. Stripping the paper away, she gazed uncomprehendingly at the gilded dragon. "I—I don't understand," she stammered. "What is it?"

Instead of telling her, Rebecca took the dragon from her cousin's hands and squeezed its neck. *Click!* And a tongue of fire shot from its mouth. Andrea laughed.

"I love it!" she said, taking the lighter back from Rebecca and trying it herself. "Where did you ever find it? It's wonderful!" Rummaging in her purse, she found a package of cigarettes at the bottom, pulled one out, and lit it from the dragon's mouth. "Now if anyone says I have dragon breath, at least they'll be right!"

"You mean you really like it?" Rebecca asked. "It's all right?"

"It's perfect," Andrea assured her. Then she glanced around. "Now I feel even worse about taking your room."

"It's not my room," Rebecca reminded her. "It's yours. And the one downstairs is fine for me. I don't need much. I'll bet I don't have nearly as many clothes as you, and I won't have to listen to Aunt Martha snore anymore." She instantly clapped her hands over her mouth as she realized she'd once more spoken without thinking, but Andrea only laughed again.

"Is it really bad?"

Rebecca nodded. "Sometimes I have to wear earplugs in order to sleep."

"Oh, Lord," Andrea moaned, flopping back onto the bed. "Maybe I'm actually doing you a favor after all."

She sat up again, then held the pack of cigarettes out to Rebecca. "Want one?"

Rebecca shook her head. "Smoking's not good for you."

Andrea laughed, but this time the sound was bitter. "Life hasn't been very good for me. No job, no husband, no place to live, and pregnant. So where's the good part?"

"You're having a baby?" Rebecca asked. "But that's wonderful, Andrea. Babies are always good, aren't they?" Then her eyes fell on the cigarette from which Andrea was inhaling deeply. "But now you really shouldn't smoke," she went on. "It's really bad for the baby."

The last faint feeling of optimism that the gift had brought to Andrea dropped away. "What the hell would you know about it?" she asked. Then, unwilling to witness the pain her words inflicted on Rebecca, she stood up and went to the window, gazing out at the dark, rainy afternoon.

Rebecca, stinging from Andrea's rebuff, went to the door. Hand on the knob, she turned back, hopefully, but when Andrea made no move even to look at her, she shook her head. "I'm sorry," she said. "I didn't mean to upset you. I just—well, I just say things, that's all. I'm really sorry."

"Just leave me alone, Rebecca. Okay?"

A moment later Andrea heard the door open and close, and knew that she was once again alone in the room. She went back to the bed, dropped down onto it once more, and picked up the lighter.

Clicking it on and off, she watched the dragon's flaming tongue flick in and out of its gilded mouth. As the flame flared then died away, flared and died once more, she thought about the baby growing in her womb.

Then, with a sharp *click* that made the dragon spit its flame again, she made up her mind what she was going to do.

Chapter 4

*M*artha Ward left her house at dawn the next morning. She hadn't slept well, which she always took as a sign that her soul was troubled. This morning, her private prayer session in her own chapel wouldn't be enough. Dressed in the dark blue suit she invariably wore to church, and with her hat and veil pinned carefully in place, she used her key to bolt the front door. Both Rebecca and Andrea were asleep inside the house, and though she was well aware that both of them were already steeped in sin, she was always mindful that there were men in Blackstone—just as there were men everywhere—whose hearts were filled with lust.

Satisfied that the door was firmly locked, she left the porch, buttoned her coat to her chin as the sharp wind cut into her, then made her way down Harvard Street. Her feet, misshapen from the arthritis that had been one of her crosses for the last twenty years, were hurting badly by the time she'd gone a block, but she ignored the pain, silently repeating her rosary. This morning she was saying St. Benedict's—one of her favorite rosaries—and the rhythms of the Latin words eased her pain slightly. If her Savior had been able to bear His cross through the streets of Jerusalem with graceful dignity, surely she could carry the pain of her arthritis with dignified grace. When Charles VanDeventer stopped to offer her a ride, she barely acknowledged him before turning her head firmly away from temptation.

When she arrived at the Catholic church on the town square, she noted with satisfaction that the door was already unlocked despite the early hour. Indeed, since Monsignor Vernon had come to Blackstone several years ago, seven o'clock mass was celebrated daily. Though she well knew that there were those in town who felt that the monsignor's Catholicism was out of step with their own, Martha Ward was not among them. From the day he arrived—from some small town out in Washington State, she recalled—Martha knew she'd found a kindred spirit. "I always leave the church open for prayer," he'd told her, "and I'll always be available to hear your confession." Not that Martha had much to confess. She made it a point to live a life of virtue. Still, she often found it comforting to talk to Monsignor.

Inside the church, Martha dipped her fingers in the font of holy water, genuflected, then walked slowly down the aisle, her eyes fixed on the face of the crucified Christ that loomed above the altar. Genuflecting again, she slipped into the first pew, dropped to her knees and began the first of her prayers. A few minutes later, catching a glimpse of movement out of the corner of her eye, she knew that Monsignor Vernon was in the confessional, waiting for her.

"Something is preying on you this morning," the priest said softly when Martha's confession was done and he'd handed down her penance, then absolved her. "I can feel that your heart is heavy."

Martha sat silently for a few seconds, her fingers working at her beads, hesitant to reveal her shame. But what choice had she? "It's my daughter," she whispered, her voice quavering. "She is pregnant, Father. But she isn't married." Did she hear a shocked gasp? She was almost certain she did.

She clutched the beads more tightly.

"You must pray," the priest said, his voice low but distinct. "Your daughter has committed a mortal sin, and you must pray for her. Pray for her to see the error of her ways. Pray for her to turn away from sin and find her way back to the Church. Pray for her to find her way into the arms of the Lord so her baby may be saved."

Martha waited, but no other words came to her from the other side of the screen. When she finally left the confessional, the church was once again empty, except for her. Returning to the pew, she dropped to her knees.

The words she'd heard in the confessional echoed in her mind.

Pray for her to find her way into the arms of the Lord so her baby may be saved.

Over and over again the monsignor's resonant voice echoed in her mind, until the words took on the cadence of a chant that resounded louder and louder, filling the entire church and penetrating to the very core of her being.

It was as if she'd been spoken to by the Lord Himself. Martha Ward felt transfigured.

The Lord would show her the way.

Andrea would be saved.

As soon as she was wide enough awake to remember where she was and why she was there, Andrea Ward felt her good intentions of the previous day evaporate. She reached over to the nightstand, felt for her cigarettes, and lit one with the dragon's head lighter her cousin had given her yesterday afternoon. Sucking the first puff of smoke deep into her lungs, she choked, then fell victim to a fit of coughing. When the coughing finally subsided, she dropped back onto the single thin pillow that had been allotted to the bed—her mother had never believed that more than one could possibly be necessary—and wondered why she'd bothered to wake up at all.

Nothing had changed overnight. She was still pregnant, still jobless, and Gary had still run out on her. But now she was back home in Blackstone, and her mother was condemning her for her sins, and Rebecca—

Rebecca! Christ! Though it was true that her cousin had tried to be nice to her, so what? Since her accident, Rebecca was even more useless than she'd been before, if that was possible. Sweet, maybe, but useless. Which meant Rebecca wasn't going to be any good to her at all.

Stop it! Andrea commanded herself. None of this is Rebecca's fault. You got yourself into this mess, so now it's up to you to get yourself out of it!

Stubbing the cigarette out in the soap dish she'd commandeered from the bathroom to serve as an ashtray, Andrea slid off the bed, only to feel a wave of nausea break over her as she stood. Running to the bathroom, she made it just in time to throw up into the toilet. Groping, she found the handle on the side of the tank and flushed the bowl, but as she started to get to her feet, her stomach recoiled again, a foul mixture of acid and bile rising in her throat, and she sank again to her knees. Whimpering, she stayed crouched on the floor waiting for the nausea to pass, and after retching two more times, decided to risk standing up once again. She was turning on the water to rinse the residue of vomit from her mouth when she heard a tapping at the door, immediately followed by Rebecca's voice.

"Are you all right, Andrea? Can I help?"

"No one can help," Andrea groaned. "Just go away, okay?"

There was a silence, followed by the sound of her cousin's footsteps retreating back toward the staircase. She stared at herself in the mirror. Her eyes were bloodshot, and her hair, darkening badly at the roots, lay against her scalp in a limp, oily tangle. To her own eye, she looked at least ten years older than she was. She looked worn. She looked the way she felt. Hopeless.

How on earth would she manage to keep all the promises she'd made yesterday?

Andrea went back to her room, put on the same blouse and faded jeans she'd worn the day before, and finally went downstairs. She found Rebecca in the kitchen. Two places were set at the table. As Andrea sank down into one of the chairs, Rebecca put a glass of orange juice in front of her, and a plate containing an English muffin thickly coated with butter and bright orange marmalade.

Just the sight of it made Andrea's stomach churn again. "All I want is a cup of coffee," she pleaded.

The welcoming smile on Rebecca's face faded into a look of uncertainty. "Is that good for the baby? I think I read—"

Andrea glared at her cousin. "I have news for you," she said. "I don't give a good goddamn what you *read*." As Rebecca's eyes glistened with tears, Andrea felt a twinge of guilt. "Look, I'm sorry, okay? But it hasn't been a great morning so far. I didn't sleep more than an hour, and then I started puking my brains out. Right now my life isn't going real well, you know? Anyway, I'm sorry I snapped at you."

"It's all right." Rebecca picked up the plate and glass and moved them to the counter, then poured her cousin a cup of coffee.

"Where's Mother?" Andrea asked. "She can't be asleep—she always thought being in bed after six was some kind of sin."

"Sometimes she goes to church," Rebecca explained. "Especially when she's worried about something."

Andrea rolled her eyes. "Well, I think we can both guess what she's praying about this morning, huh? What'll you bet she starts in on me the minute she gets home?"

"Aunt Martha's been good to me," Rebecca said. "And she only wants what's best for you too. She worries about you all the time."

"Worries about *me*?" Andrea cried, her voice mocking. Her hands shaking with sudden anger, she lit another cigarette. "Let me tell you something, Rebecca. Mother never worried about anyone in her whole life. All she worries about is who's sinning, and whether she's going to Heaven or not. Well, I have a news flash for her too—if Heaven is where nice, loving mothers go, then it's way too late for her already!"

Rebecca recoiled from Andrea's venom. "She's not that bad."

"Isn't she?" Andrea shot back. "Let me show you something." Standing so abruptly she nearly toppled her chair, Andrea left the kitchen and walked quickly through the house until she came to the closed doors to the room that had once been her father's den. Shoving the doors open, she stepped inside. "Did you know this is where I grew up?" she asked. Using the dragon's head, she began lighting the candles lined up on her mother's small altar, then lit the ones that stood beneath the icons of the Holy Mother and half a dozen saints.

"This is the way it always was, Rebecca," she said as the dark room began to glow with the shadowy light of the shimmering candle flames. "Ever since I was a little girl, this is how it was. I had to come in here and pray every morning, and every day after school, and every night before I went to bed. And you know what, Rebecca? I never even got to see what it looked like in real light. Well, let's find out, shall we?"

Crossing the room first to the window on the left of the altar, then to the one on the right, Andrea pulled the heavy drapes back. As the bright daylight washed away the candles' glow, the room seemed to change. The walls—once painted white—were grimy with the soot of the thousands of candles that had been burned in the chapel, and the upholstery on the prie-dieu was revealed to be stained and threadbare. The statues of the saints, their colors showing garishly in the daylight, were as grime-streaked as the walls. "Why wouldn't I have gotten out of here as soon as I could? What kind of woman would raise a child in a place like this?"

"But she loves you—" Rebecca began.

Andrea didn't let her finish. "It wasn't love, Rebecca! It was insanity. Don't you get it? She's nuts. Or isn't it just her anymore? Has she gotten to you too now? Or was it the accident? Did it make you so stupid you can't see what she's like? God! Why did I come back here?" Throwing her cigarette onto the carpet, she ground it out with her heel, then stormed out of the room, and raced up the stairs.

Rebecca picked up the cigarette butt and did her best to scratch the burned surface of the carpet away, then hurriedly pulled the drapes, plunging the room once more into the gloom that hid its flaws. Blowing out the candles, she pulled the chapel door closed just as Andrea reappeared at the foot of the stairs, wearing a coat and clutching the keys to her car in her hand.

"Where are you going?" Rebecca asked.

Andrea's eyes fixed darkly on her for a brief second. "Why would you care?" she demanded. Then, before Rebecca could reply, she was gone.

An hour later Rebecca had cleaned up the kitchen, her room next to the dining room, and Andrea's room too. She'd been on her way downstairs to have a last cup of coffee before going to work, but when she heard the music in the chapel begin and realized her aunt was back from church, she changed her mind and started down Harvard Street toward the library instead. She was still half an hour early, though, and since Germaine Wagner had never given her a key to the library, she decided to go over to the Red Hen and have her cup of coffee there. She was just pulling the door to the diner open when she heard a car horn honk and turned to see Oliver Metcalf nosing his car into an empty slot in front of the movie theater next to the diner.

"If you sit with me, I'll pay," Oliver said after he'd parked and approached her.

"You don't have to do that," Rebecca replied. "I have my own money, you know."

"Great," Oliver said, holding the diner's door open. "Then you can pay. How's that?"

"That would be nice," Rebecca told him. "Everybody's always offering to pay for me, like I'm still a little girl. And it's stupid, since I'm almost thirty."

Oliver feigned shock. "I had no idea," he said. "If you're that old, then you can buy me a doughnut too." They settled onto a pair of stools at the counter, and Oliver smiled at her. "How did Andrea like her present?"

Rebecca's brow furrowed. "I'm not sure," she replied. "I thought she liked it when I gave it to her last night, but this morning she just seemed to be mad about everything." As Oliver listened, she recounted everything that had happened since she'd seen him yesterday. "I just don't understand," she finished a few minutes later. "If she hates Aunt Martha so much and thinks she's crazy, why did she come home?"

"It doesn't sound like she had anyplace else to go," Oliver replied. "And if I were you, I wouldn't worry too much about what happened this morning. She's had a bad time, and it must seem to her like her life is nothing but problems. You just happened to be there when she had to blow off some steam, that's all."

Rebecca glanced at Oliver, but her gaze quickly shifted away. "But she sounded like she really meant it when she said I was so stupid I can't see what Aunt Martha's like." She was silent for a second, and then, still not looking at Oliver, asked, "Is it true, Oliver? Am I stupid?"

As he had in the car the day before, Oliver turned Rebecca's face toward him so she had no choice but to look at him. "Of course it's not true, Rebecca," he said, his voice gentle. "And I don't think Andrea meant it. She

was just upset, and people say things they don't mean
when they're upset. So the best thing for you to do is just
forget it." Then, acting on an impulse before letting himself think about it, he leaned forward and kissed her
softly on the lips. "You're not stupid," he whispered into
her ear. "You're a wonderful, lovely woman, and I love
you very much." Then, feeling his face flush with embarrassment, he quickly stood and looked at his watch. "I'm
late," he said. Dropping some money on the counter, and
feeling every eye in the diner watching him, he hurried
out the door.

Chapter 5

Oliver pulled his car into the parking lot of the white building that had housed Blackstone Memorial Hospital for the last twenty years. There were only three beds, and even they were rarely used: anyone who needed long-term care went either up to Manchester or down to Boston. For the last few months, though, the hospital had been busier than usual; first with Elizabeth McGuire's tragic miscarriage, then with taking care of Madeline Hartwick. Jules Hartwick's body had been taken first to Blackstone Memorial too, but even as the ambulance carried it downhill, everyone knew it was only going there as a matter of legal formality.

Oliver was still haunted by that terrible night when he'd found Jules on the steps of the Asylum and seen him plunge the knife deep into his own belly. It seemed to Oliver as if his headaches had been getting even worse lately, and yesterday, when his hand reflexively jerked away from the cigarette lighter Rebecca had bought for Andrea at the flea market, he'd been far more frightened than he let on.

Perhaps, if he hadn't been suffering from the blinding headaches, he might not have been so frightened by the false message of searing heat that his involuntary nervous system had received. But in combination with the headaches, an idea had begun forming in his mind, and though he told himself it was ridiculous, he hadn't been able to shake it all night long.

Brain tumor.

How else to explain the sudden onset of the unbearable migraines—when he'd rarely suffered from even mild headaches his whole life? How else to account for the odd flashes of vision—hallucinations—that seemed to accompany the hammering pain, though he could never quite recall their content after the headache passed. And yesterday . . . When he touched the lighter, he hadn't had a headache. Yet he could still clearly remember the searing heat he'd felt in the brief instant when his fingers first touched the object.

The searing heat that—impossibly—was no longer there a second later, when Rebecca put the lighter into his hand.

Well, Phil Margolis would undoubtedly have an answer for him. Getting out of the Volvo, Oliver went into the hospital.

"All this does is take a picture of your brain," Dr. Margolis explained. The CAT scanner sat in a small room that had been renovated specifically to house it after the doctor succeeded in putting together enough funds to buy the used machine five years ago. Serving not only Blackstone, but half a dozen other towns, the scanner had brought in enough money to allow the tiny hospital to operate in the black for the first time in its history. "Lie down on the table, and I'll strap you in."

"Do you have to?" Oliver asked. The moment he'd stepped into the room, he felt a wave of panic begin to build inside him. Now, his eyes fixed on the heavy nylon restraining straps, and his palms went suddenly clammy.

"I have to hold you immobile," Margolis explained. "Any movement of your head, and the images will be spoiled. It's easiest if you're strapped down."

Oliver hesitated, wondering where the panic was coming from. He'd never been claustrophobic—at least he didn't think he had—but for some reason the idea of being strapped to the bed terrified him. But why? It couldn't have anything to do with Phil Margolis—he'd known the doctor for years.

Could it be he was just frightened of what the CAT scan might show? But that was ridiculous—if there was something wrong with him, he wanted to know about it! "All right," he said, lying down on the table. Fists clenched, he shut his eyes and steeled himself against the fear that instantly gripped him as the doctor began fastening the straps that would hold him immobile. His heart raced; he could feel the sweat on his palms.

"You okay, Oliver?" the doctor asked.

"Fine." But he wasn't fine; he wasn't fine at all. A terrible fear was overtaking him, an unreasoning terror.

"Okay, we're all set," Phil Margolis told him. He stepped out of the room, and a moment later the machine came to life, the scanner starting to move down over his head as it began taking thousands of pictures from every possible angle, which a computer would then knit together to form a perfect image of his brain.

And anything that might be growing inside it.

Then it happened.

With no warning at all, a blinding pain slashed through Oliver's head, and the room seemed to fill with a brilliant white light that faded to utter blackness in an instant. And then, out of the blackness, an image appeared.

The boy is in a small room, staring at a table to which heavy leather straps are attached. The man, looming above him, is waiting impatiently for the boy to get onto the table. In his hand, the man holds something.

Something the boy has seen before.

Something that terrifies him.

Instead of getting on the table, the boy retreats to cower in a corner of the room.

As the man raises the object, with two shining metal

*studs protruding from a long tube at one end, the boy
whimpers, already anticipating the pain to come.*

*As the man advances toward the boy, the child,
screaming now, starts to run. The man's large, mus-
cled arm reaches out—*

"That's it," Philip Margolis said as he came back into
the room. He unfastened the straps that held Oliver to the
table. "That wasn't so terrible, was it?"

Oliver hesitated. The fact was, he couldn't really
remember much of the scan at all. There had been a
moment of panic, but then . . .

What?

A headache? One of the strange hallucinations?

Something—some kind of vague memory—was flitting
about the edges of his consciousness, but as he reached out
for it, trying to grasp it, the memory slipped away.

Oliver managed a grin as he sat up, the straps having
released their grip. "Not so bad," he agreed. "Not so bad
at all."

Chapter 6

*A*ndrea drove slowly, searching for the impossible: an empty parking spot in Boston. She'd already passed the red brick building three times, twice going this direction, once the other. Should she try the other side again, or give up hoping to find a spot within a few steps of the building, and try one of the side streets?

Or should she just turn around and drive back to Blackstone?

She rejected the last idea immediately. She'd thought it all through too many times to back out now. If she didn't go through with it now, she never would. Her mother would start in on her, and this time there would be no escape. Sooner or later she'd give in. And whatever Martha decided, it wouldn't be good for her, and it wouldn't be good for the baby.

It would be good only for Martha Ward, who would then spend the next few years exacting emotional payment for having "gotten you out of that mess, even though I had nothing to do with getting you into it!" A three-way bank shot, the kind Andrea knew her mother loved best, leaving Andrea feeling guilty, grateful, and indebted, all at the same time.

But not this time. This time Andrea was going to take care of it—take charge of her own life. Her mind made up, she turned off onto a side street, resuming her search for a parking spot. She finally found one three blocks from her destination, pulled into it, and automatically locked the rusting Toyota, even though she suspected it was worth more stolen than not. Hunched against the cold drizzle that had begun an hour before, Andrea trudged back toward the clinic, her steps heavy, her eyes fixed on the pavement in front of her.

The doctor's office was on the third floor. To Andrea's surprise, the door was unlocked. There were several women in the waiting room. Only one, a neatly dressed Asian woman several years younger than she, glanced up when she came in. The woman smiled briefly, then quickly lowered her eyes again to the magazine she was leafing through. A white-coated receptionist behind a glass partition looked up and said to Andrea, "May I help you?"

Andrea hesitated. There was still time to change her mind, still time to turn around and just walk out.

But then what?

Then, nothing.

No school, no decent job, no life.

Ever.

"I was wondering if Dr. Randall has an opening today," she asked.

The nurse glanced down at the appointment calendar that was spread open before her. "Can you come back at two?"

Andrea nodded, gave the nurse her name, then filled out a medical history form, and filled in her MasterCard number, uttering a silent prayer that Gary had neither canceled the card nor run it past its credit limit. The first was doubtful; the second not at all unlikely. Leaving the office, she went back to the street, spotted a Starbucks half a block down on the other side, and settled in for the long wait.

When she returned to the office at exactly two that afternoon, the waiting room was empty. "Right on time," the nurse said, smiling at her again. She opened the inner door and led Andrea into the doctor's office, where a man of about forty, with a blond crew cut, the build of a football player, and a ruggedly handsome face rose and offered her his hand.

"I'm Bob Randall."

As Andrea sank into the chair opposite the doctor, he reached for the forms she'd filled out, and she saw the gold wedding band on his finger. Damn.

"Do you want to talk about this?" Randall asked.

Andrea groaned to herself. Now what? Was she going to have to explain herself to the doctor too? What business was it of his? The operation was perfectly legal—hundreds of women had it every day, and thousands more, she believed, should have.

The doctor seemed to read her mind. "I don't mean about having the abortion," he said. "I just mean about the procedure itself."

"You mean you're not going to guilt-trip me?" Andrea asked.

Randall shrugged. "It's your life, and your body, and nobody but you has the right to tell you what to do with it. You're old enough to know what you're doing, and if you're as healthy as you say you are, there shouldn't be any problems. You'll be out of here in little more than an hour."

For just a moment, Andrea hesitated. Even though she'd been told Dr. Randall wouldn't lecture her, she hadn't really believed it.

But this was it.

No questions, no arguments.

She nodded her head. "Let's do it."

The doctor took her into another room, left her alone while she changed into a hospital gown, and then came back, this time with the nurse. He checked Andrea's blood pressure and pulse, her respiration and reflexes. He listened to her chest, palpated her stomach, then told her to stretch out on her back and put her feet in stirrups.

"Last chance to change your mind," he told her.

"Go ahead," Andrea said. "Let's just get it over with."

Fifteen minutes later it was all over. There had been surprisingly little discomfort; the worst had been when he'd dilated her cervix, but even that hadn't hurt badly. "Is that it?" she asked as the nurse began cleaning up the small operating room.

"That's all there is," the doctor replied. "I'd like you to lie down and relax for half an hour or so, and then I'll take a look to make sure there aren't any problems, but I can't really imagine that there are going to be any. It's a very simple procedure, and I know what I'm doing."

Forty minutes later Andrea was dressed and back out on the street. It had stopped drizzling. The first thing she did when she was out of the brick building in which she'd at least solved the worst of her problems was to reach into her purse and pull out a cigarette.

A cigarette, and the lighter that Rebecca had given her yesterday.

She squeezed the trigger concealed in the dragon's throat, lit the cigarette, and sucked the smoke deep into her lungs, at last feeling a loosening of the tension she'd had all day.

Rebecca.

She'd have to apologize to Rebecca for what she'd said this morning.

And thank her for the lighter too. She was still holding it in her hand, and now, as the sun broke through the clouds overhead, it glinted brightly. She held it up, gazed at its red eyes, and once again squeezed its neck.

Click. Its flaming tongue appeared, flickering in the light breeze.

Andrea gazed at the lighter for a long time. Its red eyes glinted at her with a fiery light that seemed to come, not from the sun, but from deep within the dragon's golden body. Glowing crimson, the eyes held her mesmerized. Then, almost unaware of what she was doing, she held her other hand up too.

Very slowly she moved her hand toward the dragon's fiery tongue.

When the flame touched her skin, it didn't hurt.

It didn't hurt at all.

Chapter 7

*D*usk had fallen as Andrea pulled up in front of her mother's house. In all the other houses on the block, except for the Hartwicks' next door, windows were already glowing with light, and thin curtains revealed glimpses of warm, inviting interiors. Only her mother's house was dark; save for the dim porch light that might provide a measure of safety to someone climbing the front steps, but offered no real welcome, the house appeared to be deserted. Yet Andrea was certain her mother was at home. She could almost feel Martha's unforgiving presence inside, almost see her kneeling on the prie-dieu, her fingers clicking through her rosary beads while her lips formed the words, *Hail Mary, Mother of God. Pray for us now and in the hour of . . .* Except that it would be the Ave Maria her mother was reciting, repeating the prayer over and over again in the original Latin, understanding no more of the prayers she uttered than she understood the daughter she'd raised.

Andrea shut off the car's engine, but instead of getting out of the Toyota, she reached into her purse, found her cigarettes, and used the dragon to light one. As she sat in the car, smoking her cigarette, she idly flicked the lighter on and off, watching the tongue of flame flare quickly, then die away. The cigarette was only half smoked when she was startled by a rap on the glass and glanced over to see Rebecca peering worriedly through the curbside window.

224

"Andrea? Are you all right?"

Stubbing the cigarette out in the car's ashtray, Andrea got out. "I'm okay, I guess." She sighed, knowing she wasn't okay at all. The first terrible doubt about what she'd done had set in even before she'd gotten back in her car. Over and over, she'd tried to convince herself that she'd done the right thing, but she still hadn't been able to rid herself of the nagging feeling that she could have coped with the situation another way. Surely she could have found some kind of job: pregnant women worked all the time—lots of them right up until a week or so before they were ready to deliver. And after the baby was born, there would have been lots of options. She could have put the baby up for adoption, or maybe even kept it and—

Stop it, she commanded herself. It's over and done with.

Rebecca was still looking at her anxiously. Andrea forced herself to smile as she came around to the curb. "Hey, it's all right," she said. "I'm going to be okay. And look, I'm sorry about this morning, okay? I mean, I was having morning sickness and feeling like a mess, and—well, you were there, so I took it all out on you. So I'm sorry. And I really like the lighter. I've been using it all day."

"But with the baby—" Rebecca began, but Andrea didn't let her finish.

"Will you stop worrying? I said everything's going to be okay. All right?" They were on the porch now, and as Rebecca opened the front door, Andrea smelled the familiar, choking scent of incense and candle smoke, and heard the drone of the recorded chanting. "She's praying, isn't she?"

Rebecca nodded. "I was just starting supper."

"I'll help." Andrea hung her coat in the closet, then followed Rebecca into the kitchen, where the table was set for two.

Rebecca, seeing Andrea's eyes fix on the two places,

reddened. "I didn't know whether you were going to be here or not," she said quickly. "I'll set another—"

"For God's sake, Rebecca, take it easy. I'll set another place." She eyed the small table at which she and her mother had eaten all their meals since her father had left, and at which, presumably, Rebecca and her mother had been eating for the last twelve years. "I have an idea. What do you say we use the dining room?"

Rebecca's eyes widened. "I don't think Aunt Martha would like that."

"Who cares what Mother would like?" Andrea countered. "What about what you and I would like? Haven't you ever wanted to eat in the dining room?" Without waiting for an answer, Andrea scooped the two place settings off the kitchen table and put them back in the cabinet to the right of the sink. "And I think we'll just use the good silver tonight too," she announced.

Half an hour later Rebecca dished the warmed-up pot roast, left over from the night before, onto the good china. Just as she and Andrea were carrying the plates in from the kitchen, the chanting from the chapel stopped abruptly and Martha Ward appeared at the end of the hall. Before her mother could say a word, Andrea spoke.

"We're eating in the dining room tonight, Mother."

"We never eat in the dining room," Martha stated.

"Well, we are tonight. The kitchen table's too small, and what's the point of having a dining room if we never use it?"

"The dining room is for company," Martha said coldly.

"Come on, Mother. When was the last time you had company?"

Martha's lips pursed in disapproval, but she said nothing until she came into the dining room and surveyed the table. Andrea had not only set it with the good silver, but had put a cloth on the table, and candles in the twin candelabra that had stood unused on the sideboard for a quarter of a century. Rebecca hovered near the door, certain that Martha was going to demand that supper be moved to the kitchen and the dining room table be cleared instantly. When her aunt finally spoke, though, the chill in her voice had softened slightly.

"Perhaps we can consider this a celebration of Andrea's homecoming," she said. The tension in the room eased slightly, and Rebecca and Andrea took their seats on opposite sides of the table as Martha settled herself into the chair at the head. "But only for tonight," she went on. "I'm sure the three of us can fit around the kitchen table perfectly comfortably. Shall we say grace?"

Martha bowed her head. Andrea winked conspiratorially at Rebecca, who quickly tilted her own head forward and clasped her hands as her aunt muttered the prayer. When Martha was done, she picked up her knife and fork, cut a piece of pot roast, and put it in her mouth. She chewed it for a long time, finally swallowed it, then fixed her eyes on her daughter. "I spoke to Monsignor Vernon this morning, Andrea."

Andrea looked at her mother guardedly. "Oh?"

"He says I must pray for you."

Andrea tensed, girding herself for the lecture she knew her mother was preparing to deliver. "I'm afraid it's a little late for that," Andrea ventured. "I haven't been as good as you about going to church."

Martha regarded her daughter sadly, as if contemplating whether it was already far too late for her to find redemption. Still, she thought, she must follow her priest's instructions. "Monsignor Vernon says I must pray that you will find a way to return to the arms of the Lord. For the sake of the baby," she added pointedly, lest Andrea mistake her purpose.

Andrea, about to put a bite of food in her mouth, slowly put down her fork, then looked directly at her mother. "If you're planning to pray for my baby," she said, "you don't need to waste your time. There isn't going to be a baby. I went back down to Boston today and had it taken care of."

Martha Ward's face paled. "Taken care of?" she repeated, her voice barely audible. "Exactly what do you mean, Andrea?"

Andrea searched her mother's face for any trace of sympathy for what she'd been going through, any hint that her mother might understand why she'd done what she had. But there was none, and suddenly the doubts she'd had about the abortion vanished as she realized the future her child would have had: Her mother would have found some way—any way—to take the baby away from her. Then the child would have grown up in this house, suffocated by her mother's fanaticism, believing that it was conceived in sin and damned for all eternity.

With a certainty proved by the unforgiving sanctimony of her mother's expression, Andrea knew she'd made the right decision.

"I mean I had an abortion this afternoon, Mother."

A stifling shroud of silence fell over the dining room as Martha and Andrea stared at each other. Finally, Martha rose from her chair and pointed an accusing finger at her daughter. "Murderess," she hissed. Then her voice rose. "Murderess! May you burn in Hell!"

Turning her back on her daughter, Martha Ward strode out of the room. Within seconds the sound of Gregorian chants swelled through the house.

"She's praying for you," Rebecca said softly.

"No she isn't," Andrea replied. "She's praying for herself. She doesn't give a damn about me."

"That isn't true," Rebecca said. "She loves you."

Now Andrea too was on her feet. "No she doesn't, Rebecca. She doesn't love anyone." Tears streaming down her cheeks, Andrea fled from the dining room.

As the house filled with the mysterious droning rhythm of the chanting, Rebecca sadly cleared the dining room table and wondered if it would ever be used again.

* * *

Rebecca wasn't certain what woke her up; indeed, at first she wasn't sure she'd fallen asleep at all. Though the doors to her small room were closed, she could still hear the music emanating from the chapel, just as it had been when she'd gone to bed. Rolling over, she glanced at the little travel alarm clock she'd brought down from Andrea's room yesterday afternoon.

Three o'clock.

Three o'clock?

She sat up in bed, wide-awake now, and for the first time noticed something else.

There was a smell in the house; not the normal sickly sweet smell of her aunt's incense, but the acrid odor of the smoke that had filled the living room the one time she'd tried to use the fireplace, only to discover that her aunt had long ago had the chimney blocked to keep the house from losing heat.

Smoke?

Getting out of bed, Rebecca pulled on her bathrobe as she went to the pocket doors that separated her sleeping room from the dining room beyond. Before the panels were even inches apart, the acrid smell grew stronger, and she choked as she drew in a breath of smoky air. Throwing the doors wide open, she ran to the foot of the stairs.

The smoke was far thicker there. She watched in horror as more of it billowed down from the floor above.

"Fire!" she yelled up the stairs. "Andrea, get out! The house is on fire!" When there was no reply, she started up the stairs, but the smoke immediately drove her back down, coughing and gasping for breath. Her mind racing, she shouted again, this time to her aunt, then ran back to the kitchen to snatch up the phone. Fumbling twice, she finally managed to punch 911 into the keypad. Dropping to the floor to avoid the smoke that was now pouring into the kitchen from the hallway, she yelled into the phone the moment the emergency operator came on the line: "It's Rebecca Morrison—please! Help! The house is burning. I live at—" Suddenly, Rebecca's mind blanked, and she felt panic rising in her. Then she heard the operator's voice.

"I already have the address," the operator told her. "You're at 527 Harvard. The engines are on the way."

Dropping the phone, Rebecca ran out of the kitchen and back down the hall. At the foot of the stairs she shouted for her cousin once more, then charged through to the other side of the house, jerking open the door to her aunt's chapel.

All the candles were lit, and her aunt was on her knees at the prie-dieu, her head bowed, her fingers clutching her rosary.

"Aunt Martha!" Rebecca shouted. "The house is on fire! We have to get out!"

Slowly, almost as if in a trance, Martha Ward turned her head and gazed at Rebecca. "It's all right, child," she said softly. "The Lord will look after us."

Ignoring her aunt's words, Rebecca grabbed Martha Ward's arm and, with all her strength tugged her to her feet, then out of the candlelit room and into the foyer. Jerking the front door open, she shoved her aunt out onto the porch, then stumbled after her. Rain had begun to fall, but Rebecca ignored it as she pulled Martha off the porch and out into the yard as sirens wailed in the night. Rebecca looked up to the second floor, once again calling out her cousin's name. But even as she shouted to Andrea, she knew it might already be too late: unlike any of the other windows in the house, Andrea's were glowing orange from the flames that danced within.

Rebecca sank to her knees on the front lawn. Oblivious to the rain and the cold, with tears streaming down her face, she joined her aunt in prayer.

Chapter 8

*R*ebecca sat trembling in the waiting room of Blackstone Memorial. She was doing her best to answer all the questions she was being asked. Most of what had happened was still clear in her mind. She recalled waking up and smelling smoke, then calling out to her aunt and cousin to warn them that the house was burning. After that, as events started moving faster and faster, her memories were jumbled. She remembered calling 911, and getting her aunt out of the house. But then it became a blur. The fire engines began arriving, and a police car, and people had come out of the other houses. That was when they started asking her questions, but there were so many people and so many questions, she couldn't keep them sorted out. Finally, when Andrea was carried out of the house and put in the ambulance, Rebecca had begged to be allowed to go to the hospital with her.

She'd crouched on the floor of the ambulance, trying to stay out of the way of the medics, who were putting an IV in Andrea's arm. When she got her first good look at her cousin, she almost screamed out loud. Andrea's face was badly burned; her eyebrows were gone, and flesh was peeling from her cheeks and nose. The skin on her arms and shoulders was blackened, and all her hair was gone, except for a charred stubble on her blistered scalp. Though Rebecca quickly looked away, she felt a terrible hopelessness flood over her, wondering if Andrea would survive even long enough for them to get to the hospital.

But when the ambulance had finally screeched to a stop, her cousin was still breathing, and Rebecca scrambled out of the ambulance fast enough not to delay the medics. A few seconds later they pushed past her with the stretcher bearing Andrea's body, and Rebecca thought she heard a faint moan.

Rebecca had been clinging to that sound ever since, while the waiting room quickly filled with people and the questions began all over again. This time, though, it was the deputy sheriff, Steve Driver, who had put his hands on her shoulders to stop her trembling, and was gazing down intently at her.

"Is there anything else you can remember, Rebecca? Anything at all?"

She shook her head. "I've told it all."

Driver shifted his gaze to Martha Ward, who was sitting next to her niece, her rosary clutched in her fingers, her lips working as she silently recited her prayers. "What about you, Mrs. Ward? Did you hear anything? If you were awake—"

"She was praying," Rebecca said quietly. "When she prays, she never hears anything at all. She didn't even hear me when I came into the chapel to get her out of the house."

Steve Driver reached out and touched Martha's arm. "Mrs. Ward? I need to talk to you. It's really important." When Martha only kept on praying, he squeezed her arm and shook her slightly. "Mrs. Ward!"

As if jerked out of a deep sleep, Martha suddenly looked up. There was an odd, empty look in her eyes, but then her hands dropped into her lap and she shook her head sorrowfully. "It was God's will," she pronounced.

Steve Driver frowned, glanced at Rebecca, then turned his attention back to Martha. Leaning forward, he took her hands in his. "Mrs. Ward? Can you hear me?"

Martha seemed to gather herself together, taking a deep breath and straightening in the plastic chair on which she was perched. "Of course I can hear you. And I'm telling you what happened. God has punished Andrea for her sin."

The deputy's frown deepened. "Her sin?"

"She killed her child," Martha said, her voice strong now, and carrying throughout the waiting room. "And God has stricken her down."

The deputy sheriff cast a questioning glance at Rebecca.

"Andrea had an abortion," she explained. "Aunt Martha didn't approve of it, and—"

Martha drew up still straighter, and now her eyes fixed angrily on her niece. "God didn't approve," she declared. "God judges, not I. All I can do is pray for the soul of the child she murdered." Her fingers tightened once more on her beads. "We shall pray. We shall—"

Before she could finish, the door separating the waiting room from the emergency room opened and a nurse appeared. Spotting Rebecca, she hurried over and knelt down. "Your cousin's awake, and she's asking to see you," she said.

"Me?" Rebecca asked, her voice puzzled. "Shouldn't Aunt Martha—"

"It's you she's asking for, Rebecca," the nurse said.

"How is she?" Steve Driver asked, rising to his feet. "Is she going to make it?"

"We don't know," the nurse said quickly. "She has third-degree burns on most of her body." She shook her head. "She must be in terrible pain." She turned back to Rebecca. "But she's awake, and she's asking for you. It's going to be very difficult for you, but—"

"It's all right," Rebecca assured her. "It can't be nearly as bad for me as it is for Andrea."

She followed the nurse through the double doors and into the emergency treatment room. Andrea was lying on an examining table. There was a large bottle attached to the IV that the medic had put in her arm while she was still in the ambulance, and there was another tube in her nose. Dr. Margolis and two of the medics were carefully picking what looked like dead skin from Andrea's body, but as she drew closer to the bed, Rebecca realized it wasn't skin at all, but the remains of the nylon nightgown Andrea had been wearing when the fire broke out. Rebecca winced as one of the medics lifted a scrap of the material loose, taking a small patch of burned skin as well.

"I—I'm lucky," Andrea breathed, her voice barely audible. "I can't feel it yet."

Rebecca started to reach out to take her cousin's hand, stopping herself just in time. "Thank God you're still alive," Rebecca whispered. "And you're going to be all right."

She saw a barely perceptible shake of her cousin's head. "I don't think so," Andrea whispered. "I just—" She fell silent, winced as she tried to take a breath, then managed to utter a few more words. "My fault," she breathed. "Fell asleep with . . . cigarette. Dumb, huh?"

"It's all right, Andrea," Rebecca told her. "It wasn't your fault. It was an accident."

"No accident," Andrea whispered. "Mother said—"

"It doesn't matter what Aunt Martha said," Rebecca told her. "The only thing that matters is that you're alive, and you're going to get well."

For a long time Andrea said nothing, and Rebecca thought she must have gone to sleep. Then she spoke one more time. "The dragon," she breathed. "Don't let—"

Rebecca leaned forward, straining to hear what her cousin was saying. Andrea struggled, then her charred lips worked again. "M-Mother," she whispered. "Don't—" But before she could finish, the sedatives that had been added to the IV took hold and Andrea drifted into unconsciousness. She lay so still that finally Rebecca looked up at the nurse.

"What happened? Did she—"

"She's asleep," the nurse said. "If you'd like to go back to the waiting room . . ."

Rebecca shook her head, her eyes never leaving Andrea's ruined face. "Can't I stay here?" she asked. "What if she wakes up again? If I'm here, maybe she won't be so frightened."

The nurse hesitated, then indicated a chair close to the door. "Of course you can stay with her, Rebecca," she said. As Rebecca lowered herself into the chair, the nurse went back to work, helping the medics and Dr. Margolis clean the worst of Andrea's wounds and treat them with Silvadene ointment to try to prevent infection.

Rebecca, feeling utterly helpless, could only watch in silence.

Oliver Metcalf stood up and stretched, then stepped outside to suck a few breaths of morning air into his lungs. He'd been at the hospital for four hours, arriving minutes after Rebecca had been taken in to see Andrea.

He'd collected every scrap of information about the fire he could get. He and Steve Driver had come to the same conclusion. The fire had undoubtedly been an accident, caused by Andrea's habit of smoking in bed. The crew that had put the fire out had found an ashtray next to the bed, and though it was overturned, there were half a dozen sodden cigarette butts scattered around the floor in the same area. The only thing that saved Martha Ward was that she'd been praying in her downstairs chapel, and even that might not have saved her if Rebecca hadn't awakened.

"It could have been a lot worse," Driver said as he and Oliver finished comparing notes.

With nothing more that could be accomplished at the hospital, Driver had left. As the night wore on, the waiting room slowly emptied, until only Oliver and Martha Ward were still there. Though Oliver had tried several times to speak to Martha, she utterly ignored him as she concentrated on a seemingly endless repetition of her prayers. Eventually the rain stopped and the day dawned, the sun shining outside.

Half an hour before, Philip Margolis had come into the waiting room to ask Martha Ward if she wanted to see her daughter. Martha shook her head.

"I am praying for her," she said. "For her and her child both. I don't need to see her."

The doctor, nearly exhausted after hours of trying to save Andrea's life, turned away in disgust and started back to his patient. Oliver stopped him.

"How's she doing?" he asked, but even as he uttered the question, the expression on the doctor's face told him all he needed to know.

"I don't see how she can hold out much longer," Margolis said. He looked carefully at Oliver. "What about you? How are you feeling? Any more of those headaches?"

Oliver shook his head.

"Well, there's nothing in your CAT scan to worry about. I was going to call you later this morning. I had a friend up in Manchester take a look at your pictures, and he couldn't find anything wrong. Says you're perfectly normal." The doctor forced a tired smile. " 'Course, he doesn't know you as well as I do, does he?"

Before Oliver could reply to the weak joke, an alarm sounded from beyond the double doors and Margolis hurried out. Oliver sank back onto the sagging Naugahyde sofa, then restlessly stood up and walked outside. Now, as he turned to go back into the waiting room, he saw Rebecca Morrison emerging through the double doors. Her eyes were red, and tears stained her cheeks. Hurrying back into the waiting room, he put his arms around her and held her close. "It's over?" he asked quietly, though he already knew the answer. He felt her nod, then she pulled back a little and looked up into his face.

"It was so strange," she said. "First she was breathing,

and I thought she was going to be all right, and then she wasn't. She just stopped breathing, Oliver. Why do things like that happen?"

"I don't know," Oliver said quietly. "It was just a terrible accident." He gently smoothed a lock of hair back from Rebecca's forehead, then brushed a tear from her cheek. "Sometimes things happen—" he began. Martha Ward's voice interrupted him.

"Things do not just happen," she declared. "There is such a thing as divine retribution, and it has been visited upon Andrea. God's will has been done. Rebecca, it is time for us to go home."

Oliver felt Rebecca freeze in his arms, then pull away from him.

"Yes, Aunt Martha," she said softly. "I'm sure Oliver will take us."

Nodding curtly to Oliver, Martha said, "You may take us home," then turned and without looking back strode out into the morning sun.

Rebecca was about to follow her, but Oliver held her back.

"What's going on?" he asked. "Does she even realize what's happened?"

Rebecca nodded. "She thinks Andrea was punished for getting an abortion. But I don't think God would do something like that, do you?"

Oliver shook his head. "And I don't think you ought to be living with her anymore, either. Isn't there some other place you can go? You could come and stay with me. I'll—"

"It's all right, Oliver," Rebecca said. "I can't leave Aunt Martha now. She doesn't have anyone else, and she's been so good to me for so long."

"But—"

"Please, Oliver? Just take us home?"

Five minutes later Oliver pulled into the driveway of Martha Ward's house. Amazingly, the only outward signs of the fire from this side of the house were the damage to the lawn and shrubbery, which had been inflicted by the hoses the firemen dragged from the trucks into the house and up to the second floor.

"You're sure you want to do this?" Oliver asked once again. "Even if the house is livable, it's going to smell—"

But Martha Ward was already out of the car and striding toward her house. As she reached the steps to the porch she turned back. "Come, Rebecca," she commanded.

Like a dog, Oliver thought angrily. She treats her like a dog.

But before he could say anything, Rebecca too had slipped out of the car, and a moment later both Martha and Rebecca disappeared inside.

Oliver knew he'd made a mistake as soon as he opened the door of the Red Hen. But he'd been so intent on satisfying the hunger in his stomach that he'd momentarily forgotten the equally strong hunger of the regular morning crowd who came to the diner to begin their day—not a hunger for the crullers and coffee for which the diner was famous, but a hunger for information.

"Information" was what they called it, since they were men. Their wives—far more accurately—would have called it "gossip."

Either way, almost every voice in the Red Hen fell silent as Oliver entered, and nearly every eye shifted to fix expectantly on him. After scanning the faces, he chose the table where Ed Becker and Bill McGuire were involved in a conversation that was suspended only long enough to beckon him over. As Oliver slid into the booth next to the attorney, Bill McGuire looked at him questioningly.

"Andrea Ward died about half an hour ago," he told them in answer to Bill's unspoken question.

The contractor winced. "What the hell's going on around here?" he asked.

Ed Becker signaled to the waitress for more coffee. "Nothing's going on," he said, and his tone was enough to tell Oliver that last night's fire wasn't all they'd been talking about.

McGuire shook his head dolefully as the waitress refilled his cup. "How can you say that?"

"Because it's true," the lawyer replied, then turned to Oliver. "Bill's starting to sound like he thinks there's some kind of curse on the town or something."

"I didn't say that," McGuire interjected a little too quickly.

"All right, maybe you didn't say it in those exact words," Becker conceded. "But when you start trying to connect a bunch of things that can't be connected, isn't some kind of curse what you're talking about?"

McGuire shook his head doggedly. "All I'm saying is that it's getting really weird around here. First the bank gets in trouble and Jules goes nuts and kills himself, and now Andrea Ward comes home after years away and burns to death the next day."

Though no one mentioned what had happened to Elizabeth McGuire, they didn't need to. Her suicide, so shortly preceding Jules Hartwick's, still hung over Bill like a specter, and though he hadn't spoken her name, he didn't have to.

"The fire was an accident, pure and simple," Oliver told the other two men. But after he'd filled them in on everything he'd learned over the past few hours, Bill McGuire was still shaking his head doubtfully.

"A few months ago I might have believed it wasn't anything more than Andrea falling asleep with a cigarette, but now . . ." His voice trailed off into a long sigh.

"Maybe it wasn't an accident," Ed Becker suggested. "Maybe Martha torched her."

"*Torched* her?" Oliver echoed, recoiling from the word. "Jesus, Ed, maybe you did criminal law too long. Why on earth would Martha Ward want to kill her own daughter?"

"Well, you said yourself she didn't seem to be too sorry Andrea had died. Didn't you say something about it being God's will?"

" 'Divine retribution,' was the way she put it," Oliver corrected him. "Martha's a religious fanatic. You know she sees the hand of God in practically everything."

"Sometimes people like that decide they *are* the hand of God," Becker said pointedly.

"Come on, Ed," Oliver said, lowering his voice and glancing around at the other patrons in the diner. "You know how gossip spreads around here. If anybody hears you, it'll be all over town by this afternoon."

"Let it!" Ed Becker said, leaning back and smiling mischievously. "Personally, I never could stand Martha Ward. Even when I was a kid, I always thought she wasn't just holier-than-thou. She was just plain mean. What I can't figure out is why Andrea came back at all."

"No place else to go, according to Rebecca," Oliver replied. He was about to tell them about the abortion Andrea had had yesterday, but stopped himself as he remembered that it was the miscarriage Bill's wife, Elizabeth, had suffered that led to her suicide, just days after losing their baby son. "I, on the other hand, *do* have places to go," he announced, sliding out of the booth. "And so does Bill, unless he's planning to drag the remodeling of my office out until all the problems at the bank are cleared up."

McGuire smiled for the first time that morning. "Finally figured it out, huh? Well, just don't tell your uncle, okay?"

Oliver eyed the contractor sardonically. "You think he

hasn't figured it out too? Why do you think he keeps coming up with new ideas every couple of weeks? Come on. Let's go figure out a whole new idea about what my office is going to look like, just on the off chance that Melissa Holloway gets the bank straightened out and you can finally get to work on the Center. And let's not talk about curses or dire plots, all right? I'm a journalist, not a fiction writer."

The two men hadn't been gone more than a minute before the Red Hen was once again buzzing with low voices, each of them passing on whatever scrap of Oliver's conversation they'd overheard.

Finally, Leonard Wilkins spoke. A crusty seventy, he had run the drive-in theater for thirty years before it closed and the grounds were given over to the flea market.

"You ask me," he said, "I think we should be keeping an eye on Oliver Metcalf."

"Come on," someone else said. "Oliver's solid as a rock."

"Maybe so," Wilkins replied. "But we still don't know just what it was that happened to his sister back when they were kids. Lately, since the ·trouble around here started, it seems to me that boy's been acting strange. And I heard from my Trudy that he was talking to Phil Margolis about headaches the other day. Bad headaches."

After only the shortest of pauses, the buzz in the diner resumed.

But now they were no longer talking about the fire that had killed Andrea Ward.

Now they were talking about Oliver Metcalf.

Chapter 9

*I*t wasn't just the look of the room, though that was bad enough. The bed—the one Rebecca had slept in nearly every night of the last twelve years—was a sodden, blackened ruin. Even from the doorway—Rebecca hadn't yet found the courage to actually go into the room—she could see that the fire must have started in the bed and spread from there. She shuddered as she imagined Andrea falling asleep, a cigarette between her fingers. The cigarette must have dropped onto the coverlet, slowly burned its way through the blankets, sheets, and pad, and eventually burrowed into the mattress itself.

But why hadn't Andrea awakened? Wouldn't she have begun choking on the smoke filling the room? Or had she just gone from sleep directly into unconsciousness, utterly oblivious to what was happening to her? She must have, or surely she would have awakened as the fire had spread out from the bed, crawling across the carpet, then climbing up the curtains around the windows. The paint on the window frames was badly charred, and the wallpaper hung in scorched shreds. Everything in the room would have to go, and the paper and paint peeled down to the bare wood.

It was the smell that truly made Rebecca shiver. The terrible smell that was nothing like the friendly odor of a fire burning on a hearth. This was an odor she would never forget. From the moment she and her aunt had come back into the house, it filled her nostrils, every breath bringing back the memory of awakening in the middle of the night and realizing that the house was on fire.

Though Martha Ward objected, Rebecca had gone through every room of the house save the chapel, opening the windows as wide as she could and propping open all the doors to prevent any of them from blowing shut and cutting off the breeze. The cold air was eliminating at least the worst of the acrid smell. She'd stripped her bed, and her aunt's too, and put the linens into the big washing machine down in the basement, but even as she began the first batch of laundry, she'd known that it was going to be endless. Every piece of clothing would have to be washed, every stick of furniture cleaned. Every rug would have to be taken to the cleaners. Even then, she was certain the smell would remain, which meant that every time she entered the house, the whole terrifying scene from last night would come back to her like a nightmare from which she would never escape.

She was still standing at the door to Andrea's room, willing herself to go in, when she heard her aunt calling to her from downstairs: "Rebecca? Rebecca! This house won't get clean by itself."

Rebecca was about to turn away from the door to Andrea's room when something caught her eye.

Something that glittered in odd contrast to the charred blackness of the room.

Something that was almost hidden beneath the bed.

Even as she went into the room to pick the object up, she knew what it was.

The cigarette lighter she'd given Andrea the day before yesterday, in the shape of a dragon's head.

Wiping away the worst of the soot, she turned the shining object over in her hands. The dragon's red eyes glared up at her, and though there were still some smudges of soot on the creature's golden scales, it seemed undamaged by the fire.

When she pressed the trigger in its neck, a tongue of flame immediately appeared.

"Rebecca? Rebecca! I am waiting for you!"

Her aunt's commanding voice startled her, and Rebecca scurried out of the ruined room and down the stairs. Martha was waiting in the foyer, a bucket of soapy water at her feet. She handed Rebecca a rag. "Start here. I shall start in the kitchen."

Rebecca glanced at the soot-stained paper on the walls. "It will ruin the paper, Aunt Martha."

"The paper will not be ruined," Martha pronounced. "The Lord will cleanse our house as surely as He punished Andrea for her sins." Then her eyes fell on the object in Rebecca's hand. "What is that?" she demanded.

Rebecca's first impulse was to slip the dragon into her pocket, to keep it out of her aunt's sight, but she knew it was already too late. Reluctantly, she placed the golden dragon in her aunt's hand. "It's just a cigarette lighter," she said softly. "I gave it to Andrea on Sunday, when she came back."

Martha Ward held the lighter up, turning it and examining it from every angle. "Where did this come from?" she asked, her eyes still fixed on the dragon.

"The flea market," Rebecca replied. "Oliver and I found it, and—"

"Oliver?" Martha cut in. "Oliver Metcalf?"

Rebecca shrank back from the opprobrium in her aunt's voice. "Oliver is my friend," she said, but the words were uttered so quietly they were almost inaudible.

"I might have expected Oliver Metcalf to find something like this," Martha said, her fingers tightening around the dragon for a moment before she deposited it in the pocket of her apron. "I shall dispose of this."

"But it's not yours, Aunt Martha. I gave it to Andrea, and—" Her voice broke. "And I'd just—well, I'd just like to keep it."

Martha Ward's expression hardened into the same

dark mask of condemnation that had appeared on her face at dinner the evening before, when Andrea told her what she'd done in Boston. "It is a graven image, and a tool of the Devil," she pronounced. "I shall decide how best to dispose of it."

She turned away and disappeared down the hall toward the kitchen.

Rebecca dipped the rag into the bucket of soapy water, wrung it out, and began wiping the layer of soot from the woodwork around the front door. But even as she worked she knew it was useless. No matter how long they might scrub, the terrible stench of the fire would never be removed from the house.

But her aunt, she also knew, would never let her stop trying.

Chapter 10

*I*n the silence of the night, Martha Ward moved slowly through the rooms of her house. She had lived in it all her life; the past was hidden in every corner. It had been years since she'd gone in search of the memories though, having long since confined herself to the rooms in which she felt safest.

Her room. Not her parents' room, where she and Fred Ward had slept in the few short years before he deserted her, but her own childhood room, where she'd lived when she was still an innocent, before she allowed herself to be tempted into sin. The room she'd moved back into the day Fred Ward left, to tempt her no more.

She had been lucky, or so she'd thought. She, at least, had married Fred Ward before allowing him to lead her away from the path of righteousness.

Not like her younger sister, who had given birth to Rebecca only five months after marrying Mick Morrison.

And certainly not like her older sister, who had allowed Tommy Gardner to show her the ways of evil, and never married her at all.

In the course of her bitter catechism, Martha had come to understand the wages of sin, and all the forms of retribution that God's will could take.

Certainly His divine will had been visited on her family many times over the years, and in many ways.

First, there was her older sister, who had been banished from the house as soon as her sin was discovered. But

Martha herself was a small child then, and hadn't understood Marilyn's sin. She had simply thought her sister was sick, and that was why she'd been taken to the hospital on the top of the hill. Finally, after Marilyn had been gone a very long time, Martha opened her piggy bank, took out all the money, and bought her sister a present. It was a cigarette lighter, and to her six-year-old eyes it had been beautiful, with its golden scales and its ruby eyes. She had gazed lovingly at it before taking it up to the front door of the big stone hospital and giving it to the first person she'd seen, who had promised to deliver it to her sister.

Her father had been very angry when he found out what she'd done. He'd beaten her, and kept her in her room for a week, and when finally she'd been allowed out, he told her that she would never see her sister again.

It wasn't until years later that she finally learned what had happened to her sister, and when she'd gone to her priest to confess the sin of having given her sister the instrument with which Marilyn had killed herself, the priest had reassured her. "It was God's will," he told her. "Your sister sinned grievously, and the gift you offered her was no more than a tool of divine intervention. You are blessed, for God chose to act through you."

Though her older sister had been promptly punished for her sin, Martha's younger sister's punishment had not been meted out by the hand of God for sixteen years. Yet when the "accident" had finally come, Martha quickly understood that it had been no accident at all. In the flickering candlelight of the chapel, with the Gregorian chants numbing her mind to all other sound but God's voice, Martha had quickly come to understand that Rebecca's parents had finally been punished for their sin. She had also understood that it was her duty to take Rebecca—the fruit of that long-ago sin—into her home and shelter her from the ways of evil.

Martha had done her best to do just that.

She had given Rebecca her own daughter's room, and tried to keep her on the path from which even Andrea had strayed.

Two of the rooms—the room in which her parents, and even she and Fred Ward, had lain together, and the room in which Rebecca's mother had lain with Mick Morrison— she refused to set foot in. Others, such as the dining room and living room, which her parents had used for entertaining their godless friends, she simply avoided.

Rebecca kept them clean of course, for Martha had been careful in her instruction of the girl, instilling in her not only the virtue of chastity but of cleanliness as well.

For herself, Martha used only her childhood bedroom, where she knew no sin had ever been committed, and the chapel, in which she prayed for salvation and the guidance to keep herself and Rebecca free of sin.

And it had been working. As the years of prayer and devotion went by, Martha slowly felt a purity coming into the house, the same purity she felt in her own blessed soul, and she had grown secure in the knowledge that she, at least, was safe from the damnation that had befallen both her sisters.

Two days ago, when Andrea—unbidden and unwelcome—had returned, Martha knew she should have closed her doors to her, refused even to look upon her harlot's face. But she had not. Instead she allowed Andrea to enter the house, and Satan had slipped in with her.

Adultery with a married man.

A child unblessed by wedlock.

Abortion!

Why had she tolerated it?

And now, as she roamed sleeplessly through the rooms of the house, all the memories came back. In the living room she could still feel her older sister's presence, even smell the perfume she'd used to draw the Devil—in the form of Tommy Gardner—near.

In the big bedroom upstairs, unused for decades, she could hear her younger sister's moans of pleasure as she'd given herself to the false joys of sin in the arms of Mick Morrison.

Despite Martha's years of prayer and atonement, Satan still resided here. Even the smell of the smoke from the fire in which Andrea had died couldn't cover the stench of sin, which drenched the house in a sulfurous fog.

Finally, Martha went into the chapel. Lighting all the candles, she turned on the music of the Gregorian chants, keeping it soft enough not to awaken Rebecca, then sank onto the prie-dieu. The rosary draped from her fingers, she began silently reciting the decades of her prayers. As the candles flickered and the chanting droned, she opened her mind to the voice of God and fixed her eyes on the face of her Savior. But as the minutes of prayer ticked by and slowly turned into hours, the face that Martha Ward beheld began to change.

The face of her Savior was transfigured, and now she was gazing into the eyes of the dragon.

As she gazed deep into the ruby eyes, a voice came to her, and told her what she must do.

Martha Ward rose and left the chapel.

Rebecca ignored the first drop of water that fell onto her face. It was a perfect spring day, the kind she loved the best, when the sun was shining brightly in a soft blue sky, the trees were covered with the pale green of newly spreading leaves, the last of the crocuses were still in bloom, and the barely opened daffodils were showing the first traces of yellow. Birds were singing and a gentle breeze was blowing, carrying the pungent fragrance of the pine woods behind the house through her window, and she breathed deeply of it. Sighing, she shifted her position, squirming contentedly under her light coverlet.

Another drop hit her face, and then another.

Rain?

But how could it be rain?

She was in her room, and even though the window was open and a cool breeze was wafting in, she could see that the morning sky was perfectly clear.

But then another drop hit her face, and yet another.

She squirmed again, then rolled over, trying to escape the rain that was spoiling the perfect morning.

The sunlight was fading away, and as darkness gathered around her, the breeze died, and with it the pine scent it had carried. The fresh, perfumed air she had thrilled to only a moment ago now had an acrid quality to it that made her want to turn her head away.

Even the rain had changed; it no longer felt like rain at all.

The birdsong had shifted too, dropping from the merry tune of a moment ago into a low murmur of sounds that were familiar but not quite identifiable.

She rolled over again. Suddenly she was coughing and choking. Her nostrils were flooded with the acrid odor. She jerked awake and the last remnants of the dream gave way to consciousness.

It wasn't morning at all: the only light in the room came from the moon that hung low in the sky outside.

Nor had she felt a breeze, for the window was tightly closed against the cold March night.

But the rain? What had caused her to dream of rain?

Then she realized that the bedding around her was cold and wet, clammy with something that smelled like . . .

Turpentine?

But it wasn't possible. Why would—

Only then did she notice the movement in the room, and hear the muttering that in her dream had sounded like the singing of birds.

Her heart pounding, Rebecca freed herself of the clinging bedding and groped for the switch on the small reading lamp on the table next to the daybed. She blinked in the glare, but then her eyes focused and she recognized her aunt.

Her eyes wide and unblinking, gazing into the distance upon something that Rebecca couldn't see at all, Martha Ward was moving around the room, pouring turpentine from a large can onto the curtains and the walls. The smell of it was so strong that it utterly obliterated the smoky odor that had filled the room when Rebecca went to sleep. Instinctively, Rebecca clutched the sheet to her nose and mouth to filter out the noxious fumes, only to begin coughing once again. As her gorge rose in response to the bitter taste of the turpentine she'd sucked into her mouth, she shoved the soaked covers away.

"Aunt Martha, don't!" she begged, the words rasping in her throat. "What are—"

She left the question unfinished as she realized her aunt was as deaf to her voice as she seemed blind to the light that Rebecca had turned on.

"Cleansed," she heard her aunt muttering. "We must be cleansed of our sins that we may live in the presence of the Lord!"

Shaking the last of the turpentine from the can, Martha hesitated for a moment, looking at the container almost as if she didn't understand why the fluid had stopped flowing from it. Then she turned abruptly and strode from the room, pulling the pocket doors to the dining room closed behind her.

A second later Rebecca heard the click of the lock as her aunt twisted the key.

Leaping from the bed, Rebecca ran to the doors, pulled and pounded, trying to pry them open.

"Aunt Martha!" Fear bloomed in her as she realized she was trapped in the little room. "Aunt Martha, let me out!"

Instead of a response to her pleas, Rebecca heard only the sound of her aunt's mumbled prayers, now muffled by the thick wood of the closed and locked doors.

Out!

She had to get out, and get help!

Snatching her bathrobe from the hook in the little room's single tiny closet, Rebecca pulled it on, jammed her feet into a pair of worn sneakers, then ran to the window. Though the lock at the top of the lower casement finally turned, the window frame had long ago been painted shut. No matter how hard she tried, Rebecca couldn't jerk it loose. Finally she picked up the small reading lamp, smashed the lower pane, then knocked the broken shards away until it was safe for her to climb out. Dropping to the ground only a few feet below, she hesitated.

Where was she going to go?

Memories flashed through her mind—memories of the strange looks her aunt's neighbors, the VanDeventers, had given her over the years; of remarks they'd made when they thought she couldn't hear them.

Poor Rebecca.

Hasn't been quite right since the accident.

Afraid it left her just a little bit touched in the head.

What would they say if she pounded on their doors in the middle of the night, saying her aunt was going to burn her house down?

Oliver!

Oliver would listen to her! He was her friend, and he didn't think she was crazy!

Instead of heading for the front of the house, Rebecca ran across the backyard to the edge of the woods, where a narrow trail edged the Hartwicks', then hooked up with the path that led to the Asylum. Though there were still a few clouds in the sky, there was enough moonlight so Rebecca was able to run all but the few yards where the path was so soggy and muddy that she had to slow almost to a stop and pick her way through. By the time she arrived at Oliver's front door and began pounding and shouting to him, her sneakers were sodden and heavy with mud, and her legs were streaked with it as well. The cold night air had long since penetrated the thin material of her bathrobe, and though she was panting from running, she was shivering from the cold as well.

When there was no immediate response to her pounding on the door, Rebecca pressed her finger on the bell, banged once more, then stepped back to shout up toward the second floor. "Oliver! Oliver, wake up! It's Rebecca!"

It seemed like forever before the porch light came on, the front door was thrown open, and Oliver peered out. "Rebecca? What is it? What—"

Rebecca, finally overcome by the cold, the darkness, and the terror she'd only barely been able to control long enough to get there, began sobbing. "She locked me in," she began. "She tried . . . I mean she wants . . ." She paused, forced herself to take a deep breath, then lost control again.

Oliver pulled her into the house and closed the door, shutting out the cold. "It's all right, Rebecca," he soothed. "You're safe now. Just try to tell me what happened."

"It's Aunt Martha," Rebecca finally managed to say. "She's . . . oh, Oliver, I think she's gone crazy!"

Chapter 11

*A*ll was ready.

Save for her beloved Gregorian chants, the only music that had ever been able to soothe her soul, Martha Ward's house was silent.

Though she harbored a vague memory of Rebecca calling out to her a while ago, her niece's voice had quickly fallen silent.

God's hand, Martha was certain, had muted the sinful girl.

She gazed at herself in the mirror one last time—chiding herself for her vanity, but secure in the knowledge that she would be forgiven, as she would be forgiven all her sins in a few more minutes—and smiled, recognizing how beautiful she looked.

The image in the mirror perfectly reflected Martha's vision of herself: her youth restored, her cheeks rosy and her lips full, her eyes wide and filled with childlike innocence. Though her dress had been worn once before—the day she'd married Fred Ward—in the mirror it appeared as pristinely new as the day she'd bought it, and indeed, as she gazed at the seed pearls scattered across its bosom, and the perfect virtue expressed in its flowing expanse of pure white, its long sleeves and high neck, she had no memory of ever having seen it before.

A tiara of pearls held a veil to her head, and as she pulled the thin layer of tulle down over her face, Martha's image took on an ethereal, almost saintly

254

quality. Satisfied that all was in order, she turned at last away from the mirror and from vanity itself, knowing she would never look at her reflection again. Picking up the single object she would carry to the ceremony awaiting her, she left her bedroom, gently closing the door behind her.

Downstairs she paused outside the chapel, composed herself, then opened the door and let herself inside. The room was dark but for a single perfect light shining on the face of Christ, which seemed to float in the darkness above the altar. Genuflecting deeply, Martha moved slowly toward the altar, her eyes never leaving the face that hovered above her. Finally, when she was very close to the altar, she squeezed the object in her hands with trembling fingers.

A tongue of fire leaped from the dragon's mouth.

Holding tight to the gilded beast, she began to light the candles on the altar, moving steadily from one to another, uttering a silent prayer over each.

She prayed for her mother and her father.

For her elder sister, Marilyn, whose sins had taken her to an early death.

For Tommy Gardner, whom Satan had sent to tempt Marilyn.

For Margaret and Mick Morrison, the fruit of whose sin Martha herself had taken into her home.

The dragon's tongue touched candle after candle, for Martha knew well that Blackstone was filled with sinners, and on this night above all others, redemption must be begged for each of them.

When all the candles on the altar were glowing brightly, Martha turned to the saints in their alcoves, lighting a candle for each of them, that they might bear witness to the glory of this night.

Martha lit the candles in front of the Blessed Virgin, kneeling in front of the statue and praying that she might be found worthy of the saint's only son.

When all the prayers were said, Martha rose to her feet once more. She started once again toward the altar, hesitated, then realized there was one more thing she must do.

Going first to one of the windows, then the other, she drew back the heavy draperies, securing them carefully with the velvet ties that had hung unused for more than two decades. She opened the sheers as well, and though the rotted material tore to shreds in her fingers, she was unaware of anything but the glory of her surroundings, open at last to the world outside so that anyone who wished might watch and bear witness to her final salvation. As she returned to face the altar and her Savior this ultimate time, she was utterly unaware of the siren that had started to wail outside and the lights that were going on in her neighbors' homes as they rose from their beds to see what new tragedy might have befallen their town.

Dropping to her knees, Martha silently began the vows that would tie her to her Savior for all eternity.

Oliver Metcalf's Volvo pulled up to the curb in front of Martha Ward's house only seconds after the police car whose siren had already awakened the neighbors. As Rebecca tried to explain her aunt's strange behavior to Steve Driver, the occupants of the neighboring houses began to appear, some of them still clad in their nightclothes, others having pulled on overcoats, still others having hastily dressed. They clustered around Rebecca, whispering to each other as first one, then another, picked up a fragment of the peculiar tale she was relating. But even before she had finished, someone noticed the two windows that were glowing brightly in the otherwise darkened house.

Swept along with the gathering of neighbors, Rebecca and Oliver moved closer to the Hartwicks' driveway, their gazes following those of everyone else. Through the uncurtained windows they could clearly see Martha

Ward standing in her wedding dress in front of her altar, her veiled face tilted upward, her entire figure bathed in the golden glow of the flickering candles.

"What's she doing?" someone asked.

No one answered.

Her vows completed, Martha Ward knelt one last time. Her eyes still fixed on the face of the figure above the altar, her fingers tightened on the dragon's neck.

For the last time the dragon's flame came alive.

Martha Ward reached down and touched the reptile's tongue to the turpentine-soaked carpet. As the flames spread quickly around her, she cast the dragon from her hand and rose once more to her full height. Lifting the veil from her face, she felt herself filled with a rapturous exaltation. As the fire consumed her sins, she felt her spirit being uplifted, and she raised her arms in unutterable joy.

As the medieval voices of her beloved chants gave way to the crackling of the spreading flames, Martha Ward's soul rose to meet the destiny for which she had always prayed.

"Don't watch it," Oliver said. He drew Rebecca to him, pressing her face into his shoulder to shield her from the horror unfolding within the house.

A silence descended upon the crowd as they watched Martha Ward's last moments, a silence now broken by a gasp as flames suddenly rose around her. As the fire grew, some of the women began to sob and some of the men swore softly, but no one made any move to stop the fire, to put an end to the conflagration that was already spreading through the house, destroying everything in its path.

More sirens tore apart the night, but even when the volunteer engines arrived, their crews did nothing to quench the flames, but only stood by to protect the homes next door.

Within minutes the entire structure was engulfed, the heat enough to drive even the bravest to the opposite side of the street. Finally the entire structure collapsed in upon itself, and a tower of sparks rose into the night sky as if in some strange and macabre celebration.

A pile of smoldering rubble was all that remained of Martha Ward's house.

As dawn broke, Oliver watched in fascination while the crowd that had gathered in the night to watch the fire quickly dispersed, as if they felt exposed by the morning light and were embarrassed to have the morbidness of their curiosity further revealed.

The firemen were circling the wreckage of the house like a band of hunters warily inspecting fallen prey, knowing it was mortally wounded, but all too aware that it was still capable of inflicting damage upon anyone who ventured too close.

"Do you have anyplace to go?" Oliver finally asked Rebecca. She was next to him, her hand holding on to his arm, but her eyes still fixed on the blackened ruin that had been her home. For a long time she said nothing, and he was about to repeat the question when he heard a voice behind him.

"She'll come to live with me. It's what her aunt would have wanted."

Turning, Oliver saw Germaine Wagner standing a few feet away, a gray woolen overcoat buttoned up to her neck, a grayer scarf wrapped around her head.

Oliver turned back to Rebecca, whose wide, frightened eyes made it clear she had no idea what to do. "You can stay with me if you'd like," he said softly. "I have an extra room."

Rebecca glanced uncertainly at Germaine Wagner, then back to Oliver, but before she could say anything, the librarian spoke again.

"That's not a good idea, Oliver. You know as well as I do that it would cause talk." Her lips pursed disapprovingly. "The very idea—you and Rebecca? It's—" She hesitated, and Oliver wondered if she was going to finish her thought. But then her eyes fixed on his. "Well, you know what I mean, don't you? Surely I don't have to spell it out for you."

Just as they had in the library on the December day when he'd gone in to research the Asylum's history under Germaine's stern stare, the old memories now rushed back at him once again, memories of the people who used to glance at him out of the corner of their eye and whisper about him behind his back. If Rebecca came to live with him, would it all start up again?

Of course it would.

The only difference would be that this time the whispers would be about Rebecca instead of his sister.

For himself, it didn't really matter. But for Rebecca?

He wouldn't put her through it.

"No," he said at last, "you don't have to spell it out for me."

He watched in silence as Germaine Wagner led Rebecca toward her car, and wondered if she was also walking away from him forever. Sighing heavily, he realized that if Germaine had anything to do with it, she might very well be.

A few minutes later, as he too drove away from the wreckage of Martha Ward's house, Oliver realized that his head was starting to ache again.

This time, though, he was fairly sure he knew the reason why.

* * *

Enough rain had fallen on Blackstone in the weeks since Martha Ward had turned the tongue of the dragon upon herself that the smell of the fire had finally begun to be washed away, its acrid stench slowly replaced with the sweet aroma of the first flowers of spring. Behind the thick stone walls of the Asylum, though, the same stale, musty odor of mildew and mold that had permeated every hidden corner of the building for the last several decades still hung heavily in the air.

The dankness was of no concern to the dark figure that moved through the shadowed rooms, as oblivious to the still and moldering atmosphere within the walls as he was to the freshly vibrant breezes beyond.

He was in his museum once more, carefully—almost lovingly—pasting Oliver Metcalf's account of Martha Ward's last moments into the leather-bound ledger he had found two months ago. Satisfied with his work only when his latex-covered fingers had perfectly trimmed every edge and smoothed out every wrinkle, he read the story one more time, then put the cherished book aside.

Now, before the full moon began to fade, it was time to decide which of his treasures next to give away. His fingers moved over them slowly and sensuously, feeling the details his eyes could not discern in the dim light, until at last he came to the one he knew should next be sent to work its evil.

A handkerchief, woven from the finest linen, edged in the daintiest of lace, and perfectly embroidered with a single ornate initial.

An initial that would guide this cherished article to its target as surely as if it were an arrow shot from a bow.

To be continued . . .

PART 4
IN THE SHADOW OF EVIL:
THE
HANDKERCHIEF

Prelude

*O*nce again the time had come.

The moon, high in the early spring sky, silvered the long-concealed room with a glow that lent the objects within the quality of a bas relief. The dark figure, though, saw nothing this night save the handkerchief. Its soft folds hung gracefully from his surgically gloved fingers, its pale linen seeming to shine with a luminescence of its own. Nor was he aware that beyond the stone walls the winter's stillness was occasionally pierced by the first tentative mating calls of insects and frogs slowly emerging from their seasonal torpor; within the building's dark confines the silence of nearly half a century still reigned.

Enclosed in that silvery silence, the dark figure stroked the linen lovingly, and from the depths of his mind, a memory began to emerge. . . .

Prologue

*T*he *woman rose languorously from her bed, letting her fingers trail over the smoothness of the silk sheets and caress the softness of the cashmere blankets before she drifted across the room to gaze out the window. It was late in the afternoon. Below, two of her gardeners tended to the rosebushes she'd laid out last year, while another trimmed the low box hedge. Some of her guests were playing badminton on the broad lawn beyond the rose garden, and when one of them looked up, she waved gaily. For a moment she toyed with the idea of dressing and going out to join them, but then she changed her mind.*

Better to stay in her boudoir, resting and enjoying her privacy before tonight's festivities began.

What was it to be tonight?

A formal dinner, with dancing afterward?

Or a fancy-dress ball, with supper at midnight and a champagne breakfast served just after dawn?

She couldn't remember just now, but it didn't matter really, for one of her maids would remind her when it was time for her to dress for the evening.

Turning away from the window, she wafted back to the bed and stretched out once more, picking up the square of finest linen she'd been embroidering for several weeks now.

It was edged with lace, every stitch perfectly worked into a floral design so exquisitely wrought that she could almost smell the flowers' scent. In one corner she was working a single initial, an ornate R to signify the rank of the handkerchief's eventual recipient. Regina.

The queen would be pleased with her gift, and perhaps even summon her to court—a most pleasurable diversion, inasmuch as it had been months since she'd been away from her own country seat.

Spreading the handkerchief on her lap, she set about the final embroidery. Surrounding the R was another intricate pattern of flowers, these woven into the linen in the finest and palest of silk thread, lending the handkerchief a faint aura of color that was almost more illusion than reality. The stitching was so delicate that it seemed to emerge from the weave itself, and each side was as perfect as the other. Even the monogram had been mirrored so the handkerchief had no wrong side.

An hour later, as she worked the last thread into the design, then snipped its end away so deftly that it instantly disappeared into the pattern, she heard a sharp rap at the door, announcing the arrival of her maid. Setting the handkerchief aside, she drew her robe more tightly around her throat. "You may come in," she announced.

The door opened and the servant appeared, bearing a silver tray upon which she could see a plate covered by an ornately engraved silver dome.

An afternoon repast.

Which meant that tonight would be the fancy-dress ball. She must begin thinking about a costume.

"What have you brought me, Marie?" the woman asked. "A pâté perhaps? Some caviar?"

The nurse's hands tightened on the metal tray.

Pâté?

Caviar?

Not likely.

And not that it mattered either. Even if she'd brought half a pound of pâté de foie gras or a whole can of Beluga caviar, it wouldn't be good enough for this one! She hadn't eaten anything at all for a week. And how many times had she told the woman her name was Clara, not Marie? "It's spaghetti," *she said as she bent at the waist, intending to set the tray down on the woman's lap.* "With some nice salad with oranges, and a roll."

"Be careful!" *the woman ordered, her voice sharp.* "This robe was handmade for me, and if you stain it—"

"I know." *The nurse sighed, straightening again, the tray still in her hands.* "I'll be dismissed." *She eyed the rough terry-cloth robe the patient wore over her flannel nightgown, and wondered just what material the woman's delusions had created. Silk? Ermine? Who knew? Or cared?* "And if you spill it all over yourself, don't try to blame me. It won't be anybody's fault but your own."

The patient drew herself up, her eyes narrowing into slits of anger. "I will not be spoken to like—"

"You'll be spoken to any way I want," *the nurse interrupted.* "And if you're smart, you'll eat this."

Finally setting the metal tray on the patient's lap, she lifted the cover off the plate.

The silver dome lifted to reveal a tangle of worms writhing in a pool of blood, and a rat, its red eyes glaring balefully up at her. As she hurled the silver tray off her lap and flung it aside, the rat leaped away to scuttle across the floor, and the blood and worms cascaded down Marie's uniform. Feeling no sympathy at all for the servant who had subjected her to such torture, the woman reached out to slap the hapless girl, but to her utter astonishment, the maid caught her wrist, immobi-

lizing it in a grip so strong the woman was suddenly ter-rified her bones might break.

"How dare—" she began, but the maid cut in without letting her finish.

"Don't 'how dare' me, Miss High-and-Mighty! I've had just about enough of your acting like I'm your ser-vant. Look what you've done to my uniform! How would you like it if these were your clothes?"

Rendered speechless by the impertinence, the woman watched as the maid dropped her wrist, then reached out and snatched up the handkerchief she'd finished embroi-dering only a few minutes ago. As the woman looked on in horror from her bed, the servant pressed the fine linen square to her chest, using it to soak up the blood on her uniform.

"Stop that!" she demanded. "Stop that this instant! You'll ruin it!"

The nurse glowered furiously at the patient as she wiped away the mess of spaghetti and tomato sauce that was still dripping down her brand new uniform. She'd bought it only last week and was wearing it for the first time that day. "You think you can get away with anything, don't you?" she asked. "Well, you're about to find out who runs this place, and it isn't you." Leaving the patient cowering in her bed, the nurse strode out of the room, returning a few moments later with an orderly and a doctor. While the orderly mopped the splatter of spa-ghetti off the linoleum floor, the nurse recounted the inci-dent to the doctor. "I suppose if she won't eat, it's really none of my business," she finished. "But I don't have to stand for her throwing her food at me."

The doctor, whose eyes had been fixed on the patient throughout the nurse's recitation, smiled thinly. "No," he agreed, "you certainly don't. And it's certainly time she began eating too, don't you think?"

For a moment the nurse said nothing, but then, as she realized what the doctor was saying, she smiled for the first time since entering the room a few minutes earlier. "Yes," she said, "I certainly do!"

With the aid of two more orderlies, the doctor and the nurse secured the struggling patient to her bed with thick nylon straps. When the woman was totally immobilized, the doctor instructed the aides to hold the patient's mouth open.

As the woman moaned and struggled, then began to gag, the doctor inserted a thick plastic feeding tube through her mouth, down her throat, and into her stomach.

"There," he said. "That should do it."

Before he left the nurse to begin feeding the immobilized patient, he stooped down and picked up the soiled handkerchief from the floor. Holding it gingerly between his thumb and forefinger, he gazed at the elaborately embroidered initial and the perfectly worked lace. "Interesting," he said, more to himself than to the nurse. "I wonder who she thought she was making it for." Crushing the handkerchief into a shapeless mass, he stuffed it into the pocket of his white coat and left the room.

The woman in the bed tried to cry out, tried to beg him not to take away the beautiful handkerchief she'd spent so many weeks making, but the tube in her throat turned her plea into nothing more than an incomprehensible moan.

She never saw the handkerchief again.

A month later, when she was finally released from the bonds that held her to the bed, she waited until she was alone, then used the belt of her terry-cloth robe to hang herself from the clothes hook on the back of her door.

*   *   *

Still gazing at the handkerchief, the dark figure let his finger trace the perfectly embroidered R that had been worked into one of its corners.

The letter itself told him who its recipient must be.

All he regretted was that he couldn't deliver it personally. Still, he knew how to guide the handkerchief to its destination, and who its bearer would be. . . .

Chapter 1

Oliver Metcalf had spring fever. There simply wasn't any other way to describe it. The first symptoms had appeared early that morning, when he found himself lingering in his kitchen over an extra cup of coffee while he watched a pair of robins begin their courtship. It was the first morning that was warm enough to open the window, and the air was redolent with the musky smell of leaves that had been slowly decomposing under the winter's finally vanished blanket of snow. Inhaling the scent of spring, he felt the first faint urge to take the day off. He ignored the urge, of course, since today was Tuesday, the deadline for putting this week's edition of the *Chronicle* to bed, but the seductive sense of lassitude that had come over him as the birds' songs drifted into his kitchen only increased a few minutes later as he set out down Harvard Street toward the village at the foot of North Hill. His pace, which he'd fully intended to keep aerobically brisk, had slowed to a leisurely stroll, and he kept pausing to admire the crocuses that were blooming everywhere, and the daffodil shoots that seemed to have shot up at least six inches just since yesterday.

By the time he came to Main Street, a stop at the Red Hen had seemed utterly imperative, and this morning's fifteen minutes of gossip disguised as "networking" had somehow managed to stretch out to half an hour. Even then, Bill McGuire and Ed Becker were still at the counter when he left, postponing the start of their workday under the guise of a serious conversation regarding the financing for Blackstone Center and when it might finally come through. That Melissa Holloway, who had officially been appointed permanent president of the bank at the last meeting of its board of directors, had told them they could count on no approvals any earlier than June seemed to cut no ice with Bill and Ed. But then, it was that kind of morning: today everyone seemed to prefer speculation over actual labor. When Oliver finally arrived at the *Chronicle*, it was more of the same.

"Everyone wants to know when you're going to run a story about what's been going on," Lois Martin said as he opened the office door. "I just got another call—this time from Edna Burnham. She says everyone in town is talking, and it's up to you to stop it."

The temperature of Oliver's pleasant springtime mood notched down to a wintry chill. He knew perfectly well what Lois was talking about: a day hadn't gone by in the month since Martha Ward had burned her own house to the ground and perished in the flames that someone hadn't called the paper demanding to know what—exactly—the connection was between the suicides of Elizabeth McGuire, Jules Hartwick, and Martha Ward. As far as Oliver could see, there was no connection at all.

A few odd coincidences, perhaps, but nothing more than that.

It was Edna's contention, Oliver knew, that there was ominous significance in the fact that all three of the suicides had occurred shortly after a full moon. But the term *lunacy* had been around in one form or another for millennia, and given that all three of Blackstone's tragic victims had been under one form of stress or another, Oliver wasn't willing to call the full moon a causative factor for any of them. A trigger, possibly, but certainly no more.

Still, if Edna Burnham was demanding answers, it meant the talk was starting to get even more serious than Oliver had thought.

"Does she have a new theory, or is she just upset?" he asked.

Lois Martin hesitated before answering his question, and when she did, her eyes didn't quite meet Oliver's. "She's wondering if it might not all go back to the Asylum somehow."

"The Asylum," Oliver repeated. "And did she say what put that idea in her mind?"

Lois's eyes finally met his. "A few things, actually," she said, picking up a pad on which she'd scribbled some notes when old Mrs. Burnham had called. The phone had been ringing off the hook when Lois arrived that morning. "First off," Lois told him, "there's the anonymous gifts. Edna claims to have heard whisperings about weird things that turned up, first at the McGuires', then at Jules's house and at Martha's. She says no one knows where they came from."

A look of disbelief came over Oliver's face. "Come on! What kind of things?"

"Well, Bill McGuire was talking about a doll that showed up in the mail a few days before Elizabeth killed herself, and Rebecca told her about a gold cigarette lighter—"

"I know where that came from," Oliver told her. "No mystery there. Rebecca and I found it at the flea market."

"I know, I know." She held up a hand to stop his protests. "Edna's been doing some sleuthing of her own. She's been over at the library, chatting with Rebecca. And it seems she asked Janice Anderson where she got it, and Janice has no memory of ever having seen that lighter before the morning Rebecca bought it."

Oliver groaned. "I suspect Janice can't remember where she got half the merchandise in her store," he said. "And the stuff she was selling at the flea market was just junk. Besides, what about Jules Hartwick? What mysterious item supposedly showed up there?"

"There was a locket," Lois replied. "Celeste found it on the lawn after the snow melted."

"Which means that anyone could have dropped it some-time between December and three weeks ago, when Celeste and Madeline got back from Boston," Oliver pointed out. "I would hardly call that conclusive evidence of anything."

"Hey, don't shoot the messenger," Lois protested. "I'm just reporting what Edna Burnham said."

"She *said* a great deal," Oliver remarked dryly. "But what actually is she getting at? Does she think there's some kind of curse on these things?"

Lois Martin shrugged elaborately. "You said it, not me." She hesitated, but then decided she might as well tell him everything Edna had said. "She also said some-thing about Rebecca having seen someone at the Hartwicks' the night of the party—presumably the someone who left the locket, I suppose. Furthermore, Edna maintains that each and every one of the families who received these objects has some connection to the Asylum. Or at least did have, back when it was open."

"Aha!" Oliver said, as if Lois had finally delivered incontrovertible proof of the ludicrous nature of Edna Burnham's speculations. "Find me a family in Black-stone that *didn't*." Oliver's eyes glittered with challenge. "The Asylum was the mainstay of the economy around here for years. Everyone in town had a relative working there, and half of them had relatives who were *in* the place, for God's sake!"

Lois held up her hands as if to fend off his words. "Hey, I'm not the one you have to convince. It's Edna—" She paused, then grinned with malicious enjoyment. "—and the hundred or so other people she's probably convinced by now."

"Oh, Lord." Oliver groaned again. "What am I sup-posed to do? Write an article about some ancient evil that's suddenly come forth from the Asylum to wreak havoc on us all?"

"Hey, that's not bad," Lois deadpanned. "I can see the headline now: 'Beware the Blackstone Curse.'"

"How about this one instead," Oliver shot back. " 'Beware the Unemployed Assistant Editor.' "

He was smiling as he turned and headed toward the rear of the building to the renovated office that Bill McGuire had finally finished last week. He busied himself readying the paper for the press, but try as he did to put Edna Burnham's outrageous theory out of his thoughts, Oliver found himself coming back to it over and over again. As the day wore on, and Edna's speculations kept popping unbidden back into his mind, he knew the idea must be churning around other minds in Blackstone as well.

Finally, shortly after noon, with this week's *Chronicle* put to bed but his thoughts still restless, he gave up. "I'm going home," he told Lois. "I might even go up to the Asylum and take a look around." He managed a grin he didn't quite feel. "Who knows? Maybe I'll even find something that will prove Edna's right."

"Better if you can find something that proves she's wrong," Lois replied.

"More likely, I won't find anything at all."

Leaving the office, he thought about stopping into the library to see Rebecca Morrison, then remembered the dark glares he'd received from Germaine Wagner the last few times he'd turned up during working hours. Better to come back at closing time, when Germaine might not approve but at least would have no reason to object if Rebecca chose to let him walk her home.

Walk her home? He sounded like a high school kid. Obviously, the spring fever was back!

As he started up North Hill, Oliver found himself eyeing a few crocuses he might just steal for Rebecca later on in the afternoon. But then, when he came to the gates of the Asylum and stopped to look directly at the building, his good mood vanished.

Just the idea of entering the deserted building was enough to make his stomach cramp, and it wasn't until he had turned away from the Asylum, walked back down the hill and entered his own house that the knot of pain in his belly began to ease. But his restlessness would not be tamed. He paced the living room, wandered into the kitchen, then back, feeling as though he needed to look for something—something that eluded him.

Almost unconsciously, his eyes moved to the ceiling.

Upstairs?

What was there to search for upstairs? There were only the three bedrooms and the bathroom. Nothing unusual to be discovered there.

Still, he found himself mounting the stairs, entering each room and pulling open the doors of the closets in all three bedrooms, looking for . . . what?

He'd been through these closets dozens of times—maybe hundreds—and knew exactly what was in each of them. Old clothes he hadn't wanted to throw away, boxes of Christmas decorations, his luggage. But nothing from the Asylum.

Still, he searched each one a second time, then started back toward the top of the stairs, where he paused and found himself looking up once more.

The attic?

He couldn't remember the last time he'd been up there. But as he regarded the old-fashioned, spring-loaded, pull-down ladder, it occurred to him that if there really were any old records around, they might just be up in the attic. Even if his own father hadn't stored anything up there, some of the earlier superintendents might have.

Getting the step stool from the kitchen, he reached up and jerked the ladder down. The motion sent a shiver through his spine as the old springs squealed and groaned. With a flashlight in hand, he mounted the stairs, opened the trapdoor that was the attic's only access, and climbed up into the space beneath the house's steeply pitched roof.

An old-fashioned push-button light switch was mounted on a support post. When he pressed it, a bare bulb sputtered on, filling the area with a yellowish glow.

No more than five feet away was an oak filing cabinet and two old wooden fruit crates, faded, curling labels barely clinging to their sides. Opening the top drawer of the filing cabinet, he found a stack of leather-bound ledgers, each of them containing a full year of the Asylum's bookkeeping, the entries noted in the kind of precise accountant's handwriting that has all but disappeared since the advent of the computer.

The second drawer contained more of the same, and so did the fourth. The third drawer, either jammed or locked, wouldn't budge.

He shifted his attention to the crates, testing the top of the first one. Free of nails, its surface was slightly warped and took no effort at all to lift away.

Inside the box were two stacks of file folders.

And something else.

Neatly folded on top of one of the stacks was a piece of cloth. Picking it up, Oliver gingerly unfolded it, then took it over to hold it under the light.

It was a handkerchief made of linen, and though he wasn't an expert, it looked as though the lace around its edges was handmade. In addition to the delicate lace edging, a pattern of flowers in colors so pale he could hardly discern them had been embroidered into the material, forming an intricate wreath all around the handkerchief's perimeter and spreading out to encircle an ornate symbol that had been worked into one corner. For a moment Oliver wasn't sure what the symbol was, but then, when he turned the handkerchief over and discovered that the other side was as flawlessly embroidered as the first, he understood.

The symbol was actually two R's worked carefully back to back, so that each side of the monogrammed handkerchief would be exactly the same.

No right side.

No wrong side.

Refolding the handkerchief, he put it back into the

crate, then hefted the wooden box itself and carefully inched his way down the ladder. After going back for the second crate, he closed the trapdoor, folded the ladder back up against the ceiling, then took the boxes into one of the spare bedrooms and began unpacking their contents onto the bed. Just as he'd hoped, they turned out to be old patient files.

For the rest of the afternoon, his fascination growing as he read, Oliver pored over the old files, marveling not only at the strange diagnoses that had been made in the early days of the Asylum but at the cruel treatments that were prescribed.

Bed restraints had been commonplace.

Straitjackets had been ordinary.

Even detailed accounts of ice-water baths and prefrontal lobotomies were recorded with no more emotion than might have been used in lab reports describing the dissection of an insect or the interaction between two chemicals.

His revulsion growing with every page he read, Oliver slowly began to understand his horror of the Asylum, even after all the years that had gone by since it was closed down.

A torture chamber.

That was what it had been. A place of unspeakable sadness and pain.

Even now he could imagine the screams that must have echoed inside the building.

Screams, he suddenly realized, that he surely would have heard when he was a child, living here, in the superintendent's cottage, no more than fifty yards away. Yet he had no memory of them.

But shouldn't he have heard the agonized howls that would have clawed through his open windows on summer nights, ripping into his dreams, turning them into nightmares?

The answer came to him as quickly as had the question: the records he had found were far older than he, Oliver realized, and when his father had taken over the Asylum, the inhumanity must have ended.

The solution brought no satisfaction, however. For if the horrors that had taken place within the Asylum's walls had truly ended when his father became superintendent, then why couldn't he bring himself to go into the building?

Other memories! There must be other memories, too horrible for him to face!

Suddenly unwilling to delve any deeper into the files, Oliver replaced them carefully in the crate. As he did so, he spotted the handkerchief again and picked it up, marveling anew at the perfection of the work, and wondering who had sewn it. Most likely not a patient—such delicate work required skill and concentration hard to imagine in someone mentally disturbed.

Surely, he thought, it must have been made by one of the staff members, filling the endless empty hours of the night shifts.

He held its soft fabric in his fingers, and once more his eye fell on the double-sided R that had been worked so cleverly into one corner.

Instantly he knew what he would do with the handkerchief.

As he found some paper with which to wrap his gift, Oliver imagined the look of delight on the recipient's face as she opened it.

Even if old Edna Burnham was right, he thought, and the gifts that had apparently come from nowhere to the homes of Elizabeth McGuire and Jules Hartwick and Martha Ward had brought with them some kind of evil, there could be no doubt where *this* gift had come from.

It had come from his own attic, where it had been stored for more years than he could remember.

And Rebecca would love it.

Chapter 2

"*R*ebecca? *Rebecca!* I want you!"

Rebecca Morrison cringed as the querulous voice ricocheted from the floor above, immediately followed by the hollow thumping of a rubber-tipped cane pounding against bare hardwood planks. She had come home from the library early today, sent by Germaine to clean out the cupboards under the sink. She wasn't certain exactly why this chore had to be accomplished today, since it didn't look to her as if anyone had cleaned anything out from under the kitchen sink for at least twenty years, but it was what Germaine wanted her to do, and she knew she owed Germaine a very great deal. Germaine, after all, had explained it to her the day after the fire that had destroyed her aunt's home.

"I hope you understand what a sacrifice Mother and I are making," Germaine had said. She was perched on the edge of the single straight-backed chair that, save for the bed, was the only place to sit in the small attic room that Rebecca had been given. "Except for the cleaning girl, Mother isn't used to having anyone but me in the house. However, if you're very quiet, she might get used to you. We'll have to let the cleaning girl go, of course, but with your extra hands to help us out, I don't think we'll miss her too much, will we?"

Rebecca shook her head, as she knew she was expected to do, and when she spoke, it was in the hushed tone she'd learned to use in the library. "I'll be careful not to disturb Mrs. Wagner at all," she said.

"You mustn't call Mother 'Mrs. Wagner,' " Germaine had instructed her. "After all, you're not the cleaning girl, are you? I think if you call her Miss Clara, that will be fine." Rebecca thought calling a widow who was nearly eighty "Miss" was a little strange, but after having worked for Germaine at the library, she knew better than to argue with her. "We'll be just like a little family, taking care of each other," Germaine said with a sigh of satisfaction, and for a moment Rebecca thought the woman might just reach out and pat her on the knee. Instead, she rose from the chair and, in the tone of a grande dame, added, "It isn't everyone who would have taken you in, Rebecca. You should be very grateful to Mother for allowing you to live here."

"Oh, I am," Rebecca quickly assured her. "And I really like this room, Germaine. I mean, what would I put in the dressers and closets in all the big bedrooms downstairs?"

For some reason, her words seemed to make Germaine angry; Rebecca saw her lips tighten into the thin line she used to silence rowdy children in the library, but then she'd turned and left.

Left alone, Rebecca had unpacked her few belongings. All her clothes and possessions had perished in the fire, but she'd purchased some necessary items, and Bonnie Becker, Ed's wife, had brought over some clothing that morning. ("I won't hear of your refusing me," Bonnie had said to her. "These things are almost brand new and they just don't fit. They'll be absolutely perfect on you.") After Rebecca hung up the four blouses, one skirt, and two pairs of jeans, and stowed the meager supply of underwear in the tiny pine chest that squatted beneath the one dormer window in the attic room, she started back downstairs. Clara Wagner's shrill voice stopped her just as she was passing the old woman's open door on the second floor, near the foot of the stairs leading to the attic.

"You will bring me a pot of coffee every morning," the old woman had instructed her from the wheelchair in which she was sitting. "Not so hot it will burn my tongue, but not cold either. Do you understand?"

For the next two weeks, Rebecca had done her best, and finally got it right. But more often than not, satisfying Miss Clara's exacting tastes meant running up and down the stairs at least three times every morning before she and Germaine were finally able to leave for work at the library. During the evenings, and on her days off from the library, she'd been busy catching up on all the housework the cleaning girl never seemed to have gotten around to doing.

Now, her unsuccessful attempt to scrub away the cupboard stains was interrupted by Clara Wagner's voice piercing through the vast reaches of the house. Rebecca stood up, stretched her aching back, and let the rag she'd been using drop back into the sink, which was filled with a mixture of hot water, detergent, and bleach.

Leaving the kitchen, she made her way through the walnut-paneled dining room, then into the immense foyer. The pride of the house, the entry hall rose a majestic three stories, crowned by an immense stained-glass skylight set in the roof above, its sunburst pattern filling the huge space with a rainbow of color. On the second-floor level, a broad mezzanine circled the foyer. At the end of the hall opposite the double front doors rose a sweeping staircase that split halfway up, branching in both directions. Sometime after the house had been built, an elevator had been installed on the left side of the foyer, directly opposite the marble-manteled fireplace that dominated the right side. Rebecca had been cautioned that she was never to use the elevator; it was only to be used by Clara Wagner on her infrequent forays to the first floor of her house. Rebecca caught herself holding her breath every time the old lady pushed the button that set the machinery, hidden somewhere in the attic, to grinding ominously as the ornate brass cage rattled slowly from the first floor to the second, or back down. Someday, Rebecca was certain, the ancient contraption was going to break down. She only hoped that Clara Wagner wasn't in the cage when it happened.

As Rebecca mounted the long flight of stairs, the old woman's cane struck the floor twice more. "Rebecca!"

"I'm coming, Miss Clara," she called. "I'll be there in just a second!" Reaching the second floor, she hurried down the long mezzanine toward the room next to the attic stairs.

"Must you shout?" Clara Wagner demanded as Rebecca stepped through her open door. "I'm not deaf, you know!"

"I'm sorry, Miss Clara," Rebecca apologized. "I was in the kitchen trying to—"

"Do you think I care what you were doing?" Clara demanded. Her wheelchair was drawn up close to the room's fireplace, in which a few embers were glowing brightly. With one clawlike hand she pulled her shawl tighter around her thin shoulders, while she used the other to jab her cane toward a glass that sat on a table no more than two feet away.

"Hand me that glass," she said. "And put some more wood on the fire. It's freezing in here."

"Would you like me to turn the heat up?" Rebecca offered.

Clara glared at her. "Do you have any idea what oil costs these days? No, of course you don't! Why would you? You always had your aunt to take care of you, didn't you?"

"Heating oil costs a dollar a gallon," Rebecca offered.

"Don't you dare mock me, Rebecca Morrison!" the old woman snapped. "You might get away with it with my fool of a daughter, but I won't tolerate it. As long as you're living under my roof, you'll keep a civil tongue in your head!"

Rebecca's face burned with shame. "I'm so sorry, Miss Clara," she began. "I didn't mean to—"

Clara jabbed her sharply with the cane. "Don't tell me what you meant and what you didn't mean! Now, what are you waiting for? Hand me that glass, and do something about that fire. And mind you, don't leave the door open when you bring the wood in! I hate a draft as much as I hate laziness," she added, glaring pointedly at Rebecca.

Rebecca handed her the glass from the table, then hurried out of the room and downstairs. The woodpile was back behind the garage; Germaine had forbidden her to move any of the firewood closer to the laundry room door, where it would have been much handier. "The woodpile has always been behind the garage, Rebecca," Germaine had explained. "And that is where it will stay. Mother doesn't like to see things out of their usual place."

Rebecca, though, was fairly sure that Clara Wagner hadn't been anywhere near the laundry room in years. Except for her brief public appearance at Elizabeth McGuire's funeral, Rebecca doubted the old woman had even been outside the house in years. Well, she certainly wasn't going to argue with either of the women who had been kind enough to take her into their own home. Picking up the leather sling that was the only thing Germaine allowed her to carry wood in, she went out to the backyard, stacked five pieces of wood into the carrier, and returned to Clara's room.

"That's hardly enough to keep me warm for the evening," the old woman observed tartly as Rebecca piled three of the logs onto the fire, then used a bellows to fan the embers back to life.

"I'll bring more later on," Rebecca promised. Glancing at the clock, she saw that it was nearly five. "Right now I have to finish in the kitchen. Germaine wanted the cupboard under the sink clean before she came home today."

"Then I suggest you don't waste any more time chattering," Clara told her. "And I shall have tea this afternoon. In the front parlor. Have it ready at six. And I don't mean ready in the kitchen at six, Rebecca. Have it in the *parlor* at six!"

"Yes, Miss Clara," Rebecca replied, scurrying out of the room.

As she returned to the kitchen, she wondered—not for the first time—if perhaps she'd made a mistake moving in here. But where else could she go? Oliver had offered to take her in—he was so sweet—but Germaine made it clear that such an improper arrangement simply would not do. Even now Rebecca could remember Germaine's words as she'd brought her into the house the night of the fire.

"There aren't many people who would do this for you, Rebecca. So I suggest you make everything as easy for Mother and me as you possibly can."

Since then, Rebecca had been laboring to please Germaine and her mother, and she would continue to. But sometimes it seemed that no matter what she did, it was never quite enough.

As she lowered herself back down to her hands and knees, determined to go after the stain under the sink and vanquish it, Rebecca chastised herself for her ingratitude.

She would just have to try a little harder to please Miss Clara, and everything would be all right.

They would be just like a little family—just the way Germaine had said.

Oliver's timing was almost perfect: he'd added fifteen extra minutes to his estimate of the time it would take him to stroll along the path through the woods to the top of Harvard Street, then down to Main and over to the library. Ten minutes had been added in response to his spring fever, which had noticeably worsened as the weather improved throughout the afternoon. He'd tacked on another five to account for a few minutes to survey again the ruins of Martha Ward's house: he was still trying to fathom the twists of psychosis that had led to that strange night a month ago when Martha had burned the place down around herself while she prayed in the flickering light of her votive candles, surrounded by her beloved religious icons. The fire chief determined that the blaze had been deliberate, but no one had yet found any trace of the dragon-shaped cigarette lighter, although Rebecca guessed that they'd find it in the ashes that were all that remained of her aunt's chapel. While he'd said nothing to Rebecca, Oliver privately suspected that someone—perhaps one of the volunteer firemen—had indeed found it, and simply pocketed it as a macabre souvenir of that terrible night. Still, after circling the blackened pit where the house had once stood, he'd poked among the ashes for a minute or so on the off chance that he might stumble upon it.

He hadn't.

Now, at precisely five minutes before the library was due to close, he jogged up the steps and pushed through the double set of doors. As usual, Germaine Wagner glanced up as Oliver entered her domain; also as usual, her expression hardened into a thin-lipped grimace as she recognized him. Since Rebecca had moved into the Wagners' house, Oliver had decided, Germaine's disapproval of him had grown stronger than ever. When a quick glance around didn't reveal Rebecca, he forced himself to give Germaine a friendly smile and approached the counter.

"Is Rebecca around?" he asked, hoping to seem casual, though he did not feel at all nonchalant.

"No," Germaine replied. For a moment there was an impasse as the editor and the librarian gazed at each other, neither of them willing to impart any more information than absolutely necessary.

Oliver broke first. "She isn't sick, is she? Did she come to work?"

Germaine Wagner seemed to weigh the possibility of getting him to leave without pressing her with endless questions but quickly decided the chances were close to nil. "Rebecca's fine," she reported. "She simply left early today. There were some chores at home she needed to complete."

Needed to complete? She made it sound as though Rebecca was late with her homework, Oliver thought. He wondered if Germaine used the same patronizing tone when she talked directly to Rebecca as she invariably did when she talked *about* her, and whether it annoyed Rebecca as much as it did him. But of course it wouldn't—it was exactly the sort of trait Rebecca always managed not to notice in people, let alone find offensive.

Not for the first time, Oliver reflected that if Martha Ward had really been as interested in saints as she claimed to be, she should have been able to recognize that she had one living in her own house. Martha Ward, though, had been just as condescending to Rebecca as Germaine Wagner was.

"Well, maybe I'll just stop over and say hello," he said, deliberately keeping his gaze steadily on Germaine, waiting to see if she would object. This time it was she who broke, turning brusquely back to her work, but gripping her pencil so hard Oliver could see her knuckles turning white.

As he left the library, Oliver wondered once again exactly what Germaine Wagner's problem really was. Was it him? Rebecca? Both of them? But as he emerged back into the warmth of the late afternoon, he decided he didn't really care—it was far too nice an April day to waste much energy on worrying about Germaine Wagner.

Walking up Princeton Street, he crossed Maple, then turned right on Elm. It was just a few minutes after five o'clock when he raised the knocker on the front door of Clara Wagner's house. Rapping it twice, he waited a moment, then pressed the button next to the door. Before the chimes had quite died away, Rebecca opened the door. The questioning look in her eyes as she pulled the door open instantly gave way to a warm smile. The smile disappeared as quickly as it had come, as Clara Wagner's voice called down from above.

"Rebecca? Who is it? Who's at the door?"

Rebecca glanced anxiously over her shoulder. As she hesitated, it occurred to Oliver that she was going to close the door in his face. But then she opened it farther, quickly pulled him inside, and, maneuvering around him, shut the door.

"It's Oliver, Miss Clara," she called to the upper reaches of the house. "Oliver Metcalf!"

Oliver stepped farther into the foyer. From this vantage point he could see Germaine's mother. Sitting in her wheelchair, a shawl clutched tightly around her shoulders, she was glaring down from the mezzanine.

"What does he want? And don't shout, Rebecca. I'm not deaf, you know!"

"Hello, Mrs. Wagner," Oliver said, nodding to her. "Isn't it a lovely day?"

It was as if he hadn't spoken. "I'm going to need more firewood, Rebecca," Clara Wagner said. "My room is no warmer than it was an hour ago!" Turning her chair away from the balustrade, she wheeled herself back into her room. Oliver and Rebecca heard her door close with an angry thud.

"Is she always that charming?" Oliver asked.

Rebecca's eyes clouded slightly. "She's old, and she doesn't get out very much, and—"

"And she can still be polite," Oliver cut in, but as Rebecca flinched at his words, he wished he could take

them back. "I'm sorry," he said. "I know you're right."
He grinned lopsidedly. "I guess I'm just not quite as nice
as you are, am I?"

"Oh, no!" Rebecca protested. "You're very nice! It's
just—well, she and Germaine have been so good to me,
and she really *is* very old, and—"

Oliver put his forefinger gently to Rebecca's lips.
"Enough," he said softly. Then: "I went by the library. I
was going to walk you home and try to convince you that
you ought to let me take you out for dinner tonight. We
could go to the Red Hen, or even drive up to Manchester,
or—" Feeling flustered, he broke off, then spoke again.
"Maybe I better find out if you want to go at all."

Now it was Rebecca who seemed flustered. Involuntarily, she glanced up at the gallery where Clara Wagner
had been only a moment ago, then back toward the
kitchen. "I don't know," she fretted. "I've got so much
to do."

"I can bring the firewood in," Oliver told her, breaking
in again before she could totally refuse his invitation.
"And you can let whatever else you were doing wait."

Now Rebecca looked utterly at a loss. "I'd love to go,
Oliver, but Germaine wanted me to get the stain out
of . . ." Again her words died away, this time because a
car had pulled into the driveway. As they heard its door
slam shut, Oliver took her hands in his own.

"Rebecca, you can go out to dinner with me if you
want to. Germaine and Clara don't own you. I know you
feel grateful to them for giving you a place to live, but
that doesn't mean you can't have a life of your own."

Before Rebecca could reply, the front door opened and
Germaine Wagner came in. Though Oliver was almost
certain he saw a flash of anger in her eyes, it disappeared
so quickly he couldn't quite be sure it had been there at
all. One thing he did know: the smile on her lips was far
less genuine than she obviously intended it to appear.

"Isn't this nice," Germaine said. "You have a gentleman

caller!" She turned to Oliver. "Like in *The Glass Menagerie*."

Oliver glanced at Rebecca, who appeared to wish she could disappear through the floor. "I just came by to ask Rebecca if she'd like to have dinner with me," he said.

Germaine's eyes darted toward Rebecca, then shifted back to Oliver. "And what did she say?"

"She hasn't said anything yet," Oliver replied. Then, knowing that if he stayed in the house much longer he would say something he'd regret, he opened the front door. "Why don't I wait for you outside?" he told Rebecca. "Even if you decide not to have dinner with me, at least we can take a walk."

As he closed the door, he could already hear Germaine starting to lecture Rebecca. When Rebecca came outside several minutes later, he could not only read her decision on her face but see her unhappiness as well.

"I really can't go with you, Oliver," she said. "There's so much I have to do, and I promised Miss Clara I'd make tea for her." She peered anxiously at him. "You understand, don't you?"

For a second Oliver was tempted to argue with her, then just as quickly he realized that his words wouldn't change her mind, but would only upset her more. "Of course I understand," he said. Reaching into his pocket, he pulled out the package he'd wrapped for her. "I brought you this," he said. "I found it in my attic today, and—well, you'll understand when you see what it is."

Her expression instantly clearing, Rebecca carefully removed the wrapping paper from the package, then opened the box Oliver had found for the handkerchief. As she lifted it out, her eyes widened in a gaze of delight at the delicate lace and embroidery. "Oh, Oliver, it's beautiful," she breathed. Her finger traced the mirrored R emblazoned in one corner. "And it has my initial! I've never had anything with my initial on it before."

"Then from now on, finding you presents is going to

be easy," Oliver replied. "All I have to do is look for R's." Leaning over, he kissed her quickly on the cheek, then started down the steps. "Promise me you'll have dinner with me one night next week?"

Rebecca hesitated, then smiled. "I promise," she said. "And I won't change my mind either. I'll just do it."

"Is he gone?" Germaine asked as Rebecca came back into the house.

Rebecca nodded. "I told him I'd go out with him next week," she said. "And look! He gave me a present!"

Germaine took the handkerchief from Rebecca. She could see at a glance that although it was spotless and carefully pressed, it was very old. As she examined both the lace and the embroidery, she realized something else: not only was the work flawless, but it had all been done by hand. "It's beautiful," she pronounced, bringing a happy smile to Rebecca's face. Then she smiled herself. "Mother will love it."

Rebecca's pleasure at Germaine's compliment for the handkerchief instantly collapsed. "Your mother? But Oliver gave it to me."

Germaine clucked her tongue as if chiding a child who was being deliberately dense. "But what would you do with it? You'd only lose it, or ruin it. A work of fine craftsmanship like this should be enjoyed by someone who can truly appreciate it. And I can't think of anyone better than Mother." She paused a moment, then: "Can you?"

Rebecca hesitated; she reminded herself of how kind Germaine and Clara Wagner had been to her. "No," she said at last. "I'm sure she'll love it as much as I did."

As Germaine started up the stairs to present the beautiful handkerchief to her mother, Rebecca returned to the back of the house. First she would bring in the firewood, then she'd fix tea for Miss Clara.

And she would console herself with the memory of the look on Oliver's face when he gave her the present she didn't get to keep.

Germaine paused outside the door to her mother's room, girding herself to face the woman whose only goal in life appeared to be to make her daughter's life as miserable as her own. How long had it been since her mother had announced one morning that she could no longer walk? Fifteen years? Closer to twenty, Germaine suspected, though she'd long ago given up keeping track. After all, what was the point? Nothing was ever going to change until her mother had passed to her heavenly reward, and Clara Wagner was showing no signs of joining her Maker anytime in the near future.

Germaine had always suspected that nothing was wrong with her mother when Clara suddenly announced her status as an invalid; indeed, none of the many specialists Germaine had taken her mother to had been able to find any physiological cause for the woman's paralysis. But Clara had insisted she could no longer move her legs, and by now it was undoubtedly true. Certainly her mother had grown smaller over the years, her whole skeleton seeming to shrink as her body adapted to the cramped contours of the wheelchair. Her muscles had quickly atrophied from lack of exercise, her legs turning into useless sticks. The pounds had dropped from her once stocky frame, and Germaine was sure she no longer weighed even a hundred pounds. Her eyes had sunk deep into their sockets, and her skin hung in wrinkled folds from her cheeks and arms. But the strength of Clara's voice had never failed her over the years, nor had her will to dominate everything—and everyone—around her.

Most of all, Germaine.

The years had ground slowly by as Germaine waited on her invalid mother. She prepared her meals and kept her bathed. At first, when she'd still believed that Clara would either recover or quickly die, she tried to keep her entertained as well. She'd gotten her to movies and concerts, even taken her on trips. But it had never been good enough. There was something wrong with everything they did and every place they went. After a while, when it became clear that Clara was neither on the verge of recovery nor hovering on the doorstep of death, Germaine had given up. It was no longer worth the effort to try to cajole and plead and lift and push her mother into activities that Clara showed no sign of appreciating. Her father had left just enough money to keep up the house, and Germaine's paycheck, while not generous, yielded just enough for her to hire a part-time cleaning girl, giving her at least a partial respite from her mother's complaints each day.

But every day when Germaine came home from the library, Clara demanded to know what she had brought her, like a spoiled child asking for candy.

Well, today she had something to offer, even if it was only the little gift that Oliver Metcalf had given to Rebecca.

She would have to do something about that situation. When the idea of inviting Rebecca to live with her had come to her in a flash of inspiration as she watched Martha Ward's house burn to the ground, it hadn't occurred to her that Oliver Metcalf might be a problem. Indeed, it had seemed to Germaine that Rebecca would be the perfect solution for her. She would take Rebecca in, and a grateful Rebecca could take over not only the duties of the cleaning girl—thus allowing her to save a dollar or two—but much of the care of her mother as well.

It also hadn't occurred to her how quickly she would

become annoyed by everything about Rebecca. The girl never complained about anything, and always seemed able to find the good in everything. As far as Germaine was concerned, that made her a fool.

But it was Oliver Metcalf who bothered her more. He was starting to hang around—a situation that could lead to no good at all in Germaine's estimation. Well, she would simply forbid Rebecca to see him anymore, and that would be that. At least Rebecca—unlike her mother—would do as she told her to do.

"Germaine? Is that you?"

She flinched as her mother's voice jabbed into her reverie as sharply as needles stuck into flesh. "Yes, Mother," she said, finally stepping through the doorway to face the old woman.

Clara's hooded eyes fixed on her. "What were you doing out there? Were you spying on me?"

Germaine cast around in her mind for an excuse for having lingered outside the door, but knew there was none that would satisfy her mother. "I wasn't doing anything," she finally admitted.

"You were spying on me," Clara accused.

"For Heaven's sake, Mother, why would I do that?" Too late, Germaine realized she'd let her exasperation be revealed by her voice.

"Don't use that tone on me, young lady," Clara snapped. "I'm your mother, and you'll show proper respect." Her eyes narrowed suspiciously. "You didn't bring me anything today, did you?"

"You're wrong," Germaine said. "I brought you something wonderful today. Look!" Crossing to the wheelchair, Germaine knelt and placed the handkerchief in her mother's lap.

Clara stared at the handkerchief for a long moment, then her gaze shifted and the bright black eyes fixed sharply on Germaine.

"Where?" she asked. "Where did you get this?"

Germaine's jaw tightened in anger. Was that all her mother cared about? Where it had come from? Next she would be demanding to know how much she'd paid for it. Well, if that was all that counted, fine! "I found it in Janice Anderson's shop," she said.

"Liar!" Clara rasped. Then, with no warning at all, she spat in her daughter's face.

As Germaine fled from the room, Clara's voice rose in a furious howl that pursued her down the stairs. "Liar! *Liar! LIAR!*"

Chapter 3

*O*liver Metcalf wasn't sure exactly what it was about the file that caught his eye. He hadn't really been thinking about what he was doing; indeed, more of his attention had been focused on his growing concern about Germaine Wagner's influence over Rebecca Morrison than on the task of packing the old files he'd brought down from the attic back into their box. Yet the moment he'd picked up the faded folder he was now holding, he knew there was something different about it.

The folder itself was made of the same buff manila paper as all the others, mottled with age, its edges softened and fraying. The tab on the edge showed a discoloration where the identifying sticker had once been glued, but the label had long ago fallen away.

Dropping onto the straight-backed chair that he had positioned next to the guest room's single window, Oliver opened the file. As he scanned its first page, he felt the pangs of a headache coming on. Absently, he rubbed his fingers against his temple, as if hoping to massage the pain away before it took root, and focused on the handwritten notes.

The first page bore nothing more than the patient's vital statistics. Her name—Lavinia Willoughby—meant nothing to Oliver, and her home had been someplace in South Carolina called Devereaux. Complaining of depression, she had been brought to the Asylum by her husband, and was admitted in 1948.

According to the record, she had died in the Asylum four years later.

The year Oliver was born.

As he began reading Lavinia Willoughby's case history, Oliver unconsciously pressed the fingers of his right hand harder against his temple, which was starting to throb with pain. Mrs. Willoughby was diagnosed as manic-depressive, and the treatment prescribed for her had been typical of her time. There had been some counseling, with a great deal of emphasis put on her relationship with her father. As her counseling progressed, it became clear that Lavinia's doctor had concluded that there had been an incestuous relationship between Lavinia and her father.

Lavinia Willoughby, though, had apparently not agreed with the doctor, for there was a notation on the same page that the patient was "in denial and refusing to deal with the possibility."

A few pages further on, the doctor began exploring the suggestion that Lavinia herself had initiated the incestuous relationship, though it was duly noted that the patient also denied that possibility. After that session, the doctor prescribed hydrotherapy for his patient.

Oliver's headache spread from his right temple to the back of his head as he read the account of Lavinia Willoughby's three sessions in the hydrotherapy room. The first one had lasted an hour, after which the patient developed "pneumonia unrelated to her therapy session." When she had recovered from her illness, her therapy resumed, and after the third session, in which she'd been immersed in cold water for three hours, her therapy had proved successful. The next day, in her regular counseling session, Lavinia Willoughby had remembered that her father had, indeed, molested her when she was a small child.

Looking up from the file as the afternoon light began to fade, Oliver's eyes moved to the looming form of the

Asylum atop the hill. Its gray walls seemed almost prison-like this afternoon, and though neither the room nor the day was cold, Oliver found himself shivering as he imagined what incarceration there must have been like for Lavinia Willoughby. He scanned the blank and filthy windows of the ancient stone building, wondering which of them might have been Lavinia Willoughby's, which of those barred portals might have stood between her and the world outside the Asylum's walls.

How had she stood it? How had any of them stood it? Even if they weren't insane when they entered that building, surely they would have been after only a few months' stay.

His headache spreading into his left temple now, Oliver switched on the lamp that was on the table between the bed and the chair in which he sat, and went back to Lavinia Willoughby's file.

It was after her acknowledgment of her relationship with her father—and her admission that she had initiated it—that electroconvulsive therapy had been prescribed for Lavinia.

As Oliver began reading the description of the treatment that had been administered to her, a blinding stab of pain slashed through his head and a shroud of utter blackness closed around him.

The boy is looking straight up, watching the pattern of light and shadow on the ceiling change. He knows it is useless to struggle against the thick leather straps that hold him to the gurney: even if he could work his arms and legs free, there is no place to run to, for he knows there is no way to escape the people who have tied him down, let alone escape the building itself.

He tries not to think about where they might be taking him, but it doesn't matter.

All of the rooms are the same.

All of them terrify him.

The gurney stops, and the boy is able to shift his eyes just enough to see a door. A plaque is mounted on it, with three letters:

E. C. T.

The boy doesn't know what the letters mean, but he instantly knows that all the rooms are not the same and this is the worst of all of them.

He can feel a scream building in his throat, but he struggles against it, knowing if he shows how terrified he is, it will only be worse. Besides, even if anyone heard him scream, they wouldn't come to help him.

They never do.

One of the orderlies opens the door, and the other one pushes the gurney inside. The boy catches a glimpse of the box on a table against one of the walls, and feels the knot in his stomach turn into a ball of fire.

And suddenly he has to go to the bathroom.

He tries to tell the orderly, but now he is so terrified that his mouth has gone dry, and the only sound that comes out is a choking sob as he struggles not to cry.

He shuts his eyes: maybe if he doesn't watch, it won't happen.

When he hears the door open and close, and the familiar voice ask if everything is ready, he squeezes his eyes shut tighter, as if by closing out more of the light he might close out the sound of the voice as well.

The darkness, though, is even more frightening than what he has seen, and when he finally risks a peek, he knows it is going to happen again.

The wooden box is open, and the man is taking the bright metal plates out of it.

Though the boy tries not to watch, he can't help himself, and his eyes never leave the metal contacts as the man applies a gooey substance to them, then snaps them into a heavy band of rubber.

One of the orderlies fastens the band around the boy's head.

As the boy braces himself, the orderlies bend over him, pressing his body down against the gurney. He squeezes his eyes shut again.

The first shock jolts through him, and every muscle in his body convulses, jerking his limbs against the restraining straps with so much force he thinks his legs and arms must be broken.

But even worse is the hot wetness spreading from his crotch and the stink coming from behind his buttocks.

Crying as much from shame as from the pain, the boy waits for the next shock.

And the next.

And the next . . .

Melissa Holloway exited the front door of the bank just as Ed Becker's Buick pulled up to the curb.

"See how prompt I am?" Bill McGuire got out of the passenger seat and held the door for Melissa. "Give me a schedule, and I adhere to it."

Though his inflection was bantering, the nervous look in the contractor's eyes belied his tone, and as Melissa waved him into the front seat while she herself got into the back of the big sedan, she tried to allay his obvious fears.

"This is only a formality, Bill," she said. "I just think I ought to at least take one good look at the project, since suddenly it's going to be *my* name signing off on the final approval for the loan."

"Yours, and the board's," Ed Becker reminded her.

"Mine and the board's," Melissa agreed. "But why don't I think it's the board that's going to get fired if anything goes wrong?"

"Nothing's going to go wrong," Bill McGuire assured her as Ed turned up Amherst Street. "Jules was all set to fund the loan when—"

"Jules isn't here anymore," Melissa cut in, deciding it was time for her to assert herself a little more strongly. "And let's not forget that we're not quite out of the woods on the audit yet. If the loan has to hinge solely on Jules's last recommendation, I'm afraid it's not going to fly." She saw the two men in the front seat glance uneasily at each other, but neither of them said anything. "Let's also not forget that it was the way Jules ran the bank that got us into trouble in the first place."

"But the Center Project is perfectly sound—" Bill McGuire began. This time it was Ed Becker who cut him off.

"Melissa knows the math better than either one of us," the lawyer told him. "She knows it works on paper. But a good banker wants to know it's going to work in the real world too."

"I know." Bill sighed. "It's just that ever since this whole thing began ... well, you both know what I'm saying."

Though neither Ed Becker nor Melissa Holloway replied, they did, indeed, know exactly what Bill was saying. For the last four months, ever since Bill's wife had miscarried their second child, only to kill herself a few days later, a sense of foreboding had fallen over the town. When the news had spread that there were problems at the bank, and then Jules Hartwick disemboweled himself on the steps of the Asylum, the foreboding had turned to apprehension. No one, though, had expected

Martha Ward to be next. Her fiery death ignited a conflagration of fear and suspicion in Blackstone. The very atmosphere throbbed with anxiety. Neighbors who for years had greeted each other with cheerful hellos had now begun to cast wary eyes on their fellow townsmen, as if trying to ferret out who might next fall victim to whatever curse had been visited upon the town.

And each of them prayed that he might be spared.

Their arrival at the Asylum did nothing to dispel the mood that had descended over all three of them. As Melissa Holloway got out of the Buick's backseat and gazed up at the building's grimy stone facade, an unbidden vision of the hospital in which she herself had once been confined came into her mind, and she wondered if she really wanted to venture through the great oaken doors. But as Bill McGuire turned the key in the lock and the heavy door creaked open, Melissa firmly put her memories aside, reminding herself that what had happened in Secret Cove when she was a child had nothing to do with Blackstone today. Taking a deep breath—a breath that almost succeeded in calming her nerves— she followed Ed Becker and Bill McGuire as they led the way into the Asylum.

Little was left of the splendor that had graced the building in the days before it had been converted from a private mansion into a hospital for the insane. What had once been a series of large, elegant rooms had at some point been subdivided into a warren of tiny offices. Bill McGuire led them from room to room explaining the building's original floor plan and describing what it would look like when the reconstruction was completed. "This will become an atrium," he said as they returned to the entry hall. As they threaded their way through the maze of empty rooms on the west side of the building, the fading sunlight that filtered through the dirt-encrusted windows did little to dispel the ominousness of the place. Finally, toward the rear of the building, they came to the foot of what once must have been an impressive staircase.

"The stairs are original," Bill pointed out, "but somewhere along the line the mahogany banisters and balustrades were replaced with metal ones. Probably at the same time the sprinkler system was put in." He gazed sourly up at the network of pipes suspended from a Celotex ceiling of the kind that had been popular back in the late forties and early fifties. "The last remodeling was done only a couple of years before they closed the place."

"Why *did* they close it?" Melissa asked.

Bill McGuire and Ed Becker exchanged glances. In the silence that followed, each of them seemed to be waiting for the other to speak. It was Ed who finally said, "No one really knows exactly what happened." He paused. "Oliver Metcalf's father was the superintendent, and when Oliver and his twin sister were almost four, his sister died. There were all kinds of rumors at the time. Most people thought it was an accident, but some people blamed Oliver. There were even a few who blamed Dr. Metcalf. It was before my time, of course, but local lore has it that things went downhill from there. Metcalf never really recovered from the tragedy. Over time, many of the patients were moved to other places, and there weren't any new ones. In the end, when Metcalf died, the trustees decided to shut it down instead of trying to find a new director."

"So the building just sat empty for forty years?" Melissa asked. "What a waste."

"On the other hand, at least they didn't tear it down," Bill McGuire said. He had started up the stairs and motioned for them to follow. "There's still enough left that it can be restored and expanded." As he led them up to the second floor, he explained how the reconstruction would be done, first by restoring the original entry hall and returning both the second and third floors to the galleries they had once been. "The bedrooms up here were huge, but they got chopped up into cubicles just like the rooms on the ground floor. They'll make terrific shops, and down on the first floor, the kitchen's still almost up to commercial standards. We've found enough pictures of the original dining room that we can restore it almost perfectly."

As the light continued to drain away, Bill McGuire flipped on the flashlight he'd brought along. Moving steadily through the rooms on the second floor, he carefully explained to Melissa the plans for every area, and what kind of shops had already agreed to lease space. Then, on the third floor, they discovered some rooms that weren't quite empty. In one of the old patients' rooms there was still a Formica-topped table and a chair; in another they discovered an old oak dresser. Its finish was nearly gone and its top surface slightly warped, but its frame was still solid, its brass fittings and pulls still intact though blackened with age.

Ed Becker pulled one of the curved drawers out of the dresser and took it to the window, where enough light was still leaking through for him to examine the dovetail joinery that a craftsman had used to fit the corners together. Though the light was nearly gone, he could see that the joinery had all been done by hand, and that its gracefully curved expanse had been carved from a single block of wood, not fitted together from pieces.

"What are you going to do with this?" he asked.

Bill McGuire shrugged.

"Any chance of buying it?"

"You'd do better to ask Melissa than me," Bill said.

"What was done with the rest of the furniture?" the young banker asked.

"I had Corelli Brothers come and haul it out a few months ago. It was all auctioned off, and the money was put into the Center account. They must have just missed a few things up here."

Melissa's brow furrowed. "Well, there's not enough left to be worth an auctioneer's time. What do you think it's worth?" Ed Becker eyed the dresser, calculating how much of an underestimation of its value he might get away with, but Melissa seemed to read his mind. "Given that it's hand-carved, I don't see that it would go for much less than a thousand at auction, do you, Bill?"

"I think she's on to you, Ed," the contractor said, grinning. "But look at it this way—by the time you finish restoring it, it'll be worth twice that."

Ed Becker's eyes moved over the dresser, appraising its workmanship again. Though he and Bonnie couldn't afford quite that much right now, he knew the chest was worth at least the thousand Melissa had suggested. Moreover, there was something about it—something he couldn't quite put his finger on—that made him feel he had to own it. It was a beauty, after all.

Whatever the reason, he wanted the dresser. "No slack, huh?" he asked.

Melissa and Bill shook their heads. "You'll have to clear the purchase with the rest of the Center's board of directors," she told him, a smile playing over her face. "They might claim you have a conflict of interest."

Ed Becker rolled his eyes. "They'll be so happy to get a thousand dollars out of me, they won't argue for a second." Putting the drawer back in the dresser, he moved to follow Bill McGuire and Melissa Holloway out of the room, but turned back at the doorway to look at the old piece of furniture one more time.

Even at a thousand dollars, he decided, it was still a hell of a deal. From the zippered portfolio he was carrying, he extracted a legal pad and pen and wrote in bold capitals: PROPERTY OF ED BECKER. DO NOT REMOVE. And folding the paper so it would hang from the drawer when closed, he staked his claim.

But as he turned away from the chest once more, he

felt a sudden chill, as if he'd been struck by a draft from an open window.

He glanced around the room again, but the window was closed tight and none of the panes was even cracked, let alone broken.

As he hurried to catch up with Bill and Melissa, he dismissed the strange chill, telling himself it must have been nothing more than his imagination.

Chapter 4

Clara Wagner gazed down at the handkerchief that still lay in her lap, exactly where Germaine had left it. Since her daughter had left the room half an hour before, Clara hadn't moved at all. The fire on the hearth had burned low, but for once she hadn't called out, hadn't banged her cane on the floor to bring Germaine or Rebecca running to do her bidding.

For half an hour she'd done nothing at all except sit in her chair, gazing at the handkerchief.

Why did it look so familiar to her?

And why did the very sight of it so frighten her?

Somewhere deep in the recesses of her mind, this small scrap of linen with its elaborate floral design had stirred a memory, but no matter how she tried, she couldn't quite grasp it, couldn't get it quite close enough to pull into the light. Annoyingly—maddeningly—its significance hovered in the blurry fringes of her memory, refusing to come into focus.

Was it possible that Germaine hadn't been lying, and that she'd actually found the handkerchief in Janice Anderson's antique shop?

She supposed it was barely possible, though she'd never admit as much to Germaine. A strong and certain sense within told her she had seen this handkerchief before. And it came from no shop.

The handkerchief had stirred her memory the moment she laid eyes on it. And not a pleasant memory either.

Her stomach—delicate even when she was feeling at her best—had instantly churned, and bile boiled up into her throat, leaving a sour taste in her mouth. For a moment she'd even thought she might vomit. She hadn't, of course; instead she'd sat motionless, willing her body to respond to her wishes, just as she'd willed it to respond when she decided she no longer wished to walk. That memory still made her smile, for when Germaine had brought Dr. Margolis to see her, he hadn't been able even to find a reflex in the legs she'd decided never again to use. Philip Margolis—and a host of neurologists and orthopedists to whom Germaine had dragged her— agreed that she couldn't walk. None of them could determine the cause. The wheelchair—and Germaine—had become her legs.

Precisely as she'd intended.

Ever since that day eighteen years ago, Clara had felt completely in control of everything about her life. Her daughter did her bidding, and her cleaning girl did her bidding.

Now Rebecca Morrison too did her bidding.

But for some reason—a reason she couldn't quite fathom—the handkerchief was upsetting her. Picking it up as gingerly as if it could have burned her, she held it under her reading light, examining it more closely.

It had indeed been skillfully done, every loop and knot of the tatting perfectly even, every tiny stitch of embroidery executed with such remarkable precision that she could find neither a knot nor a tag end of the fine silk thread showing anywhere.

Suddenly an image from the past flashed through her mind. An image of a woman, clad in nothing more than a thin cotton nightgown, sitting on the edge of a metal-framed bed, gazing straight ahead, seemingly at nothing.

But in her lap, her fingers were working so quickly they were little more than a blur as she wove silken thread into a square of fine linen.

Clara's fingers tightened on the handkerchief. But of course the idea that was forming in her mind was impossible. More than half a century had passed since Clara had so much as set foot in that building! Whatever that woman had been working on had disappeared as utterly as had the woman herself.

Despite her own logic, Clara examined the handkerchief yet again, unable to take her eyes from it, searching for . . . what?

Something that—once again—she couldn't quite grasp. As her memory refused to respond to her demands, and the recollection she sought remained hidden in the shadows, her frustration grew. For a moment she was tempted to hurl the handkerchief into the fireplace. She crumpled it in her hands, squeezing it hard, as if she might be able to wring the memory from its folds, then drew her hand back in preparation for tossing it into the dying flames. At the last second she changed her mind.

She wouldn't destroy the handkerchief—yet.

First she would remember.

Then she would burn it.

As the clock on the mantel above the fireplace struck six, she shoved the handkerchief deep into the pocket of her dress, then placed her right hand on the wheelchair's control panel. With a nearly inaudible hum, the wheelchair rolled out of the room onto the mezzanine.

"For Heaven's sake, Rebecca, can't you be more careful? If you drop it, Mother will kill you."

Rebecca tightened her grip on the silver tray bearing the teapot, three cups and saucers, a pitcher of cream, a sugar bowl, a basket of scones, and a box of candy. Germaine had been insistent that she couldn't use the tea cart in the butler's pantry—she must carry the tray in herself, and she mustn't let even a single drop of either the tea or the cream spill. Still, Rebecca knew she had steady hands, and Germaine's reluctance to let her use the cart was no more strange than her demands regarding the preparation of the tea, which she insisted on tasting and had made Rebecca prepare no fewer than four times before declaring that it was satisfactorily brewed.

As she followed Germaine out of the kitchen and through the dining room to the foyer, Rebecca took tiny, careful steps so the surface of the cream barely even moved, let alone threatened to slop over onto the tray. She stopped just outside the dining room door, just as Germaine had instructed. A clanking, followed immediately by the sound of the machinery in the attic coming alive, announced Clara Wagner's imminent arrival. As she and Germaine waited side by side, the brass elevator slowly descended from the mezzanine to the first floor, its door opened, and Clara, her small frame sitting absolutely erect in her wheelchair, emerged from the metal cage. Her eyes fixed balefully on Germaine and Rebecca, almost as if she was sorry they were waiting for her. Rolling the wheelchair across the enormous Oriental carpet that covered all but the edges of the entry hall's walnut floor, Clara inspected the tray. Rebecca could almost feel her searching for something to complain about, and it took her only a moment to find it.

"The sugar bowl isn't full," she announced at the exact second she lifted its lid.

"I'm sorry, Miss Clara," Rebecca said, her face reddening. Why hadn't Germaine told her to fill it? "I'll fill it right away."

"You won't," Clara Wagner declared. "Germaine will do it while you set the tea table."

Rebecca saw a vein in Germaine's forehead throbbing, but she said nothing as Germaine picked the offending sugar bowl off the tray and retreated back toward the kitchen. Rebecca herself followed Clara Wagner as she led the way to the front parlor, where a tea table waited, which Rebecca had already set with three places. Clara eyed them suspiciously, but Rebecca had been careful to get each utensil straight. The damask napkins were folded perfectly. She held her breath as Clara's eyes moved from the china to the jam pots to the butter dish, but those too seemed to meet her standards.

"You may set the tray down," she decreed.

They waited in silence until Germaine arrived with the sugar bowl. Rebecca carefully fixed its level in her mind, determined not to make the same mistake again.

Germaine poured the first cup of tea and set it in front of her mother. "Why don't you show Rebecca the handkerchief I gave you?" she asked, her eyes flicking toward Rebecca as if to see if the younger woman would contradict her.

She *did* give it to her mother, Rebecca reminded herself. Oliver gave it to me, but it was Germaine who gave it to Miss Clara. "Thank you," she said as Germaine finally passed her a cup of tea. Then she turned to Clara. "I'd love to see the handkerchief."

Clara Wagner's hand moved automatically to the pocket into which she'd stuffed the handkerchief. "I didn't bring it downstairs," she said. "I don't like it."

The vein in Germaine's forehead began throbbing again as she saw the lump in her mother's pocket and instantly understood what it was. Still stinging from her humiliation over the sugar bowl, she glared at her mother. "If you don't like it, why don't you give it back to me?"

Clara's eyes met her daughter's. "I don't have it," she insisted.

"You do," Germaine replied coldly. She reached over to take the handkerchief out of her mother's pocket, but Clara's fingers closed on her wrist. For a long moment mother and daughter glared at each other. "Are you going to call me a liar again, Mother?" Germaine asked.

Suddenly Clara's hand released Germaine's wrist and

she pulled the handkerchief out of her pocket. "Very well," she said, her voice rasping. "If you want it that badly, have it! Have it with my blessing!" Crushing the handkerchief into a wad, she hurled it in her daughter's face.

Rebecca held her breath, bracing herself for the scene she was certain was to ensue, but to her relief, Germaine didn't respond to her mother's fury. She merely retrieved the handkerchief from the floor where it had fallen, spread it flat on the table, then folded it carefully. She slipped it into the breast pocket of her blouse so the mirrored R showed perfectly. "There," she said, her eyes fixing once more on Rebecca. "Isn't it pretty?"

Without waiting for an answer, Germaine lifted the lid off the box of chocolates. To her horror, she found no candy inside. Instead of the array of chocolates she'd been expecting, she saw nothing but a pulsating mass of ants, gnats, and flies. Her eyes widened in terror as a cloud of insects swarmed up from the box, flying directly at her face. Screaming, Germaine leaped up from her chair, overturning it in her haste to escape the horde of insects still pouring from the open box. Instinctively, she lashed out at the teeming mass, trying to fend it off, and succeeded only in overturning the teapot. As scalding tea gushed across the table and into Clara's lap, Germaine backed away from the table, but her terror only increased as she spotted the tangle of snakes writhing on the floor around her feet.

Another scream emerged from her throat, and she fled, sobbing and stumbling, from the room.

Rebecca, stunned by Germaine's sudden, unexplained outburst, was frozen in her chair until Clara Wagner's voice penetrated her shock and she realized that the old woman was shouting at her, "Help me! Help me!"

Her dazed confusion broken, Rebecca jumped up and began blotting at Clara Wagner's skirt with a napkin. Her mind was groping for some explanation, but all she could think of was that suddenly, in no more than the blink of an eye, Germaine had gone crazy. But that was impossible, wasn't it?

"What was it?" she asked. "What happened?"

Irritably brushing Rebecca away, Clara Wagner picked up another napkin and started working on her skirt herself. "What does it matter?" she asked. "She's ruined my tea." Without another word, Clara backed away from the table and left the parlor.

Oliver's head snapped up as the file slipped from his lap to the floor, and he bent down to pick it up. His headache was finally loosening its grip, but his whole body hurt, as if he'd just put himself through a punishing workout. His skin was covered with a cold sheen of sweat, and he felt utterly exhausted. It was only as he bent to gather the contents of the file together again that he glanced out the window and noticed that the last of the daylight had slipped away.

Darkness and shadows had enshrouded Blackstone, and the Asylum, looming at the top of the hill, cast the darkest shadow of all. As he gazed at the silhouette of the structure for which his father had been the final overseer, Oliver tried to imagine Malcolm Metcalf committing the kind of atrocities that had been so coldly and clinically described in the case history he now held in his hand.

He could not make himself believe it, despite the conclusive evidence in the pages he had just read—pages of precise notations in his father's own distinctive handwriting.

Accept it, he told himself, accept that the treatments he had prescribed for that patient were far from uncommon back then; indeed, they were considered the most advanced thinking in the treatment of mental illness. Why, then, shouldn't his father have used them?

His thoughts were interrupted by a flash of light from

the top of the hill. Oliver froze, but then decided it had been an illusion.

He saw another flash of light—barely more than a flicker—illuminating one of the third-floor windows for a second, only to disappear as quickly as had the first.

A moment later he saw it again, and then again.

For the tiniest fraction of a second reason completely deserted him and he felt an absolute certainty that he knew who was walking in the Asylum this night.

It was his father.

His father, somehow come back to prowl the darkened corridors of his long-silent domain while he himself read of the sadistic "treatments" in which Malcolm Metcalf had once indulged.

But as quickly as the terrifying sensation came over him, it drained away, and he realized the truth.

He was seeing nothing more than the beam of a flashlight as someone explored the Asylum's empty rooms. Peering out the window, he spotted the dim shape of a car parked close by the Asylum's entrance, and then remembered that this was the day Bill McGuire and Ed Becker were going to take Melissa Holloway through the building.

Straightening the file and putting it back in the box with the others, Oliver went downstairs, took a light jacket from a hook by the front door, and went out into the gathering night. Even if he couldn't bring himself to go into the Asylum, he could certainly wait on the steps for his friends to emerge. But as he started up the slope toward the dark stone structure, he began to feel the familiar throbbing in his right temple.

With every step the pain grew worse, but Oliver kept moving doggedly onward, refusing to give in to the agony in his head. As he reached the bottom step of the short flight leading to the Asylum's front door, a wave of nausea rose in his stomach and he lurched to a stop, dropping to his knees as he felt a clammy sweat break out over his entire body.

Nausea twisted at his guts. Oliver struggled to breathe, then staggered back to his feet. He gazed up at the double oaken doors at the top of the steps. They seemed to grow before his very eyes, doubling in size, then quadrupling. A gurgle of terror bubbling in his throat, Oliver recoiled backward as the great doors began to tip toward him, and he knew that if he stayed where he was even a second longer, he would surely be crushed. Fighting the keening scream that was about to explode from his throat, he turned and fled into the darkness.

Melissa Holloway hesitated at the top of the stairs leading to the Asylum's basement. A shiver passed through her and she felt an odd sense of being suddenly close to some incomprehensible evil.

"We don't have to go down there," Bill McGuire offered, sensing her discomfort. "If you'd rather—"

"It's all right," Melissa quickly cut in. "I came here to see the building, and I'd like to see it all." But as she gazed down at the black pool into which the steps led, she wondered if she really did want to see what was down there. A moment later, though, as the flashlights Ed Becker and Bill McGuire were carrying washed enough of the darkness away to reveal nothing more threatening than what appeared to be a perfectly ordinary corridor, her fears eased. Yet as she followed the two men down the stairs, their footsteps echoing hollowly, her sense of an evil presence grew stronger.

"Are you sure there's no one here but us?" she asked, and immediately regretting her question, reproached herself for sounding like a skittish girl.

"You never really know, do you?" Ed Becker suggested, playfully picking up on her nervousness. "Who knows what evil once roamed these . . ." His words died away as Bill McGuire cast the beam of his light into one of the rooms that opened off the corridor and they saw the shackles hanging from its walls. "Jesus," the lawyer whispered. "You don't think they actually used those things on people, do you?"

Melissa Holloway stared at the thick leather cuffs that hung from the ends of heavy chains bolted to the wall. "Can you think of another purpose for them?"

Neither of the men made a reply, but Bill McGuire shifted his light quickly back to the corridor.

The next two doors were both pierced with small windows, and when Bill McGuire opened one of them, Melissa and Ed Becker both knew why.

Little more than cells, there were still remnants of padding hanging from their walls.

There was no furniture.

The three of them gazed wordlessly at the room for a moment, then moved on.

The room next to the padded cell was equipped with three large porcelain tubs, each of them big enough for an adult to stretch out in. All three had heavy wooden covers. The covers were notched at one end. Ed Becker stared at them, puzzled.

Again, it was as if Melissa Holloway read his mind. "For the patients' heads," she said softly. "No one stays in a tub of cold water voluntarily. So they used covers to hold them in."

Ed Becker stared open-mouthed at the tubs and tried to imagine what it would be like to be closed into one of them. The cold water would be horrible; the immobility and helplessness even worse. Shuddering, he turned away. "What the hell kind of place was this?" he muttered as he moved quickly back into the hall.

"No different from hundreds of others, I suspect," Melissa Holloway replied.

The three of them finished their tour of the basement in

silence, as if compelled to investigate every one of the dank rooms, all of them used for purposes that none of them really wanted to talk about.

As they finally turned back toward the stairs, Melissa shook her head sadly. "I wonder if we're really doing the right thing," she said, remembering not only the rooms they had just inspected but the ones upstairs as well. "Maybe it would be better just to tear the whole place down."

Bill McGuire and Ed Becker glanced at each other. "Too late for that," the lawyer replied. "The structure's sound. Besides, if it was going to be torn down, it should have been done a long time ago." A grim smile played over his lips. "I know it's spooky, Melissa—frankly, I'm a bit spooked by it myself—but whatever went on here happened so long ago that practically everyone's forgotten about it. All it is now is an historical building. In fact," he added as they emerged back onto the first floor, "it's a registered landmark building, so even if we wanted to, we couldn't tear it down."

When they came to the front door, Melissa took one last glance back at the shadowy interior. A shudder passed through her, as though some indefinable evil that lurked within the building's dark stone walls were making its presence known. "I don't know," she said, shaking the feeling off, "I guess sometimes I just wonder if places like this should really be saved. It's as if so much unhappiness lived here that it seeped into the walls themselves. And I wonder if anything we do will ever really change that."

Bill McGuire glanced anxiously at the banker. "You're not changing your mind about the loan, are you?" he asked.

Melissa hesitated, then chuckled. "No," she assured him. "I'm not. I'm just musing, that's all. As a person, the whole place gives me the willies. But as a banker, I have to say it looks like a terrific investment."

A moment later they drove out of the Asylum grounds, totally unaware that only a few minutes before, Oliver Metcalf had stood on the porch, waiting for them—then fled.

The headache slowly eased, the nausea passed, and the black veil of terror that had fallen over Oliver lifted.

Yet he was still nearly blind, for only a faint glimmer of starlight broke the darkness that surrounded him.

He was running. But where? And from what?

His foot struck something. Tripping, he lunged uncontrollably forward, then sprawled facedown on the ground.

Instinctively throwing his right hand out to break his fall, it too struck something—something hard and rough—and a second later his other hand found something else. Gasping to catch his breath, fighting the urge to leap to his feet once again and flee whatever nameless thing might be pursuing him, he made himself stay on the ground, forced himself not to give in again to the panic that had overcome him on the Asylum steps, and concentrated on calming his fraying nerves.

There's nothing, he told himself. *Nothing chasing you. Nothing to be afraid of. Nothing at all!*

As his breathing and pulse slowly returned to normal, he sat up, reached out, and finally understood where he was.

The cemetery.

The little plot of land where for nearly half a century the unclaimed bodies of patients whose families had abandoned them to the confines of the Asylum's walls had been laid to rest once their tortured journeys through life had finally come to an end.

A potter's field, really, for it was as filled with the

homeless and the friendless as any other paupers' graveyard might be.

Except that not only the long-forgotten patients of the
Asylum had been buried here.

Finally getting to his feet, Oliver found himself threading his way among the weathered granite grave markers
toward the far corner, where, in a small area set off by a
rusting wrought-iron fence, his father was buried. Pausing at the gate, he gazed down at the headstone that was
barely visible beneath the night sky.

> Malcolm Metcalf
> Born February 25, 1914
> Died March 19, 1959

Why had his father killed himself?

And why had he chosen to die on that particular date?

Always—since he was a small boy—Oliver had assumed his father had chosen the date out of grief for his
lost child.

But what if it had been something else?

Oliver didn't know; would probably never know.

Even now, nearly forty years later, he remembered
practically nothing of any of it.

Whatever memories he had were buried as deeply in
his subconscious as his father was buried in the dark,
cold ground.

For a long time Oliver stood in the quiet of the night,
staring down at the grave marker. Then snatches of the
medical record he'd read only a little while ago began to
drift through his mind.

*Restraints . . . ice-cold baths . . . electroconvulsive
therapy.*

"What did you do, Father?" The words forming in his
mind were barely audible on his lips. But then, as the

import of the question grew, he repeated it aloud: "What did you do?"

Still the question swelled, taking on the force of a drumbeat, growing louder, louder in his mind, and once more he uttered it. This time, though, it wasn't a whisper. This time it was a howl of anguish, bellowed into the darkening night.

"WHAT DID YOU DO?"

Chapter 5

*G*ermaine Wagner huddled in her bed, her blanket wrapped around her, struggling against the panic that had overwhelmed her in the front parlor. She had neither turned on the light when she came into the room nor changed into her nightgown before retreating to the bed, so terrified was she of what she might see in the bright light of the chandelier, or hidden in the shadows of her closet. For a time—a long time—she sat trembling in the darkness, her heart pounding so hard she could hear nothing else, the vein in her forehead pulsing so strongly she feared she might have a stroke.

But as the endless minutes ticked by, the adrenaline in her blood began to be reabsorbed and her pulse to calm. As she emerged from the shock of her terror, her wits slowly came back to her and she began consciously to try to relax, to ease the tension that had led her to draw her legs up against her chest and to wrap her arms tightly around her knees.

This is not me, she told herself. *I don't react like this. Not to anything.*

But a second later, as her memory released a vision of the flies and gnats that had swarmed around her, and the snakes that writhed on the floor of the parlor, another wave of panic towered over her. This time, though, Germaine retained her self-control.

It didn't happen, she silently insisted. *Whatever it was, I only imagined it.*

320

Germaine Wagner knew she was not the type to imagine things. She had always prided herself on her ability to see things clearly, and exactly as they were. Even when she'd been a child and her playmates had gazed up into the sky to envision elephants and tigers and other wondrous creatures soaring overhead, Germaine had seen nothing but stratus, cumulus, and cumulonimbus clouds drifting on the wind. The mind, she knew, was intended to be an analytical tool, and she believed in keeping it well honed, abstaining from ingesting any chemical that might interfere with its workings. She had never had a drink, never smoked a marijuana cigarette, and had certainly never experimented with any of the drugs that—

Drugs?

She turned the possibility over in her mind. Was it possible that Rebecca Morrison might have put something in the tea? Of course it was!

It was Rebecca's revenge, a spiteful reaction for having taken the handkerchief from her before she could ruin it!

As her fear gave way to anger, Germaine touched the pocket of her blouse to be certain the handkerchief was still there. It would have been just like Rebecca to snatch it from her pocket while she was still under the influence of whatever substance the ungrateful girl had put into the tea. Finding that the handkerchief was still there, Germaine slipped it out of the pocket of her blouse and into her bra.

Her anger, though, was unassuaged. Obviously it had been a mistake to take Rebecca into her home. To repay her kindness—not to mention her mother's!—with such a trick was unconscionable. Utterly unacceptable. Rebecca would simply have to find another place to live.

The decision made—and made unalterably, as were all her decisions—Germaine saw no point in putting off telling Rebecca that she would have to find another place to stay.

Tonight would be the girl's last under her roof.

Throwing back the blanket, Germaine started to rise, and then she heard a noise.

A faint scratching sound, as if something were trying to claw through the screen outside her window. Satisfied that she'd identified the sound, Germaine sat up and swung her feet off the bed.

The sound came again, only this time it wasn't outside her window.

It was in the room.

A tiny clicking and scraping noise, as if something—something small—had scurried across the bare hardwood that was exposed around the edges of the antique rag rug that covered most of the floor.

A mouse?

Germaine's feet jerked reflexively, then went firmly back down as she realized her terror had driven her into her bed without even taking off her shoes. As she stood, she heard the skittering sound again. This time, though, she ignored it, reaching for the electrified hurricane lamp that sat on her night table. She switched it on, and the warm glow of its light banished the darkness.

For just a moment Germaine relaxed. But then she heard the scampering again, and saw a flicker of motion out of the corner of her eye. She jerked her head toward the movement so quickly that she felt a spasm of pain in her neck, and reached up to rub at the spot.

Something wriggled under her fingers!

She turned again, frantically trying to brush away the thing on her neck, and this time caught a glimpse of herself in the mirror above her dresser.

A centipede, its dozens of tiny legs moving in smooth waves, was creeping up her neck. Gasping, Germaine brushed it off and tried to step on it, but it disappeared under the bed.

Dropping to her hands and knees, she lifted the bed's skirt and peered beneath the metal frame, reaching for her slipper, intent on smashing the repulsive little creature.

But her slipper was gone. In its place was a large rat, its red eyes glaring at her, hissing as it crouched, ready to leap. Her heart racing, a tiny shriek escaped Germaine's lips as she jerked her hand back. Then she saw another movement out of the corner of her eye, and lost her balance as she ducked away. As she sprawled out onto the rug, she felt something brush against her hair.

She rolled over, panic welling up uncontrollably, and tried to get to her feet. With a rush, something darted at her out of the corner of the room—a bat, she thought—and she ducked away again. Her foot catching on the rug, she plunged forward, her forehead smashing against the edge of her dresser.

A jagged spear of pain slashed through her head, and when she rubbed at the sore spot, she felt the warm stickiness of blood. A cry as much of fear as of pain erupted from her throat. Terrified, she tried to struggle to her feet.

Now the bat was back, fluttering around her head. She tried to swat it away but it swooped in close to her, then disappeared into the folds of the curtains that covered her window. Groping for something—anything—with which to protect herself from the bat, Germaine's hand closed on an alabaster pot of face powder. She hurled it at the spot where she was certain she'd seen the bat. It smashed against the window, shattering into a hundred pieces, sending a cloud of powder boiling up from the broken pot, releasing a swarm of gnats and flies, countless times the number that had risen from the chocolate box downstairs. Millions of them, a dense, dark, choking cloud that swirled toward her. A moan of terror erupted from Germaine's throat, and she backed away from the dark swarm, screaming, choking as they invaded her open mouth. Coughing, beating them back with flailing arms, she dropped to her hands and knees.

Hundreds of mice ran out from under the bed; Germaine jerked her hands away as they stampeded over her fingers. Her knuckles smashed against the metal bed frame, tearing the skin away. As her stinging fingers began to bleed, the rat darted out into the open. Grabbing the bed lamp, Germaine smashed it down at the rodent. The glass shattered against the floor, shards flying up into her face, lacerating her skin.

The air was thick with insects, alive with bats, their wings beating, sharp teeth bared. With a scream that emerged as no more than a gagging sound, Germaine struggled to her feet and stumbled to her bathroom, slammed the door behind her, then groped for the light switch.

Brilliant white light flooded the room. Germaine stared into the mirror over the sink. But what she saw bore no resemblance to her own image. A gargoyle's face stared back at her, blood oozing from its eyes, worms clinging to its cheeks. As it opened its toothless mouth, a serpent erupted from the dark hole, striking out at her with dripping fangs as the monster in the mirror reached out with clawed and scaled fingers.

With her own fists, Germaine smashed the mirror, sending broken glass cascading to the sink and floor. A glimmering scimitar slashed at her leg as it fell, then tumbled onward, glistening with blood, only to shatter on the tiles.

Every droplet of her blood seemed to come alive so that the floor was crawling with red ants. Germaine sank to her knees, sobbing, helplessly watching as the ants swarmed over her skin, feeling the fire of their millions upon millions of bites.

Crawling out of the bathroom, she lurched once more to her feet and staggered toward the door, finally escaping from her room onto the mezzanine. She peered over the balustrade, gazing down into the vast entry hall below. Where the huge Oriental carpet had been spread all her life, now Germaine saw nothing but a terrifying pit filled with writhing snakes.

Sinking to her knees, she vomited onto the floor. The contents of her stomach spewed from her mouth, instantly turning into wriggling maggots and pulsing slugs, spreading around her, then turning to creep back toward her.

Out!

She had to get out!

But there was no way out, no escape save the staircase that led down to the pit of vipers.

There was no choice. Everywhere she looked, she saw some new threat advancing on her. She edged backward, her throat burning with acid, her stomach heaving. At the top of the stairs she peered down.

The steps cascaded away from her, dropping endlessly, the bottom unreachably far away.

She hesitated, and something dropped from the ceiling into her hair.

Twisting her neck to look up, she saw the spiders.

They were everywhere, their webs hanging from the chandelier and the skylight, covering the walls and the moldings. The spiders, black and shiny, the red hourglasses on their underbellies glimmering brightly, crept toward her.

She could hear their mandibles clicking, see the drops of poison that soon would be coursing through her veins.

Whimpering, nearly insane with fear, Germaine Wagner began scrabbling her way down the stairs toward the writhing mass of serpents that waited below.

Chapter 6

*T*hough the graveyard that adjoined the Congregational church was surrounded by no less than four of Blackstone's old-fashioned streetlights, none of them cast enough illumination into the two-acre plot to penetrate the shadows in its center. Oliver paused as he came to the gate in the white picket fence, wondering if the headache that had been plaguing him all day would strike again.

Across the street someone was making his way through the square, but from where Oliver stood, the figure was no more than an indistinct dark silhouette that soon disappeared entirely. Suddenly feeling oddly exposed even in the dim glow cast by the converted gas lamps, Oliver stepped through the gate, closed it behind him, and made his way along the paths that twisted between the gravestones until he came to the weathered marble mausoleum that Charles Connally had built in 1927, when he and every one of his five sisters had made up their minds that they would not be buried in the edifice their father had already constructed for himself, his wife, and their six offspring.

An edifice in which old Jonas Connally—Harvey Connally's grandfather and Oliver's great-grandfather—had deliberately provided no space for the men his daughters had married, let alone Charles's wife or any of their progeny.

To this day, the bodies of Jonas and Charity Connally lay in lonely splendor in an immense white limestone building at the exact center of the cemetery, their mausoleum empty save for the two of them.

Their son and daughters—along with their own husbands, Charles's wife Eleanor, and at least a few of every generation of their further descendants—were housed in six separate edifices, each of them built so that it faced away from the structure that Jonas Connally had erected, an eternal reminder that just as they had in life finally turned their backs on the patriarch of the Connally clan, so also had they turned away from him in death.

Oliver had always thought there was something almost inexpressibly sad in the manner in which the arrangement of the mausoleums bore eternal testament to the long-forgotten grudge that had existed between Jonas Connally, his son, Charles, and his five daughters, but of all the structures, he found the one built by Charles, Oliver's own grandfather and the man who had erected the great mansion on North Hill, to be the saddest.

Though Charles Connally died long before Oliver had been born, his uncle Harvey had often told him of the elder Connally's unflagging enthusiasm and optimism, which had extended even to the mausoleum he'd constructed with enough space for himself and his wife Eleanor, his children and their spouses, and a dozen grandchildren as well. But even after all these years, only four of the mausoleum's crypts were occupied—and, Oliver thought grimly, only two more ever would be.

The pale marble structure glowed in the dim light, almost as if it were lit from within rather than by the four distant streetlights. As he approached it, Oliver gazed at the motto that had been etched deeply in the marble that formed the three steps leading to the crypts:

ALL ARE WELCOMED — NONE COMMANDED

Still another rebuke to his great-grandfather. As he did every time he read the words, Oliver wondered if he would ever know what the quarrel between Jonas and his children had truly been about.

That quarrel, though, had nothing to do with the reason he was here tonight. Mounting the steps, he stood facing the two crypts that were beneath and to the left of those occupied by his grandparents. Each of them bore a small plaque:

Olivia Connally Metcalf Born March 19, 1923 Died April 24, 1952	Mallory Connally Metcalf Born April 24, 1952 Died March 19, 1956

His mother and his sister, lying side by side.

He knew how his mother had died, of course. Giving birth to himself and Mallory proved to be too much for her, and in the end she lost her life so that both of her children might live.

A little girl, named for her husband.

A little boy, named for her.

The death of his sister, though, was as shrouded in mystery now as it had been on the day it occurred.

Pictures of both of them had been mounted into the stone, protected by thick glass, but long since faded to near invisibility. Yet Oliver knew every feature.

He reached out, laying his hand on his mother's image, and, as always happened, felt his eyes moisten with tears. "Why?" he whispered. "Why did you have to leave us?" He fell silent, as if waiting for an answer to his oft-asked question; the silence of the graveyard wrapped around him like an icy sheet, making him shiver in the darkness.

His hand moved to the image of his sister, whose death had occurred on what would have been their mother's thirty-third birthday.

This time a vision from the past came to his mind,

welling up from his memory as vividly as if he'd seen it all only yesterday.

He and Mallory were both very small—no more than three or so—and he was holding on to her hand as they ran across the lawn toward the forest. There was a spring in the woods, and the two of them used to love to go hide in the shrubbery that bordered the clear, racing stream and watch raccoons washing their food in the rushing water. Sometimes deer drank from its crystal surface.

If they were feeling particularly brave, he and Mallory would sometimes take off their shoes and socks and wade in the cold water welling out of the ground, even though their father had warned them that if they slipped and fell in, they could easily drown.

But they hadn't ever slipped; hadn't ever—

The stab of pain slashed through Oliver's head so suddenly that he staggered back from the crypt, and the vision of his sister vanished in the blackness that instantly closed around him.

A point of light appears in the blackness.

The boy stares at it. As he focuses his mind on it, the point slowly begins to expand.

Now it is as if he is looking into a tunnel.

At the end of the tunnel he sees a coffin.

The boy emerges from the tunnel. He is in a church, staring at a coffin.

A small coffin.

Small enough that even he would barely fit in it.

Hands lift him up, holding him high, so that he can look down into the coffin.

He sees a face.

His sister's face.

As he stares at it, his eyes wide, blood oozes from his sister's neck.

Shuddering as the headache slowly released him from its grip, Oliver pressed his hand against the glass covering his sister's image.

"Oh, God, why can't I remember? What's happening to me?" he cried, his voice breaking.

His eyes streaming with tears, his breath catching in his throat, Oliver turned away from the mausoleum and started the long walk back home.

Germaine had no idea how long it had taken her to descend the apparently endless staircase. Time itself lost its meaning as she flailed against the terrors that surrounded her. Cowering at the foot of the stairs, she gazed into the pit, mesmerized. What had been an enormous and lush Oriental carpet bearing an intricate pattern of flowers, vines, leaves and birds was now a pulsating, writhing, living mass that throbbed with a hypnotic rhythm and threatened to draw her irretrievably into its deadly grasp. Vines grew before her very eyes, their tendrils reaching out to twist around her ankles. Snakes slithered among the vines, their undulating bodies nearly indistinguishable from the sinews of the plants themselves. A whimper escaped Germaine's lips as she tried to turn away from the hideous vision, but the jungle before her held her in its thrall.

A glistening drop of saliva oozed from the corner of her mouth, but Germaine was as oblivious to it as she now was to the blood that dripped from the gashes on her legs.

The jungle dropped away, consumed by the black bottomless pit that opened before her. A wave of vertigo struck Germaine as she stared into the abyss, and she flung one arm out to try to steady herself, succeeding only in smashing her hand against the hard wood of the newel-post at the base of the stairs. The sudden bone-jarring pain in her hand cost her what little was left of her equilibrium. Her balance deserted her.

Screaming, she plunged into the blackness far below. As she fell she could see the writhing snakes, their mouths gaping, fangs dripping with venom, straining upward as if to strike her even before she crashed to the ground.

Then they were all over her, twisting around her, binding her arms and legs. She couldn't breathe; her skin was crawling. Twisting. Turning. Screaming. Vipers churning over her. She tried to move her arms, her legs. Trapped. Immobile. Paralyzed. Screaming—screams of pain and terror. Then only utter despair.

Clara Wagner finally picked up the remote control and muted the volume on her television set. As the sound of the late news died away, the wailing from beyond her door became clearer, and her brow furrowed in irritation. What on earth was going on out there?

Was someone crying, or shouting?

It must be Germaine and Rebecca.

What on earth were they doing?

But of course she knew! Rebecca had undoubtedly done something stupid again, and Germaine would have corrected her. Now the silly child was crying. Well, it would have to stop.

Now.

Turning her chair toward the door, she rolled across the room, then struggled to open the heavy mahogany panel, one hand clutching the doorknob while she used the other to manipulate the chair's controls. As the door slowly swung open, the sounds grew louder. "For heaven's sake,"

Clara began as she rolled the chair out onto the broad mezzanine that encircled the huge entry hall below. "What on earth—"

The words died on her lips. Below her, she saw Germaine writhing on the carpet that was spread out over the broad expanse between the front door and the base of the stairs.

What in heaven's name was she doing? Had she fallen down the stairs?

"Germaine? *Germaine!*"

The screech echoing through the jungle galvanized Germaine. She lunged to her feet as she heard the as-yet-unseen beast crash toward her. Though the snakes still clung to her, and her vision was a red blur, with a preternatural strength born of sheer terror she jerked her limbs loose from the clutching vines and writhing vipers.

Hide.

She had to find someplace to hide.

Frantically turning first one way and then another, Germaine searched for someplace—anyplace—that would shelter her from the beast that was coming ever closer. Then, at last, she saw something.

A tree—a hollow tree.

Not much, but at least something.

The vines still dragging at her, the snakes still twisting around her, she struggled toward the shelter, finally dropping to all fours to slog her way across the mire the floor had become.

Then, as the beast roared again, she whimpered and redoubled her efforts.

* * *

"Germaine!"

Clara Wagner glared furiously down at her daughter. What on earth was she doing? Obviously she wasn't badly hurt, since she'd gotten up, taken a few steps, then dropped back down as if she were simply too dizzy to stand.

Dizzy!

Of course!

Germaine was drunk! That had to be it! After the scene she'd caused in the parlor, she'd gone back to her room and begun drinking.

It didn't surprise Clara—didn't surprise her at all. She'd always suspected Germaine was a secret drinker. Typical of the kind of person Germaine had turned out to be, despite how hard she had worked to raise her properly, and the sacrifices she'd made to make certain that Germaine had all the advantages. But the girl had always been a disappointment.

Maybe if she'd been pretty enough to snare a husband—

Too late now! Germaine would never be anything but an old-maid librarian.

But she would not be a drunk!

"I'm coming down there, Germaine!" Clara called over the edge of the mezzanine. "I'm coming down, and if I find out you've been drinking . . ."

She left the sentence hanging unfinished as she maneuvered the wheelchair toward the elevator. Angrily, she jerked at the accordion door of the brass cage. Finally pulling it open, she wheeled herself inside, then jabbed at the button that would send the cage down to the first floor.

The renewed roaring of the beast spurring her on, Germaine burst free of the vines and scrabbled across to the shelter of the hollow tree, no more than a rotting stump, its bark filled with holes. Drawing her knees to her breast and wrapping her arms around them, she closed her eyes and rocked back and forth. Her breath was coming in short gasps; every part of her body hurt now. Her skin felt as if millions of insects were crawling over it, and blood was smeared everywhere.

Sobbing and whimpering, she tried to shrink herself into an even smaller ball and clamp both her eyes and her ears shut against the terrors that surrounded her. Then a new sound penetrated the fog that was gathering in her mind.

A terrible clanking and groaning. The beast! Moving toward her. Against her will, she opened her eyes and looked up.

An enormous boulder—so huge it filled the entire hollowed trunk of the tree—was dropping toward her.

Germaine screamed in terror.

As her daughter's scream pierced the armor of anger in which Clara Wagner had wrapped herself, she realized with horror exactly where Germaine had chosen to hide from her mother's wrath. She reached out for the elevator's control, but the wheelchair had lodged itself against the back wall, one wheel jammed firmly into a crevice in the metal latticework, and her fingers hovered just short of the button that would stop the cage's descent. She fumbled wildly for the panel on the chair's right arm, but Clara's now-trembling fingers missed their target, and her heart began to beat erratically as she realized what was about to happen.

Then her fingers found the wheelchair's controls and pushed hard.

The motor hummed; the chair shuddered but did not

budge. The back wheel remained tightly jammed between the ornate ironwork struts of the cage.

Clara struggled harder, pushing at the cage itself in an effort to free the chair, but she had long ago let her muscles go far too flaccid to obey her commands now.

She leaned forward, stretching toward the elevator button, her heart racing wildly.

A stab of pain slashed through her head and her whole body stiffened. Then, as Germaine uttered yet another howl of pure terror, a great fist of pain smote Clara's head and she slumped in her chair.

Germaine's terrified howl rose into a scream of pure agony.

The cry built, rising through the great entry hall, expanding to fill the house. The air trembled with it, and then, so suddenly that even the silence that followed seemed to echo, it ended.

So also did the clanking of the elevator, and the grinding of the machine that ran it.

For a moment that seemed to stretch into eternity, silence reigned.

Then, as the pain that had crashed down on her slowly lifted, Clara Wagner moaned.

She tried to cry out—tried to call for help—but no words emerged from her lips.

Instead there was only an unintelligible stream of meaningless sound.

She tried to move.

As the worst terror she had ever felt closed around her, Clara Wagner realized that she was no longer in her wheelchair by choice.

Chapter 7

*R*ebecca was running, and even though she couldn't see her pursuer, she knew exactly what it was.

The dark figure, the same one she'd seen the night of the Hartwicks' party, moving silently down their driveway, then disappearing into the whirling snow so completely that it was almost as if he'd never been there at all.

But he was here tonight, chasing her. There was no way to escape him.

She was in the street, and there were houses on both sides, all of them brightly lit, all of them filled with people. But when Rebecca tried to scream, tried to call out for help, her throat constricted, and no sound emerged.

Her legs and feet seemed to work no better than her voice. Though she was running as hard as she could, she was barely moving at all, for her feet felt as if they were mired in mud, and every muscle in her legs ached from exhaustion. And every second the dark figure was looming closer to her.

Suddenly, the houses around her disappeared, leaving her in utter darkness. Terror clutching at her throat, she sensed the threatening figure lurch ever closer, and she redoubled her efforts, plunging through the darkness, unheeding of where she might be running to, so long as she was escaping her pursuer.

Now she felt hands reaching out, grasping at her, and

336

she tried to pull away, but the hands closed on her, and then she fell, a muffled scream escaping her lips, and—

Rebecca listened to the rapid beating of her heart, a thudding in the silence of the house.

She had no idea what time it was, no idea how long she'd slept. After taking the tea things back to the kitchen and retreating to her room, she'd stretched out on her bed, intending only to close her eyes for a minute or two—to try to relax—but when she'd jerked awake from the nightmare a few minutes ago, her mind was as foggy as if she'd been sleeping for hours. She wasn't even certain whether the muffled cry that ended her sleep had come from somewhere downstairs or only been the end of the terrible dream in which—

But the dream had vanished from her mind, every detail of it erased so completely that had she not still been in the last, weakening clutches of its terror, she might have wondered if she'd had the dream at all. Yet she was sure it was the nightmare that had awakened her, and as the mist in her mind slowly cleared away, other sounds filtered in. A few minutes ago she'd heard a crash coming from the second floor.

She'd almost gone downstairs to investigate. Then she remembered the beautiful handkerchief that Oliver had given her, and that Germaine had promptly snatched away to give to her mother. *It doesn't matter,* she told herself. *Germaine has been very kind to you, and if she wanted the handkerchief for Miss Clara, you shouldn't begrudge it.* But when Miss Clara hadn't wanted it after all, why had Germaine insisted on keeping it for herself?

Even so, she reminded herself, *if something is wrong downstairs, you should go see if you can help.*

Still she hesitated, the strange scene she'd witnessed in the parlor fresh in her memory. What had come over

Germaine? From the moment she'd opened the box of chocolates, it had been as if . . .

Even in the privacy of her own mind, Rebecca hesitated to use the word that had popped into her head. Yet there was no other way to describe it.

It was as if Germaine suddenly had gone crazy.

Although it had been no more than a minute or two before Germaine fled the room, the scene had terrified Rebecca. When she'd taken the tea tray back to the kitchen, her hands were trembling so badly that she was afraid she might drop it. And she still had no idea at all what had happened to Germaine.

She recalled, then, hearing glass breaking, followed by a sound that was part scream and part moan. Had she not been so badly frightened by the terrible scene in the parlor, Rebecca knew she would have hurried to see what had happened.

But what if Germaine really had gone crazy? What if she would have attacked her?

The house had fallen silent for a few minutes, but then the noise started up again. She heard Miss Clara shouting, and decided that Germaine was no longer in her room and that she and her mother must be having a fight. Better not to interfere, she'd thought.

For the first time since she'd awakened, Rebecca felt the tension in her body ease a little. When she heard the grinding of the gears that operated the elevator, Rebecca concluded that the argument must be over.

A sudden scream—a scream so terrifying it made Rebecca's blood run cold—erupted through the house. At almost exactly the same instant, the elevator's machinery fell silent.

Finally, the terrible quiet.

It held Rebecca in a strange thrall. She stood motionless at her bedside, one hand on the iron footboard, straining to hear anything that might reveal whatever terrible tragedy had brought forth that final, awful, ear-splitting scream.

The silence seemed to turn into a living thing, taking on a terrifying, suffocating quality, and slowly it came to Rebecca that only she could end it. Unconsciously holding her breath, she finally gathered her courage to leave her room and walk to the top of the steep and narrow flight of stairs leading down to the second floor.

Her steps echoing hollowly, she descended the bare wood stairs and gazed down into the hall below. Though she saw nothing, she sensed that it was not empty.

It was as she started toward the head of the great sweeping staircase at the far end of the mezzanine that the silence was finally broken.

A sound—nothing more than a gurgling whimper—drifted up from below.

As she came to the elevator shaft, Rebecca paused and peered down. A glistening pool of blood was spreading across the floor in front of the elevator door.

Her heart pounding now, Rebecca ran to the head of the stairs. For one terrible moment she hesitated, instinctively knowing that whatever awaited her below was going to be far worse than anything she might be able to imagine, and wanting desperately to turn away from it, to go back to her room, to hide herself from whatever horror had transpired below.

But she knew she couldn't. Whatever it was had to be faced.

Gathering her strength, Rebecca walked down the stairs and gazed upon the elevator.

Clara Wagner was slumped in her wheelchair inside the cage. Her eyes were open and seemed to be staring at Rebecca, but her jaw hung slack, and spittle dripped from the corner of her mouth.

Rebecca was certain she was dead.

The pool of blood was still spreading out from beneath

the elevator, and for one brief instant Rebecca failed to understand exactly what had happened.

Then she saw it.

From beneath the narrow space between the bottom of the elevator and the floor itself, an arm protruded.

Clutched in the fingers of the hand, Rebecca saw the handkerchief.

The handkerchief that Oliver had given her.

Her mind utterly numbed by the terrible vision spread before her, Rebecca moved across the broad sweep of the Oriental carpet, bent down and reached for the handkerchief.

Germaine Wagner's fingers, even in death, seemed to tighten on the scrap of linen for a moment, but then relaxed.

Suddenly, a stream of strangled, unintelligible sounds gurgled out of Clara Wagner's throat.

Jumping as if she'd received a jolt of electricity, Rebecca gasped, then whirled to face the old woman in the wheelchair.

Clara Wagner's eyes were glowing malevolently now, and the fingers of her right hand were twitching spasmodically, as if she were still trying to make her wheelchair respond to her bidding.

Terrified by the specter of the old woman who seemed to have come back from the dead before her very eyes, Rebecca backed away a step or two, then fled out into the night.

Help!

She had to find help!

She ran down the sidewalk into the street, then hesitated, wondering where to go.

Oliver!

If she could just get to Oliver, he would be able to help her!

Racing to the corner, she started up Amherst Street.

And the memory of the dream—the memory that had

vanished so completely when she'd awakened only a little while ago—came flooding back.

A terrible, unreasoning panic rose in Rebecca, and suddenly she was caught up in the nightmare once more. The darkness of the night closed around her; even the houses on either side of the street seemed to shrink away, retreating beyond her reach.

Once more her feet seemed to be mired in sludge, and every muscle in her legs was aching.

Now she could feel a presence—a terrifying, evil presence—close behind her.

She opened her mouth to cry out, to scream for someone to help her, but just as in the dream, her throat was constricted and no sound emerged.

Her heart pounding, her lungs failing her, she forced her legs to move, lunging up the hill into the darkness.

An arm reached out of the darkness, sliding around her neck, and then, as she finally found her voice, a hand clamped over her mouth.

A hand made slick by a latex glove.

Chapter 8

*T*he dark figure prowled the cold stone building like a panther patrolling his domain, every nerve on edge, every muscle tense.

He could sense the trespassers everywhere; it was as if their very scent was in the air. Every room they had entered seemed somehow violated, as if that which was rightfully his had been taken away.

Yet nothing was gone.

Everything was exactly as it had been before, save for the dust that was disturbed as they tramped from one room to another.

Opening doors they had no right to open.

Touching things that were never meant for any fingers but his own.

Peering into every closet and drawer, trying to ferret out his secrets.

What right had they to invade his realm?

He tracked them as easily as a carnivore stalking its prey, knowing where they'd been with as much certainty as if they were still there, and he were slinking after them, watching them with a wary eye.

The third floor was where they'd spent the least of their time, barely stopping at some of the rooms, entering only a few. But why not? There was nothing much here—never had been.

What little it contained were castoffs, things of little interest and even smaller value.

They'd explored the rooms on the second floor more thoroughly, entering every one, running their fingers over every object—*his* objects.

He sensed at once what they were doing, of course.

Placing values on every object they found, trying to determine what each one might be worth. But what did it matter what the building's contents were worth?

The things within the Asylum were not theirs to sell.

All of it—every bit of it!—was his.

It wasn't so bad on the ground floor. The rooms on that floor, shielded from the world outside by the two great oaken doors, had always been filled with strangers, and the three who had been there that day made little difference. Indeed, as he moved quickly through the rooms, it was almost as if their presence had made no difference at all.

It was in the lowest rooms of all, the chambers that had been hidden away in the basement by purposeful design, that he most sharply felt the ravages of the invasion that had taken place that day.

Their voices seemed still to echo within the tiled walls of those wondrous chambers in which the work had been performed. As he moved from one to another, remembering perfectly the specific use for which each had been designed, the rage simmering within him began to boil, for he knew deep within his soul that the interlopers had not looked upon these rooms with the respect they deserved.

They had been repulsed by what they found here. Even now their condemnation hung like a poisonous vapor in the air. As he completed his inspection, his indignation swelled, for he knew that despite what they had felt, these petty, conniving fools had no real idea at all of what transpired in these rooms, to what uses these sacred spaces had actually been put.

How, he wondered, would they feel if they truly understood?

Well, soon they would, for he was going to show them.

With satisfaction, he tested the concealed entrance to the most important room of all, and found it undisturbed.

This room, still, was known to no one but himself.

This room, which contained his most cherished treasures.

From one of the shelves he took a large mahogany box, and set it on the table. Opening the box, he lifted an ancient stereoscope from the larger of the box's two compartments, and a stack of curled and yellowed cards from the smaller. Gently placing one of the cards in the rack at one end of the stereoscope, he held the instrument to his eyes and peered through the lenses.

There was just enough light filtering through the window from the waning moon to illuminate the image.

Before him was an old-fashioned room, filled with overstuffed sofas and chairs, and ornate tables covered with bric-a-brac. The illusion of three dimensions was so perfect that he almost felt as if he might be able to reach into the room itself, pick up one of the objects, and handle it.

But of course he couldn't.

After all, the stereoscope was only an amusement, and the images it offered no more than illusions of reality.

Still, it was a toy that would make a perfect gift. . . .

To be continued . . .

PART 5
DAY OF RECKONING: THE STEREOSCOPE

Prelude

To any creature of the daylight, the dark shape would have been all but invisible as it moved through the inky corridors of the ancient stone building. Nor would any but the sharpest ears have heard it, so certain were its footsteps, so easily did it avoid any of the floorboards that might have betrayed its presence with the slightest creak.

Yet even in its silence and invisibility, the figure carried with it an aura of evil that spread before it like a chill wind, reaching into every room it neared, lingering even after the figure had passed by.

But unlike the dark figure's forays on earlier nights, when it had moved with eagerness through the halls and passages of its domain, on this night it crept almost reluctantly from its lair, drifting slowly through the corridors as if it had no wish to reach its destination. And indeed it did not, for tonight it would part with one of its most precious treasures, and though it was eager to revel in the madness the stereoscope would cause, still it was loath to give up the cherished memories the object held for it.

Prologue

Though he was barely eighteen, the boy had the heavy bones of a man who had long since reached his full maturity, and his large frame easily bore the muscles he had spent every day of the last four years building into indestructibility. Even now, though both his wrists and ankles were shackled to chains that were in turn affixed to heavy iron eyebolts mounted in the room's thick stone outer wall, he still exercised his body every day, maintaining his strength toward the time when he would escape from this room, slip free of the gray walls that surrounded him, and return to the world beyond.

The world where all his fantasies—all his darkest dreams—could once again be brought to life.

The room in which he was shackled held nothing more than the barest necessities:

A metal cot, as firmly fixed to the wall as the eyebolts that secured his chains.

A metal chair, screwed to the floor next to a metal table just large enough to hold the tray on which his food was brought.

A single barred window that pierced the wall, allowing him to gaze upon the village at the bottom of the hill with malevolent eyes.

A lone bulb, unshaded but protected by a thick glass and metal casing, was mounted in the exact center of the ceiling. The glaring light never dimmed, depriving him nightly of a haven of darkness in which to sleep.

A peephole in the door allowed the staff to keep watch on him. Though he could never see the eyes that observed him, he always knew when they were there.

He had been allowed only a single object to distract him from the endless empty hours his life had become: a stereoscope, brought to him by his grandmother.

"He's a good boy," the old woman had told his doctor. "He didn't do what they say. It's not possible. I'll never believe it." She had pleaded long and hard, and finally the doctor, convinced more by the size of the check she left behind than by her entreaties, agreed: the boy could have the instrument, along with the dozen images his grandmother had provided.

Since that day, the boy had whiled away most of his waking hours staring through the lenses of the stereoscope at the three-dimensional images. They were all pictures of home—the home they said he would never see again.

All the rooms were there for him to behold:

The big formal living room in which his parents entertained their friends.

The dining room, where two dozen people had often gathered for holiday feasts.

The nursery in which he'd spent the first two years of his life, before his brother had been born.

There were exterior views of the house too, of the enormous yard filled with spreading trees. Beneath these branches, he had first begun dreaming his wonderful fantasies.

His favorite image, though, was the one he was gazing upon today.

It was of his room.

Not this room, but his room at home, the room he'd grown up in, the room that had provided him refuge when the fantasies began.

The room in which he'd brought his darkest dreams to life.

It had been easy at first. No one noticed when the squirrels that had always annoyed him so much began to disappear from the trees outside his window; even the disappearance of a few yowling cats hadn't caused any trouble.

The next-door neighbors, though, and the people down the street had come looking for their dogs. Of course, he denied knowing anything. Why, after all, should he have told anyone that he'd skinned their pets alive, and hidden their bodies in the back of his closet?

When his best friend vanished, he had shed the proper tears—though he didn't really feel any emotion except relief that one more annoyance was removed from his life—and afterward decided not to bother with friends anymore.

For a while things had been all right. Soon, though, the little girl—his sister—started to annoy him, and he began to fantasize about sending her to join the others.

It made him furious when they finally came and took him away from his room. He struggled, but there were too many of them. Despite his screams and his shouted denials, they brought him up here and chained him to the wall.

They watched him.

He'd screamed every time they came near him, pouring out vivid threats of exactly what he'd do when he got loose and had his knives back. Finally, it seemed they decided to leave him alone. Except for the orderly who slid his meals through the slot in the door, he hadn't seen anyone for a long time.

Which was fine with him.

At least if they stayed away, he wouldn't have to kill them.

Not that he'd mind killing them, since killing what annoyed him had turned out to be the perfect way not only of satisfying his anger but of realizing his dreams.

He was still gazing at the image of his room at home, constructing a wonderful fantasy of what he might do if he were there right now, when he heard a noise at the door. Startled, he turned to see three men entering his room. He dropped the stereoscope and stood up, his fury at their invasion of his space already blazing from his eyes.

"Take it easy," one of the men said, glancing at the chains warily as if expecting the boy might free himself from his shackles. "We're only here to help you."

The boy's eyes narrowed, his jaw tightened, and he crouched low, ready to strike the moment they came within range of his fists. If he could just wrap one of his chains around one of their necks . . .

For interminable seconds no one in the room moved. Then, very slowly, the three men began edging closer.

Every muscle in his body tensed; his face contorted with fury.

"You can't win," one of the men said softly. "You might as well not even try." With a flick of his right hand that signaled his colleagues to act, he lunged for the boy.

Twenty minutes later, when the battle finally ended, the boy lay strapped to a gurney with thick bands of leather, his eyes still glittering with rage, his muscles knotting as he struggled against his bonds. Of the three men who had come for him, two had broken noses and the third a crushed hand. Although the patient had finally been controlled, he still had not been subdued.

"Do you understand what is going to happen to you?" the doctor asked. The boy glared up from the gurney and made no reply, except to spit in the doctor's face. The doctor impassively wiped the glob of phlegm away from his cheek, then began reading aloud from a document that had been issued by the court six weeks earlier. When

he finished his recitation, he glanced at the team around him. The three injured orderlies had been replaced by three others, and two nurses stood by. "Shall we proceed?"

The team in the operating room nodded their agreement. The orderlies moved the gurney into position next to an operating bench that had been constructed specifically for the procedure the doctor was about to carry out. A notch was cut in the bench, allowing the end of the gurney to slip under the open jaws of a large viselike clamp.

The boy's head was held immobile as the jaws were tightened on his temples.

Using a pair of electrodes, the doctor administered a quick series of shocks to the boy's head, and then, before the temporary anesthetic the shocks had provided could wear off, he went to work.

As a nurse peeled the boy's right eyelid back, the doctor found his tear duct and inserted the needlelike point of a long pick into it. With a sharp rap to the other end of the pick, he drove the point of the instrument through the orbital plate. Measuring the distance carefully, the doctor slid the pick into the soft tissue inside the boy's skull until its tip had sunk two full inches into his brain.

Satisfied that the tool was properly placed, the doctor expertly flicked it through a twenty-degree arc, tearing through the nerves of the frontal lobe.

The boy's body relaxed on the gurney, and his twisted grimace of rage softened into a gentle smile.

The doctor withdrew the pick from the boy's tear duct and nodded to one of the nurses. "That's it. His eye might be sore for a day or so, but frankly, I doubt that he'll even notice it." His work done, the doctor left the operating room.

One of the nurses swabbed the boy's eye with alcohol; the other taped a bandage over it.

While one of the orderlies released the clamps that held the boy's head immobile, the other two loosened the leather straps that bound him.

The boy did nothing more than smile up at them.

Three days later, when the bandage was removed from the boy's eye, he picked up the stereoscope and peered once more through its lenses.

The image of his room was still there, but it no longer looked the same, for when the doctor had plunged the pick into the boy's brain, it had cut through the optic nerve. He no longer saw in three dimensions, so the illusion provided by the stereoscope was gone. It didn't matter, though, for everything inside the boy's head had changed.

His fantasies were gone. Never again would he be able to make his dreams come true.

The dark figure lingered in the cold, silent room, his fingers stroking the smooth mahogany of the stereoscope's case. But he knew the moment had come. Reluctantly, with a last, loving caress to the satiny dark wood, he bent and placed the stereoscope in the fourth drawer of the oaken chest, sliding the drawer closed.

Soon—very soon—his gift would be in other hands. The hands carefully selected to receive it. Once more the past would return to haunt Blackstone.

Chapter 1

*E*d Becker shuddered as he gazed up at the grimy stone facade of the Asylum. "Sometimes I wonder if the whole idea of trying to turn this monstrosity into something nice makes any sense at all." Though it was an early Friday morning that promised a perfect spring day, even the bright sunlight couldn't wash away the ominous aura that seemed to him to hang over the building. "I have an awful feeling we might all wind up taking a bath on this deal."

Bill McGuire got out and slammed the door of his pickup truck. He barely glanced at the looming form of the building as he dropped the tailgate down and pulled the hand truck out of its bed. "You've been reading too many novels," he told Becker. "It's just an old building. By the time I'm done renovating it, you won't even recognize it."

"Maybe so." Becker sighed as they mounted the front steps. He and Bill, along with others, had returned here on Wednesday, and again yesterday, to search the cold, dark rooms and every inch of the ten-acre grounds for Rebecca Morrison, with no success. Now he said, "I'm starting to wonder if Edna Burnham's right and whatever's going on around here has something to do with this place."

As the contractor's face flushed with anger, the attorney wished he'd kept his thought to himself. It was too late now. "Look, Bill, I'm sorry," he said quickly. "I

354

didn't mean to imply that what happened to Elizabeth was—well . . ." He floundered, struggling to find a way to extricate himself from his gaffe, but decided anything more he might add would only make matters worse. "I'm sorry," he said again. "I should have kept my mouth shut." For a second or two he braced himself, thinking McGuire might take a swing at him, but then saw the anger drain from the contractor's expression.

"Forget it," McGuire said. "I don't know why I still let it get to me. I mean, it's not as if I'm not hearing those ugly whispers from everyone else in town. It's not just Edna Burnham anymore."

It was true. In the two days since Germaine Wagner's body had been discovered crushed beneath the elevator in her own house, rumors had been sweeping through Blackstone like a virus, a contagion of fear and suspicion. Clara Wagner had been moved to a nursing home in Manchester only yesterday. Witness to her daughter's hideous death, she had suffered a massive stroke that robbed her of language; Clara would never reveal the events of that awful night her daughter had died. Germaine had been quietly buried as soon as the coroner had finished the examination of the body. By her own request, found neatly filed among Germaine's papers, there had been no funeral.

Steve Driver, the deputy sheriff, had searched every corner of Clara Wagner's house with as much energy as the fire chief had expended in sifting through the ruins of Martha Ward's place after it had been destroyed in a devastating conflagration a few weeks earlier. But his investigation proved equally fruitless.

There was obvious evidence of violence: nearly everything in Germaine Wagner's bedroom was overturned, her bathroom mirror shattered, blood everywhere. But even the criminalist Steve had immediately called in from Manchester had found no signs that anyone but Germaine had been involved. Blood samples from the bedroom and bathroom, from the stairs, from the Oriental carpet on the floor of the great entry hall were the same: all were Germaine Wagner's.

Most disturbing of all, Rebecca Morrison had disappeared. The only possible witness who might be able to describe these terrible events had vanished. Where was she—and was she in danger, if indeed she was still alive? Had Rebecca witnessed a dreadful accident—or a horrible crime? Had she fled in terror—or in guilt? Or had some unspeakable tragedy befallen her as well as the Wagner women? Searches of the town and the surrounding countryside had produced no trace of her, nor had appeals for information brought forth any clue. Even the Asylum had been combed, to no avail. Speculation burned like wildfire: Some said Rebecca had suffered a mental breakdown and turned on her benefactor. Others recalled that there was a dark side to Germaine Wagner's generosity, and that while it was true that she had employed Rebecca and given her a home when Rebecca's had burned down, she had also been treating Rebecca for years with the kind of patronizing attitude that no one but Rebecca would have tolerated for more than a minute.

Had Rebecca finally been pushed too far, into an act of cold-blooded murder from which she had fled?

Steve Driver found these whispered theories ridiculous. He'd known both Rebecca Morrison and Germaine Wagner for better than twenty years. He was unable to imagine Rebecca in the role of murderess. Moreover, she would never have been able to inflict the kind of wounds Germaine had sustained without injuring herself as well. The litter of broken glass in the bathroom alone gave the lie to that idea. Nor had he been able to find even a sliver of evidence that anyone except the three people who lived in the house were there that night.

Blackstone was pressing for answers, no one more so than Oliver Metcalf, and Driver had none, not a single thing that made any sense. On Thursday evening Oliver had burst yet again into the deputy's office, demanding a report of Driver's progress. At a loss, and before he could stop himself, Driver sardonically suggested that maybe Germaine had been the recipient of the same kind of "gift" that had brought tragedy into three other Blackstone houses over the last few months. To his utter shock, Oliver Metcalf's face paled.

"Oh my God," Oliver whispered. "It was *my* fault. I gave Rebecca a handkerchief. It had an R embroidered on it. . . . I—I thought it would be perfect for her."

"For Christ's sake, Oliver!" Driver said, astonished. "I was kidding! Don't tell me even you believe that crap Edna Burnham's been spreading around!"

Though both men would have been willing to swear they'd been alone in the deputy's office, the rumor of another "cursed" gift had swept like a plague through the town.

When the latest rumors had reached Bill McGuire, though, he'd dismissed them in disgust. Now he repeated to Ed Becker the same words he'd spoken to Velma Tuesday afternoon when he'd stopped in at the Red Hen for a piece of pecan pie and a cup of coffee after his tour of the Asylum with Ed and Melissa Holloway. "What happened to Elizabeth was a direct result of her miscarriage. It had nothing at all to do with the doll that showed up at our house. Megan still has the doll, and nothing's happened to her, has it?"

"Of course not," Ed Becker agreed. "And nothing's going to either."

Bill McGuire unlocked the Asylum's huge front door. As it swung open, Ed Becker felt a chill as a mass of cold air rushed from the building. Unbidden memories of stories he'd read as a boy blossomed in his mind, and he shivered as he remembered that a mass of cold air in a room invariably presaged a ghostly presence.

Or merely a lack of heat in a big old building on a

warm morning, he told himself as the chill passed as quickly as it had come. But when he stepped inside, it seized him again. The door closed, shutting the bright sunlight out, and the gloom closed around him like a suffocating shroud.

Suddenly he wondered if he really wanted the oak dresser they'd come to pick up.

"Getting to you?" Bill McGuire asked, grinning at the lawyer's obvious discomfort. "Maybe you'd like to wait outside while I go up and get the dresser."

"I'm fine," Ed Becker insisted, hearing too late the extra emphasis that belied his words. "All right, so I think it's a little creepy in here. So sue me."

McGuire laughed. "Spoken like a true lawyer." But then he too shivered, and found himself wishing he could just turn on the lights and wash the dark shadows from the rooms they were passing through.

Both men breathed a little easier as they came to the stairs to the second floor, if only because of the sunlight flooding through the windows behind the staircase. Yet even here they found a grim reminder of the building's last use, for the thick metal grill that had been placed over the windows decades earlier still cast forbidding prison-bar shadows on the bare wood floor.

It was as Ed Becker came to the top of the stairs that the hairs on the back of his neck stood on end and goose bumps rose on both his arms.

He knew, as surely as he knew his own name, that he and Bill McGuire were not alone.

An instant later, as McGuire too froze, he heard a sound.

It was faint, barely audible, but it was there.

"Did you hear that?" McGuire asked, his hand closing on Becker's forearm.

"I—I'm not sure," Ed Becker whispered, unwilling to admit how frightened he was. "Maybe . . ." His words died on his lips as he heard the sound again. This time there was no mistaking it.

Somewhere down the hall, in one of the long-abandoned rooms, someone—or some*thing*—was moving.

Ed Becker tried to swallow the lump of fear that blocked his throat.

The sound came a third time. It seemed to echo from one of the rooms on the left side of the wide corridor, halfway down the hall.

The room where the dresser is, Ed Becker thought, and his fear instantly notched a level higher.

Moving to the left so he was pressed protectively close to the wall, Bill McGuire began edging slowly down the corridor. Ed Becker followed hesitantly, his movement motivated less by bravery than by terror at the idea of remaining in the hall by himself.

As they drew closer to the room, they heard the sound yet again.

A scratching, as if something were trying to get through a door.

The door, which stood slightly ajar, suddenly moved.

Not much, but enough so that both of them saw it.

"Who is it?" McGuire called out. "Who's there?"

The scratching sound instantly stopped.

Seconds that seemed to Ed Becker like minutes crept by, and then Bill McGuire, closer to the door than Becker, motioned to the lawyer to stay where he was. Treading so lightly that he created no sound at all, McGuire inched closer to the door. He paused for a moment, then leaped toward the door and hurled it all the way open. There was a loud crash as the door smashed against the wall, then Bill McGuire jumped aside as a raccoon burst through the doorway, raced past Ed Becker, and disappeared up the stairs.

"Jesus." Ed Becker swore softly, utterly disgusted with himself for the terror he had felt only a moment ago. "Let's get the damn dresser and get out of here before we both have a heart attack." Retrieving the hand truck from the landing, he followed Bill McGuire into the room.

The chest of drawers was exactly where it had been on Tuesday afternoon, apparently untouched by anything more sinister than the raccoon.

Five minutes later, with the dresser strapped firmly to the hand truck, they reemerged into the bright morning sunlight to find Oliver Metcalf waiting by the truck. As they loaded it into the back of the pickup without bothering to unstrap it from the hand truck, Oliver eyed the old oak chest.

"You actually want that thing?" he asked as Ed Becker carefully shut the tailgate.

"Wait'll you see it after I'm done with it," Becker replied. "You'll wish you'd kept it yourself."

Oliver shook his head. "Not me," he said, his gaze shifting to the Asylum. "As far as I'm concerned, anything that comes out of there should go straight to the dump."

Ed Becker looked quizzically at him. "Come on, Oliver. It's only a piece of furniture."

Oliver Metcalf's brows arched doubtfully. "Maybe so," he agreed. "But I still wouldn't have it in my house." Then: "You guys want a cup of coffee?"

Becker shook his head. "I promised Bonnie I wouldn't be gone more than half an hour. Amy's home from school with sniffles and driving Bonnie crazy. How about a rain check?"

"Anytime," Oliver said.

Ed Becker and Bill McGuire got into the truck. As they drove away, Oliver caught one last glimpse of the oak dresser that stood in the truck's bed.

And as the image registered on his brain, a stab of pain slashed through his head.

*   *   *

The boy stares at the hypodermic needle that sits on the chest, not certain what is about to happen, but still terrified.

The man picks up the needle and comes toward the boy.

Though the boy cowers back, he knows there is no escape. He does his best not to cry out as the man plunges the needle into his arm.

Then blackness closes around him.

By the time the pain in his head had eased and Oliver was able to start back to his house, the truck had disappeared down Amherst Street, as completely as the image had disappeared from Oliver's memory.

Chapter 2

*R*ebecca Morrison had no idea where she was, no idea how long she'd been there.

Her last truly clear memory was of awakening from a nightmare to hear terrible noises coming from downstairs. She remembered leaving her little room in the attic, but after that her mind could provide her with only a jumble of images:

Germaine's room. A broken lamp on the floor. Bright red bloodstains.

More bloodstains on the stairs. On the carpet.

And an arm.

She clearly remembered an arm, sticking out from under the elevator.

Had Miss Clara been in the elevator?

She thought so, but even that wasn't clear.

She remembered running out into the night—she must have been trying to get help—but after that, everything was a blank.

The next thing she remembered was slowly waking up, not knowing whether she was awake or trapped in a dream of wakefulness.

She'd been cloaked in darkness, plunged into a blackness so deep it had seemed she was drowning in it, unable even to catch her breath. When her mind had cleared enough for her to realize she was not dreaming, was not dying, but was awakening instead in some strange, lightless place, her first terrified thought was that she'd been buried alive.

A wave of panic overwhelmed her. She tried to scream, but all that emerged was a muffled groan that jammed in her throat, causing her to cough and choke.

Taped!

Her mouth was taped, so she couldn't give vent to the coughing, and for a second it seemed as if her head might actually explode. Finally, though, she'd managed to control the coughing—she still wasn't sure how.

Slowly—very slowly—her panic had eased, only to give way to something even worse.

The tape wasn't just over her mouth—it bound her wrists and ankles as well.

She was on a floor—a hard floor, covered with no rugs or carpeting. In the total blackness, she could not judge how large or small the room she was in might be.

A silence as deep as the blackness surrounded her. As time crawled endlessly on, the eerie quiet became as frightening as the dark.

Then the cold began to wrap itself around her.

It was a cold she'd barely noticed when she first came awake. But as the minutes and hours slithered by, and she could neither hear nor see, the cold, her sole companion, edged closer and closer, engulfing her in its clammy arms, slowly invading not only her body but her spirit as well.

Soon it had seeped into her very bones so her whole body ached. No matter how she tried to writhe away from it, there was no escape.

Sleep became impossible, for whenever exhaustion and terror overcame her, and her mind finally retreated into unconsciousness for a moment or two, the nightmares that thrived on the cold chased after her, torturing her even in her sleep so that when once again she came awake, body and spirit woke even more debilitated than before.

Her sense of time deserted her; day and night had long since lost their meaning.

In the first hours—or perhaps even days—she'd thought she might starve to death. When she first awakened, she had been far too terrified even to think about food or water, but even fear must eventually give way to hunger. At some point the ache induced by the increasing cold had been punctuated by pangs of hunger, stabbings that eventually settled into a dull agony that attacked her mind as efficiently as it ravaged her body.

With the hunger had come thirst, a parching so powerful she thought she would die from it. How long would it take to die? How much longer before hunger, or thirst, or some unnamed evil that would strike from out of the darkness brought deliverance from this unending agony?

The hunger and thirst, and the terror of the darkness, the emptiness, and the nightmares would go on until she finally sank into an oblivion that, she knew, would be welcome once it came.

But until then . . .

A sob rose in her throat, but she quickly put it down, knowing it would only choke her once it rose high enough. And when she felt hot wetness flooding her eyes, she battled against it, refusing to waste so much as a single drop of water on something as useless as tears.

The very effort required to wrestle against her raging emotions somehow put her terror under control, and after an interminable period of time—Rebecca had no idea how long it might have been—she finally conquered the worst of the demons that had come to her out of the darkness.

Over and over again she told herself that she was still alive, and that soon—very soon—someone would come and rescue her.

But how long would *soon* be?

There was no way of knowing.

Again, she shook off a demon nightmare brought on by the cold and roused herself from the fitful sleep into which she'd fallen. But the moment she came awake, she knew that something had changed.

Something in the quality of the darkness was different, and she knew with utter certainty that she was no longer alone.

She lay perfectly still, holding every muscle in check, not daring even to breathe as she listened to the silence.

It too had changed.

No longer the empty, eerie silence she had awakened into before, now there seemed to be something— something not-quite-audible—lurking just beyond the range of her hearing.

And her skin was crawling, as if some primeval sixth sense detected watching eyes that her own could not see.

Her heart raced; her pulse throbbed in her ears.

Whatever lurked in the darkness drew closer.

An icy sheen of sweat oozed from Rebecca's pores, making her skin slick with fear.

And then she felt the touch.

A shriek rose in her throat as something so feather-light as almost not to be there at all brushed against her face, but once again the tape securing her mouth cut off her cry, and her howl of terror was strangled into a whimper.

The touch came again, and then, finally, the silence was broken.

"The beginning. This is only the beginning." The words were spoken with so little voice that they could have been no more than the whisper of a breeze, but in the silent darkness they echoed and resounded, filling Rebecca once more with indescribable terror.

The voice whispered again.

"Cry out if you want to. No one can hear you. No one would care if they could."

Then she felt the touch once more.

It was firmer this time, and it instantly brought back a terrible memory.

She had fled the house to get help. She was racing up Amherst Street, intent on getting to Oliver's house at the very top, just inside the gates to the old Asylum. And suddenly—with no warning—an arm had snaked around her neck and a hand had clamped over her mouth.

A hand, she had realized just before terror overcame her, that was covered in thin latex.

The same thin latex that covered the unseen finger now stroking her cheek.

The tape was ripped from her mouth.

Instinctively, Rebecca opened her mouth to scream, but before even the slightest sound came out, a voice inside her head gave her a warning:

He wants you to scream. He wants to hear your fear.

Exercising the control she had somehow gathered around her during the endless hours of cold and darkness, Rebecca remained utterly silent.

As she had for hours—perhaps days—she waited quietly in the dark.

The silence grew—stretched endlessly on. Though she could hear nothing, Rebecca could sense the growing fury of her tormentor.

She decided she would not give him whatever it was he wanted from her.

Not now.

Not ever.

Finally she spoke.

"You might as well kill me," she said, somehow managing to keep her voice from quavering even a little bit. "If that's what you're going to do, you might as well do it right now."

Again silence hung in the darkness like an almost palpable mass, but just as Rebecca thought she could stand it no more, the whisper drifted out of the void.

"You'll wish I had," it breathed. "Soon you'll wish I had."

She'd braced herself then, uncertain what to expect next.

All that happened was that the tape was put back on her mouth, and the hours of silence and darkness began again.

Now and then he came back.

He brought her water.

He brought her food.

He did not speak.

Neither did she.

Slowly, she explored the room in which she was being held, creeping across the floor like some kind of larva, snuffling in the corners with her nose, touching what she could with her fingers, though her wrists were still bound behind her back.

Every surface she touched was cold and smooth.

The room was totally empty.

She no longer knew how many times she had crept around its perimeter and crisscrossed its floor, searching for something—anything—that might tell her where she was.

There was nothing.

Then, a little while ago, the silence had finally been truly broken.

She heard footsteps, and the muffled sound of voices, and for the first time since she'd found herself in the silent blackness, she tried to cry out.

Tried, and failed, frustrated by the thick tape that covered her mouth.

A little later she heard the muffled sounds again, and once more she struggled against the tape, trying to rub it off against the floor, but finding nothing that would catch its edge long enough for her to rip it free.

Then the voices faded away, and the black silence once again closed around her.

Chapter 3

"Go all the way down by the garage," Ed Becker told Bill McGuire. "My back's already starting to hurt, and the closer we get to the basement stairs, the better."

Bill McGuire glanced over at the attorney. "Still got a coal bin? Maybe we could just slide it right on down. At least then it'll be in the right place when you decide to shove it in the furnace."

"Very funny," Becker groused. "But when I'm done, you won't even recognize it."

"Exactly my point," the contractor taunted. He slowed the pickup to a stop about ten feet from the Beckers' garage, and swung out of the cab just as the back door flew open and Ed's five-year-old daughter, Amy, came barreling out, closely followed by Riley, a six-month-old Labrador puppy that Amy had managed to convince her parents was "absolutely the only thing I want for Christmas. If I can just have a puppy, I promise I'll never ask for anything else as long as I live so-help-me-God." While the campaign had worked sufficiently well so that the puppy had, indeed, taken up residence in the Becker house, Amy's father had yet to overcome the fear of dogs from which he'd suffered since he was his daughter's age. As the comparatively nonthreatening eight-week-old ball of fluff that Riley had been upon arrival developed into the immensely menacing—at least to Ed Becker—forty-pound medicine-ball-with-feet that Riley now was, Ed had become increasingly wary of his daughter's pet. Now, as Riley did his best to climb into Ed's arms and administer one of his specialty soggy face licks, the attorney who had never quailed before the most irate judge or angry client cowered away from the puppy's enthusiastic onslaught.

"Put him in the house, Amy," Ed ordered, reaching for authority although his guts seemed to have turned to Jell-O.

"He won't hurt you, Daddy," Amy replied with enough scorn to make her father blush. "He's just being friendly. He loves you!"

"Well, I don't love him," Ed muttered, now fending the dog off with both arms.

Riley, yapping happily and utterly unaware of the havoc he was wreaking on Ed's intestines, kept leaping at Ed's chest, enjoying the intricacies of this new game.

"Riley, *down*!" Bonnie Becker commanded as she thrust open the back door and joined the group around the pickup truck. The dog instantly dropped to the ground, though his entire body quivered with barely suppressed excitement as he gazed adoringly up at Ed. "Take him inside, Amy," Bonnie told her daughter. "Can't you see he's scaring your father half to death?"

Ed's embarrassed flush deepened as his daughter grasped the dog by the collar and began pulling him toward the house. Though the Lab, only a few inches shorter and no lighter than the little girl, could have dug in and refused to go, he happily submitted to his small mistress's tugging. Child and pet disappeared back into the house, and Ed, his courage fully restored now that the puppy was nowhere to be seen, attempted to recover a little of his dignity. "I am *not* afraid of him," he declared. "It's just that he's so big, he could hurt someone! He has to learn not to jump all over people!"

His wife nodded gravely. "You're absolutely right," Bonnie agreed. "Why don't you train him?"

Ed attempted a scathing look, failed miserably, then

flushed even redder when Bonnie giggled. "It's not funny!" he insisted, though now his own lips were starting to twitch. "He could really hurt someone!"

"Oh, he really could," Bill McGuire agreed, his expression deliberately deadpan. "I know I was scared out of my mind." He winked at Bonnie. "Did you see the nasty way his tail was wagging?"

"And the way his lips curled back when he tried to lick Ed's face," Bonnie added. "That was pretty scary."

"Oh, all right," Ed groused, finally recognizing he was going to get no sympathy. "So when it comes to dogs, I'm a wimp. So sue me." He went around to the tailgate of the truck, pulled it down, and began struggling with the big oak dresser. "You two going to help me with this, or would you rather just poke fun at me all day?"

"Poking fun sounds good to me," Bill McGuire said. "How about you, Bonnie?"

"I always think poking fun beats hauling junk furniture around," Bonnie agreed.

"It's not junk," Ed informed her. "It's solid oak, and it's at least a hundred years old, and—"

"And if it's not junk, then how come they gave it to you?" Bonnie asked.

"*Gave* it to him?" Bill McGuire asked, the question popping out of his mouth before he'd bothered to think of the implications of Bonnie's question. "Did he tell you we *gave* it—" Too late, he realized his mistake, then looked away so he could pretend he didn't see Ed glaring at him.

"How much?" Bonnie asked, suddenly far more interested in the dresser than she'd been even half a minute earlier. Moving closer to the pickup, she eyed the battered oak chest like a prizefighter sizing up an opponent, then offered her opening gambit. "I can't believe anybody would have the nerve to take money for this thing."

"You just don't know anything about antiques," Ed

parried, faking an offense as he tried to prepare his defense.

"Or Melissa Holloway," Bill McGuire added, though he wasn't certain whether his words would help or hinder his friend's cause.

Bonnie arched an eyebrow. "Melissa, huh? It's going to be even worse than I thought."

"That's hardly fair," Ed began, hoping to edge his wife into an entirely different arena. "In fact, it has all the earmarks of a very sexist remark."

Bonnie rolled her eyes. "It means I know Melissa, and frankly, if I had to place a bet on you or Melissa as a negotiator, I'm afraid I'd pick her. I love you very much, Ed, but I have a horrible feeling you paid a lot more than you should have for that dresser."

Seeing the slimmest chance at escape, Ed darted toward the opening Bonnie had given him. "What do you think I should have paid?"

Bonnie eyed her husband, then the dresser, then her husband once more, calculating how much he might have paid. A hundred? Maybe two? Surely not any more. She decided to let him off the hook. "Four hundred," she ventured, ready to repair his male ego by praising his shrewd bargaining when he proudly told her how much less he'd shelled out. When she saw him wince, she knew she'd guessed wrong.

"All right." She sighed. "The truth."

"A thousand," Ed told her, unable to look her in the eye.

Bonnie flinched, but then remembered the terror in Ed's eyes when they'd gone to pick up the puppy his daughter had wanted so badly. Moving closer to the truck, she pulled open one of the dresser's drawers and touched the dovetail joinery. "You might actually have made a good deal," she conceded. "When you get it restored, I'll bet you can sell it for twice that."

For the first time since he'd gotten out of the truck, Ed

Becker relaxed. "See?" he told Bill McGuire. "Even Bonnie can see how good a piece it is."

Ten minutes later, after Bill McGuire had unstrapped the dresser from the hand truck, helped Ed maneuver the heavy piece into his basement workshop, and headed back up the street to his own house, Ed began pulling the drawers out of the dresser, examining each one and assessing just how much work it was really going to take to bring the carved chest back to the beauty it had been a hundred years earlier.

It was in the fourth drawer that he discovered the mahogany box. Taking it out, he set it on top of the chest, then opened it as his wife entered the workshop. "My God." He whistled softly. "When was the last time you saw one of these?" Lifting the stereoscope out of the box, he held it carefully in both hands, turning it over so he could examine it from every angle. "It's perfect," he said. "Look—there's not a scratch on it."

Taking the instrument from Ed's hands, Bonnie held it up to her eyes and peered through the lenses, though there was no image to see. She tried working the focusing knob and the rack that would hold the cards, which moved easily along its track. And just as Ed had said, neither the brass fittings nor the leather and mahogany of which the stereoscope had been constructed bore any damage at all. With a little polish, the brass would gleam like new, and saddle soap would bring the leather back in just a few treatments. "Are there any pictures?" she asked.

"About a dozen," Ed replied. "Why don't you take it upstairs and show it to Amy? I'll be up as soon as I get the rest of the drawers out."

"Keep an eye out for treasure," Bonnie admonished him as she started for the basement stairs. "Who knows? Maybe some loony hid a fortune in there!" Easily ducking away from the mock swing Ed aimed at her, she picked up the mahogany box and took both it and the stereoscope upstairs.

Twenty minutes later, when Ed found Bonnie in the living room with Amy, both his wife and his daughter were absorbed in looking at the pictures. As he came into the room, Bonnie was handing the stereoscope to Amy. "What about this one?" he heard her ask.

Amy held the stereoscope up and peered through the lenses. "My room," she announced.

"Excuse me?" Ed asked. "What did she just say?"

"Her room," Bonnie told him. "It's what the picture's of."

Frowning, Ed crossed to the sofa where his wife and daughter were sitting. "What are you talking about?"

Bonnie looked at him. "It's the strangest thing," she said. "But all the pictures look like they're of this house."

Ed's frown deepened. "But that doesn't make any sense," he began. "Why would they be—"

"I didn't say it made sense," Bonnie told him. "In fact, I think—" She had been about to say she thought it was very, very weird, but remembered just in time that Amy never missed anything either of them said. "I think it's quite a coincidence," she finished, pointedly glancing at Amy, who was still peering through the stereoscope's lenses. "Let Daddy look," she said.

Reluctantly, Amy passed the stereoscope to her father, and Ed held it up to his eyes. All he saw was a large room furnished in Victorian style. "This doesn't look anything at all like Amy's room," he said.

"Not the way it is now," Bonnie agreed. "But take a look at this one." She lifted the card out of the stereoscope's rack, replacing it with another. "Look at the fireplace, and the bookcases, and the windows and door. Don't pay any attention to the furniture."

Ed gazed through the lenses at the three-dimensional image of a Victorian living room, filled with overstuffed furniture, tables covered with knickknacks, and ornate lamps with heavily fringed shades. But as he looked past the furniture at the features of the room itself, he began to realize that it appeared vaguely familiar. Then, slowly, it came into focus in his mind.

Take away the intricately patterned wallpaper, remove the thick velvet drapes, add paint to some of the wood-work, and completely refurnish it, and the room in the picture would be exactly like the one in which he was sitting.

Bonnie put another picture in the rack, and Ed Becker quickly recognized an earlier incarnation of his own dining room.

She changed the picture again, and he saw the back-yard, when the trees were smaller and the clapboards had been a darker shade than the pale gray they now were.

Finally he returned to the picture Amy had been looking at when he came in. Now he could see that it was, indeed, his daughter's room. His daughter's room as it might have been . . . when?

A hundred years ago?

Fifty?

He knew he had to find out.

Chapter 4

Steve Driver was seriously worried. His worries had been multiplying exponentially since Wednesday morning when Charlie Carruthers had arrived at the Wagners' to deliver their mail and discovered the door standing wide open and the house apparently deserted. It hadn't helped that instead of calling him immediately, old Charlie had followed his instincts and gone into the house, where he'd found Clara Wagner barely alive in her wheelchair and Germaine crushed under the elevator. In helping old Clara out of the elevator—a perfectly reasonable thing to do—he might well have destroyed evidence of an intruder. Evidence that could have stopped the clacking tongues that were, increasingly, suggesting that Rebecca Morrison was somehow to blame.

For all intents and purposes, the young woman had simply vanished off the face of the planet. God knows, he and Oliver, Bill McGuire, Ed Becker, and a party of other volunteers from Blackstone and even the surrounding towns had searched into the night on Wednesday and again all day yesterday before giving up.

Driver himself was absolutely certain that Germaine Wagner's hideous death had been a freak accident—though he still had no theory to explain why she'd been inside the elevator shaft in the first place—but he had no answers for those who were suggesting that Rebecca must have had something to do with it. After all, they asked, if she was innocent, why had she run away? Without doubt, some terrible scene had been enacted in Germaine's bedroom, but all the evidence indicated that whatever struggle occurred there, Germaine had been alone. The county coroner—a woman with a genius for excavating even the faintest evidence of a fight—had found nothing to implicate Rebecca Morrison, or anyone else.

Nothing had been scraped from beneath Germaine's fingernails; no telltale hairs or foreign fibers were found clinging to her clothes.

Which left Steve Driver, as well as everyone else in Blackstone, unable to account for Rebecca's disappearance. If she was abducted by someone who had killed Germaine, how had the killer managed to leave no trace of his presence behind?

And if she killed Germaine herself and then fled, why had she taken nothing with her? And left the door standing wide open, a sure signal to the first person who saw it that something was amiss inside the house?

Still, Rebecca was gone, he had no leads, and every hour the gossip was getting worse. Now, as he walked from his office to the bank, he wondered how best to conduct this interview. Would it be better to do it right out in front of everyone, where a few people might either overhear his questions or read his lips? Or should he conduct this part of his investigation in private, thus leaving everyone free to speculate about the questions he'd asked? He knew that technically the conversation should take place in private, but he also knew that there was one certain truth in places like Blackstone: people who talked behind closed doors had something to hide, and their conversations were therefore fair game for speculation.

Still, better to follow the rules, even if it did cause more talk.

"I wondered when you'd be in," Melissa Holloway said, rising from her chair as Ellen Golding showed him into the office Melissa now occupied in Jules Hartwick's place. "And I suspect I know what you want."

"Activity on Rebecca Morrison's accounts," Driver said as he lowered himself into the chair in front of Melissa's desk. He handed her a copy of the court order he'd gotten that morning instructing the bank to give him its cooperation.

"None, as of yesterday afternoon," Melissa told him.

"You already checked?"

Melissa nodded. "It struck me that if Rebecca were really trying to run away, she'd have to have some money. And she hasn't touched a dime."

"Nothing?" Driver asked. "Are you sure?"

"I'll check again." Melissa turned to her keyboard and typed rapidly. "But as of yesterday there hadn't been any withdrawals of cash, any checks, or any bank-card trans-actions." She fell silent for a moment as the screen in front of her came to life, then turned back to the deputy sheriff. "Still nothing."

Nor, Driver knew, could Rebecca have had much cash on hand, for even if she'd been in the habit of squirreling money away at home, whatever she might have hoarded would have gone up in the flames that consumed her aunt's house. In the few weeks she'd been living at the Wagners', there wouldn't have been time to build up any new reserves. "The truth of the matter is that I can't really imagine Rebecca running away from anything, anyway." Driver let out a sigh. "Knowing her, if she'd done anything to Germaine at all, she'd have called me herself."

"Then what happened?"

"If I knew, I wouldn't be here," Driver observed sourly. "It just doesn't make any damn sense. There isn't any evidence of a break-in, and even if an intruder had managed not to leave anything behind, I can't believe Rebecca wouldn't have screamed bloody murder."

"Or put up a fight," Melissa added as Steve, shaking

his head in a gesture of bewilderment and frustration, stood to end the interview. "Maybe it's the curse Edna Burnham keeps talking about," she went on, smiling as she rose to see him out of her office. Then, seeing the look on the deputy's face, she quickly apologized. "It was just a joke," she assured him. "But not a very funny one, huh?"

"No," Steve Driver agreed. "Not a very funny one at all."

The oak dresser was turning out to be a bigger project than Ed Becker had originally bargained for. A lot bigger. He'd come down to the basement right after dinner, expecting that within an hour or so he would have the dresser disassembled and all its hardware off. But after more than two hours, he was still wrestling with the top.

Of the eighteen screws that had secured the top to the dresser—a number Ed had initially regarded as a sign of "the kind of craftsmanship you just don't see anymore"—he had so far succeeded in removing only eleven. By now the "craftsmanship" Ed had admired only a couple of hours earlier had become "the kind of overkill only an idiot would indulge in!" Until Ed had begun swearing at the screws, Amy had been playing Daddy's helper, but then Bonnie summoned Amy upstairs, out of earshot of his four-letter imprecations. For the last half hour he'd been alone in the basement, with no one even to soothe his complaints. As he struggled with screw number twelve—whose recalcitrance was threatening to defeat him altogether—his mind was focused as closely on the work at hand as it had ever been on the most complicated of his legal cases, so when the door to the basement stairs opened, he didn't hear it.

Thus it came as a complete shock to him when Riley's

forty pounds of pure canine enthusiasm struck him a full broadside.

Three things happened nearly simultaneously:

His head reflexively jerked up, smashing hard against the frame of the dresser.

He sprawled out onto the basement floor, smashing his left knee hard on the concrete.

The point of the chisel he was clutching in his right hand sank deep into the flesh of his left palm.

Any one of the three would have been enough to make Ed yell; the combination of them all, piled onto the frustration he was already fighting, made him explode with fury. "AMY!" he bellowed. "Get this goddamn dog out of here! *Right now!*"

A second later his daughter came charging down the stairs. "Riley! Here, Riley! Come on, boy!" Wrapping her arms protectively around the big puppy, who was now happily licking his mistress's face, Amy glared at her father. "He wasn't trying to hurt you. He was only being friendly."

"I don't care what he was trying to do!" Ed snapped, getting to his feet and clamping the fingers of his right hand over the deep gouge the chisel had dug in his left palm. "Just get him out of here. If you can't control him, you can't keep him!" As Amy led the dog upstairs, her chin trembling as she struggled not to burst into tears, Ed moved to the laundry sink, wincing, to wash the blood from his left hand. He was rummaging around for something to wrap around his injured hand when Bonnie came down the stairs.

"For Heaven's sake, Ed, what happened down here? Amy's crying and says you threatened to take Riley away from her!"

"Well, if she can't control him—"

"She's not even six years old, Ed! And Riley's not even six *months*. Maybe you should learn to control your temper!"

Ed spun around. "And maybe—" But as he saw the anger in Bonnie's eyes dissolve into alarm at the sight of the blood oozing from his left hand, his own rage drained away. "It's okay," he quickly assured her. "The chisel gouged me, but it's not nearly as bad as it looks." Then, as Bonnie found a clean rag to wrap around his injured hand, he tried to apologize. "I'm really sorry," he said. "You're right. Riley wasn't trying to hurt me, and certainly none of it was Amy's fault. I—"

"Let's just get you upstairs and bandaged, all right?" Bonnie said. As they passed the dresser, she glared at it, already having decided that the damn thing was to blame for her husband's bleeding hand. "Incidentally," she said, "I think I know how the pictures got into the Asylum."

"Come on." Ed looked at her, surprised. "We just found them a few hours ago. How could you find out where they came from?"

"Edna Burnham, of course," Bonnie told him. "While you've been downstairs playing with your toys—"

"They're not toys," Ed interrupted. "They're tools—"

"Whatever," Bonnie said. "Anyway, while you've been playing with them, I've been on the phone. And according to Edna Burnham, you had a rather unsavory great-uncle."

In the back of Ed's mind, a dim memory stirred. "Paul," he said, more to himself than to Bonnie.

"You mean Mrs. Burnham's right?" Bonnie asked, astonished. "Who was he? And what did he do?"

"He was my grandfather's brother," Ed said. "And I'm not sure what he did. But I sort of remember Mom telling me about him once—how if anyone said anything to me at school, I shouldn't tell Grandpa. But nobody ever did, and I guess I forgot all about him."

"But why was he committed to the Asylum? What was he supposed to have done?" Bonnie pressed.

Ed shrugged. "Who knows? They could have locked

him up for anything, I suppose. Maybe he had a nervous breakdown."

"Or maybe he was a mass murderer," Bonnie suggested, her voice teasing. "After all, your fascination with criminal law had to come from somewhere."

They were in the bathroom now, and Ed winced as Bonnie peeled the rag away from his wound and began washing it with soap and water. "Don't you think if he'd killed someone, I would have heard about it?" But then an image of his grandparents came suddenly to mind: Stiff, emotionless people, the kind of New Englanders who never would have dreamed of airing any of the family's dirty laundry, even in private. If they'd had such a relative, neither one of them ever would have mentioned it. Indeed, they'd have probably stopped acknowledging his very existence on the day he'd gone into the Asylum.

The bizarre idea Bonnie had planted stayed with him for the rest of the evening. What if she was right? Not that Uncle Paul was likely to have been a mass murderer, of course, but what if he *had* actually killed someone? Maybe he'd heard more about his uncle than he now consciously remembered.

As he and Bonnie went to bed a few hours later, he was still searching his memory for any other scraps of information about his all-but-forgotten great-uncle, but whatever he might have been told had long since slipped away.

Every eye in the courtroom was on him, and Ed Becker resisted the urge to strut with pleasure at the discomfort he was causing the witness.

A cop was sitting in the witness box, just the kind of cop Ed hated most: a detective sergeant, the sort who assumed that anyone who'd been arrested must be guilty, and who therefore concentrated on searching only for evidence that would lend credence to his preconceived idea. Well, it wasn't going to work this time.

This time, the cop had gone after Ed's own great-uncle, and it was Ed's intention today to destroy not merely the detective's case but his credibility as well. By the time Ed was done with him, the detective would never be willing to get on a witness stand again, at least not in any courtroom where Ed Becker practiced.

And this courtroom was one of Ed Becker's favorites. Large and airy, it was in the corner of the building, and had four immense windows, all of which were open today to allow the sweet spring breeze to wash away the last of winter's mustiness.

But even in the cool breeze, the witness before Ed Becker was starting to sweat. Like a predator on the attack, Ed had caught the scent of the detective's fear.

Turning away from the witness for a moment, Ed gave his great-uncle Paul a confident smile, a smile designed to let Paul Becker know, along with everyone else in the courtroom, that for all intents and purposes the verdict was already won. When Ed was finished with this witness, the state would undoubtedly drop its case altogether. With another smile, this one accompanied by an almost fraternal wink to the jurors, Ed turned back to the witness.

"Isn't it true that you have absolutely no hard evidence that a crime was even committed?" he demanded.

The witness's expression turned truculent, his jaw setting angrily. "We found blood," he said. "A lot of blood."

"A lot?" Ed asked, his tone dripping with sarcasm. "What do you mean by a lot? A gallon? Half a gallon? A quart?" As the detective squirmed, Ed pressed harder. "How about a pint? Did you find a pint of blood?"

"Stains," the witness said. "We found stains on the defendant's knife, and on his bed, and on his rug."

Ed leaned forward, his face coming so close to the

detective's that the witness pulled back slightly. "So you didn't find a lot of blood," Ed said, his voice deadly quiet. "All you found were a few stains."

Suddenly, from a courtroom that Ed knew should be absolutely silent, tensed to hear what his next question would be, he sensed a stirring, followed by a ripple of laughter.

He spun around, searching for the source of the distraction.

And beheld his daughter's dog walking down the aisle from the door, carrying something in his mouth.

A second later Ed recognized the object that Riley was carrying. It was a leg.

A human leg.

On the foot, Ed could clearly see a white sock and a patent leather Mary Jane shoe.

The other end of the leg, cut off midway up the thigh, was still dripping with blood.

As Ed watched in horror, Riley pushed open the low gate that separated the spectators from the court, turned, and went to the defense table. Rearing up on his hind legs and wagging his tail, the dog dropped the bloody leg on the table in front of Paul Becker, then trotted from the courtroom.

Silence now. Deadly silence. Ed felt every eye in the room on him; they were waiting to see what he would do.

"It doesn't mean anything," he began, but before he could finish, another murmur ran through the room, and Ed turned toward the back of the courtroom, though he knew he was making a mistake even by looking.

"Guess maybe we just found some more blood, lawyer," he heard the witness say. Spinning around, he glared at the detective.

"It means nothing," Ed said, but his voice sounded shrill, even to himself. "The dog could have found—" But now he heard the courtroom door swinging open and he pivoted again, to see Riley coming down the aisle once more.

This time, carrying it as if he were bearing the crown at a coronation, the huge puppy held a head in his mouth.

A child's head.

A little girl's head.

The head of the little girl that Ed Becker's great-uncle Paul was accused of killing.

A great rage welled up in Ed Becker as he watched the Labrador puppy carry the head toward the table at which his uncle sat.

No!

He couldn't let it happen!

Not when he was this close!

Not when he'd had the jury in the palm of his hand and the prosecution's primary witness on the verge of admitting he had no real evidence at all.

His fury cresting, the lawyer charged toward the defense table and lifted the huge dog off his feet. With the animal still clutching the child's head in his mouth, Ed carried him to one of the open windows and hurled him out. He was already turning back to face the courtroom when he heard the blast of an air horn, followed by a howl of pain that chilled his very soul. Whirling back around, he leaned out the window and looked down.

All that was left of the dog was a shapeless mass of black fur, stained scarlet by the blood that was now oozing from his mouth.

A few feet away, the head the dog had been carrying lay on the pavement, staring straight up. But it was no longer the face of the little girl his uncle was accused of killing.

It was his daughter's face.

Amy's face.

A howl now rising in Ed's own throat, he turned away from the window, unable to look for even a second longer into his daughter's accusing eyes. But suddenly everything in the courtroom had changed.

He was no longer on the floor before the bench.

Now he was in the witness box, and everywhere he looked, his daughter was staring at him.

Amy sat at the prosecution table, gazing at him with condemning eyes.

Amy was on the bench, clad in black robes, already judging him.

Amy was everywhere, filling every seat, standing at every door, watching him from every direction.

She knew what he'd done.

She had seen it.

And now she was charging him, and prosecuting him, and judging him, and finding him guilty.

He rose up. "No!" he cried. "No!"

Suddenly, Ed Becker was wide awake, sitting straight up in bed, his body covered with a sheen of sweat. "No!" he said once more, but already the dream was releasing him from its grip. He felt exhausted, and flopped back on the bed, his heart pounding, his breathing ragged.

"Ed?" Bonnie said, sitting up and switching on the lamp next to her side of the bed. "Ed, what happened? Are you all right?"

He was silent for a long time, but finally nodded. "I—I think so. It was just a bad dream."

Bonnie propped herself up on one elbow. "Do you want to tell me about it?"

Ed hesitated, but already many of the details had slipped away from him and all he could really remember was the last moment, when everywhere he looked he'd seen Amy, staring at him, knowing what he'd done. "Go back to sleep, honey," he said, wrapping his arms around his wife. "It was only a dream. Something about a trial, and I think I did something to Riley. I can hardly even remember it."

Bonnie reached out and switched off the light, and

within a minute Ed felt her breathing fall back into the easy rhythm of sleep.

But he lay awake in the darkness for a long time. And even in the darkness, he could still see Amy's accusing eyes.

Chapter 5

*O*liver Metcalf was not sleeping well. Images were flickering all around him, as if he were in a carnival fun house gone dreadfully wrong: no matter where he turned, how he twisted, he could neither escape them nor see them clearly. But they frightened him nonetheless, for though they hovered around the edges of his vision, never coming into perfect focus, there was something familiar about all of them.

Painfully familiar.

He moaned with the effort just to *see*, the low guttural sound of a man exerting all the effort he can muster, to no avail. No matter how he tried, Oliver simply couldn't get a grasp on the images that floated maddeningly around him like smoke drifting in mirrors.

Finally, his frustration culminated in a spasmodic contraction of nearly every muscle in his body, and he came abruptly awake. Even before he opened his eyes, he knew something was terribly wrong.

Every bone in his body was aching with cold.

His eyes blinked open and for a split second he felt certain he was still caught in the nightmare, for around him he saw none of the familiar sights to which he usually awoke. Instead of the wall of his bedroom and the budding branches of the maple tree outside, he was staring at the silhouette of the Asylum, etched against a leaden sky. He was not in his house, but outside it.

387

Shaking off the last cobwebs of his uneasy sleep, Oliver slowly sat up, stretching first his arms and then his legs.

It was as he stood that he realized that not only did his limbs ache but his head did too. He braced himself against the great stab of agony that often followed the first telltale pang of one of his headaches, but the onslaught did not come. Instead, the dull ache in his head slowly ebbed away. He moved toward his house, but before going inside, felt an urge to look back just once at the Asylum. As his eyes scanned the dark building that loomed over his cottage—and his entire life—the strange images flickered once more through his mind.

But what did they mean? And why, since they were obviously embedded deep within his memory, could he not call them up as anything other than ghostly fragments of a past that seemed to be deliberately hiding from him? Turning away from the building at the top of the hill and closing the door firmly behind him, Oliver made his way to the kitchen and put on a pot of water for coffee.

As he waited for the water to boil, he glanced up at the clock: just after six A.M. Far too early to call Phil Margolis, even if the doctor would see him on a Saturday. But why call the doctor anyway? Whatever was causing his headaches was not a physical problem: the CAT scan had proved that.

No, it had to do with memories, and with the Asylum. And it had to do with his father.

As he poured the boiling water over the coffee grounds in his old-fashioned Silex, he remembered the case history he'd read a few days ago—a case history that had shown him just how little he'd really known about his father. Since then, he'd gone through most of the files he'd found in the attic, to discover they shared a sickening similarity. For years, patients in the Asylum had been subjected to the worst kinds of treatment, treatment that must have been utterly unbearable for them.

All of it done under his father's supervision.

Oliver absently poured himself a cup of coffee and took small sips of the hot brew as he thought.

Almost against his will, he found himself going to the window and once more looking up at the grimy stone building. What else had gone on inside it? What was hidden behind its walls that was so horrifying it prevented him from entering the building? Even as the question formed in his mind, he knew who would have the answer.

Draining the rest of his coffee in two big gulps—gulps that threatened to scald his throat—Oliver pulled a jacket off the hook next to the door to the garage and got into his car before he could change his mind.

Five minutes later he pulled up in front of the big house on Elm Street, just a little west of Harvard, in which his uncle had spent his entire life. Harvey Connally had been born in the master bedroom on the second floor of the Cape Cod–style house, and often announced that he had every intention of dying in the same room. "A man can travel the world all he wants," Harvey had been heard to say more than once, "but when he's ready to die, he shouldn't be far from where he was born." Though there were those in Blackstone who thought Harvey Connally's determination to die in the very bed in which he'd been born was a bit excessive, the old-fashioned sentiment was more typical of the town than not.

The house itself had become all but invisible from the street over the years, hidden behind a hedge that had been allowed to grow far beyond the basic demands of privacy. Whenever Oliver suggested that it be trimmed, though, his uncle shook his head. "After I die, you can do what you want with it. For now, I'll just leave it alone. I've got no reason to see what's going on outside it, and other people certainly have no need to look at me!"

Now Oliver opened the gate, then let himself into the

house with his own key, calling out to his uncle as soon as he was in the foyer.

"In the library," the old man's reedy voice called back. A moment later, as Oliver entered the book-lined room—his uncle's favorite in the house, and his own as well—Harvey Connally eyed him suspiciously. "A mite early for a social call, don't you think?" he asked. "I don't generally stir the martinis until the sun has set."

"I wasn't even sure you'd be up," Oliver admitted.

"I'm always up by five these days," Harvey replied. "An old man doesn't need as much sleep as a young one," he added pointedly. When Oliver made no reply, his uncle nodded to a silver tray that sat on a table in front of the wing-backed chair in which he was seated. "Help yourself," he said.

As Oliver poured himself a cup of steaming coffee, he felt his uncle watching him appraisingly, and as Oliver sat down, the old man issued his judgment. "You look tired, Oliver. Peaked. As if you're not sleeping well."

"I'm not," Oliver confessed. "And there's something I need to talk to you about." Though his uncle said nothing, Oliver was certain the old man's posture changed, that he became wary. "It's my father," he went on. "I want to know—"

"There's nothing you need to know about that man," his uncle snapped, his eyes flashing with anger. "After he died, I raised you to be a Connally, not a Metcalf! Do you understand? A Connally, like your mother! Like me! The less said about the man who was your father, the better." Harvey Connally's gaze fixed on Oliver with an intensity that warned the younger man he was treading on ground even more dangerous than he had expected, but he went on anyway.

"I need to talk about my father," he repeated. Choosing his words carefully, he told his uncle about the headaches he'd been having, and the strange half memories that seemed to accompany them.

"You should talk to Phil Margolis about this," the old man growled, his eyes hooding as he pressed deeper into his chair, almost as if he was seeking protection from his nephew.

"I did," Oliver said quietly. "And he hasn't been able to find anything wrong. But there *is* something wrong, Uncle Harvey. There are things I can't remember that I think I have to remember."

The old man snorted impatiently. "When you get to be my age, you'll know that some things are best *not* remembered." His eyes remained fixed on Oliver like those of an old wolf staring down a younger one. But Oliver didn't waver.

"I still need to know. I need to know what happened to my father. And I need to know what happened to my sister."

Harvey Connally studied his nephew for several long seconds, as if taking his measure. Finally, he seemed to come to a decision. "Your father killed himself," he said.

"I knew that," Oliver replied. "But I don't know why. Was it because he missed my mother so much?"

"I really have no idea," Harvey said, his tone betraying his reluctance to discuss the matter at all. "I suppose it could have been that. I also suppose"—and his voice hardened—"it could have been because the trustees had decided to close the Asylum."

Oliver felt his pulse quicken slightly. "I thought the decision to close the Asylum was made after my father died."

Harvey's head tipped slightly in assent. "There was no reason to tell you otherwise," he said.

"They fired him, didn't they?" Oliver asked. "The trustees found out what he'd been doing and fired him."

Again Harvey Connally's head tilted a fraction of an inch, but he said nothing more.

"And what about my sister?" Oliver said. "What happened to her?"

Harvey's attention shifted away from Oliver, as he pondered something.

"Did my father have something to do with my sister's death?" Oliver pressed.

Harvey Connally's gaze snapped back to Oliver. "I only know what he told me," he said.

"And what was that?" Oliver asked. "What did he tell you?"

Silence hung in the room for a long time. Finally, Harvey spoke, and though his words were uttered very quietly, they exploded in Oliver's head like blasts of dynamite. "It was your fault," his uncle told him. "It was just an accident, but it was your fault."

Oliver slumped in his chair, unable to speak.

Amy Becker's fists were firmly planted on her hips as she glared at her father with stormy eyes. "Why can't I go too?" she demanded.

"Because there isn't anything for you to do, and you'd just be bored," Ed assured her. "And I'll be gone only a couple of hours. When I get back, you and I can go for a hike. Maybe up in the woods behind the old Asylum. You'd like that, wouldn't you?"

"I want to go to the office with you," Amy insisted. "I want you to teach me how to be a lawyer!"

Ed reached down and lifted his daughter up so he could look directly into her eyes. "If you want to be a lawyer, you have to go to law school. And you can't do that until you've finished college. And you can't do that—"

"Until I finish high school, and I can't do that until I finish grade school." Making a face as she completed the familiar litany, Amy pretended to try to wriggle out of her father's arms. "I'll never get to be a lawyer!"

"Sure you will," Ed told her as he put her back down.

"Unless you decide to be something more fun, like a fireman or an astronaut. But all I'm going to do this morning is look at some papers. Okay?"

Amy sighed as if she were being asked to take the weight of the entire world onto her little shoulders, but then shrugged. "Okay. I'll play with Riley until you get back. But as soon as you come home, we're going for a hike in the woods. You promised!"

"I promised," Ed agreed, leaning over to kiss his daughter on the head. He straightened up as Amy skittered out the back door, then moved toward the kitchen sink, where Bonnie was rinsing the breakfast dishes. "And maybe when we get back from the hike . . ." he began, nuzzling the back of her neck as he slipped his arms around her waist.

"Ooh, promises, promises," Bonnie replied, letting her body shimmy against his. "Promise you won't stay more than a couple of hours?"

"Promise," Ed repeated. "I just have to review the final financing package for the Center so Melissa can give it to the feds. Should have done it yesterday," he added with a sheepish smile before Bonnie could remind him that he'd put in more time on the chest of drawers than his paperwork. Then, briskly: "In another week, maybe we can all start breathing a little easier around here."

Bonnie sighed. "I hope so, but sometimes I wonder if maybe we shouldn't just tear that horrible old place down and be done with it."

"Oh, Lord," Ed groaned. "Not you too! You're starting to sound like Edna Burnham!"

"I am not!" Bonnie protested. "Well, maybe a little bit. But I'm starting to think the whole idea of turning an insane asylum into a shopping center is a little creepy."

"It was Charles Connally's home before it was a mental hospital," Ed reminded her.

"I *still* think it's creepy," Bonnie insisted. Then she smiled. "On the other hand, if it'll help everyone in town earn a decent living for a change, then who cares what I think? *I* don't even care. Go get those papers done so we can all get on with our lives."

Giving Bonnie one more kiss, this time on the lips, Ed went out to the garage and got into the Buick.

Just as he always did, he started the car, glanced in the rearview mirror, and put the transmission into Reverse in a nearly seamless series of motions, then pressed lightly on the gas pedal.

The rear door had just cleared the garage when Ed felt a bump, followed instantly by a yelp of pain, then a scream of anguish. Instinctively slamming on the brakes, he jammed the transmission into Park and leaped out of the car, his first awful thought being that somehow he had hit his own daughter. A second later, though, as he saw Amy standing in the driveway and realized she was unhurt, he felt a wave of relief. His relief, however, was replaced with horror as he heard what Amy was shouting.

"You killed him! You killed Riley!"

Ed saw the black mass that was half-hidden under the car, and in an instant he was back in his dream, standing at the courthouse window, staring at the mangled body of Riley smashed on the pavement below, crushed beneath the wheels of a truck.

But this wasn't a dream.

And Amy, now on her knees beside her injured pet, was sobbing brokenly.

"No!" Ed gasped. "I didn't—" His words died on his lips as he saw a twitch of movement in Riley's hind leg.

Now Bonnie was next to him too, brought running from the kitchen by her daughter's anguished cries.

"Help me!" Ed told her. "He's not dead! If we can get him to the vet . . ." Leaving his sentence unfinished, he carefully drew the dog out from beneath the car. A faint whimper bubbled up from the animal's throat, but then, as if to apologize for the inconvenience he was causing, he tried to lick Ed's hand. "Oh, God, Riley," Ed said, his own voice now catching with a sob. "I'm sorry. I didn't mean to—"

"The car, Ed," Bonnie urged, gently guiding Ed to his feet. "Let's just put him in the car and get going." She pulled open the back door, and Ed laid the dog on the seat, ignoring the blood oozing from the corner of the Labrador's mouth onto the upholstery. "I'll get in back with him and hold his head," Bonnie said. "Get in front with your father, Amy. And fasten your seat belt!" Then she caught sight of her husband's ashen face. "Maybe I'd better drive," she suggested.

Ed shook his head. "I'll be all right."

Less than five minutes later he pulled into the graveled parking area in front of the building that served as Cassie Winslow's office as well as her home. From behind the house came the sound of half a dozen barking dogs and the cries of twice as many birds. Even before Ed was out of the car the veterinarian appeared on the porch.

"It's Riley, Dr. Winslow," Amy cried as she scrambled out of the passenger seat next to her father. "Daddy ran over him. Don't let him die! Please?"

Cassie Winslow dashed off her front porch and pulled open the rear door of the car. The dog's breathing was shallow, and his eyes had taken on a glazed look. "Let's get him inside," she said. "Ed, go ahead and open the doors for me. I'll bring Riley."

"He's heavy," Ed protested. "I can—"

"I have him," Cassie cut in, her voice firm but soothing. "Bonnie, why don't you see if you can't find a lollipop for Amy behind the counter in the waiting room?" Picking up the dog with an ease that should have been impossible for a young woman as slim as Cassie, she followed Ed through the waiting room and directed him to the examination room between the kennels and the laboratory. Laying the dog on the table, she expertly began running her fingers over him, feeling for broken bones.

"What happened?" she asked, glancing at Ed only for the briefest of moments before returning her concentration to the suffering animal.

As quickly as he could, Ed explained. "Is he going to be all right?" he asked when he'd told her all there was to tell.

Cassie Winslow arched her brows. "I'm not sure yet," she said. "I know one of his shoulders is broken, and at least three ribs. As for internal injuries, I can't—" She fell silent as Riley, with a rattling gasp, suddenly stopped quivering and lay still. Cassie felt for a pulse, looked into the Labrador's eyes, then gently closed them with her fingers. "I'm sorry," she said, her gaze finally shifting to Ed.

His hand shaking, Ed reached out to touch the big dog's body. "I'm sorry, boy," he whispered. "I'm so sorry." For a long moment he stood perfectly motionless, his hand still on the dog, as if his very touch might bring the animal back to life. But at last his hand dropped away, and he started back to the waiting room.

As he stepped through the doorway and saw his daughter looking at him, the memory of his dream exploded in his head, and as the voice from the dream cried out at him yet again, so also did his daughter's.

"You killed him!" Amy shrieked, instantly reading the truth on her father's face. "You killed Riley! You killed my dog!"

Ed went to his daughter, kneeling beside her, trying to comfort her, but she pushed him away and buried her face in her mother's breast.

"It was an accident, darling," Bonnie said softly, gently stroking her daughter's hair. "Your father didn't mean to do it. It was just an accident. He didn't mean to—" But as she looked up at Ed, the words died on her lips. Her husband's face had gone deathly white.

"I dreamed it, Bonnie," he said, nearly strangling on the words. "Last night, I dreamed I killed Riley."

"No—" Bonnie began, but Ed cut her off.

"I did," he said. "I dreamed it. And now it's come true."

Wordlessly, desperately trying to convince himself that there could be no connection between the dream and what had happened this morning, Ed knelt next to his wife and daughter and did his best to comfort the child whose pet he had killed.

But there was no comfort. No comfort for his daughter, and none for Ed Becker.

Chapter 6

A silence hung over the Becker house, but it wasn't the kind of comfortable silence that often settles over dwellings whose occupants are happy and content with each other. This was a tense silence, the kind of quiet in which people wait nervously, knowing something is going to happen, but not knowing what.

Bonnie had finally succeeded in putting Amy to bed, though the little girl had insisted that without her dog there was no possibility at all that she would go to sleep. She refused even to say good night to her father, to whom she hadn't spoken all day. Bonnie had sat with her for almost an hour, though, and finally Amy drifted into a fitful sleep.

When Bonnie came downstairs, she found Ed sprawled on the sofa in the living room, his feet propped up on the coffee table. Though his eyes were fixed on the television, she was sure he saw nothing of the flickering image on the screen. Sitting down beside him, she took his hand in hers and gave it a reassuring squeeze. "It wasn't your fault," she said quietly. "And I know it doesn't seem like it tonight, but Amy *will* get over it. And we'll get her another dog."

At first Bonnie wasn't sure if her husband had heard her, but finally he returned her squeeze. "I know." He sighed. "What's really freaking me is that I dreamed the whole thing last night before it happened."

Bonnie shook her head. "C'mon, Ed. It wasn't the

same as your dream. The circumstances were completely different."

For the first time since that morning, Ed managed a smile, though it was little more than a wry grimace. "Now you're starting to sound like me in a courtroom," he told her. "I always could split enough hairs to get the worst kind of sleazebags off hooks they should have been left dangling from."

"It was your job," Bonnie replied, though without an enormous amount of conviction. While she loved everything about her husband, even after having been married to him for nearly ten years, there were still some things she didn't understand, not the least of which was Ed's insistence that everyone, no matter how heinous his crimes might be, deserved the best defense that could be presented. *The prosecution will always twist things against the defendant.* He'd told her this so many times, the words were permanently etched in her memory. *It's my job to twist them the other way, so that in the end the jury has a shot at coming to a fair verdict.* The problem for Bonnie had always been that Ed was so good at twisting the facts, he often was able to get acquittals for people both of them knew were guilty. The final straw was a case that left such a bad taste in both their mouths that Ed had finally decided to give up his criminal practice in Boston and come back to Blackstone and a very quiet civil career. It was a capital case in which he'd won acquittal for a defendant accused of killing three children. Ed had convinced the jury that the police had somehow framed the man. The day after the acquittal, Ed's last criminal client had gone out and killed a fourth child.

"And I was good at my job," Ed said now. "Too good, as we both well know. But the plain fact is that last night I dreamed I killed Riley, and this morning I did it. You can't change the facts."

"Dreams don't involve facts," Bonnie insisted. "They

aren't anything more than your subconscious taking out the garbage after you've gone to bed."

"Even if you're right, it doesn't make me feel any better."

"Well, I'm not going to sit here and argue about it with you all night," Bonnie told him. "In fact, I think I'll go to bed. Want to come with me?"

Ed shook his head. "I'm going to stay up for a little while," he said. "Maybe I'll even go down and work on the dresser for a couple of hours."

Bonnie leaned over and kissed him. "Suit yourself. But whatever you do, don't keep on brooding. Things are going to be fine."

After Bonnie was gone, Ed reached for the remote control, intending to turn off the television set, when he saw the old stereoscope they'd found in the dresser, along with the collection of pictures, sitting on the coffee table. Ignoring the television, he picked up the stereoscope and pictures, then stretched out on his back on the sofa so the light of the table lamp would fall fully on the faded images printed on the cards. Dropping the first one into the rack, he twisted the knob until the scene came into focus.

It was the room that was Amy's now, though in the picture it looked little like the room in which his daughter was currently sleeping. Nor did it look anything like he remembered it from when he himself had been a boy and his grandparents had still lived in this house.

Yet there was something familiar about it, something that made him feel as if somewhere deep inside him, there was a memory of the room as it was in the picture, rather than as it was now. He studied the picture for several minutes, then put in another.

Again he had the sense that there was a memory lurking just beyond the fringes of his consciousness, but again he couldn't quite grasp it, couldn't quite pull it into a bright enough light to examine it.

One by one, Ed examined all the pictures, finally returning to a scene of the room he was in—the living room. It too held that vague feeling of déjà vu, though at least in that picture he was able to identify the source of the eerie feeling: two of the pieces of furniture—an ornate Victorian sofa and a large Queen Anne chair—had been in this room when he was a little boy.

Ed was still gazing at the picture when he slowly drifted into sleep.

He was back in the basement, working on the dresser.

Opening a drawer, he found a stereoscope, exactly like the one upstairs. There was a card in its rack, and Ed picked up the instrument and peered through its lenses.

This time he was staring not at a familiar room but at a scene in which a man was crouching over a woman almost as if he were about to make love to her. But there was a knife in the man's hand, and as Ed stared at it, its blade turned red. Then he saw that the woman's chest was oozing blood from at least a dozen wounds.

Suddenly, the man's face came into focus, and Ed recognized it as the face of a man he had defended a decade earlier.

A man who had stabbed his wife a dozen times, then left her—still conscious—to bleed to death.

Shuddering at the image, he dropped the stereoscope back into the drawer and slammed it shut, but when he pulled another drawer open, he found another stereoscope. This time he hesitated before picking up the instrument, but although he willed himself to resist, his hands seemed to close on it of their own volition. The image this time was of a fast-food restaurant. He felt a momentary sense of relief as he gazed at the scene of families seated at tables, munching on hamburgers and french fries. But then—like the image he'd gazed at before—it began to change, the happy faces on the children transformed into masks of terror, the black-and-white image horrifyingly reversed to its negative. A blinding flash, and then the floor was writhing with a tangle of bodies, and now crimson blood spouted from arms, legs, torsos. The blood of the innocent.

Ed had defended the man who had abruptly appeared in the doorway of that restaurant six years ago, carrying an automatic rifle with which he'd killed a dozen people in less than ten seconds, and maimed two dozen more. Within the privilege of their relationship, the man had calmly and with no remorse told Ed that he'd done it simply because "there were too damned many people in the place, and I was sick of seeing them." Not guilty by reason of insanity. His stomach knotting, Ed slammed the second drawer closed. He wanted to get up and walk away from the dresser, but it wasn't possible—something inside him compelled him to keep opening the drawers, keep pulling out the stereoscopes, keep viewing the atrocities his clients had committed.

The drawers seemed to go on forever, but finally he closed the last one. Having witnessed the final grisly scene, and looked once more upon the guilty face of another man he'd extracted from the jaws of justice, he at last was able to turn away from the dresser.

And found himself facing the same man he'd been defending in his dream the night before.

His great-uncle stared at him through the eyes of a madman; in his hands he cradled a double-barreled shotgun. Raising the gun, Paul Becker pointed it directly at him. "You got them off," he said. "You got every one of them off! Every one of them except me!"

As if in slow motion, Ed watched Paul Becker fire the gun. An explosive roar filled the basement, and suddenly there was blood everywhere. Ed could feel it, feel its hot stickiness as it oozed from the gaping wound the shotgun had torn in his belly, feel it running down his body to puddle at his feet. Somehow it had already flowed across the basement. It was smeared across the floor; it was flowing from the beams overhead. Every surface was dripping with it.

His blood. And the blood of every victim of every murderer he'd ever defended.

Now Great-uncle Paul was raising the gun a second time, aiming it at him, but this time Ed raised his hands, crying out, "No! I'm sorry! Oh, God, I'm sorry!"

It was the sound of his own voice that tore Ed Becker from the grasp of the nightmare. As he jerked upright on the sofa, the stereoscope tumbled to the floor.

He stared at it for a long moment, then reached down and picked it up. The card he'd placed in its rack before falling asleep was still there, and he started to raise the instrument to his eyes for one last look. But as the images he'd seen in the dream suddenly flooded back to him, blood-soaked and horrifying, he abruptly changed his mind.

Leaving the stereoscope on the coffee table, he went upstairs to bed.

But the dream still haunted him, and sleep refused to come.

Go to bed, Oliver Metcalf told himself. Just go to bed and forget about what Uncle Harvey said. But even as he silently repeated the words to himself for what must have been the twentieth time, he knew he wasn't going to be able to obey his own command. All day long he'd been trying to get his uncle's words out of his head, and all day long he'd failed.

Your fault . . . it was your fault.

But how could it have been his fault? He'd been only four years old. How could he have done something that killed his sister? "All your father ever said was that somehow the two of you had gotten hold of a knife of some kind." He paused, as if searching his memory. "You were playing with it. One of you must have tripped, and the blade . . ." Harvey Connally's voice had faded into silence for a moment, but then he'd made himself finish telling his nephew the little he knew. "The blade went into your sister's neck," he said. "Apparently you were so frightened, you ran away and hid the knife."

All day, Oliver had listened to his uncle's words replay in his mind, and slowly he began to understand what had happened to him. The gaps in his memory suddenly made sense—even now, so many years later, the mental image he conjured up of two small children playing with a dangerous instrument made him shudder, and when he tried to imagine the knife plunging into his sister's neck, the horror of the image was so great, he was unable to complete it even in his imagination.

What must it have been like when he'd been only four years old?

No wonder he'd blotted it out, hiding it from himself as thoroughly as he'd managed to hide the weapon from his father, and everyone else who'd searched for it.

No wonder people had looked at him so strangely all his life. Although his uncle insisted that Malcolm Metcalf never told anyone else what had happened, and Mallory's death had been officially deemed accidental, there would have been as many rumors about his sister as there now were about what had really taken place in the Wagners' house.

As had happened so often over the days since she'd disappeared, an image of Rebecca rose in Oliver's mind. Since her mysterious disappearance, he'd felt an emptiness inside him, a hole at his very core that grew larger with each passing day. His frustration had grown too, as he'd realized there was nothing—nothing at all—he could do to help her.

But of one thing he'd become absolutely certain: when

Rebecca was found—and he wouldn't let himself even think of the possibility that she might not be found—he would ask her to marry him.

But now, as his uncle's words echoed in his mind, he knew that when Rebecca returned, he couldn't ask her to marry him. Not until he'd banished the demons—the demons that brought the blinding headaches and the terrifying blank spots in his memory. This morning he had at last found the source of those demons.

And the reason he had not been able to make himself go to bed tonight was clear: he knew that the time had finally come to face the demons, and vanquish them.

Sometime during the day it had come to him, a slow and dawning realization of the reason he could not bring himself to enter the Asylum: the certainty that the "accident," the terrible thing that had happened to Mallory, must have taken place within those dark stone walls. From the moment he realized this, he knew that until he walked through those great oaken doors, he would not sleep. Yet as the afternoon had passed and daylight gave way to darkness, the courage of the sun had yielded to the shadowy terrors the moon brings with it. Now, as the clock downstairs struck midnight, Oliver knew he could put it off no longer.

He must enter the Asylum tonight or forever abandon hope of destroying the demons that haunted him.

Forever give up the hope of Rebecca.

Pulling on a jacket, he took his flashlight from its charger, checked to be sure the beam was at its brightest, then removed the key to the Asylum's door from the hook next to his own. Even then he hesitated, but finally pulled his front door open and gazed up at the shadowed building looming atop the hill, fifty yards away.

Dark, silent, it stood against the night sky like some great brooding monster, quiescent now, but ready to come to furious life the instant it sensed an unwelcome presence. Oliver started up the path, moving carefully, stepping lightly, as if the mere sound of his feet crunching on the gravel might be enough to bring forth whatever evil lurked within the blackened stone walls.

At the foot of the steps leading to the heavy double doors, he hesitated again. Already a headache was stalking the fringes of his consciousness. As he mounted the steps and inserted the key into the lock, the first waves of pain washed over him. Steeling himself, Oliver drove the pain back into the dark hole from which it had crept, pushed the heavy oak panel open, and stepped inside.

Turning on the flashlight, he played its beam over the shadowed interior.

Where? Where should he go?

But even as the questions formed in his mind, some long-buried memory seeping out from his subconscious guided him through the warren of offices until he stopped in front of a door.

It seemed no different from any of the others, yet behind this door, he knew, were the rooms that had been his father's office. His hand trembling, Oliver reached out, turned the knob, and pushed the door open.

Still outside the threshold, he let the flashlight's beam inch through the room, searching every corner it could reach for whatever dark menaces might be lurking in wait.

But the room was empty.

His heart pounding and his right temple dully throbbing, Oliver forced himself to step through the doorway, expectant, unconsciously holding his breath.

There was nothing.

No sound. No sense of an unseen presence.

Only three bare walls, long stripped of the pictures that had once adorned them, and a fourth wall, lined with empty bookshelves.

He had no real memory of this space at all, yet still felt

as though the room should be bigger than it was. But of course the last time he would have been in this room he had still been a little boy and it would have seemed huge.

Now it seemed small, and cramped, and dingy.

Crossing to a door that led to an adjoining room, Oliver paused, searching his memory for a clue as to what might lie beyond, but there was none. At last he grasped the knob and turned it, pulling the door open.

The flashlight revealed a bathroom.

A large tiled bathroom, still equipped with an old-fashioned, claw-footed bathtub, a toilet with a flushing tank pinned high on the wall—its pull chain long since disappeared—and a pedestal sink standing below an old-fashioned medicine cabinet with a mirrored door.

Oliver played the light into every corner of the room, but once again found nothing even slightly threatening. It was just as barren and grubby as the office next door. But then, as he was turning back toward the door, the beam of the flashlight struck the mirror above the sink. Through the layer of grime that had built up over the years, Oliver caught a quick glimpse of the bathtub.

Now, in the reflected glow of the beam, it was no longer empty.

Two figures, their eyes glimmering in the light, peered back at him.

Stunned, Oliver whirled around to bathe the figures in the flashlight's brilliant beam, but even as he turned, an explosion of pain erupted in his head. He staggered, reached for the sink as he fell to his knees, then slumped to the floor. The flashlight, released from his grip, clattered on the tiles and blinked out, and the room dropped into a blackness as dark as the unconsciousness into which the agonizing pain had driven Oliver Metcalf.

The Asylum was once again as still as death.

Chapter 7

Ed Becker gazed dolefully at the glowing digits on the clock next to his bed. The last time he looked they had read 1:14 A.M. Now, unbelievably, they read 1:23 A.M. How could only nine minutes have passed in what had seemed to Ed like at least an hour? Yet the colon was flashing steadily, once a second, just as it always did.

Bonnie was sleeping peacefully beside him, not even making a movement or emitting a sound he could blame for his own sleeplessness, so he didn't have a decent excuse to wake her up. Finally giving up altogether on the idea of sleeping, he slid out of bed, pulled on his robe, and went downstairs. In the kitchen, he fished around in the refrigerator until he found a package of sliced ham, some turkey, and a loaf of bread. Five minutes later he carried his sandwich, along with a glass of milk, into the living room. Switching on the television set, he turned the volume down low enough so as not to disturb his wife and daughter, then restlessly switched it off again and picked up the latest issue of the *Blackstone Chronicle*, a special edition Oliver had hastily put out, most of it taken up with news of the death of Germaine Wagner and the disappearance of Rebecca Morrison. Though he'd elected to keep his own counsel, Ed privately agreed with those who suspected that Rebecca might have had more to do with Germaine's death than Steve Driver was currently thinking. It had been Ed's experience—and he would be the first to admit that his

408

own experiences didn't make him the most objective of observers—that often it was exactly the kind of sweet, quiet woman, such as Rebecca appeared to be, who secretly harbored an anger that could explode into violence like the carnage that had swept through the Wagner house.

Oliver Metcalf, though, had carefully slanted the story to be so sympathetic toward Rebecca that she sounded like a saint.

Ed Becker didn't believe in saints.

On the other hand, it was exactly the kind of thinking he was indulging in right now—the assumption that not only did evil lurk within even the most innocent-appearing souls, but it would inevitably manifest itself in murder—that had finally led him to give up his practice and leave the darker side of Boston behind. So maybe Rebecca was every bit as innocent as Oliver presented her.

Putting the paper aside, he swallowed the last bite of his sandwich and, rising, carried the plate and glass back to the kitchen. He was about to switch off the light when he suddenly caught a whiff of something.

Gas!

Moving to the stove, he checked to make sure all the valves were tightly closed.

Every one of them was shut. The pilot light burned steadily blue.

Frowning, Ed glanced around the kitchen, then moved toward the door to the basement stairs. Instinctively reaching for the light switch as he opened the door, he reeled back as fumes surged out of the basement, nearly choking him. He slammed the door closed again, then broke out in a cold sweat as he realized what could have happened if he'd actually turned the light on. Any spark from the switch might cause the gas to explode. Then, as he remembered there was a freezer in the basement—a freezer that switched on and off automatically several times every day and night—his heart began to pound.

Out!

He had to get Bonnie and Amy out, right now!

Racing out of the kitchen, he bounded up the stairs, taking them two at a time. "Bonnie!" Shouting his wife's name again, he slammed open the door to their bedroom. "Get out!" he yelled. "Quick!"

Jerking awake, Bonnie sat up in bed. "Ed? What—"

"Don't talk! Don't ask questions. Just get out of the house! I'll get Amy!" As Bonnie finally started to get out of bed, Ed ran down the hall to his daughter's room, throwing its door open with enough violence that he heard the plaster behind it crack and fall to the floor as the knob struck it. Amy, already sitting up, was rubbing her eyes as Ed reached down and scooped her out of bed, snagging the blanket that had been covering her as well. "Come on, honey," he said. "I have to get you out of here."

Amy, still half asleep, tried to wriggle free. "No!" she wailed. "It's still night! I don't want to get up!"

Ignoring his daughter's words but tightening his grip on her, Ed dashed out of the room, coming to the head of the stairs just as Bonnie, now clad in a robe and slippers, was emerging from the master bedroom.

"What is it?" she demanded. "What's going on?"

"Gas!" Ed shouted as he started down the stairs. "The whole basement's full of it!"

A moment later he was fumbling with the chain on the front door, but Bonnie darted in front of him, her nimble fingers instantly freeing it from its catch. Then they were out of the house and hurrying across the front lawn. Only when they were on the sidewalk did Ed finally stop and lower Amy to the ground.

"Gas?" Bonnie repeated. "What are you talking about? How did you—"

"I couldn't sleep," Ed told her. "So I went down and

made myself a sandwich, and while I was cleaning up, I smelled it. I thought it was the stove, but—"

The blast cut off his words in midsentence, and he instinctively reached down and pulled Amy back into his arms as shards of glass exploded from the small light wells that served as the basement's two windows, and the long-unused access door to the coal bin blew off its hinges, allowing an enormous ball of fire to boil out of the cellar and roll across the driveway.

Shrieking, Amy wrapped her arms around her father, and buried her face in his shoulder.

"It's all right," Ed whispered into his daughter's ear. "It's going to be all right."

But in his head he was hearing the sound of the explosion over and over again.

It sounded exactly like the blast of the gun that Paul Becker had fired at him in his dream.

Rebecca wasn't sure what had awakened her; indeed, it was only the slow process of coming back to consciousness that told her she'd been asleep at all.

She wasn't afraid anymore—at least not in any way she'd been familiar with before being brought to the place that had become her dark, cold world. The things that had once frightened her—the unidentifiable sounds of the night, which only a few days ago would send goose bumps racing up her spine, or the imagined presences that might be lurking in the shadows on the evenings she walked home alone from the library—now seemed like old friends whose reappearance would bring her comfort in the total isolation into which she'd fallen.

Crazy, she thought. *I must be going crazy.*

She had lost all sense of time; had no feeling either of night and day, or of how long she'd been in the featureless room. In the muddle of her mind, there was no longer any difference between minutes and hours, hours and days, days and weeks.

Her wrists and ankles were still bound, but now she was blindfolded, and it felt as if her eyes were covered with the same kind of heavy duct tape that sealed her lips. She was certain she knew why the blindfold had been added: so her captor could see without being seen.

Now, as she came out of the restless sleep she'd fallen into minutes—or perhaps hours—ago, she tried to fathom what it was that had brought her awake.

A sound?

But there were no sounds; the tiny chamber that was her prison was as eerily silent as the palaces of death built for the pharaohs.

Yet she was filled with foreboding, sensing that if she held perfectly still, if she held her breath so that not even her lungs would disturb the quiet in the room, she would hear something.

She waited.

And then she heard it: the scraping of a key being fitted into a lock, followed by the click of a bolt being thrown. The door itself made no sound, but Rebecca, deprived of any visual stimulus, had grown sensitive to other things, and the slight change in the air currents as the door swung open felt like wind against her cheek.

And she could feel that she was no longer alone.

Still, she waited, and though she could hear nothing, she began to sense that whatever had entered the room was behind her now.

She felt a touch against her cheek, a touch so light she could almost imagine it wasn't there at all.

Then there was a quick movement, and she felt a slash of pain across her mouth. For a moment it was as if her skin were torn away, but then she realized it was only the duct tape that had been ripped off. A tiny moan escaped her lips. Instantly, a hand clamped over her mouth, silencing her.

The hand lingered, its pressure only slowly lightening, but Rebecca made no move, and finally it dropped away. A second after that she felt something touch her lips, and then realized she was being offered water.

Greedily, she sucked it up, swallowing every drop she was allowed.

A moment later the tape was once more pressed in place, but again the fingers lingered on her skin, and now Rebecca could feel the cold smoothness of the latex that covered them.

She held perfectly still, refusing to acknowledge the touch with any reaction. Finally, one of the fingers moved.

Involuntarily, Rebecca shuddered as the finger crept across her throat like the point of a knife. . . .

Ed Becker stared mutely at his house. Beside him, Bonnie was as silent as he, though their neighbors—who had appeared on the sidewalk before the first fire truck had arrived—seemed to all be talking at once. "What happened?" Ed heard someone say.

"An explosion," someone else replied.

"I saw a flash," a third voice said. "Helluva thing—lit up our whole bedroom. Scared Myra half to death!"

"Oh, it did not," a woman's outraged voice protested. "You were more scared than I was!"

"So if there was an explosion and a flash, where's the fire?" the first voice demanded.

And that was the eerie thing. There was simply no fire.

From the moment the gas had exploded in the basement, Ed had waited for his house to burst into flames, certain that by the time the first fire truck arrived, the building would have become an inferno like the one that destroyed Martha Ward's house only a few weeks ago. But as the sound of the sirens grew louder and louder, and not just one, but three fire trucks converged on Amherst Street, the house remained silent and dark, looking for all the world as if nothing had happened. As the fire trucks braked to a stop, their sirens were abruptly cut off, then three crews began pulling hoses from the reels on the trucks. Larry Schulze pulled up in the white Chevy Blazer that served as his chief's car and hurried over to Ed.

"What happened? Where'd it start?"

"It was gas," Ed explained. "I smelled it coming out of the basement, and got Bonnie and Amy out just before it blew. But I don't get it—how come the house isn't burning?"

"You mean 'how come it isn't burning *yet*,'" the fire chief corrected him. "Just because we don't see it doesn't mean it's not on fire." Dispatching one man to shut the gas off at the main, he beckoned to two others to follow him as he started down the driveway.

"I'm coming with you," Ed said.

The fire chief turned back, his stony expression clear even in the shadowy light of the street lamps. "No you're not," he declared in a voice that carried every bit as much authority as any judge Ed had ever dealt with in a courtroom. "You're going to stay right here until I've gone around the house and then gone through it. When I'm satisfied there's no fire and that it's safe, then you can go in."

As Ed was considering the merits of trying to argue with the chief, Bonnie laid her hand on her husband's arm. "Let him do his job, Ed," she said. "Please?"

Ed nodded his thanks to Bonnie as Schulze and his men set off. In less than ten minutes they had circled the exterior and were back in front of the house. "So far it looks okay," the chief called as he mounted the steps to the front door, which was standing wide open. "Is the gas off?"

"Thirty seconds after you asked!" one of his men shouted back.

"Okay! We'll be out in a couple of minutes."

The crowd waited, finally falling silent as the fire chief inspected the house. When he emerged a few minutes later appearing just as calm as when he'd gone in, an audible murmur of relief rippled through the bystanders, except for two small boys who sounded sorely disappointed that they weren't going to see the firemen use their hoses.

"You got lucky," Schulze told Ed Becker as his men began rewinding their unused hoses onto the reels. "If you'd had the kind of trash in your basement most people do, you could have lost the whole house."

Bonnie Becker stared at the fire chief in disbelief. "You mean it's all right? It's not on fire?"

"That happens sometimes," Schulze explained. "You have to understand what goes on with gas. When it lights off, which probably happened when the freezer kicked on, it goes so fast that unless there's something in the immediate vicinity that's pretty flammable, it literally blows itself out. You lose all the windows, and the doors too, but that's about it. You can take a look now, if you want. But I'll go with you."

Ed gazed at the house, remembering just how close he'd come to dying that night. If the gas had exploded as he'd opened the basement door—

He cut the thought short, trying to shut out the image that rose in his mind of a boiling mass of fire erupting around him, snuffing his life out in an instant, or leaving him so badly burned he would have prayed to die rather than suffer the pain the flames would have inflicted.

Though he didn't want to think about what might have happened to him, he knew he had to go back into the house.

Into the basement, where the explosion had occurred.

With Larry Schulze following close behind him, Ed

started toward the front door. "Is it okay to switch on the lights?" he asked as they stepped into the foyer.

"Can't. I shut off the power, just in case. Use this."

Turning on the flashlight Schulze handed him, Ed moved cautiously through the foyer, shining the beam into every corner, barely able to believe the house had suffered no serious damage. But it seemed to be true—everything looked normal; nothing seemed even to have been disturbed. But as he entered the kitchen, he stopped short. "Jesus," he said, staring at the door to the basement.

Or, more accurately, what *had been* the door to the basement. It now was a heap of shattered lumber so torn by the explosion that it was barely recognizable as having been a door at all. All that remained within the frame were a couple of fragments of wood clinging to the hinges that had been half torn from the frame itself. "That's where I was standing not more than a minute before it blew," Ed said, his voice barely above a whisper as the unbidden vision of the exploding fireball rose in his mind once more. Stepping over the shredded wood that had been the door, he gazed down the stairs.

Oddly, the basement looked normal too. It wasn't until he'd started down the stairs that he realized he'd been expecting everything to be blackened. But apparently it had happened so fast that not even any charring had occurred.

As he came to the bottom of the stairs, he shined the light around and stopped short.

Blood!

There was blood everywhere!

His gorge rising, Ed braced himself against the wall as his knees threatened to buckle beneath him.

The blood was smeared on the walls, puddled on the floor, dripping from the beams overhead. But it was impossible! When the gas exploded, there had been no one down here!

Besides, the blood he'd seen before had existed only in a dream. Yet here it was.

First the explosion, sounding exactly like the shotgun Paul Becker had been aiming at him.

And now the blood.

The blood of the people his clients had murdered splashed through his basement as if in retribution for his having defended the undefendable.

But it was impossible! It hadn't happened! It was only a dream!

"Ed?" Larry Schulze was gripping his shoulder. "Ed, are you okay? I know the paint's a mess but—"

Paint?

Paint!

Or course! Not blood at all! Paint!

Though the fire chief was still talking, Ed Becker no longer heard his words. The strength finally coming back into his legs, he moved deeper into the basement.

As he looked around, using the flashlight to explore every corner, the same feeling of horror that had come over him when Riley died that morning crept up on him once again.

Though it hadn't been the roar of a shotgun, the explosion of the gas had sounded exactly like one.

And though the red stains on the walls and the floor and even the ceiling weren't blood, they looked no different from the terrifying crimson vision he'd witnessed in his dream.

It had happened again.

For the second time, his nightmare had come true.

Chapter 8

*T*he crowd in front of the Becker house dispersed almost as fast as it had gathered, and though Bonnie Becker knew the thought was uncharitable, she had a distinct feeling that at least a few of those who'd rushed out of their homes were just a bit disappointed that there had been so little to see. Within minutes after Ed and Larry Schulze emerged from the house, only Bill McGuire was left. Bonnie, feeling at sea, was perplexed—and perhaps just slightly resentful—that none of her neighbors had offered to take them in for the night. Was it possible they actually thought she would go back into the house tonight? Or take Amy back inside?

Bill McGuire read her expression perfectly. "You don't get invited to stay at anyone's house until you've been here for at least two generations," he explained, displaying the first semblance of a grin Bonnie had seen on his face since his wife died. "It's the price Ed has to pay for having married out of town. But don't worry—I married out of town too. You'll all stay with Megan and me. Besides, if I know Mrs. Goodrich, she'll have a pot of tea on."

Far too upset by fear and its aftermath to offer even the feeblest of polite protests, Bonnie gave Bill a hug instead. "I promise it won't be for more than a night or two," she assured him. "I just have to know it's safe."

Just as Bill had thought, the teakettle was whistling and Mrs. Goodrich was bustling about the kitchen as they

418

entered his house, which was across the street. Amy, already having converted the night into a wonderful adventure, slid onto a chair at the kitchen table and demanded a glass of milk.

"Say please," Bonnie automatically instructed her daughter, but Mrs. Goodrich was already setting a tumbler in front of the little girl.

"Please," Amy parroted as her hand snaked out to take a cookie from the plate the old housekeeper offered.

Ten minutes later, with Amy making no more than a token protest against having to go to bed, Bonnie tucked her daughter in next to Megan McGuire. Megan was fast asleep, looking angelically peaceful with her arms wrapped around the doll that had been her inseparable companion since her mother died.

"It's so beautiful," Amy breathed, gazing at the doll's porcelain face. "Can I have a doll like that?"

"We'll see," Bonnie temporized. "I'm not sure we can find one. But maybe tomorrow Megan will share hers with you. Now, go right to sleep," Bonnie told her, bending over to kiss her daughter. "And don't wake Megan up. All right?"

"All right," Amy promised. But as soon as her mother was gone, she reached over to touch the beautiful doll.

"Don't," Megan said, her voice startling Amy, whose hand jerked back before she'd made even the slightest contact. Megan's eyes were wide open, and Amy realized she hadn't been sleeping after all.

"She's mine," Megan went on, "and she doesn't like anyone else to touch her. She doesn't like it one bit."

Megan's eyes closed and she said nothing else, but for a long time Amy lay awake. She stared at the doll. In the dim light from the street lamp outside, it almost seemed to be sleeping. But Megan's words kept echoing in her mind.

She didn't try to touch the doll again.

* * *

"It happened again."

Ed and Bonnie were in the McGuire guest room. Bonnie was already in bed, and Ed was standing at the window, gazing out at the house across the street and one lot down the slope. His house. His sanctuary, meant to provide shelter from the storms of daily life as much as from winter's icy blasts. In the last twenty-four hours his refuge had become instead a place where his nightmares came true.

"What happened?" Bonnie asked, though her heart was beating faster in anticipation of his reply.

"I dreamed it." Ed turned away from the window and sat on the edge of the bed. In the shadowy darkness of the room, he told her about the dream he'd had, and what he'd seen in the basement only a little while ago, when he and Larry Schulze had gone down to assess the damage.

"But it wasn't a gunshot," Bonnie insisted when Ed was finished. "And it wasn't blood. It was *paint*, Ed. It was just a can of paint whose lid got knocked off in the explosion."

"But—"

"But darling, it really *was* just a dream." Feeling utterly exhausted as the remembered terror of the explosion closed in on her, she said softly, "It will all seem different in the morning. Can't we talk about it then? Please?"

Ed hesitated, but as Bonnie held her arms out to him, he slipped into bed beside her, holding her close. She was right, he decided as he kissed her gently. In the bright light of day, none of it would seem so terrible. And, in truth, there had been no permanent damage, nothing they wouldn't easily recover from. Tomorrow they'd look for a new puppy for Amy, and with a couple hours' work the mess in the basement would disappear as completely as if the explosion had never happened. Bill McGuire had already promised to put in an automatic detection system to guard them against another accident. In a few days everything would be back to normal. As he felt Bonnie's breathing drift into the gentle rhythm of sleep, Ed Becker closed his eyes, yielding to oblivion.

Ed stood on the sidewalk, staring at the house.

Around him the night had become eerily quiet, as if the explosion had silenced every living thing in Blackstone.

Ed knew he should turn around and go back to Bill McGuire's house, slip back into bed with Bonnie, and let himself surrender to sleep. Instead, he moved toward the house, irresistibly drawn inside.

His house—yet not his house.

In the living room, all the furniture he and Bonnie had brought with them from Boston was gone, and the heavy Victorian decorations from the long-ago days when his grandmother had lived here were all back in place. The room looked exactly as it had when he'd viewed the picture in the stereoscope. The stereoscope itself sat on a mahogany gateleg table upon which a lace cloth had been spread. Moving closer to the table, Ed lifted the cloth and ran his fingers appreciatively over the perfect satin finish. There was a drawer at one end of the table, and Ed's hands closed on its pull. He hesitated, remembering the carnage let loose when, in his dream, he'd pulled open the drawers of the oak chest from the Asylum. Yet even as his mind cried out against temptation, Ed's trembling fingers slid the drawer open.

He found himself gazing at a .38 caliber pistol.

The pistol was clutched by a hand hacked off at the wrist, blood dripping from its severed veins.

Shuddering, he slammed the drawer shut. He stood still, waiting for the sick feeling in his stomach to pass.

It was not there, he told himself. I only imagined it.

But he didn't try to open the drawer again, instead dropping the tablecloth back in place to conceal the drawer, to make it disappear.

He left the living room and moved into the dining room. A gleaming cherry-wood table surrounded by eight armchairs stood where only a few hours before his own teak table had been. Against the wall a Victorian break-front was filled with Limoges china in an ornate pattern of royal blue and gold. On one shelf three dozen heavy crystal goblets glittered in the dim light.

He reached for a glass. As he took it, it filled with blood.

Dropping it, Ed spun around. The table, bare only a moment ago, was set now as if for a feast. Twin cande-labra, each of them glowing with a dozen candles, cast a warm glow over an elegant display of silver and crystal.

At each place, a serving plate had been set, and on each plate there was a single object.

The severed heads of eight of Ed Becker's clients stared at him with empty eyes. Their lips were stretched back from their teeth in grim parodies of smiles, and pools of blood filled the plates upon which they sat.

"No!" The word caught in his throat and emerged only as a strangled grunt. Backing out of the dining room, he turned to flee, but instead of taking him out of the house, his legs carried him up the stairs until he stood at the door to the master bedroom. His heart pounded. He tried to make himself turn away from the closed door, to go back down the stairs, to leave the house.

Powerless to stop himself, he reached out and pushed the door open. As it swung back on its hinges, the room was revealed, not as the cheerful sunshine yellow space Bonnie had made it, but as a dark chamber dominated by an ornate four-poster bed, its curtains drawn back to reveal a heavy brocade coverlet.

Then he saw the figure of the man.

He recognized it instantly, for its face was bathed in silvery light pouring in from the window.

Ed Becker was staring at himself.

And he was hanging, broken-necked, from the chandelier. The hands of the lifeless corpse reached out as if to grasp the living man and draw him too into the cold grip of death.

A scream of horror rose from Ed Becker's lungs, boiling out of him, echoing through the room, shattering the night.

Chapter 9

*F*or a second Ed Becker didn't know where he was. His mind still half entangled in the nightmare, he tried to twist away from the clawlike grasp of the dream. The terrible vision remained before him; he could still hear his own howling scream. Beside him, though, Bonnie slept quietly. As he sat up, willing his heartbeat to slow, his thoughts to focus, she sighed and snuggled deeper into the quilt, but did not wake.

Imagination. These hideous images were merely the product of mental stress—the culmination of months of anxiety over the awful tragedies among his friends, his worries over the fate of the Blackstone Center, capped by the close call they'd had tonight.

Imagination—overwrought and out of control.

Ed got out of bed and went to the window, where he could just make out the silhouette of his house against the starlit darkness of the sky. "It really was just a dream," he said quietly, repeating his wife's comforting words to himself like a mantra. *A dream. Just a dream.*

But he knew he didn't believe it.

Knew he had to see for himself.

Even as he opened the front door, he could sense that something had changed.

Everything about the house was different.

424

The way it smelled.

The way it felt.

He reached for the light switch, remembering the power had been turned off only when there was no response to his touch. Making his way through the foyer, he came to the dining room door. Though it was almost pitch-black, he could see the vague outline of a table and chairs.

Big, heavy furniture, unlike the teak set he and Bonnie had brought with them from Boston.

An illusion!

It had to be an illusion, born of the darkness and the memory of the dream. But then, as he remembered the vision of his clients' severed heads displayed on the table, he backed away from the dining room. Crossing the threshold into the living room, he stopped.

The room was not empty.

He could feel the presence of someone—or some*thing*— waiting in the space that yawned before him. As in the dream, he tried to turn away and leave the house.

But also as in the dream, his body refused to respond to the desires of his mind, and he found himself drawn inexorably into the room and the blackness beyond.

And then he knew.

They were everywhere. They sat in every Victorian chair, perched on every footstool, and leaned against every gateleg table and curio cabinet.

Two of them flanked the fireplace.

He could see at once that they were all dead. Pale, motionless, they somehow managed to stare at him accusingly with their sightless eyes.

Then, the wail. A low keening that slowly built into a cacophony of pain and suffering.

Ed recognized them all, for during the last fifteen years, he had studied photographs of every one of them. They were the victims of his clients, now gathered in his home, come at last to settle their accounts with the man who had defended their killers.

His heart pounding, Ed turned away and lurched toward the front door, only to find himself staring into the empty eyes of his long-dead great-uncle Paul Becker.

"They come for us," he heard his great-uncle say, though his colorless lips stayed utterly still. "The people we kill. They come for us every night. Now they've come for you too."

A moan escaping his lips, Ed turned and shambled up the stairs. His heart was beating so wildly he felt as if his chest might explode. At the top of the stairs he stopped, his eyes darting around the hall, searching for someplace to hide.

As the sky outside continued to brighten, and the silvery dawn began to seep through the stairwell's windows, one by one the doors to each of the bedrooms opened.

In silent ranks the victims appeared and came slowly toward him, reaching out to him just as his own specter had reached out to him in the dream.

Instinctively taking a step back, Ed lost his footing. For a moment he teetered on the top step, but then fell backward, a single panicked scream bursting from his throat before his head struck the bare hardwood treads, cutting off his shout.

Rolling over and over, Ed Becker tumbled to the foot of the stairs, to sprawl in a broken heap on the floor of the foyer.

Bonnie Becker raced across the lawn and up onto the porch of their house, throwing the door open so hard that the glass panel in its center cracked. For a split second she saw nothing in the faint light, then caught sight of her husband's body lying at the foot of the stairs. "Ed!" she screamed. "Oh my God! Ed!" Dropping to her knees, she was about to gather him into her arms when she saw the strange angle at which his head lay, and knew his neck was broken.

Don't touch him! she told herself. Don't touch him. Just call for help.

Her entire body shaking, she managed to get to her feet and stumble to the phone.

Picking up the receiver, she jabbed at the keypad, her hand trembling so badly she couldn't even be certain she had punched the right buttons. But on the second ring the 911 operator answered. Moments later, as she heard the sound of sirens screaming toward her house for the second time that night, Bonnie gazed numbly around the room.

It was exactly as they had left it.

Nothing had changed; nothing was different.

Yet as Bonnie went back into the foyer to watch over her husband until the ambulance came, she knew that despite her own words to the contrary, somehow—in some way she was certain she would never understand—another of Ed's nightmares had come true.

Chapter 10

*T*he first copy of next week's *Blackstone Chronicle* lay on Oliver Metcalf's desk. Though Lois Martin had put it in front of him nearly an hour earlier, he had not yet touched it. Instead, he'd simply stared at the headline—a headline he himself had written—and wondered if he could, in good conscience, let the paper be distributed the way it stood, or whether he should try to recover every copy that had been printed, destroy them, and start all over again. He was no closer to an answer now than he had been an hour ago. Yet the headline—together with its accompanying story—would not release its grip on him.

Local Attorney Injured in Fall

In the latest in a series of apparently coincidental tragedies, Blackstone attorney Edward Becker was seriously injured in a fall at his home early Sunday morning. The house on Amherst Street had been the site of a gas explosion several hours earlier, in which no one was hurt, and Becker, 40, his wife, Bonnie, 38, and their 5-year-old daughter, Amy, had evacuated the house.

According to Mrs. Becker, the lawyer returned to the house despite the possibility that it wasn't safe, and

apparently stumbled at the top of the stairs. Fire Chief
Larry Schulze states that both the gas and electricity to
the house had been cut off for safety reasons. "I don't
have any idea why Ed went back before dawn," Schulze
said in an interview with this newspaper.

Suffering breaks in three vertebrae, Becker . . .

The rest of the story disappeared under the fold of the
paper, but it didn't really matter: every word of it was
etched in Oliver's mind.

Every not-quite-true word.

He'd spent two hours talking to Bonnie Becker at the
hospital the morning after Ed had fallen, listening to her
strange story of Ed's growing conviction that his dreams
were somehow coming true, and how she'd awakened
sometime before dawn to find him gone and had rushed
across the street to discover the accident.

She'd also talked of a stereoscope that they found in
the dresser Ed had taken out of the Asylum Friday
morning.

Bonnie, exhausted and red-eyed, had looked at Oliver
bleakly. "I know it's crazy, but I keep remembering the
gifts people are talking about. . . ." Her voice trailed off,
and then she shook her head. "Forget I said that, Oliver.
What happened to Ed was an accident. It didn't have
anything to do with the dresser, or the stereoscope, or
anything else."

But Oliver had known even as she spoke that Bonnie
didn't quite believe her own words. Nor did he. Yet when
he sat down to write the story, he decided to "forget" the
ruminations, as Bonnie had requested. No sense setting
more tongues to wagging than already were.

And there was, of course, no proof.

No proof that the tragedies that had befallen the
McGuires and the Hartwicks, Martha Ward and Ger-

maine Wagner, and now Ed Becker were connected in any way. There wasn't—couldn't be—any connection between Rebecca's disappearance and Ed Becker's near-fatal accident. Yet Oliver couldn't help wondering. Still, despite his own doubts, despite the disturbing way his heart seemed to lurch in his chest every time he thought about Rebecca, it would be irresponsible to fan the fires of speculation. No point making people more frightened than they already were.

But Oliver Metcalf was frightened. Frightened nearly to death.

As the deepest shadows of night crept through the empty rooms of the cold stone building, the dark figure slipped one more time into the hidden chamber in which his treasures were stored. He didn't linger tonight, for already the hour was late and there was much to do. Lifting a shallow, oblong box from the topmost shelf, he wiped it clean of the thick layer of dust that had settled over it, then released its latches and carefully opened it.

With latex-covered fingers, he removed a tortoiseshell object from the box's velvet-lined interior and held it lovingly up to the few rays of moonlight that filtered through the window.

Its blade glittered brightly. So brightly, it almost seemed new. In the dimness of the light, he could only barely see the blood with which it was stained.

To be continued . . .

PART 6
ASYLUM

Prelude

Night lay over Blackstone like a heavy, suffocating shroud, but it was not merely the darkness that had driven the town's citizens from Main and Elm Streets, from the locked and shuttered library and the cozy camaraderie of the Red Hen.

Fear, as well as night, now held the people of Blackstone in its clutches. Terror had spread through the village like a virus, infecting first one person, and then another, until at last no one had escaped its icy touch.

Every night when they locked their doors, the people of Blackstone prayed that this would not be the night when evil came to prey on them. If it had to feed, let it find succor within someone else's walls, destroy the lives of someone else's family.

The fever of fear was no longer limited to the hours of darkness, for even in the bright sunshine of a springtime afternoon, there wasn't a soul in Blackstone who couldn't feel his neighbors' eyes watching. Watching, and wondering.

Who would be next?

And how would it come?

The universal custom of honoring birthdays and anniversaries with gifts had abruptly stopped in Blackstone, for everyone in town had heard that any object, even the most innocent-seeming gift, could carry the curse—a doll, a handkerchief, a silver locket—*anything* could bring home the reign of terror.

The flea market had been abandoned, for everyone had heard about the dragon-shaped lighter that Rebecca Morrison had given to her cousin. Janice Anderson hadn't seen a customer in a week. The post office had begun returning packages of every description to their senders, all of them marked with the same message: DELIVERY REFUSED.

Every day the tension grew, and soon families who had been neighbors and friends for more generations than they could remember were looking at one another with undisguised suspicion. But it was at night that nerves jumped and heartbeats hammered, at night when everyone retreated to their homes and tried to bar their doors against fear. Behind their locks and barricades they knew precautions were useless, of course, for deep in their souls, each of them understood that if the madness came to invade his home, no locks would keep it out, no shutters hold it at bay.

It would slither in through the crevices and cracks, and by morning—

But none of them wanted to think about morning.

Just to get through the night was enough.

And this night—a night filled with moonless blackness made palpable by heavy fog—was the worst of all. On most other nights the people of Blackstone had been able to peek from their windows, searching the pools of light around the street lamps for signs of danger.

Tonight there was only darkness, and the viscous mist that turned keen eyes blind.

Through the fog and darkness a single figure moved, slipping unseen from the door of the Asylum, its cloak thrown loose around its shoulders. It drifted through the ebony night with wraithlike grace, a presence that crept from house to house.

In every house, the figure caught a glimpse of terror as it peered unseen through a forgotten shade or slightly parted curtain with a perfect, sinuous stealth that never betrayed its presence for an instant. The watcher could almost smell the fear, and shivers of excitement ran over its skin like a lover's fingers. Moving, silently stalking. A shadow that briefly crossed from one window to the next. Savoring the suffering. Delighting in the disease it had unleashed upon the town.

It was close to dawn when finally the triumphal tour was near an end, and the figure came to the house upon whose step it would leave its most important gift.

At this house, the figure lingered long, gazing up at the darkened windows from which no light spilled. There was no movement within, nor was there the scent of fear that issued from every other house it had visited. As the cloaked intruder circled this house, rage began to build inside it, until, reflecting upon the vengeance this gift would wreak upon this house's only occupant, the fury slowly ebbed away, leaving in its place a shiver of strangely erotic excitement.

Soon, soon, the wrath would descend upon this place too.

Caressing the gift one last time, the dark figure laid it lovingly at the front door, then faded into the blackness as silently as it had come.

Chapter 1

Numb.

Every part of Rebecca Morrison seemed to have
gone numb.

A chill had crept over her that she'd never experienced
before. She had always known what it felt like to be cold,
of course, for growing up in New Hampshire meant win-
ters wading through snowbanks and temperatures that
sank far below zero. When she was a little girl, she loved
those days. Her mother would bundle her up in a thick
woolen snowsuit, and put mittens on her hands and a
stocking cap on her head, and Rebecca would hurl herself into the snowy paradise outside with an excitement
that sometimes made her feel like she would simply burst
with joy. She would flop down into the snow, wave her
arms and spread her legs, then jump up to admire the
angel she had made. Sometimes she'd even leap right
into a big drift and bury her face in the cold white cot-
tony fluff because the frozen, wet purity was so
refreshing, its aftertingle so deliciously shivery. Best of
all were "snow days," when school was closed, grown-
ups stayed inside their warm kitchens, and she would go
off in search of other kids to play with. Inevitably, she'd
wind up in a snowball fight that—inevitably—required

her to shed her mittens since everyone knew you couldn't make a proper snowball with mittens on. By the time the grown-ups came to chase everyone inside, Rebecca's fingers would be freezing, and snow would have worked its way inside her sleeves as well. The cold she'd felt then had been an exciting cold, a happy, carefree cold that always vanished deliciously with a cup of hot cocoa covered with marshmallows, sipped in front of the fire blazing in the living room hearth of her parents' house on Maple Street.

There had been other kinds of cold, though, that hadn't been nearly as much fun.

The cold she'd felt when there weren't enough blankets on the bed and Aunt Martha turned the thermostat low, to save money and save Rebecca's "spendthrift soul."

The icy cold of the first dip into the quarry in spring, when the water was barely above freezing.

The clammy chill when she'd gotten caught in a rainstorm with neither raincoat nor umbrella to protect her from getting soaked through to the skin.

That kind of cold, though, could be banished with an extra comforter, or a thick terry-cloth towel, or a change into dry clothes.

Even the chill of a fever that could rattle her teeth and turn her skin clammy was nothing like what she was feeling now, for even when she'd been in a fever's grip, she always knew it was only a temporary thing, that in a few hours, perhaps even a day, it would pass and she would feel warm again.

The cold she felt now had crept up on her so slowly that she couldn't really remember when it began; indeed, it was as if it had always been there. Every part of her body either had gone so numb that she had no feeling at all or ached with a dull pain, an ache that had burrowed into every muscle, spread through every bone. She wasn't frozen; she knew that. She could still move her arms and legs, still twist her neck and flex her back. But every movement was agonizing, every twitch of every muscle over which she had managed to retain control brought her a new sensation of pain.

The cold had even seeped into her mind, slowing her wits and confusing her so badly that she was no longer sure when she was awake and when she was sleeping; could not determine which of the sensations she felt were real, and which were the products of the dark nightmares that seized her whenever she slept.

It was the cold of death.

Rebecca knew that, knew it with a strange certainty that had grown in her mind until she'd all but given up any hope of surviving the ordeal that began when she'd fled from Germaine Wagner's house.

How long had it been?

She had no idea, for time itself no longer meant anything to her.

Not only was there no longer any distinction between night and day, but the difference between a minute and an hour, a day and a week, a month and a year, had disappeared. An hour might be a lifetime, and a month no more than a minute.

It didn't matter, for in the world into which Rebecca had plummeted—if it was this world at all—there was no longer any time.

Only cold.

The cold of the grave.

There were times when she thought she must have

died, when the darkness around her was so deep that she knew she must be buried in the earth. But then some brief sensation would penetrate the numbing cold; a sound perhaps, or a sharp twinge of pain that would rouse her, however briefly, from the strange not-quite-sleep into which she'd sunk.

For a while she tried to keep track of the passing time, tried to count the seconds that had turned into small eternities, but even that had become impossible, for there was no way to remember how many seconds she'd counted, no way to mark the passing minutes and hours.

The Tormentor—that was how she thought of her captor now, as almost an abstraction of a being, rather than a man with a face hidden by darkness and a personality concealed by silence. The Tormentor came and went, and Rebecca had long since ceased to feel any reaction to him.

Not surprise.

Not terror.

Not even apprehension anymore.

At first, in a time grown dim and distant in her memory, she had feared his coming, her heart pounding when she heard his scraping step or even sensed his presence when no sound betrayed that he was there.

He brought her food and water, though, for which she was grateful, though his whispered words made her flesh crawl no less than did his touch. But as the cold had tunneled deeper within her mind and her body and her spirit, Rebecca even stopped thinking about what it might be that he wanted from her, what reason he might have had for bringing her here.

Now, as her mind rose slowly out of the black pit of sleep, and the cold-induced nightmares loosened their grip, she sensed that he was there once more. It was nothing in the darkness that betrayed his presence; no sound of footsteps or rasping breath, no whispered words murmured in her ear, no touch of gloved fingers on her flesh.

Only a sense that she was not alone.

Then there was a minute lessening of the darkness, and like a flower turning toward the sun, she found herself turning her head, an involuntary groping for the source of the faint brightening that slightly grayed her world of darkness.

Then there was a new sensation.

Arms were picking her up. As she was lifted off the floor on which she lay, every nerve and muscle in her body screamed in protest, and a cry of anguished agony rose in her throat.

For an instant she tried to open her mouth to give vent to the erupting scream, but a tearing pain in her lips reminded her of the tape that covered her mouth. With a surge of sudden determination she managed to control her scream before it could back up in her throat, choke and strangle her and make her retch, and fill her mouth and nose with burning bile. As the wave of pain crashed over her and finally began to ebb, her cry of agonized protest emerged as nothing more than a stifled and sighing moan.

Held tightly in the Tormentor's grasp, she felt herself being carried out of the room that had been her prison, and though she could see nothing through the tape blindfold, she had a sense of walls that were close at hand on either side, and knew with an instinctive certainty that she was being borne down a long corridor. The Tormentor's pace changed, and Rebecca had a vague sensation of rising.

Stairs! She was being carried up a flight of stairs.

Another corridor, but, oddly, she sensed that this one was wider than the other, that the spaces here were larger. But how could she know? The darkness around her was only a nearly imperceptible shade lighter than the blackness into which she'd been sunk for so long.

And yet something was different.

Something had changed.

Something was about to happen.

Something terrible.

Chapter 2

*I*t was a glorious spring morning. Under normal circumstances, Oliver Metcalf would have been humming to himself as he fixed his first cup of coffee, glanced through the *Manchester Guardian*, then set off for the office, savoring every breath of the sweet air. A day when he might have paused to watch the baby robins tumbling across the lawn in front of Bill McGuire's house as their parents hopped anxiously around, cheeping their encouragement while the chicks struggled through their first clumsy flight lessons. A day when he would have dawdled at the Red Hen over an extra cup of coffee before heading to the *Chronicle* office; a sunshiny, optimistic morning that might have induced him to wonder if this would be the day that Rebecca Morrison agreed to let him take her out to dinner.

On a day like today he might even have planned a run down to Boston. But this morning, as on every morning since Rebecca disappeared, Oliver was barely aware of the fresh April breeze or the new buds on the venerable elms outside his kitchen window. From the moment he'd awakened from a restless sleep that had been disturbed by nightmares he couldn't quite remember—vaguely horrible dreams he wasn't sure he *wanted* to remember—dire thoughts of what might have happened to Rebecca were already churning through his mind. He was still trying to hold to the hope that Germaine Wagner's terrible accident had upset Rebecca so much that she'd simply fled from it. But as the days dragged by, and his heart had filled with expectation every time the phone rang, only to deflate with disappointment when it was not Rebecca's voice each time he picked it up, it was becoming harder and harder to cling to the faith that Rebecca would return to Blackstone—and to him— unharmed.

Surely, if she was all right, she would have called him. Unless what she'd witnessed in the Wagners' house had been so horrifying that she simply blocked it, and every- thing else, out of her memory. Except that Oliver knew just how rare amnesia really was—far more common, in fact, in romance novels and cheap thrillers than it was in real life. Unable to fly directly in the face of logic, he had finally admitted to himself that she must be in danger, perhaps deadly danger. That thought led directly to a depression into which he was sinking deeper every day. Although with every dawn that had broken since her dis- appearance, Oliver told himself that today he would at last hear from her, the self-assurances had long since begun to ring hollow.

Still, he was resolutely unwilling to grant any credi- bility to the people who thought Rebecca had finally turned on Germaine. Like everyone in town, Oliver was aware of how badly Germaine Wagner had treated Rebecca. But deep in his heart he was certain that Rebecca was incapable of violence. No, it would have been much more like Rebecca to pity Germaine for the woman's unhappiness than to turn on her for her meanness of spirit.

All that was left, then, was that something terrible had befallen Rebecca. That thought—and his inability to do anything to help her—now weighed so heavily on Oliver that he was finding it more and more difficult even to get out of bed in the morning. The combined effects of his sleepless tossing and turning, and the nightmares that plagued him when he did sleep, were taking their toll. This morning, he had almost decided to call Lois and tell her he wouldn't be in. Yet the prospect of staying alone in his house all day was even less appealing, so finally, shoulders stooped with the weight of his worry, he set out down Amherst Street toward the village.

The walk did little to pick up his spirits. Crossing Oak, he came to the part of Amherst Street where both the McGuires and the Beckers lived, and saw Megan McGuire sitting on the swing that hung from the lowest branch of an enormous oak tree in her front yard. He stopped for a moment intending to talk to her, and called out, "Good morning." At first she didn't seem to hear him. When he called her name, she looked sharply up at him, then got off the swing and started toward him, cradling a doll in her arms.

The doll that had been an anonymous gift, either for her or for the baby her mother had been about to deliver when Elizabeth McGuire had miscarried.

"It hurts every time I look at it," Bill McGuire had told Oliver a few weeks before. "But I can't bring myself to take the damn thing away from her. Since Elizabeth died, she keeps it with her all the time. Even takes it to school with her. I talked to Phil Margolis about it, but he says I should just let her be, at least for a while." The pain had misted Bill's eyes, and his voice had cracked. "Of course, that's what he said about Elizabeth too," he went on. "But I shouldn't have let her be. I should have stayed with her, every minute."

Oliver had tried to reassure him. "You can't blame yourself, Bill. All of us are responsible for our own lives, but not for other people's. And Elizabeth was . . ." He hadn't finished his sentence, but he hadn't needed to.

"Delicate?" Bill had asked, his tone tinged with bitterness. "Isn't that what Edna Burnham always says? That Elizabeth was 'delicate'?" He'd shaken his head. "She got through her sister's breakdown when she was a child, and she got through the loss of her parents a few years later. If you're 'delicate,' you don't survive tragedies like that. But losing the baby was just too much for her, and I should have known that. I should have known not to leave her alone that morning."

Unlike her father, whose grief had not abated, Megan seemed to Oliver to have sublimated her sorrow by focusing entirely on the doll, which she was clutching protectively even now, as she crossed the lawn toward him. He supposed Phil Margolis was right, and that given enough time, Megan would emerge from the shell she seemed to have formed around herself and the doll. As Megan walked slowly toward the sidewalk where he stood, Oliver could see her lips moving as she whispered to the doll.

"How are you today, Megan?" Oliver asked as the little girl stopped a few feet away from him.

"I'm all right," Megan replied. "Sam and I were playing on the swing."

" 'Sam,' " Oliver repeated. "Why did you name him Sam?"

Megan's eyes instantly darkened. "Sam's a girl," she said. "We don't like boys."

"I see," Oliver said gravely. "May I hold Sam?"

Megan shook her head. "Nobody can hold Sam but me," she said. "She's my friend, and I'm her friend, and she hates everyone else." She looked lovingly down into the doll's face. "Isn't that right, Sam?" A moment later, as if the doll had spoken to her, Megan looked up at Oliver again. "Sam wants you to go away now," she announced. "She wants you to leave us alone."

Oliver hesitated, but suddenly there was a look in Megan's eyes such as he'd never seen in a child before.

Evil.

The word rose up in his mind and took Oliver by surprise, like a right hook to the jaw. Astonished, he recovered himself to see that the demon-flash was gone. But Megan stared steadily at him, and under the child's relentless gaze it was finally he who shifted his eyes from hers.

"I'm sorry," he heard himself say, almost as if the words were coming from someone else. "I didn't mean to—" He stopped, aware that he'd been about to apologize for having *bothered* Megan. How ridiculous that he, an adult, should feel the need to apologize to this little girl merely for having spoken a few friendly words!

Worse, why did the way she was staring at him upset him so?

Saying nothing more to her, Oliver turned and continued down Amherst Street.

A moment later he was across from the Becker house. It was empty now. Bonnie and Amy had moved down to Boston, where Ed was still in intensive care. Three vertebrae in his neck had been shattered in his fall the night of the explosion in the basement, and though Ed was still alive, he was dependent on a respirator to breathe for him, and had yet to speak a word since the accident. The doctors assured Bonnie that in time he would be able to talk again, but when Oliver had gone down to Boston the day before yesterday to see Ed, he'd wondered if the doctors had told Bonnie the truth. Though Ed had been awake—Oliver had seen his eyes blink several times during the half hour he sat with Ed—he hadn't been certain whether Ed even knew he was there, much less recognized him. There was a look in the attorney's eyes—a gaze that, though not vacant, had not been focused on him either. Ed Becker appeared to have wandered into some other world, a universe buried so deep within his own mind that he was unable to find his way back to the plane of ordinary life in which he had existed before his accident.

When Oliver left the ICU, Bonnie told him about the dreams Ed had been having—dreams Ed had claimed were coming true—and about the stereoscope they'd found in the chest of drawers that Ed brought down from the Asylum.

"I keep thinking about those gifts everyone's been talking about," Bonnie said, her eyes looking almost as haunted as her husband's. "Except the stereoscope wasn't a gift at all—it just happened to be in one of the drawers in that old dresser."

Bonnie had told him about the pictures too, and when he returned to Blackstone, Oliver, curious, had gone to their house, entering with the keys she'd provided, to look for the stereoscope and view the pictures.

He'd found no trace either of the stereoscope or of the photographs Bonnie—and Amy too—had described to him. They had vanished as thoroughly as if they'd never existed, though Bonnie had directed him to the coffee table in the living room, where, she said, they'd been on the night that Ed had fallen. Oliver had searched everywhere, but they were nowhere to be found. The house itself had taken on an odd feeling of abandonment, as if it knew that Bonnie had decided she would never set foot in it again. "It isn't just what happened to Ed," she'd insisted. "I just don't think I'd ever feel safe there again. Not after the explosion. I'd never get a wink of sleep in that house. And I could never let Amy sleep there again."

But it was more than that, Oliver suspected. Bonnie, like so many other people in town, had become convinced that somehow, in some way she didn't understand, an evil force had invaded Blackstone.

There was that word again. *Evil.* The same word that had popped into his mind when he'd encountered Megan McGuire a few moments ago. But the word hadn't simply come into Oliver's mind this time. It was the word that Bonnie Becker herself had used to describe the events that had resulted in her husband's paralysis, and almost killed her and her daughter as well.

It wasn't just the house Bonnie Becker wasn't coming back to.

It was the town too.

"My family is in Boston and all my friends are here," she'd said. "I don't have any reason to go back to Blackstone." She'd hesitated, but then finished the thought. "And frankly, I don't understand why anyone would stay there, after everything that's happened." Then she had whispered the word once more. "Evil. Something evil is going on there."

Now, in the warmth of the April morning, Oliver Metcalf shivered slightly, as if a chilly presence had touched him. Of course, it couldn't possibly be true, but on the other hand . . .

He found himself counting the tragedies that had befallen his friends:

The suicide of Jules Hartwick, which he'd witnessed himself.

The burning of Martha Ward's house, in which Martha had perished and Rebecca had nearly been killed.

And the horror perpetrated in Germaine Wagner's house—Germaine's body crushed beneath the elevator, her elderly wheelchair-bound mother trapped inside the cage and felled by a massive stroke—the night Rebecca had vanished.

Oliver knew that it wasn't just Bonnie Becker who was whispering about a curse that had befallen Blackstone. The rumors were rampaging through the town like a disease, and everywhere he went, he could feel everyone watching everyone else, as if searching for some sign—some mark—that would tell them who might be next.

There were explanations—reasonable explanations—for everything that had happened in Blackstone. There had to be. And he would find them.

But of one thing he was certain.

There was no evil, no curse. Things like that simply didn't exist.

And yet, as he continued down the hill into the village and started across the square toward the *Chronicle* office, he found himself turning to gaze back at the Asylum, looming above the town as it had for nearly a century. And he found himself thinking once more about the outrages that he now knew had been practiced within its walls. *That* was evil—evil that cloaked itself in the guise of medical science.

If such an evil could prevail, an evil that could turn the Hippocratic oath to acts of unspeakable horror, then perhaps evil *did* exist and could inhabit other forms, take on other unknowable black shapes.

Turning away from the Asylum's brooding stare just as he'd turned away from Megan McGuire's gaze a few minutes ago, Oliver tried to put the unsettling idea out of his mind.

He couldn't.

The seed was planted. Already, it was starting to grow.

Chapter 3

By the time Harvey Connally had entered his ninth
decade, he'd discovered two truths: the first was that
what most people thought of as the wisdom that comes
with age was in reality little more than the realization that
most things, if left to their own devices, will take care of
themselves. That first truth had led directly to the second
one: that very little ever needed to be done right away,
and that it was therefore always best to think things over
carefully before taking any action. Thus, when he found
the package sitting on his front porch that morning,
resting next to his copy of the *Manchester Guardian*—
which, though in his opinion not nearly as good a paper
as his nephew's *Blackstone Chronicle*, at least had the
virtue of coming out on a daily basis—he chose to ignore
the plainly wrapped box, at least for the moment.
Retrieving the newspaper, he left the package on the
porch while he went to the kitchen, fixed himself the first
of the two cups of coffee he always drank in the
morning—the stingy ration of caffeine that was all that
Phil Margolis approved—and perused the *Guardian*. He
avoided the editorial page since editorials had the habit
of arousing enough outrage in him to bring on a stroke.
With his second cup of coffee, though, he folded the

paper and finally allowed his attention to turn to the package that still lay on his front porch. He'd noted that it bore no stamps, and no address, so he knew it must have been delivered sometime during the night.

Harvey Connally did not approve of people skulking about in the dark, leaving anonymous packages on other people's front porches. Yet the moment he'd seen the parcel, he'd immediately thought of Rebecca Morrison's claim that she'd seen someone in Jules Hartwick's driveway the night before he killed himself. He recalled the package that had been delivered to the McGuires' a few days before Elizabeth died. "Gifts" that Edna Burnham had declared to be the harbingers of evil.

Harvey Connally had no more patience with harbingers of evil than he had with skulkers in the night.

Whatever had happened to all those people, he was certain, had more to do with their own failings than with evil being visited upon them from some unknown source.

And yet . . .

And yet led Harvey Connally to an unaccustomed third cup of coffee. As he savored every forbidden sip of it, he found himself pondering the idea of Divine Retribution. It was a concept in which Harvey, at least until recently, had put no faith whatsoever. However, over the past few weeks, as he'd watched tragedy strike one after another of Blackstone's oldest families, he'd begun to wonder.

Every family to whom one of the mysterious "gifts" had been delivered had some connection to the Asylum, and each of the tragedies had contained elements that eerily paralleled events that had occurred in Blackstone's past. Harvey had first noted such an uncanny parallel when Jules Hartwick had disemboweled himself on the steps of the Asylum. Though everyone had agreed that it was the investigation of the bank by the Federal Reserve that triggered Jules's breakdown and suicide, Harvey had instead focused on the insane jealousy Jules had exhibited toward his wife that day.

The same raging jealousy, in fact, that Harvey remembered Jules's father exhibiting half a century ago when Hartwick had become convinced that his wife was having an affair with Malcolm Metcalf. But the elder Hartwick hadn't killed himself. Instead he had merely warned his wife that if the affair continued, he would divorce her, and make the reason for the divorce public. He had promptly banished the portrait of Louisa in her Gray Lady apron—which Harvey now suspected she intended as a gift to her lover—to the attic. And that had been that. Louisa had never again gone anywhere near the Asylum. When Malcolm Metcalf died, the Hartwicks had been conspicuous by their absence from his burial.

After making that connection, Harvey had begun to listen carefully to everything that had been said about the recent deaths in Blackstone. One by one, he began putting the pieces together. He remembered the child to whom Bill McGuire's great-aunt Laurette had given birth, a child who had disappeared into the Asylum one day, never to be seen again. It hadn't been long before Laurette, despondent at the loss of her child, had drowned while vacationing at Cape Cod. Her death had of course been attributed to an accident, but Harvey had long ago concluded that even if Laurette hadn't planned to die, neither had she done anything to save herself. Elizabeth McGuire's loss of her baby son and subsequent fatal fall seemed to Harvey a circumstance far too eerily similar to be merely coincidental.

As the months went by, each new tragedy stirred a

memory within Harvey Connally. At last, he'd become convinced that Blackstone's misfortunes were, indeed, connected to the Asylum. It was as if the sins of the fathers were being visited on the sons; as if the hand of God was finally reaching out to strike down the descendants of those whose transgressions had been hidden away within the Asylum's cold stone rooms.

Divine Retribution.

Except that Harvey Connally's mind, trained in the rigors of rationalist thought, wouldn't accept the idea of Divine Retribution. While the rest of Blackstone buzzed with speculation and gossip, Harvey Connally kept his own counsel, listening, always listening, but contributing nothing to the gushing torrent of rumor that flooded the town. Instead he quietly processed each item of news or speculation through his own mind, analyzing every theory he heard, discarding the most outlandish ideas, and filing away the bits and pieces that he couldn't dismiss, as if they were the jagged parts of a complicated jigsaw puzzle and the picture would come clear once he had all the pieces gathered and sorted.

But it had not come clear. For no matter how he tried to fit the pieces together, the only shape that ever emerged, superimposed upon Harvey's mental image of Blackstone's historical landscape, was a fuzzy vision of Malcolm Metcalf, a man who had been dead for nearly half of Harvey Connally's life.

But Harvey did not believe in ghosts any more than he believed in Divine Retribution.

When he finished the third cup of coffee, he slowly returned to the front porch, stooped stiffly down, and picked up the package. Holding the parcel carefully, he took it to his study, set it on his desk, and examined it from every angle. Finding no clue as to its origin, nor anything that he would consider a distinguishing mark, he momentarily entertained the idea of calling young Steven Driver, but dismissed the thought almost immediately: there was far too great a possibility that the sheriff's deputy would, on the pretext of protecting him, confiscate the contents. That issue decided, Harvey Connally carefully opened the package, doing as little damage to the paper in which it was wrapped as he could. As the wrapping fell away, the old man found himself gazing at an object of a kind he hadn't seen in years.

He recognized it instantly. It was an old-fashioned razor case, very much like the one his father had owned when Harvey was a boy. Instinctively, he reached out to caress the box, just as he had when he was a small boy and his father had told him he could touch the case, but never open it. Now, as the old man's fingers traced the pattern of ivory and ebony that had been inlaid into the box's mahogany lid, a profusion of memories was unleashed in his mind. He saw himself back in the bathroom of the house on Amherst Street where he'd grown up, his mother having refused to live in the enormous mansion on top of North Hill that his father had constructed for his first wife. Even seventy-five years later, he could smell the pungent odor of his father's shaving soap; feel the steam rising from the washbasin as his father enjoyed his morning shaving ritual.

Could this actually *be* his father's case?

But no. His father's razor case had been adorned with a gold medallion set into the center of the lid, a medallion that was engraved with the same two ornately intertwined C's with which everything Charles Connally owned had been monogrammed.

On this case there was only a simple ivory medallion.

Yet he was certain he'd seen it before.

Lifting the lid to expose a blue velvet lining, he gazed for a moment at the tortoiseshell handle of the straight razor that lay within, then picked the instrument up and opened its blade.

For just a second he didn't understand what the brown stains on the gleaming metal were. But then, as he saw the two M's etched into the tortoiseshell of the handle, he knew, in a rush of understanding that came at him like a gale force wind, exactly where he'd seen this case before.

It had belonged to his brother-in-law, Malcolm Metcalf. It had been a wedding gift from Harvey's sister, Olivia. Harvey himself had helped Olivia select it for her fiancé.

As he stared at the brown stains on the razor's blade, Harvey slowly understood their origin too.

Blood.

The blood of his niece, Mallory Metcalf?

Was it possible that after all these years, he was holding in his hands the long-missing instrument of Oliver's sister's death?

Why had it been delivered to him?

What was he being told?

And by whom?

For a long time Harvey Connally sat at his desk, the razor clasped in his suddenly palsied fingers. Over and over again he reviewed the pieces of the puzzle that he had gathered in his mind during the past weeks. Over and over again, the only face that emerged from the mists of the past was that of Malcolm Metcalf.

But he knew that wasn't quite true, for on the day that

Mallory had died—on the day that the razor Harvey was now holding had slashed across her throat and ended her life—there had been another person present.

A person for whom this instrument—this gift from the past—might hold far more meaning than it did even for him.

Laying the razor gently back in its case and snapping shut the mahogany lid, Harvey Connally came to a decision.

And picked up the telephone.

Chapter 4

*I*t was a day in mid-March—not the worst of weather, but far from the best. Though for the last few days it seemed as if the harsh winds of winter had finally died away, they reappeared this morning, whipping out of the northeast with a chill that threatened to freeze the buds on the still-bare trees before they had a chance to open. The few tiny crocuses that had dared to poke their heads up so early in the year cowered in the cold as though trying to retreat into the safety of the scarcely thawed earth. Harvey Connally was getting ready to drive up to Manchester for a board meeting—it seemed there were more board meetings to attend every month—though he was sorely tempted to plead illness, build a fire in his library, and curl up with his worn copy of **Billy Budd**, to Harvey's mind a far superior work to the more celebrated but nearly unreadable **Moby-Dick**. Harvey Connally, however, was not the sort to follow the tide of popular opinion. He had been brought up with a sense of duty as solid as the granite beneath the soil of New Hampshire, and even as temptation whispered to him, he knew he would turn away from its siren call.

Billy Budd would simply have to wait, perhaps even until next winter.

He was just about to leave the house when the extension telephone he'd had installed in the kitchen—a luxury to which he had quickly become accustomed—rang shrilly, with a tone that set off an alarm in Harvey's mind. Though his keenly honed rationality told him it was impossible for that bell to have a different ring in an emergency than under normal circumstances, he nevertheless felt a faint foreboding as he picked the receiver off the hook and held it to his ear.

"Harvey? Is that you?"

Harvey Connally recognized the voice coming through the line instantly, though it was far louder than usual, and quavering badly. As badly, in fact, as it had quavered the night four years ago when it informed him of the death of his sister.

"I'm here, Malcolm," he replied, nothing in his voice betraying the knot of apprehension that had already clutched his belly.

"I need you, Harvey. I need you to come to my office right away."

Harvey Connally did not ask why Malcolm Metcalf needed to see him at that very minute, for there were things—many things—one simply did not discuss on the telephone. His brother-in-law's strained urgency told Harvey that this was one of those things. "I'll be there in five minutes," he said. Without another word, he pressed the telephone's hook with his forefinger as he glanced at his watch. Dialing the operator, he asked for a number in Manchester, explained that he was unavoidably detained in Blackstone, and promised to make it to the board meeting if it proved at all possible. The man he was talking to—his roommate at Dartmouth twenty-odd years ago—asked no questions, knowing that only the most dire emergency could prevent Harvey Connally from keeping a commitment. His calendar cleared, Harvey left his house through the kitchen door, got into the DeSoto he'd purchased three weeks before, backed out of his driveway, drove along Elm Street to Amherst, turned left, and started up the hill toward the Asylum.

Harvey Connally hated the Asylum.

He hated every part of it, and always had.

Hated the building, although his own father had built it.

Certainly, he hated what went on there, convinced in his own mind that there had to be better ways to treat the mentally ill than by the use of the therapies dispensed within the blackened stone walls of the building that had become his brother-in-law's domain.

Most of all, Harvey Connally hated his brother-in-law, though nothing in his demeanor, actions, or words had ever betrayed the true depth of his feelings. Indeed, the only words he had ever spoken that might have revealed how he felt were said to his sister shortly before she married Malcolm Metcalf.

"I just want to be sure you've thought this through and are certain he's the right man for you," Harvey had told Olivia the morning after she and Malcolm announced their engagement. When Olivia assured him that she'd thought about it very carefully and was deeply in love with Malcolm Metcalf, Harvey considered the matter closed. He had not resigned his position on the Board of Trustees of the Asylum—an action that would have revealed his feelings—but as a trustee, he had removed himself from discussion of any matter relating directly to the director of the Asylum on the grounds of a conflict of interest between his roles as trustee and as the director's brother-in-law. Even after Olivia's death, Harvey had

kept his feelings to himself, and Malcolm Metcalf, despite his reputation not only as a psychiatrist but as a perceptive, sensitive, and intuitive human being, had no clue that Harvey Connally hated him.

Which was exactly as Harvey Connally intended it.

As he parked the DeSoto in front of the Asylum, Harvey gazed up at the hideous facade and tried yet again to understand his father's motives in having built this immense edifice. Far larger than any other house ever built in Blackstone, the construction of this building had been an act of ostentation previously unknown in Blackstone, and totally out of character for Charles Connally. That he had turned it into a hospital for the mentally ill only a few years after having built it was just as out of character, and though Harvey Connally had spent a good deal of time searching for clues as to his father's motivations for both those peculiar actions, he'd never found answers to any of his questions.

Unconsciously taking a deep breath as he pulled the heavy front door open, Harvey stepped into the gloomy foyer, and wondered—not for the first time—how anyone could be expected to recover from an illness, mental or physical, within these cold, forbidding confines. He passed through the waiting room, and avoided looking directly at the group who huddled there—three shamefaced, obviously embarrassed people whose eyes were averted from his. The action told Harvey more than he wanted to know: they were either about to commit one of their relatives to his brother-in-law's care, or already had.

He made his way to Malcolm Metcalf's office. The latest of the director's secretaries—they never seemed to last more than a few months, and Harvey had long since *given up trying to remember their names—waved him directly into the room.*

His brother-in-law was pacing the floor, his face ashen.

"What is it, Malcolm?" Harvey Connally asked. "What's happened?"

Malcolm Metcalf's mouth worked for a moment, and finally he managed to stammer a word or two. "Mallory . . ." he said. "Oliver—"

Harvey glanced around the room, but saw no sign of either his niece or his nephew. Then he saw Malcolm Metcalf's eyes flick toward the bathroom that adjoined his office. Frowning, Harvey went to the door and pulled it open.

Red.

There was red everywhere.

It was smeared on the white-painted walls, and on the tiled floor.

There was a towel, also stained bright red, lying in a sodden heap next to the sink.

A movement, so faint he almost missed it, caught Harvey's attention, and he turned to see his four-year-old nephew cowering in a corner, his face as white as his father's and streaked with tears, his arms wrapped around his knees.

His thin form was naked, and his pale skin was also streaked with red.

And then, for the first time, Harvey Metcalf saw the bathtub.

Huge, sitting on four claw-foot legs, it was filled nearly to the rim, the water a ghastly pink.

Submerged in the bloody water, also naked, facedown, was a body.

Oliver's twin sister, Mallory.

His reason abandoning him, Harvey Connally followed the instincts that took him in two great strides from the door to the tub, where he leaned down and, plunging his arms into the gruesome liquid, lifted his niece from the water. Laying her on the floor, he turned her over to begin artificial respiration, then froze in horror.

More than a wound, the slash extended from one ear almost to the other. The child's throat had been laid open in a gash that had almost separated her head from her torso.

Harvey Connally's gorge rose in a hot flood that threatened to choke him as he stared at his dead niece, and a terrible vision flashed before him.

It was a vision of Mallory—heart-faced like her mother, with soft blond curls framing her gentle features. But instead of laughing as she so often had, her mouth was open in a dreadful, silent scream, and her eyes were wide with terror.

And from the dark, gaping wound in her throat, blood gushed in great crimson gouts as her heart quickly pumped her life away.

Onto the walls.

Onto the floor.

Into the water in which she'd been bathing.

The vision, mercifully, vanished as quickly as it had come, and Harvey Connally, knowing it was far too late to do anything for his niece, scooped his nephew from the corner. As Oliver sobbed and shook in his arms, Harvey returned to the office where his brother-in-law still stood bracing himself against the wall.

"What happened?" Harvey demanded, his voice low, almost dangerous. "Tell me what happened."

"Accident," Malcolm gasped, barely able to speak. "It was—"

"An accident?" Harvey Connally repeated. "For God's sake, Malcolm, how could you—"

Malcolm Metcalf's mouth worked spasmodically for another moment before he was able to produce any other words. Then: "Oliver," he whispered. "It wasn't me, Harvey. It was Oliver."

Harvey Connally's eyes narrowed. "How?" he demanded. "Tell me how!"

Still holding his shivering, sobbing nephew, Harvey listened as Malcolm Metcalf brokenly described what he had seen.

"They were in the tub. They loved to take baths together. And I was in here. And then I heard something. A sound—oh, God, Harvey, you can't imagine it. It was like—I don't know—a gurgling, like water going down a drain. I called to them, but—" He fell silent for a moment, then went on. "I went to the door to see what was going on. And I saw her! Oh, Lord, Harvey, I saw her die. She was in the water, and her neck was cut, and she was bleeding." Malcolm Metcalf was sobbing now, choking on his words as he struggled to get them out. "She was hanging on to the edge of the tub. I tried to help her, tried to stop the bleeding with a towel. But it was too late. She was already dying, and . . ." His words trailed off.

"And what about Oliver?" Harvey Connally asked. "Where was he?"

Malcolm Metcalf hesitated, as if wishing he didn't have to speak the words. But finally, reluctantly, they came: *"Gone,"* he whispered. *"When I realized there wasn't anything I could do for Mallory, I looked for Oliver. He—He'd gone down my private stairs, the ones that used to be the service stairs, and I found him."*

"Where was he?" Harvey asked. Almost protectively, he held his nephew tighter.

There was a long silence, then Malcolm Metcalf finally spoke again. *"Hiding,"* he said so softly that Harvey could barely hear him. *"He was in one of the treatment rooms downstairs."* He paused again, then: *"My razor's missing,"* he went on, his voice dull. *"I suppose Oliver must have been playing with it, and he and Mallory must have gotten into a tussle."* He shook his head, his eyes welling with tears. *"It was an accident,"* he said. *"I can't believe it could have been anything else! But Oliver was so scared, he ran away and hid the razor. You can't blame him. He—He's just a little boy, Harvey. It was an accident."*

For a long time Harvey Connally gazed into his brother-in-law's eyes. Then he slowly lowered his nephew to the floor and knelt down so his face was level with the little boy's. *"Is that true, Oliver?"* he asked. *"Is what your father said true?"*

Oliver Metcalf, his eyes huge, his face ashen, his whole body shaking with terror, gazed into his uncle's face.

Chapter 5

Oliver pushed open the gate in front of his uncle's house and brushed past the overgrown laurel hedge. Unless something was done this year, its branches would soon block the entrance. Not, Oliver was sure, that his uncle really cared if the gate became impassable. More and more, Harvey Connally had retreated from the life of the town, content, it seemed, to be by himself in the company of his memories. It seemed to Oliver that over the past few months, his uncle had withdrawn nearly completely from the community in which he'd lived his entire life. Oliver was uncertain as to whether Harvey Connally's self-imposed isolation was a natural result of his advancing years or a reaction to the series of tragedies that had befallen the town. The truth, he thought as he climbed the steps of his uncle's front porch, lay somewhere in between.

Not bothering to ring the bell, Oliver tried the door and discovered that it was, as always, unlocked. "Locks were invented to keep honest people out," Harvey had instructed him years ago. "They don't do a damn thing to prevent dishonest people from getting in." It was a maxim few people followed anymore; and in Blackstone, given the events of the past few months, it was a rare door indeed that was left unsecured for more than a moment or two, despite the utter lack of evidence that there was anything more than coincidence to the plague of death that had spread through the town. What had once seemed the quirky opinion of an old man trying to preserve old-fashioned ways now had the ring of prescient wisdom, Oliver thought as he stepped into the hall: none of Blackstone's locks had yet kept anyone safe.

"Uncle Harvey?" Oliver called out as he closed the door behind him. Silence. He opened his mouth to call out again, but even as he was forming his uncle's name, a cold chill of foreboding stopped him.

Something in the house was not right. He was about to start toward the kitchen, where his uncle habitually sat while he sipped his two cups of coffee and read the paper, when the old hall clock began striking the hour of ten. By this time, Harvey Connally would have finished his coffee and been at his desk, tending to the business of an elderly man: his stock portfolio and his correspondence.

Instead of turning into the dining room, Oliver moved past the base of the staircase to his uncle's study. The door was open. Harvey Connally was sitting rigidly in the leather chair behind the desk, his face ashen, his lips stretched into a tight rictus of pain.

Oliver gasped. "Uncle Harvey? What is it? What's wrong?" He moved quickly toward his uncle, his hand instinctively reaching for the telephone to summon help. Before he could lift the receiver, his uncle reached out and laid his right hand on the instrument, holding it firmly in its place.

"Not yet," he said. His voice was strained, and Oliver could see the old man's fingers trembling even as they held the receiver on its cradle. He was obviously in a great deal of pain, yet there was something in his voice that made Oliver abandon the idea of taking the telephone forcibly from his uncle's grasp. As Oliver's hands dropped to his sides, his uncle's eyes, as clear and sharp as ever, despite the old man's age and obvious pain, fixed on his. "Something was left for me this morning," he said. His lips twisted into a grimace that was intended to be a smile. "I'm not sure what it means, but I have a feeling it wasn't meant for me at all. I think it was probably meant for you." His hand moved from the telephone to the polished mahogany box that still lay on his desktop. As Oliver automatically reached for it, Harvey Connally shook his head slightly and left his hand where it was, preventing Oliver from taking the box, just as a moment ago he'd prevented his nephew from lifting the telephone. "Not yet," he said softly. Then he nodded to the chair opposite him. "Sit for a moment, Oliver."

Oliver made no move toward the chair. "Uncle Harvey, you have to let me call Dr. Margolis. You look like you're about to—" He abruptly cut off his words, but his uncle managed another smile. The piercing gaze did not waver.

"About to die?" he asked. "I think that's exactly what I'm about to do, and if you do anything—anything at all—to keep me from it, I shall do everything in my power to make your life as miserable as possible for however much longer I live. I'm old, and I'm tired; I don't mind dying. But before I go, I need to tell you something."

Slowly, reluctantly, Oliver sank into the chair across from his uncle. The old man's gaze remained fixed on him, and Oliver had an eerie feeling that his uncle was peering inside him, right to the depths of his soul. Finally, apparently satisfied by whatever he'd seen, Harvey spoke once more.

"I have always tried to do my best by you, Oliver," he said. "I'm afraid I was not always successful, but I want you to know that I did my best, and that I never believed what your father told me. Never." He fell silent for a moment, and cocked his head as if listening to words that were coming from a distant country, a place deep in the past. Then he shook his head and spoke again. "You were never a bad boy, Oliver. You were always as good as you knew how to be." He paused, and now his eyes drifted to the mahogany box. "After I'm gone, you're going to have to deal with what is in this box. I won't try to tell you how to deal with it. You might choose simply to put it away somewhere. If you do, I advise you to put it where it cannot possibly ever again be found. If you choose to deal with it by opening the box, then I want you to keep one thing in mind."

Once again Harvey Connally's eyes fixed on Oliver's, but this time they burned with an intensity greater than Oliver had ever seen before.

"I raised you to be a Connally, Oliver," the old man said. "After your father died, and you were all I had left, I did my best to raise you as my own son." He paused again, and Oliver could see him searching for the exact words he wanted to say. Then, wincing against the pain in his chest, he made his pronouncement: "It's not your name that matters, Oliver. It's what you are inside that counts. And deep inside, Oliver, I know you are not a Metcalf. You are a Connally. You may be of his issue, but you are not your father's son!"

Suddenly, Harvey Connally's head snapped back and his eyes opened wide in an expression of surprise. Clutching his chest, he slumped in his chair as Oliver rose to his feet and gathered his uncle into an embrace.

"No, Uncle Harvey," he begged. "Don't die! Please. You're going to be all right. I'll—"

Harvey Connally's right hand closed on his nephew's arm. "Remember, Oliver. A Connally! Always remember that I raised you to be a Connally!" His fingers tightened on Oliver's arm, sinking deep into the younger man's flesh, and then, with a deep gasp, he exhaled his last breath and his head sank down, his chin resting on his chest. As life slipped away from Harvey Connally, his grip on Oliver's arm slowly relaxed and his hand fell away. For long seconds Oliver stood still, gazing at his uncle.

Even in death, Harvey Connally's face retained its strength of character. Oliver studied that craggy, once handsome face—the face of the man who had been his only relative, his sole source of unconditional affection since the age of seven.

Always remember that I raised you to be a Connally!

Reaching down, Oliver gently closed his uncle's blue eyes, the light inside them having finally faded. As he straightened, his glance fell on the mahogany box that still sat on his uncle's desk. His first instinct was to open it and see what was inside, but even as he reached toward it, his uncle's words echoed in his memory:

You might choose simply to put it away somewhere. If you do, I advise you to put it where it cannot possibly ever again be found. . . .

Oliver's hand hovered over the box, then moved toward the telephone. Lifting the receiver from the hook, he dialed Philip Margolis's private number. The doctor picked up the phone on the third ring. "It's Oliver, Phil," he said to Margolis. "My uncle has died. I'd appreciate it if you could come over. I'm at his house."

Chapter 6

Silence at last hung over Harvey Connally's house on Elm Street. For the last two hours, as first Philip Margolis and then Steve Driver arrived, the rooms had rung with the comings and goings that attended the business of death. After Dr. Margolis's preliminary examination of the body, Harvey Connally's remains had been carried out of the house, to be transported not to Broder's Funeral Parlor but to Blackstone Memorial, where an autopsy would be performed.

"It's not really a legal necessity," the doctor had explained to Oliver, "but given recent events, I think you ought to let me do it. If I can say I did a thorough autopsy, and the cause of your uncle's death was the massive heart attack it obviously appears to be, then that should put an end to any talk." With a smile and shrug, he added, "Or at least keep it down to a dull roar, since there won't be any way to shut Edna Burnham up short of a restraining order."

Oliver managed a faint smile that conveyed his resignation in the face of the inevitable rumormongering the old lady would shortly be embarking on. "Somehow I don't think even a court order would stop Edna from . . ." His voice trailed off, but he didn't have to say any more. Even without Edna Burnham fueling the fire, there was bound to be speculation that there was more to Harvey Connally's sudden death than appeared on the surface. That assumption had already been borne out by the crowd that had begun to assemble within minutes after Steve Driver's arrival. Though no one inside the house was aware of the neighbors and passersby beyond the laurel hedge when Jeff Broder had arrived to discuss the funeral arrangements with Oliver, Broder reported that at least a dozen people were gathered on the sidewalk outside the gate. While the funeral director, whose family had been burying the dead of Blackstone for three generations, calmly went over the arrangements that Harvey Connally had made for himself several years earlier, Steve Driver went outside to try to clear the onlookers away.

He'd had no success.

Now, however, with Oliver's uncle's body gone, it seemed to Oliver as if the lodestone had been removed. By the time the last of those who had legitimate business at the house had left, the crowd too began to fall away. Their curiosity had been satisfied: they'd watched in somber silence as Harvey Connally left his house for the last time.

Oliver closed the front door after seeing Jeff Broder out. Left in the quiet of the house, he felt more alone than ever before in his life.

He began wandering slowly through the deserted rooms, acutely aware of the absence of his uncle.

After his father died, this house had been his home, at least during the times when he wasn't away, first at boarding school or at summer camp, then at college. Every room contained memories. The kitchen, where he'd sat on a stool watching his uncle's housekeeper, old

Mrs. Perry, stir the pots from which magical aromas wafted into his nostrils. The dining room, where he and his uncle had sat eating the meals Mrs. Perry fixed, and talking over anything that came into Oliver's mind. In the living room, the melodies Harvey Connally had picked out on the grand piano seemed still to hang in the air, and upstairs, in the room that had been Oliver's, he could still summon the smell of a blossom-laden summer breeze drifting in through the open window as he lay in his boyhood bed. Now, of course, the room was tinged with mustiness, the scent of disuse and abandonment, for after Mrs. Perry died, his uncle decided to look after himself, pleading that he was far too old to accustom himself to a stranger in his house.

Finally, after Oliver had wandered restlessly through every other room in the house, he could no longer put off returning to the study, where the flat mahogany box still sat on the bookshelf where he'd put it after calling Phil Margolis.

He hadn't mentioned the box to either the doctor or Steve Driver. The presence of yet another mysterious package would only become new grist for the gossip mill that was already grinding at full speed in Blackstone.

Nor had he yet opened it.

Now, as he touched its smooth surface, a strange shock ran through him, as if the case had been charged with electricity.

Had it happened before, when he'd picked up the box to move it from the desk to the bookshelf? He couldn't recall. His uncle's ominous words, swiftly followed by his sudden passing, had made the rest of the morning a blur for Oliver.

I never believed what your father told me. Never. The statement still echoed through Oliver's head.

A moment later the strange sensation passed. He picked up the box, moved back to his uncle's desk, and set it down.

As he gazed at it, he realized that it looked vaguely familiar. Examining it more closely, seeing the ornately worked medallion that was inlaid in the lid, he suddenly knew why it seemed familiar.

His father's.

It had been his father's.

But what could be in it?

He reached for it again, this time to open it, but just as his fingers touched the latches that secured the box's lid, something stopped him.

Not here!

The voice was so distinct that Oliver, startled, found himself glancing around the room to see who had uttered the words. But the room, like the house itself, was empty save for him.

Home. Take the box home.

Again the words were so clear that it was hard for Oliver to believe they'd risen from his own mind. Nonetheless, he found himself obeying them. Picking up the box, he left his uncle's house. But instead of leaving by the front door, he went out through the kitchen, down the driveway, then turned onto Harvard Street. The box, which for some reason he didn't quite understand he'd slipped under his jacket, felt almost warm, its heat penetrating his thin shirt to his skin, though he knew the warmth could be nothing more than an illusion. Quickening his step, he strode up the hill, but as he came to the burned-out wreckage of Martha Ward's house, he stopped.

Again, there was the strange sensation—almost a vibration coursing through him.

Standing stock-still, Oliver gazed at the charred remains of the house from which Rebecca Morrison had fled only a few short weeks ago. In his mind's eye, but so vividly he could have been watching the fire itself, he once more saw the flames consuming it.

Suddenly, the sound of laughter penetrated his reverie. He spun around to see who was there.

The street and sidewalk were empty.

His heartbeat speeding, Oliver continued on his way up the hill, passing the Hartwicks' but neither stopping nor even glancing at it. At the path that would lead him through the woods to the Asylum's grounds, he left the sidewalk and, out of sight of Jules and Madeline's house, felt his pulse begin to slow. Then the odd vibrating sensation vanished so abruptly and completely that he wondered whether he'd actually felt it or whether the disconcerting tingling had been nothing more than a result of the shock of his uncle's death.

Just as he emerged from the trees onto the weed-choked grounds surrounding the Asylum's hulking mass, it began again.

A heat radiating from the mahogany case. Hotter now, pulsing.

Drop it, he told himself.

Just let go of it, drop it, and walk away.

Or better yet, smash it underfoot and scatter the pieces—and whatever might be inside the box—across the field so they'd be plowed beneath the earth when the Blackstone Center project finally got under way.

Bury it under concrete. *Put it where it cannot possibly ever again be found.*

But instead of dropping the box, Oliver realized he was clutching it tighter, pressing it against his body as if at any second someone might try to snatch it from him.

He began walking again, picking his way across the grounds, but it was not toward his house that he was moving.

Instead, he drew closer and closer to the Asylum itself. With every step he took, his pulse quickened, until he could hear the sound of his own heart pounding in his ears.

He came at last to the front steps. He hesitated there, waiting for the familiar pain in his head to begin, quickly building until either he turned and fled to the sanctuary of his house or the blackness closed around him, felling him as surely as a blow to the back of the head.

Today, though, the pain did not come. Unable to stop himself, carried forward on a wave of foreboding and fear, he mounted the stone steps and reached out to grip the great latch on the door.

He paused then, and though his hand remained on the cold bronze latch, he gazed around as if taking a last look at a landscape he might never see again. He looked down the hill at the house he'd lived in for the first seven years of his life, and the last twenty-five.

For a moment—just a moment—Oliver thought he glimpsed a face in one of its windows, and he felt his heart quicken with anticipation until he realized it was nothing more than a trick of the light.

Then, out of the corner of his eye, he saw a flicker of movement. He whirled around, and as he turned, thought he saw a small figure disappearing into the woods.

A girl. A little girl, who looked like—

Mallory?

Impossible. An illusion. It had to be no more than an illusion, just as the face in the window of his house had been a fleeting and cruel illusion, and not Rebecca at all.

Yet from somewhere—somewhere distant—he thought he could barely hear a child's voice, his sister's voice, calling out to him.

Calling for him to come to her?

Or calling a warning to him, to stay away?

A trick of the light, and now a trick of the wind? A whisper, and now, nothing but silence.

His hand tightening on the latch to the Asylum's door, Oliver turned the knob and swung the heavy oak portal open.

Motes of dust hung thickly in the air inside, and the chill of the building's interior seemed to reach out and draw him in.

Steeling himself against the whipping pain he still anticipated would lash through his head at any moment, Oliver moved through the shadowy interior of the building as if in a dream, not certain where he was going, or why, but knowing he would recognize his destination when he came to it.

His footsteps echoed in the emptiness of the building, but he was hardly aware of them, for his ears were filled with other sounds.

Ghostly sounds, out of the past.

Voices whispering, mumbling incoherently.

Terrified shrieks, floating from the floors above.

Hopeless moans, seeping up from beneath the floor, surrounding him.

Oliver moved from one room to another, until at last

he came to the room that had been his father's office. There he finally took the mahogany box from beneath his jacket, and set it gently on the floor.

With trembling fingers he loosened the latches, then raised the lid.

Oliver Metcalf gazed upon the razor, and an image rose unbidden—unwanted—from the deepest realms of his subconscious.

It was a vision of the razor's blade, gleaming so bright a silver that it nearly blinded him as it arced in the air— slicing through his sister's throat.

His hands shaking, Oliver picked up the razor and opened it.

And heard his sister's dying scream . . .

Rebecca lay inside a swirling cloud of fog, a mist that engulfed her but, strangely, did not make her feel afraid, for out of the mists was emerging an image that had appeared in her dreams and fantasies for as long as she could remember. A knight, his armor burnished to the finish of a mirror, astride a great horse. A horse as black as coal, with a flowing mane and tail that whipped in the wind as the stallion bore the knight toward her, his banner—a streaming scarlet flag woven of the finest silk—billowing in the breeze with the softness of a cloud.

Now, far in the distance, muffled by the eddying mists, she thought she could hear the horse's hooves, and a thrill of excitement ran through her as she waited for the knight to be revealed to her. His strong face. His kind eyes.

Oliver.

It would be Oliver, riding to her rescue, racing toward her through the misty twilight to lift her up and swing her onto the steed's mighty back, where she would slip her arms around him and cling to him as they sped away.

But then, as the sound of hoofbeats grew nearer, she felt the first faint stirring of apprehension.

Abruptly, the fog closed in. She could feel the danger lurking everywhere around her, hidden just beyond the limits of her vision, waiting for the fog to thicken and the twilight to turn into night before creeping close, circling her, preparing to strike.

Ghostly faces appeared.

Eyes, feral and glinting with the fire of evil.

Snouts, tapering to cruel points.

Fangs, dripping with yellow saliva.

More eyes, yellow, and sunk deep beneath coarse brows, fixing on her with a glare of hatred.

Demons in search of souls to consume.

She tried to scream, but her throat constricted. Deafening shrieks of clattering laughter beat at her ears as if a pack of hyenas was closing on its prey, attacking, tearing it to shreds.

Rebecca turned to flee, to run from the hellhounds that drew closer with every passing second.

She twisted, turning first one way and then the other. No escape, no place to run.

The terror that had been escalating inside her erupted into panic. She threw herself hard to one side. A sharp pain shot through her shoulder, and a muffled screech of agony filled her throat, causing her to gag. Her breath caught in her lungs with a terrible, wracking heaving that convulsed her whole body—and brought her abruptly out of the clutches of the nightmare. But she awakened into the numbing fear that had held her for what seemed to be an eternity.

She became aware again of the tape that covered her eyes and mouth, blinding her and imprisoning the hacking coughs that continued to convulse her lungs until she thought her chest might actually explode.

Now, fully awake, she felt once more the aching cold that had slowly taken possession of every cell in her body, and for a moment she almost wished she could retreat into the fog of her dream. But then, as the fearsome, leering faces she'd seen in the mists rose before her once again, she knew that sleep—and the terrors it would bring—could no longer protect her from the horror to which she had fallen victim. Banishing the visions from her subconscious, Rebecca slowly regained control over her weakening body. The queasiness in her stomach began to ease, and the tightness in her chest to loosen. Her shoulder, which she'd smashed against the hard, cold surface next to her when she'd tried to thrash her way out of the grip of the nightmare, was throbbing painfully, but she knew that with time even that ache would slowly fade.

Unless, of course, she died.

It was going to happen; she knew that now. Sooner or later, she would succumb to something that was finally too much for her to bear. Silently, lying still in the darkness, she prayed that her body would fail her first, for she had already glimpsed the terrors she would face if it was her mind that finally betrayed her. Hell could hold no horrors worse than to be submerged forever in the dreams that tormented her, or the cold, dark prison in which she lived.

Then, so slowly she was barely aware it was happening, her racing pulse at last began to slow, and one by one she began to put her terrors aside.

She was not dead yet, nor had she lost her mind.

Somewhere, she told herself, beyond the blackness and the bonds that held her, Oliver was still searching for her, would still come to rescue her from the eternal night into which she'd vanished. But even as she clung to that sweet thought, she heard once more the echoing hooves of her nightmare, and for an instant thought that perhaps her mind had failed her after all.

Not the beat of hooves sounding in the darkness.

Footsteps.

The Tormentor was drawing close.

To feed her?

To slake her thirst?

Or to offer her up to some new terror she would not be able to anticipate until it was actually upon her?

Click.

She heard the latch of the door release, then the creak of unoiled hinges.

The sound of leather soles on a hard floor.

She sensed him now, standing above her.

Could he see her?

Did he know who she was?

Did he even care?

Or was she only someone who had come to hand? As she'd run through the darkness of that night that was now nearly lost in the dim recesses of her memory, fleeing the Wagners' in hope of getting help, had her abductor found her by accident?

Rebecca held herself perfectly still, and uttered no

sound at all, determined to let him know nothing of her fear or her pain.

If he sensed her weakness, surely he would kill her.

The dark figure gazed down upon his prize. Everything was almost right, everything in readiness.

Yet not quite.

Things were not exactly as they had been, not precisely as he saw them in his mind's eye.

He reached down and turned a tap.

The tub in which his prisoner lay slowly began to fill.

Then he turned away, having no need to watch until the climactic moment came.

The moment for which he'd waited, had prepared for so many years ago, and that now had finally arrived.

But not yet.

Not quite yet.

Not until the tub was filled.

And every memory savored.

For a moment, when she heard the trickle of water from a tap, Rebecca felt a flash of hope—he'd come to give her water.

But then, when no fingers tore the tape from her mouth or held a glass to her lips, she realized that it was something else.

And when she felt the icy water touch her legs, felt the freeze of winter truly begin to numb her flesh, she realized what her fate was going to be.

She understood the cold smoothness of the surface her face had touched, grasped the meaning of the hardness of everything around her. She was lying in a tub, and the Tormentor was filling it with water.

He was going to drown her.

Unless, before she drowned, the chill of the near-frozen water killed her first.

She felt the courage and determination she'd mustered only a few moments ago drain away, and knew, at long last, that the end was near.

Chapter 7

Oliver stared at the razor in his hand. Everything around it was lost in darkness. He could see nothing but the razor's glistening blade and, on its bright steel surface, the blood. The blood glimmering in the dark, slick and fresh, scarlet and thick. As he stared at it, it seemed to come alive, flowing across the blade toward the fingers that clutched the razor's handle.

His fingers.

Yet, strangely, not his fingers.

Then he heard a voice: "Daddy? Daddy, I don't want to! I want to go outside!"

The voice echoed in Oliver's head. A frightened, small voice. A stranger's voice, yet not unfamiliar.

"Please?" the voice begged. "Please can't I go outside?"

The voice sounded more familiar now, and a shiver of fear crept down his back, but still he couldn't quite place it.

Then another voice spoke, with a timbre that was hard and unyielding and instantly recognizable, though he hadn't heard it in nearly forty years. "You're a bad boy," the voice said. "You're a very bad boy, and you'll do as I say!"

Oliver's fear congealed into a terror that crawled up

484

from his subconscious like a demon from Hell, reaching out to grasp him in its sharp-clawed fingers. His father's voice.

"Tell me what you did, Oliver."

Oliver tried to shrink away into the darkness—shrink from the voice, cower away from the demon inside that was quickly taking possession of him, draining his strength, twisting his reason, threatening to destroy his mind. But there was no escape, no place to hide, neither from his father's voice nor from the terror within.

"Tell me, Oliver," his father's voice commanded again. "Tell me what you are. Tell me what you did."

"I'm a bad boy," the little boy's voice said again, and now Oliver recognized it clearly.

His voice.

He was hearing his own voice.

"I'm a very bad boy."

"That's right," his father's voice replied. "You're a very, very bad boy."

The darkness around the gleaming razor began to fade to the silvery gray of dawn, and slowly the razor and its glistening coat of blood began to fall from focus. But the light kept brightening, until finally Oliver had to squeeze his eyes closed against it. Then he heard his father's voice once more, and knew he was powerless to disobey.

"Open your eyes, Oliver," Malcolm Metcalf's voice commanded. "Open them."

Oliver is standing just inside the front door to the Asylum. His father's hand is squeezing his own so tightly it hurts, but Oliver knows there is no way he can pull his hand free and run from his father into the sunshine outside.

He flinches as the huge oak door swings closed behind him with a thud that seems to echo through the great open room forever.

No one else, though, seems to hear it.

His father is moving now, taking such great long strides that Oliver, even though his stubby legs are moving as fast as he can make them, can barely keep up with him.

There are people all around him.

Some of them he recognizes. Women in white clothes. Nurses. Men in white coats. Doctors. There are others too, whose clothes look to Oliver just like the ones the doctors wear, but he knows they aren't doctors.

Until a little while ago, he hadn't known what the other ones—the ones who weren't doctors—did.

But now he knows, and when one of them says hello to him, Oliver doesn't say hello back.

There are other people too, people dressed in pajamas and bathrobes even though it isn't even close to bedtime, even for Oliver.

Finally, they come to the top of a long flight of stairs, steep stairs that descend into darkness. Oliver's heart begins to thump and it's hard for him to breathe. Down. They go down the stairs into the blackness below until they come to the bottom and his father leads him down a long hall. There are closed doors on both sides of the hall, and Oliver tries not to look at any of them, fearful of what might lie beyond.

At last, his father opens one of the doors.

"No, Daddy," Oliver whimpers. "Please, Daddy, don't make me—"

But it is too late. His father drags him through the door, then closes it behind them.

There is a sharp click as the lock slides home.

His father lets go of his hand, and Oliver, so terrified that his legs have lost their strength, falls to the floor, then scuttles back against the wall. Whimpering with fear, he watches as his father goes to a cabinet, opens its door, and takes out a long metal tube, from one end of which two shiny metal nubs stick out.

"No, Daddy," Oliver whispers. "No . . ."

As Oliver cowers against the wall, his father presses the end of the metal tube against the bare skin of Oliver's leg.

"Don't talk back to me, Oliver," Malcolm Metcalf says, his voice harsh. "Don't ever talk back to me!"

A jolt of electricity shoots through Oliver's leg. He shrieks as the muscles of his leg jerk spasmodically, and his foot strikes his father's shin.

"Don't kick," Malcolm Metcalf commands. "Don't you dare kick me!"

Again the metal tube touches Oliver, this time on the other leg, and instantly a second shock buzzes through him. His foot smashes painfully against the tiled wall, and another squeal erupts from his throat.

His father towers over him. "Be quiet! Take it like a man!"

As the terrible metal tube hovers near him, Oliver tries to scuttle away. He is crying now, partly from fear, partly from the burning sting of the prod, as his father comes after him with the metal stick.

Shock after shock jolts through him; his muscles contract spasmodically with each one until he is wailing, a high, keening cry, punctuated with screams of pain every time a shock courses through him.

"Be quiet, Oliver!" his father demands. "You must learn to do as I tell you!"

Oliver tries once more to wriggle away from his father's wrath, but there is no escaping the towering figure.

Zap!

Another shock. Another spasm.

On all fours, Oliver tries to crawl between his father's legs.

Zap!

His arms and legs splay in every direction, and he drops onto his stomach.

Zap!

He rolls over, curling into a tight ball.

Zap!

He feels a hot wetness spread from his crotch, and begins to sob.

Zap! "Stop crying, Oliver!"

Zap! "I told you to stop crying!"

Zap! Zap! Zap!

Oliver's bowels suddenly turn to liquid, and a terrible odor fills his nostrils as one more jab of the prod costs him the last of his self-control.

Sobbing, lying in his own filth, he wraps his arms around his legs and clamps his eyes shut. His whole body shakes as he waits for the next shock. It does not come. Instead there is his father's voice.

"What are you?" Malcolm Metcalf asks.

"A bad boy," Oliver whispers. "I'm a very bad boy."

Without another word, his father unlocks the door

and leaves the room. When the door closes, Oliver has just the briefest moment of hope, but then he hears the click of the lock as his father turns it from the outside.

Crying softly, the little boy remains on the floor for a few more minutes, waiting for the pain in his body to subside. Then, knowing what he must do before the door will be unlocked again, he begins cleaning up the mess on the floor, using his shirt as a towel, washing it out over and over again at the little sink that is bolted to one of the room's walls.

He is, he knows, a very bad boy indeed.

So bad that neither his father, nor anyone else, will ever love him again.

The darkness closed around him, and once again all Oliver could see in the blackness was the glimmering blade of the razor.

The razor, and the blood of his sister.

Chapter 8

*E*verything had changed.

It seemed to Oliver that he was hanging, suspended, in some netherworld that had no relationship to Blackstone, or to the life he had lived there.

It wasn't dark—not exactly—and yet he couldn't see.

He felt as if he were deaf, yet there was no sense of sound at all, no feeling of vibration in his head, or distant muffled noises that he thought he should have heard more clearly.

His sense of touch had deserted him too, and he couldn't be certain whether he was moving or standing still.

He could have been sitting, or lying down, or even curled up, his arms wrapped around his knees the way he'd liked to sleep when he was a little boy.

A little boy . . .

The thought hung with him in the void.

That's what he was: a boy. A little boy. He was no longer Oliver Metcalf, forty-five and a responsible adult, editor of the town newspaper. Somehow, he had been transported into some other world, the world of his childhood that, without knowing it, he had years ago closed off behind a curtain of blackness. But now the curtain was parting. Before him, as he waited, the gray half-light brightened.

The first thing he knew was that he was afraid.

Afraid because he'd done something wrong.

Bad! He was a bad boy! A very bad boy!

He was a bad boy, and his father was going to punish him.

And he deserved to be punished.

Oliver waited quietly in the not-quite-dark, not-quite-light. Somehow he knew that was the right thing to do. Sometimes his father didn't come for a long time, and sometimes he came right away.

But Oliver knew he must be quiet, and he must wait. Because if he was bad, more bad things would happen.

Scraps of images began to float around him, and suddenly, the light was momentarily brighter again and he was able to catch glimpses of things.

A little girl.

She had a pretty face, framed by long blond hair, and she was holding something in her hands. A doll. A doll with a pretty porcelain face and golden hair.

Suddenly, from out of the twilight silence surrounding him, Oliver heard his father's voice. But now his father wasn't speaking to him. He was speaking to the little girl. "You can't have it anymore," his father decreed. "Little boys don't play with dolls. They play with balls and bats!"

Now Oliver could hear the little girl, her sobs enveloping him the way his father's voice had a moment ago. He saw her face, saw it change, saw the blond locks fall away, heard the cries reach a crescendo then fade away, and the strange silence fell over Oliver once again, and the child's face took on the same odd grayness that was all around.

The grayness of death.

The little boy was dead.

Dead, like Oliver's sister.

And in the twilight Oliver's father was whispering. "Do you understand?" he asked. "Do you understand why he died?"

Oliver nodded, though he didn't understand at all.

"We're going to put the doll away," his father's voice whispered. "We're going to put it away in the secret place. But you're going to remember, Oliver. You're going to remember all of it."

His father's voice faded again, leaving Oliver enshrouded in the grayness where, as before, he felt as if he was hanging in a void, suspended in a world without sensations.

A world in which there was no difference between night and day, no difference between sound and silence.

No difference between life and death.

Then a point of light appeared.

"Watch the light, Oliver," his father's voice instructed, penetrating the silence from an echoing distance that was nowhere yet everywhere.

Like the twilight itself, his father's voice was simply present.

"Watch the light, Oliver," his father's voice said again. "Watch the light and see what it does."

The light reappeared, a flame now, flickering in front of Oliver's eyes.

Then the flame began to move, and now Oliver could see something else.

An arm.

An arm covered with soft skin, soft and smooth and pale. A woman's skin.

The flame moved closer and closer to the skin.

Oliver wanted to cry out, to move the flame away from the woman's skin, but the twilight held him in its thrall as tightly as if it were made with ropes and straps.

The flame licked at the skin on the arm, and then, from out of the silence, came a sound.

The roar of a dragon.

The roar sounded again, and then Oliver saw the dragon looming out of the twilight, its eyes glowing like twin rubies, its golden scales glittering even in the strange gray light. Its mouth opened, and once again it roared, a great bellow that hung in the air as a blast of fire burst from its throat.

As suddenly as it had appeared, the dragon vanished into the twilight, and all that was left was the vision of the woman's arm, the skin charred black, great chunks of it peeling off, dropping away to reveal the raw flesh beneath.

Then, from somewhere in the gray eternity around him, Oliver heard the dragon roar once more, and the flesh before his eyes burst into flame.

Now he heard his father's voice. "Do you understand, Oliver?"

"I understand," Oliver silently breathed.

"You will remember?" his father's voice demanded, and though the words were formed into a question, Oliver understood what would happen if he forgot.

"I will remember," he promised.

"We will put the dragon with the doll," his father's voice whispered. "And when next you see it, you will know to whom it should belong."

Once again time and space melded together.

Oliver hung in the gray silence.

More images flickered in front of him.

A scrap of cloth, intricately embroidered, a single letter, mirrored, worked perfectly into one of its corners.

A face appeared, and snakes writhed about him, and once again he heard his father's voice.

"Remember what I'm showing you, Oliver. Remember what I'm saying. If you forget, you know what will happen."

Oliver knew he would not forget.

And after his father had spoken, and hidden the scrap of cloth away with the doll and the dragon, those images too fell away into the gray morass, as surely as if they'd never been there at all.

"But you'll remember," his father's voice whispered. "When it's time, you will remember."

"I promise, Daddy." The words were no more than an unvoiced whimper, but they echoed in Oliver's mind as loudly as had the dragon's now-forgotten roar. "I promise . . ."

More images rose out of the gray, took focus for a moment, then disappeared so utterly that they might never have existed. And as each of them flickered through his consciousness, only to be lost again an instant later, Oliver's father's voice kept whispering.

"You'll know what to do, boy. When the time comes, you'll know what to do as surely as if you had become my own reincarnation. You are all that's left of me, and you'll do it. After they've destroyed me—after they've sent me away and destroyed my work—you will still be here. You will be my sword of vengeance. You will do exactly as I tell you, and it will be as if I'd come back myself, to destroy the destroyers.

"And do you know why you'll do it, Oliver?"

"Because I've been bad," Oliver whispered. "Because I've been a very bad boy, and I have to do whatever you want me to do."

"That's right, Oliver. You've been a bad boy." His father's words lashed out with the sting of a whip. "Killed them! Killed your mother! Killed your sister! Evil, vile child!"

Oliver tried to shrink away from the accusations, tried to find a way to drop back into the comforting silence of the twilight abyss, but there was no escape. Wherever he turned, his father's words were there, piercing into his consciousness, jabbing at him, torturing him, until finally, the last of his resistance crumpled.

"I understand, Daddy," he said. "I understand."

It was then that the darkness closed around him once again, and he sank gratefully back into an oblivion that was free not only of the strange images but of the sound of his father's voice.

It was not, though, an oblivion in which Oliver could dwell forever.

Sooner or later, consciousness would inevitably return.

Consciousness, and the evil pleasure his father demanded.

Oliver woke up in darkness.

Not the familiar darkness that blanketed his room when he woke up at night, thinking at first there was no light at all, only to find that the shadows that moved on the walls and ceiling, cast by the street lamp outside, were old friends. In that kind of darkness he could snuggle down deeper in his bed, pulling the covers up tight under his chin as he let his imagination run wild, seeing all kinds of wonderful things in the dark shapes on the walls. He liked that kind of darkness.

Some nights he imagined he was in a tent in the jungle, and the shadows he was seeing were cast by lions and tigers and elephants.

But the darkness in which he awakened this time was different.

An empty, scary kind of darkness.

The kind of darkness that made him think that things he couldn't see were watching him.

The kind of darkness that made him shiver, even though it wasn't cold.

"Daddy?" he called out, keeping his voice soft enough so that if there were any wild animals lurking in the darkness, they might not hear him.

There was no answer. As Oliver came fully awake, he realized he wasn't in his bed at all.

He wasn't even in his room.

And his whole body was sore.

The blackness turned to a funny gray color; then, as it grew brighter, became a bright, blinding white, as a powerful, naked bulb switched on.

White tiles on the floor. And on the wall.

White paint on the ceiling.

And then his father's face, looming above him, flanked by two big men in white coats.

"You're not a very good boy, Oliver," his father said. "You're a bad boy. A very bad boy, who killed his sister."

"I didn't!" Oliver cried. "I—"

Before he could finish his sentence, his father pressed a button in a wooden box. Oliver convulsed as the jolt of electricity passed through him. Then, as his body relaxed, he cried:

"No!"

His father pressed the button again. This time as the shock shuddered through him, a gush of vomit spewed from his mouth.

"Clean him," Oliver's father said, and the two men in white coats stepped over to the table and began wiping the vomit away with a towel.

His father pressed the button again. He was sobbing now, whimpering, his stomach churning, his throat filling with bile as his body reacted to the torture.

Then, in a small voice that seemed to come from somewhere outside himself, Oliver heard himself say, "I've been a bad boy. A very bad boy."

"That's right," his father said. "A very bad boy. And now I'm going to tell you why you're a bad boy, and what you did."

His breath coming in short, shallow gasps, Oliver listened as his father explained how he had taken the razor and what he had done with it. His father's voice droned on and on, and as he spoke, tears came into Oliver's eyes.

Tears of sorrow, and tears of shame.

And at last, when it was over, and he understood everything his father had told him, he slipped from the white tiled room and pulled the door closed behind him. Outside in the corridor the cries and screams that had echoed through the building for so long could still be heard, but not by Oliver Metcalf.

All he could hear as he slowly mounted the stairs toward the first floor was the sound of his father's voice, repeating over and over what he, a very bad boy, had done.

And telling him what still was left to do.

Chapter 9

*R*ebecca Morrison was staring at the face of Death.

She had no conscious memory of when the apparition had appeared; nor did she have any idea how long she had been gazing upon it.

It was simply there, hanging in front of her in the darkness.

It was a pale, bloodless face, almost lost in the folds of a deep hood whose black cloth blended into the surrounding darkness so perfectly that the face itself seemed almost to be a part of the blackness. Though there seemed to be no source of light, the face was limned in shadows, shadows that moved and seemed to shimmer with a life of their own.

Yet the face was dead.

Wattles of skin hung around the neck, and the jaw was slack, causing a lipless maw to gape wide, exposing the rotted teeth within. The tongue, covered with open sores, was coated with a yellowish goo that strung out to the broken teeth like strands of a spiderweb; a spiderlike creature, fat and mottled black-brown, lurked deep in the specter's throat, crawling out long enough for Rebecca to catch only a glimpse of it before scuttling back down into its fleshy lair. The creature set Rebecca's flesh crawling,

498

with its multiple hairy legs and the grizzly morsels that hung from its curving, dripping mandibles.

Above the maw a great beaked nose curved out from a sloping brow, its grayish skin pocked deep with ulcerations. Mucus ran thickly from its nostrils. On either side of the hooked nose, glowering eyes were sunk deep in hollowed sockets. The eyes, like the rest of the specter's mien, were gray and dead, but from somewhere deep within them, a cold harsh light—a flame of evil—flicked like the tongue of a serpent.

The cigarette lighter, Rebecca thought. The present Oliver and I found for Andrea. It's as if the dragon's tongue were caught in the eyes of Death.

She tried to turn away, tried not to look at the terrible face, but something about it held her in thrall. There was a terrible hunger in the face, a yearning in the coldly flickering eyes, a depraved lust as it gazed upon her.

It's come for me, Rebecca thought. Death wants me, and has come for me.

All her senses were playing tricks on her now.

She had no idea how long it had been since the Tormentor carried her up the stairs, no idea of what it was he wanted. When he'd finally set her down, she'd found herself lying on something hard and cold. As her hands, still bound behind her back, explored the smoothly rounded surface on which she lay, it had come to her.

A bathtub.

He'd put her in a bathtub.

And then, almost at the very instant she'd realized where she was, he'd opened the valve.

Not far.

Just enough so that the water began slowly to fill the tub. Rebecca braced herself, tried to prepare herself for what might happen if he tore her clothes from her body. She turned her mind inward, searching within herself for something to sustain her through the ordeal she was certain was coming.

Oliver!

She would think about Oliver, and no matter what the Tormentor might do to her, it wouldn't touch her.

She wouldn't feel it.

Wouldn't respond to it.

And when it was over, it would be as if it had never happened.

As the tub had filled, she conjured a picture of Oliver in her mind, imagined him smiling at her, saw his gentle eyes watching over her, felt his hands caressing her.

Listened to his voice consoling her, encouraging her, giving her strength.

The water slowly rose in the tub, covering first her feet and then her legs. The water, still carrying the icy chill of winter, numbed every part of her body it touched. Rebecca, inured to cold, turned away from the icy wetness as completely as she had turned away from the Tormentor, utterly closing her senses to it, putting herself in a place where she neither felt nor heard anything that did not emanate from within her own mind.

In her mind she was not alone.

Oliver was with her.

Oliver was looking after her.

Until, suddenly, Oliver was no longer there, and in his place the visage of Death hung before her again.

Her senses too had come alive. She could smell the fetid breath of the specter, feel the frigid water.

Was this what Aunt Martha had seen and felt as she died?

When she'd gazed transfixed upon the face of her savior, had she too seen Death leering hungrily down on her?

Had she already died?

But no—she could still feel the hardness of the tub, the wetness of the water.

The water still ran slowly into the tub. It covered her waist in an ice-cold blanket; its tentacles were reaching up toward her chest.

In the darkness surrounding her, Rebecca saw the lipless mouth of Death twist in a grisly parody of a smile.

Then, over the sound of running water, she heard something else.

A door opened.

Footsteps approached.

The Tormentor had returned.

Oliver stood in the center of his father's office, so that the great walnut desk with the huge leather chair behind it loomed directly in front of him. His father would have to look neither to the right nor to the left to see him.

That was important.

When you were going to be punished, it was important to face it straight on. His father had told him that over and over again, but it was still hard.

So hard, in fact, that Oliver hadn't quite been able to look up. But now he heard his father's voice: "Oliver."

Biting his lower lip to keep from crying out, Oliver finally looked up.

His father's chair was empty.

He glanced almost furtively around the room, certain that his father must be there somewhere, but the sofa against the wall to the left was empty, and so was the wing-backed chair that faced his father's desk. Then his eyes fell on the portrait of his mother that hung on the wall of his father's office.

There was a black ribbon draped over its frame.

He was still gazing up at the picture when he heard his father's voice again: "Come into the bathroom, Oliver. Come and look at what you've done."

Fear forcing him to obey, Oliver moved to the door cut into the wall to the right, turned its knob, and pushed it open.

He saw nothing.

"Look," his father commanded. "Look in the mirror, and see what you've done."

Oliver moved to the sink and stared into the mirror that hung on the wall above it. But instead of seeing his own face, he found himself gazing upon the face of his father.

The face in the mirror was covered with a soapy lather, and one cheek had been scraped clean.

Then, from behind him, Oliver heard the sound of laughter.

The laughter of children.

Spinning around, he found himself once again staring at his four-year-old self.

He was in the bathtub, and his sister was with him. They sat at opposite ends of the great claw-footed tub, laughing happily as they splashed each other, then smeared each other's faces with soapy bubbles.

"Stop that," he heard his father's voice say.

In the tub, Oliver and Mallory kept splashing, kept laughing.

"I said, stop that!" His father's voice was angry now.

In the bathtub, Oliver and Mallory, caught up in their game, ignored their father's command.

Then Mallory, with a silvery peal of happy laughter, stood up in the tub and used both her little hands to heave a great splash of soapy water at her father.

The little Oliver in the tub, stunned by what his sister had done, froze, his wide and fearful eyes fixing on his father.

And Oliver Metcalf, still standing at the sink, raised his right arm. In his hand, the blade of the razor he'd brought into the Asylum less than two hours ago glinted brightly.

Rage filled Oliver as he heard his father's voice once more, trembling with cold fury as he glowered down at his little daughter. "Don't you dare laugh!" he thundered. "After what you've done, don't you dare laugh!"

But Mallory, caught up in her game, only splashed the water harder, her laughter growing louder and louder.

Suddenly, Oliver's arm flashed out, and then—

The stab of pain seared through his head, wiping out the vision he'd just seen, plunging him into the familiar abyss of darkness. But even as he felt himself sinking into unconsciousness, he heard his father's voice.

"No, Oliver! Open your eyes! Open your eyes and see what you have done!"

Slowly the blackness faded away, and the pain in Oliver's head subsided. He opened his eyes.

And found himself gazing at his sister's naked body, submerged facedown in the tub.

He was out of the tub now, and his father was putting the razor into his hand.

"Look what you've done, Oliver," his father told him. "It wasn't me, Oliver. It was you! All of it is your fault! Your fault that your mother died, Oliver! She didn't die giving birth to Mallory, Oliver! She died giving birth to *you*! And now you've killed Mallory too. Killed her, Oliver. Killed your sister!" His father's voice grew louder and louder, until the words pounded in Oliver's head, each one striking him like a blow. "Killed her, Oliver! Killed her!"

"No," Oliver whimpered. "No, Daddy, I didn't—"

"Killer!" Malcolm Metcalf roared. "Killer! *Killer! KILLER!*" His voice kept rising, and the word became a chant, then divided itself into two words: "Killer . . . killer . . . kill her! *Kill her! KILL HER!*"

Oliver reached down, grasped his sister, lifting her from the tub, turning her over to gaze into her face.

Still his father's voice roared in his head. "Kill her! Kill her!"

He raised the blade high, his hand trembling as he prepared to obey his father's order: "KILL HER!"

Rebecca tensed as she felt the touch of fingers on her flesh. But it was different this time: the cold slickness of latex was gone. Her body was being lifted out of the tub, and a second later the tape was torn from her eyes and mouth. Even the shadowy light of the bathroom blinded her for a second, but then her vision cleared and she recognized the face above her.

"Oliver!" she cried out. "Oliver!"

Then she saw the razor in his hand, the glinting blade slashing downward, and opened her mouth once more. "Oliver!"

Rebecca's scream sliced through the chaos in Oliver's mind. In an instant his father's voice fell silent. His sister's face vanished, replaced by Rebecca Morrison's sweet features. But the razor was already slashing toward her, its cutting edge ready to slice deep into her throat in obedience to his father's order.

Then, in the last instant, the blade millimeters from her neck, his arm jerked, changed course, and instead of cutting into Rebecca's flesh, the blade released her from the bonds that held her. The razor clattered to the floor. As Oliver stood, shocked into immobility by the realization of what he had nearly done, Rebecca's arms slid around his neck and she buried her face in his shoulder.

Cradling Rebecca in his arms, Oliver carried her out of the bathroom, through the empty room that had once been his father's office, and out into the corridor. A moment later he kicked the front door of the Asylum open and stepped out into the warm sunshine of the spring afternoon.

Chapter 10

Oliver set Rebecca down only long enough to open the front door to his house, then gathered her into his arms again, carried her inside, and up the stairs to the guest room. Lowering her gently onto the bed, he pulled a blanket over her. "I'll get you some towels and a robe," he said as he started toward the door.

By the time he returned, the clothing Rebecca had been wearing since the moment she'd run out of Clara and Germaine Wagner's house was lying in a heap next to the bed, and Rebecca was huddling under the covers, shivering so hard her teeth were chattering. Her skin was so pale it had taken on a bluish color, and her hair, matted, wet, and filthy, hung limply around her haggard face.

I did this, Oliver thought wretchedly. I did this to Rebecca. Dropping to his knees, he took her hand in both of his. "I'm sorry," he whispered. "Oh, God, Rebecca, I'm so sorry. I'll never—"

Rebecca frowned. "Sorry for what?" she asked. "You saved me, Oliver. You saved me from that horrible man who . . ." Her voice died away as a shudder shook her entire body at the memory of what she'd just gone through. Then, as Oliver started to speak again, she held her fingers to his lips. "Not now," she pleaded. "Please? I'm so cold, and so tired, and so hungry." Oliver choked as a sob rose to his throat, and Rebecca squeezed his hand. "Could you maybe make me some soup?" she asked. "Maybe if you could make me some soup, I could take a shower and get warmed up again, and then you can tell me all about how you found me."

Oliver felt a terrible pain in his chest—a pain that stabbed directly at his heart—and wondered if it was possible his heart could actually be physically breaking. *She doesn't understand! She doesn't understand at all!*

"Please?" Rebecca asked again. "Just not right now, Oliver."

Oliver hesitated, his mind churning, needing to make her understand the magnitude of the terrible thing he had done, but at the same time wishing there were some way he would never have to tell her at all. Even as the wish rose in his mind, he knew it was impossible. But certainly he could spare her the knowledge of what he'd done for a few more minutes. "Of course," he whispered. "I'll go find something for you. The bathroom's just through there." He started toward the door once more, but then looked back at Rebecca. "You'll be all right by yourself?" he asked anxiously.

"Of course I will," Rebecca assured him. "Besides, you'll be right downstairs. What could happen to me?"

She smiled at him then, and Oliver tried to etch that smile so deeply into his memory that he could never forget it. Once she understood what he had done, he would never see her smile again. Then he turned away and left Rebecca alone.

He found a can of chicken soup in the kitchen, opened it, and emptied its contents into a bowl, which he put in the microwave. While the soup heated, he picked up the telephone and punched Phil Margolis's number into the keypad. "It's Oliver," he said when the doctor came on the line. "I've found Rebecca." Before Margolis could ask any questions, Oliver spoke again. "She was in the Asylum. I think she's all right, but if you could come over to my house—"

"I'll be there in ten minutes," Philip Margolis broke in.

Oliver hung up, then picked the receiver up again, and this time called Steve Driver. "Steve?" he said, after explaining that Rebecca was with him. "Edna Burnham was right. It was all connected." A pause. Then: "And I know what the connection was."

There was a silence. "Is that all you're going to say?" Driver asked. "Or are you going to tell me what the connection was?"

"Me," Oliver said softly. "It was me, Steve."

Now the silence stretched out so long Oliver wondered if the deputy was still there. But then Steve Driver spoke again. "I guess I better come over."

"I guess so," Oliver said, his voice as spiritless as he suddenly felt. Hanging up the phone, he checked the soup, set the microwave to keep it warm until Rebecca came downstairs, then set a place for her at the kitchen table.

He was putting an English muffin in the toaster oven when, at almost the same moment, two cars pulled up in front of his house. After showing Philip Margolis to the room he'd given Rebecca, he led Steve Driver into the kitchen. "You want a cup of coffee or something?" His voice was as dull as it had been on the phone a few minutes earlier.

"I'd like to hear what happened," the deputy replied. "Or at least what you think happened."

Oliver cast about in his mind, trying to decide where to begin. A lot of what occurred in the Asylum that day was still jumbled in his memory. Images crowded into his mind, and he shuddered involuntarily as he remembered the scenes of his childhood suffering that had been unlocked from his memory.

"I think it started the day my sister died," he finally said.

Steve Driver, frowning, sank into one of the kitchen chairs. "That was forty years ago," he said.

Oliver nodded. "Uncle Harvey gave me something this morning, before he died." The deputy's frown deepened, but he said nothing, and Oliver continued. "It was a straight razor, in a mahogany box. He found it on his porch when he got his paper." Oliver's eyes met Steve Driver's. "It was my father's razor. My father used it to kill my sister. Then he convinced me that I did it."

Slowly, forcing himself to speak evenly and without emotion, Oliver related what had happened to him in the Asylum that day, all the memories that had come back to him. At some point, while Oliver talked, Philip Margolis joined Steve Driver at the kitchen table. The two men listened silently. Steve Driver took some notes, but never interrupted Oliver.

"That's what the headaches and the blackouts were about," Oliver explained to Margolis. "It wasn't anything physical at all. It was just too many memories that were too painful to face. And every time I went near the Asylum—every time the memories started to come to the surface—I shut them out. I gave myself headaches. I blacked out. I did everything to keep from remembering. And it was what my father wanted." He shook his head, recalling the scenes he had finally relived, the veil of blackness now forever stripped away. "All those things that started showing up the last few months?" he said. "That doll belonged to Bill McGuire's aunt. And the dragon lighter? That was Martha Ward's sister's. He showed me all those things when I was a child. And he planted it all in my mind." A bitter smile twisted his lips. "It was his revenge. *I* was his revenge. His reincarnation, he told me, all that was left of him to do his bidding. He used me to send something back to every family that ever had anything to do with that place." He fell silent for a moment, then spoke again. "It was I who kidnapped Rebecca," he said quietly. "I kidnapped her, and I tied her up in there, and I—"

"No!"

The single word was uttered with such force that all three of the men in the kitchen flinched. Then, as one, they turned to see Rebecca Morrison standing in the doorway. She was wrapped in Oliver's thick terry-cloth bathrobe, far too large for her small form, its belt sashed tightly around her waist. Her hair, clean and dry now, created a soft frame around her heart-shaped face.

Her eyes were fixed on Oliver.

"You didn't hurt me, Oliver," she said quietly. "You saved my life."

Oliver rose and took a step toward her, shaking his head. "Rebecca, you don't understand. I—"

Quickly, Rebecca crossed the kitchen and once more put her finger to Oliver's lips. "I know what you did, Oliver," she said. "I was there, remember? I was there when I was kidnapped, and I was there all the time that man held me in the Asylum. And I was there when you came for me."

"But you don't understand—" Oliver began again.

Rebecca took both his hands in her own. "I do understand," she said. "I understand that you love me, and I understand that I love you. And that's all there is." When Oliver tried to speak again, she shook her head, repeating, "That's all there is."

Oliver gazed into Rebecca's face for a long time, then finally tore his eyes away to look at Steve Driver and Philip Margolis. Regardless of what Rebecca had said, they must have understood the truth.

But Steve Driver was tearing his notes from his pad, and while he slid the notebook itself back into the inside pocket of his jacket, Philip Margolis spoke for both of them.

"It's her word against yours, Oliver," the doctor said. "And we all know that Rebecca doesn't lie. She just plain doesn't."

Finally, Oliver put his arms around Rebecca and pulled her close, his lips nuzzling her hair as she clung to him. But then he caught a glimpse of the Asylum looming on top of the hill outside the window. He released Rebecca from his embrace and his expression hardened. "I'll be back in a few minutes," he said. "There's something I've got to do."

Leaving the house, Oliver strode up the hill to the spot where the wrecking ball still stood, waiting for the work to proceed. Climbing into the seat in front of its controls, he found the starter switch, and the machine's engine roared to life. He studied the controls, then began working the various levers.

A moment later the enormous lead ball swung back on its cable, paused for an instant at the end of its arc, then moved again, gaining momentum as Oliver aimed it at the great stone edifice.

As the ball smashed into the wall, glass shattered and rock exploded in every direction.

Again and again Oliver sent the ball crashing against the Asylum's wall. With every blow a little more of the pain his father had inflicted on him when he was a boy was finally relieved.

The battering went on and on, until, too weak to stand any longer, the prisonlike wall of the Blackstone Asylum collapsed.

Oliver Metcalf at last was free.

Epilogue

*T*he white clapboard Congregational church, with its high steeple and brass bell, had stood guard over Blackstone for more than two centuries. Now, as the bell began to toll the hour of four, nearly all the citizens of Blackstone left their homes and began moving slowly toward the cemetery, as if drawn by the stately, mournful gong, inexorably, like iron filings to a magnet. They came from all directions, from the "College Streets" of Harvard, Princeton, and Amherst, north of the square, and from the less grand thoroughfares that lay in a grid to the south. As ancient custom dictated, they congregated briefly in the square itself, neighbors greeting neighbors, lifelong friends chatting quietly for a few minutes before gathering into larger groups that moved west toward the white picket fence that surrounded the graveyard.

It had been three days since Harvey Connally had died; three days since Oliver Metcalf had carried Rebecca Morrison out of the Asylum.

Three days since Oliver had taken the controls of the wrecking ball and smashed the wall of the Asylum itself.

Three days in which more rumors had crept through the streets of Blackstone, moving from house to house, passed from lip to ear in whispers so quiet that the words

513

could barely be understood. Where the tale began—
which mouth first uttered the words—no one could say,
for it is never possible to trace a rumor back to its first
seed. But by four P.M. on this cloud-darkened afternoon,
when it was finally time to lay Harvey Connally's body
to rest, there was barely a soul in Blackstone who had not
heard the story. A legend was taking root.

A legend about a man who, throughout his entire lifetime, the town had honored and held in great esteem.

A man who, in death, was taking on a new role, a role
he would undoubtedly continue to play through the
decades—perhaps even centuries—to come.

Harvey Connally, the rumor proclaimed, had been the
one who delivered the gifts, and with them the curse on
half a dozen of Blackstone's oldest families, including
his own.

"It's crazy," Bill McGuire said when someone—he
could no longer remember exactly who—had first whispered it to him. "Harvey could never have done such a
thing." But by the end of the day, when he'd gone into
the library to gaze upon the portrait of his aunt—her face
suddenly appearing to him so similar to that of the doll
with which his daughter still slept every night—he'd
wondered. Bill McGuire knew little about that aunt,
except that she'd been killed in a boating accident years
earlier—long before he was born—after some tragedy
had befallen her own child.

The details of that tragedy had never been explained
to him.

Harvey Connally, though, would have known his aunt,
and known what happened to her.

He could even have known if the doll had once belonged to her, or to her child.

Bill McGuire couldn't be sure, and though he still insisted that the doll had nothing to do with Elizabeth's death, doubt had been planted and was beginning to grow. Though Bill didn't want to believe the whispers about Harvey Connally, neither could he deny them outright. Today, as he moved toward the cemetery for the burial service, he found himself hoping that somehow, at this final moment before Harvey Connally was laid to rest, the truth might somehow be revealed.

Perhaps, Bill thought, he might simply *feel* something. Something that would tell him that the evil that had settled over Blackstone was finally coming to an end with Harvey Connally's interment.

Though she hadn't yet talked to Bill McGuire, Madeline Hartwick, with Celeste at her side, was attending the service in the cemetery for much the same reason as the contractor. She had heard the whispers about Harvey Connally only yesterday, when she had come back from Boston, where she was staying with Celeste in the small apartment they had found. Throughout a sleepless night, the first she had spent alone in the house in which Jules had terrorized her on the last night of his life, Madeline paced the chilly rooms of the mansion at the top of Harvard Street, returning time after time to the portrait of Jules's mother that she had hung on the library wall the fateful evening of the engagement party.

As she gazed at the portrait of Louisa Hartwick, she

clutched in her hand the locket that Celeste had found in the melting snow a few weeks after Jules died.

The locket that Madeline had finally opened, and discovered was engraved—in letters so tiny she'd needed a magnifying glass to read them—with twin monograms: LH and MM.

It hadn't taken Celeste long to guess what names the monograms stood for: Louisa Hartwick and Malcolm Metcalf. With the guess had come the knowledge of why the portrait of her husband's mother, wearing the apron of a volunteer at the Asylum, had been hidden away in the attic: her husband's mother must have had an affair with Oliver Metcalf's father.

And Harvey Connally, brother of Malcolm Metcalf's wife, must have found out.

Had he found the locket after all these years, and left it in her car that night, knowing it would send her husband into a paranoid rage?

But how could he have? Until that night, Jules had shown no signs at all of paranoia. But might Harvey Connally have known something about her husband's family that she did not? Might it not even be possible that some grudge, long forgotten by anyone except himself, might have been festering in Harvey Connally for years, and now, as his life drew to a close, he'd decided to try to even the score?

Madeline Hartwick, like Bill McGuire, had not quite been able to dismiss the words she'd heard about Harvey Connally, and though she didn't yet believe them, neither could she disbelieve them.

So she too had come to the service not only because

Harvey Connally had been a part of her life for so many years but because she was hoping for some kind of sign.

A sign that could lead her to the truth.

As the questions and rumors had passed from one set of lips to another, more and more small facts had been remembered about Harvey Connally.

One person reminded another that there were few secrets in Blackstone that Harvey Connally hadn't known; few families to whom, one way or another, he wasn't somehow related.

Hadn't he been a trustee of the Asylum, and in that capacity had he not known everything that had gone on there?

Hadn't his father *built* the Asylum, so Harvey would have known every room, every hidden passage, every dark niche?

What about Ed Becker? By the time of Harvey Connally's interment, everyone in town had been reminded that Ed's great-uncle had disappeared into the Asylum. It had been either that or spending his life in prison. Something about a girl who disappeared, wasn't it?

The stories had passed from house to house, been discussed in the Red Hen, whispered about in the library.

No one knew who first remembered hearing a rumor that years ago Martha Ward's sister had died in the Asylum, having burned herself so badly with a cigarette lighter that nothing could be done to save her.

A lighter like the one Rebecca had bought from Janice Anderson?

It wasn't long before at least three people were willing

to swear that they could now remember seeing Harvey Connally lurking near Janice's table just before Oliver and Rebecca bought the lighter Rebecca had given to her cousin Andrea. Though it had happened weeks earlier, their memories of Harvey's sinister presence there grew clearer with every telling, until no one in Blackstone questioned that the old man had been at the flea market that day.

Even the handkerchief that Oliver had given to Rebecca had been ascribed to Harvey. How many times had he been in Oliver's house? Couldn't it have been he who left the embroidered square in the attic for Oliver to find? He would have known that Oliver would give it to Rebecca. After all, didn't it have her initial worked perfectly into its intricate design?

By the third day, when the time had finally come to inter Harvey Connally's remains in the mausoleum his father had built, the tendrils of the legend had crept through Blackstone like a spreading vine, wrapping every citizen so tightly in its grip that only a few were still in doubt.

The most vocal of those was Edna Burnham.

She was the last to enter the cemetery behind the Congregational church that afternoon, and as she came through the gate and threaded her way slowly to the corner of the graveyard in which generations of Connallys had been buried, the mourners fell silent. Edna walked steadily, her head high, and the crowd parted before her as if submitting to her silent will.

Little Megan McGuire, her left arm wrapped tightly around her doll, shrank closer to her father as the old woman paused, looking down at her with eyes that seemed to cut right through her. When the old woman reached out as if to stroke her doll's hair, Megan's mouth tightened into a deep scowl. "Don't touch her," she said, wrenching away from the old woman. "Sam doesn't like to be touched."

Edna Burnham's fingers jerked back as if they'd touched a hot iron, but then she moved on, passing Bill McGuire and Mrs. Goodrich without speaking a word.

A few steps farther on she came to Madeline Hartwick, her daughter Celeste on one side of her, Andrew Sterling on the other. Most of the employees of the bank were clustered around Andrew and the two surviving Hartwicks. Once again Edna Burnham paused, searching their faces as if looking for something, but giving no sign as to whether she had found it. When Madeline Hartwick extended her gloved hand to Edna, the old woman took it, but still no words were exchanged.

As she moved on, Edna Burnham surveyed the silent crowd with a look both haughty and accusing. Everyone who watched had the uneasy feeling that she was searching for people who weren't there, for there was nothing left of Martha Ward's family except for Rebecca and Clara Wagner, who was slowly dying in her room at the nursing home and would never return to Blackstone again.

Edna barely glanced at Bonnie and Amy Becker as she passed them. At last she came to the marble structure in which Charles and Eleanor Connally, along with their daughter and granddaughter, had long ago been interred.

Harvey Connally's bronze coffin, bare of flowers, stood in front of the open door of the crypt; soon it would rest inside, where Harvey would sleep eternally next to his sister, Olivia.

At the head of the coffin, Lucas Iverson stood with an open Bible in his hand, though he needed no prompting to recite once more the prayers that would accompany Harvey Connally's soul to his Maker.

At the foot of the coffin stood Oliver Metcalf.

Next to him, her hand in Oliver's, stood Rebecca Morrison.

The crowd waited in silence as Edna Burnham drew close, finally stopping only a few feet from Oliver.

Her eyes fixed on Oliver for a long time, and the mourners seemed to hold their breath as they waited in tense anticipation to hear what she might say to the man about whom she had been whispering for months—the man whose reputation she had done her best to ruin.

Oliver, his face expressionless, met her granite stare, knowing that whatever she said in the next few moments would be passed from one person to another until there was no one in Blackstone who hadn't heard.

But Edna still bided her time, turning at last to Rebecca Morrison.

Rebecca Morrison, who had once humiliated her in public and now stood next to Oliver Metcalf, one of her hands in his, her face revealing nothing, her eyes clear. In her free hand she held the handkerchief Oliver had given her the day before she'd disappeared.

As she gazed first at Rebecca, and then at Oliver Metcalf, it came to Edna Burnham that the truth of what had happened inside the Asylum three days ago was never going to be revealed to her, at least not by Oliver or Rebecca.

The only other person who might have been able to tell her lay dead inside the coffin that stood in front of the mausoleum. As Lucas Iverson, the hand that held his

Bible trembling, opened his mouth to begin the service, Edna Burnham silenced him with a glance. Her gaze shifted back to Oliver. She gave him a hard appraising look, then turned to Rebecca.

The silence lengthened like a cold shadow creeping over the crowd as the citizens of Blackstone waited.

Then, as if coming to a decision, she nodded her head. "It's over," she said, resting her hand on Harvey Connally's coffin. She looked up to the Asylum, still looming atop North Hill. Though her voice rose only slightly when she spoke again, it carried easily to every corner of the cemetery. "It's time we put the past to rest." She stepped back and bowed her head as Lucas Iverson finally began to intone the last words that would be spoken over Harvey Connally.

"Ashes to ashes, dust to dust . . ."

As the prayer went on, the eyes that had been fixed on Harvey Connally's coffin shifted one by one toward the dark silhouette of the building that stood atop North Hill.

Empty at last, one of its walls shattered by the blows Oliver Metcalf had struck three days ago, it had lost its air of domination. Weakened and forlorn, stripped at last of the power it had held over Blackstone for so long. Everyone who listened to Lucas Iverson's prayer knew that Edna Burnham had, for once, finally spoken the truth.

The past, along with Harvey Connally, was finally being buried.

But it was only Oliver Metcalf who noticed the date that had been engraved on the door of his uncle's crypt.

April 24, 1997.

Until this very moment, he'd forgotten what day it was that his uncle had died.

The date of his mother's death.

The date of his own birth.

His birthday.

His forty-fifth birthday.

And the day that he had finally been released from the torture of his past.

That, he knew, had been his uncle's final gift to him.

As he stared at the date, he felt Edna Burnham standing rigidly beside him. It was only then that he realized he was not the only one staring at the date on the door of Harvey Connally's crypt.

Rebecca—and Edna Burnham—were staring at it too.

Afterword

Dear Reader,

For the past year I have lived in Blackstone, New Hampshire. Never before has a town and its citizens become so real to me. Far more than characters in a novel, the people of Blackstone have become personal friends, and as I write these words I feel an emptiness inside of me. I don't want to say good-bye to Rebecca and Oliver. I don't want to look in my rearview mirror and see North Hill and the square disappearing in the distance. I will miss my meanderings inside the library, the *Chronicle* office and, yes, even the Asylum. I shall truly miss dropping into the Red Hen for a piece of pie (pecan, of course) and a good dose of gossip. In short, I'm not sure I want to leave. But the story is over. Or, at any rate, this part of the story is over.

Writing *The Blackstone Chronicles* has been a marvelous and challenging experience. I loved being able to create a story with a beginning, a middle, and an end in a hundred pages. It was a constant challenge to sustain the suspense over a six-month period, and it was delightful to get to know my characters so well. Many of them turned out to have facets to their personalities that I knew

523

nothing about at the beginning. And I thoroughly enjoyed bringing back characters and references from other books. It was like getting in touch with old friends—even if they were as troubled as Elizabeth Conger (who finally, after all these years, got what was coming to her!), and Melissa Holloway, whose future had worried me ever since the unfortunate events that occurred in Secret Cove in *Second Child*.

But there was also an underlying apprehension that was always with me. What would happen if I got ill and couldn't finish the series? What if I created a plot problem in an already published part that couldn't be resolved in a later part? There were times when I was editing one book, writing another, and proofreading a third. Federal Express and my modem received a real workout. Artwork had to be reviewed, maps drawn, and chronologies and genealogies updated constantly. I'm sure there are those who are still wondering why it was Charles Connally rather than Jonas Connally who built the mansion on the hill. Well, it seems I goofed in the first part, and said that Harvey's father built it, when I should have said his grandfather did. But as I've thought about it, I suspect that this was not an error at all, and that the mansion was built as part of the schism between Jonas Connally and his children. I'm sure there is a story there, though I'm not yet sure what it is.

I thank my lucky stars that I had a stellar group of people working close to me. My editor, Linda Grey—to whom I have dedicated the series—was forever helping me out. My agent, Jane Rotrosen Berkey, was on call to review every book to make sure the stories were holding together. My friend, Mike Sack, who has been involved in my career from the very beginning, stood by as always and kept me moving in the right direction. Also, with his expertise in psychology, he kept the denizens of the Asylum exquisitely maniacal. My staff, Robb Miller and Lori Dickenson, spent hours maintaining detailed files that kept track of the minutiae of the people, places, and things in Blackstone.

The production of a serial novel is a major undertaking for a publisher. Far more major, I suspect, than any of us knew a year ago. A lot of the company's resources must be funneled into the project for a very long period of time. Ballantine/Fawcett as well as Random House stood behind the project all the way. Alberto Vitale, Chairman of Random House, was supportive from the start, when only he and Linda Grey knew what we were about to attempt. Within months, the group involved in Blackstone quickly grew. My copy editor, Peter Weissman, performed beyond the call of duty in keeping track of the details of Blackstone from one volume to another, ready to review each book on a moment's notice, as did managing editor Mark Rifkin. The advertising and publicity departments worked many hard hours to get the word out that Blackstone was coming, and the sales force worked with every book outlet in the country to assure that each book would be on the stands when it was due, so we didn't have different parts popping up at different times and in different places, creating chaos at the Red Hen.

The booksellers themselves performed yeoman service in making sure you could get each new part as quickly as it was released, which is no easy task when thousands of books arrive in their stores and warehouses every month.

Very special thanks go to Ellen Key Harris and Phebe Kirkham, who developed the Blackstone Web site and thereby provided many of us, myself included, with a unique experience. The Blackstone site has become a regular hangout over the last six months, and it has brought an entire new dimension to the form of the novel. Some of you may have noticed that our favorite waitress at the Red Hen diner, Velma Perkins, didn't appear in the first few books. That is because Velma was Ellen Harris's invention, and I didn't meet her until the rest of you did. By the time I'd dropped into the Red Hen a few times, Velma had become totally real to me, and soon she began showing up in the books. (I guess I stole her from you, Ellen. Sorry about that!) There are a few others I met at the Red Hen, new people who have moved to town and who are now working at the bank or assisting Oliver at his office, who aren't mentioned in the books, but you know who you are, and know how much I've appreciated getting to know you. I hope all of you keep your ear to the ground, because I have a feeling there's a lot more going on in Blackstone than any of us yet knows. As you can see, the Web site has brought you, my readers, close to me, and I have enjoyed being able to talk to you, not only at the Red Hen but through e-mail as well. The cyber-Blackstone added a whole new dimension not only to the experience of reading the novel but of writing it as well. I thank all of you who participated.

Stephen King not only opened the door for me to write a serial novel but has also been incredibly supportive throughout. When I felt overwhelmed by the complications, he assured me that I'd get through it and all would be well. I cannot express how much that support meant to me. Thanks again, Steve.

I know that there are a few minor errors that I made as I wrote the novel; errors I couldn't go back to fix since the parts in which they surfaced were already published. At one point, we actually called the printer to change a word as one of the books was in the midst of being printed. Sometimes, though, I was just too late, and a few goofs got through. Apparently this is inevitable when a book is being published before the last word has been written. Or maybe it's just that the renewal of the form is so recent that we haven't quite figured out how to do it yet.

Many of you have asked if I will write another serial. The answer is yes—if the story is right for the format. Many of you have also asked if there will be more of Blackstone. All I can say at this point is that I had a ball writing *The Blackstone Chronicles*, and while right now I'm not positive of anything, I wouldn't be at all surprised if sometime in the future you glance up at a book rack and see the shadow of a building sitting up on North Hill.

Thank you all for going on a six-month ride with me through the town of Blackstone. I only hope you've all enjoyed it as much as I have.

—JOHN SAUL
Seattle, Washington

JOIN THE CLUB!

Readers of John Saul now can join the John Saul Fan Club by writing to the address below. Members receive an autographed photo of John, newsletters, and advance information about forthcoming publications. Please send your name and address to:

The John Saul Fan Club
P.O. Box 17035
Seattle, Washington 98107

Be sure to visit John Saul at his Web site!
www.johnsaul.com

Visit the town of Blackstone on the Web!
www.randomhouse.com/blackstone
Talk with other readers, and test your wits against our quizzes to win Blackstone prizes!

© Michael Sack

ABOUT THE AUTHOR

JOHN SAUL's first novel, *Suffer the Children*, published in 1977, was an immediate million-copy bestseller. He has since written such *New York Times* bestsellers as *Guardian*, *The Homing*, *The God Project*, *Nathaniel*, *Brainchild*, *Hellfire*, *The Unwanted*, *The Unloved*, *Creature*, *Sleepwalk*, *Second Child*, *Darkness*, and *Black Lightning*, each a spine-tingling tale of supernatural, technological, or psychological terror. John Saul divides his time between Seattle, Washington, and Maui, Hawaii. His most recent novel, *The Presence*, was a Main Selection of The Book-of-the-Month Club.